BEING GOD

A Trilogy of our Near Future

by Jake Obus

BOOK 1

[BG1-PoD v2.1/ ISBN 978-0-9979613-2-4]

FRONT COVER: *"Bidwell #5"* © 2017 — a dreamscape by Jake Obus
REAR COVER: *"Emergence"* © 2017   "

To my lovely, selfless Trese

— for making my dreams come true.

THE CURIOUS CREATION OF

BEING

My calling came suddenly
— in the dead of night, between two bursts of light.

A brilliant flash interrupted one of my usual, forgettable dreams. Blinking and squinting through an ensuing, neon-green afterlight, I felt clammy…and hot…and I found myself floating in brightly lit steam. A frightening chorus of high-speed whirrings grew louder by the second, and— still blinking from that flash and now squeezing sweat from my eyes—I peered downward through the mist to see several bulbous-headed beings huddled around a raised, hospital-type bed…with…*was that me down there?* Then another flash and I awoke temporarily blind again, sitting with my back pressed into our headboard, knees to my chest, ears buzzing, heart pounding, and naked body soaked in sweat.

From then on, a chain of equally bizarre and seemingly related 3- to 5-second nightmares struck with eerie frequency, coming about every three weeks between those same two bursts of light and *always* within minutes of 2AM.

After the fourth or fifth occurrence and mostly at the urging of Trese, my highly intrigued wife, I placed a pad and pen by our bed. From then on, upon waking with the next weird characters, peculiar machines and scenes still fresh in my mind, I scribbled each episode down.

Occasionally, but to no avail, Trese and I tried to sort and sequence my growing jumble of scribblings, hoping to make sense of it all. Eventually, after what I can only describe as a procession of strangely coincidental steerings, I began meditating late at night for an hour or two in an attempt to connect with what I thought might be the possible source of my dreams, the "higher self" I'd been reading about. But aside from the drone of my nattering ego, and our old refrigerator clunking itself on or off every eighteen minutes, and the intermittent pounding of giant pinecones dropping onto our roof 'neath the Mogollon Rim, or having to scratch some fiendish itch between refrigo-clunks and pinecone bombs, I got nowhere—until rather suddenly in mid-itch as I considered reinstalling Windows on the weekend, or maybe detailing the car— my disillusioned source chose to contact me.

"Stop thinking and start listening!" chided a female voice from I don't know where, launching me ceilingward from my cushy recliner.

— ∘ ☼ ∘ —

It took the better part of three weeks before I dared meditate again, and when I finally did, I made repeated efforts to ignore or at least hush my unsilenceable ego, and *truly* listen....

— ∘ ☼ ∘ —

Roughly two weeks passed without success, until my apparently appeased, merciful chider addressed me again—this time soothingly. In a clear and succinctly, motherly tone.

"Peace be upon you, dear one."

And a calming peace befell me.

In the weeks that followed, through a nightly exercise designed to both reset my composure and prove that the voices in my head were not of my creation, I came to know my dream source: a mysterious group of etheric beings, determined *through me* to weave their perplexing, multilayered yarn.

"Why me?" I asked—silently, as the ethereans had shown me straightaway. "And what purpose might your story serve?"

"You, because you volunteered, dear one," another female of the group softly replied.

Volunteered? Half-expecting to see some fairy angel's light somewhere in the darkness of our living room's vaulted ceiling, I opened my eyes but saw nothing, and relaxed my lids again.

"You've forgotten," conveyed the next in an equally comforting, distinctly male voice. "But you did volunteer."

Really?

"Really," the second added, as though he'd read my mind. "All is, as was prearranged."

"Our 'story,' as you say," my gentle chider continued, cryptically, "is on the surface for the many, and more deeply for a few."

We then entered—guardedly at first, on both my part and theirs—what fast evolved into a fascinating, note-taking series of wee-hour Q&A sessions in which the weavers patiently interlocked and amplified my fragmented pieces of their dream-induced puzzle. And through that engrossing process, many passages of this peculiar, five-part "trilogy," I directly transcribed.

SAILBOAT SIX

CLOVELLY, NORTH DEVON, U.K.

MARCH 2013

PS: Despite my insistence that we earthlings are loathe to exercise more than ten percent of our brains, the weavers of this mysterious myth chose to introduce a myriad of interdimensional concepts, key characters and alien worlds virtually rapid-fire through the first half of Book 1. To relieve the resulting who-*is*-that?-and-where-*are*-we? befuddlements, a series of *NAVIGATOR* graphics map out each of the early chapters, so with just a glance you can see where you've just been and who you've met, and where you're going next. In addition, informative, numbered *NOTES* are detailed at the end of each corresponding chapter and are repeated in the *CONSOLIDATED* NOTES section at the back of each book, where you'll also find the

GLOSSARY, CHARTS, and *PLAYERS & WORLDS* sections—the latter being a bullet-point, who's who compilation of refresher info.

eBooks. The story's full-color digital version features an array of *hyperlinks* to the individual *NOTES* mentioned above. The books' informative back sections are also readily accessible via your device's ever-present link to the *TABLE of CONTENTS*, and PDF copies of the individual back sections are available for download via the link below. Since the trilogy's digital master is optimized for premium color devices, the more advanced your eBook reader, the more features it will recognize:

older basic models

early color models

latest devices

HARD COPIES. For hard-copies of the individual books or the complete Being God trilogy, please click on the latest purchase links to Amazon by visiting terrah.com/buy-the-trilogy. Thanks!

PDFs. For full-color PDF versions of all three books, and for free PDF copies of the Navigator series and the separate sections—such as the Glossaries only, or one-page landscapes of the split-page Charts, continuous/full-length Character Timelines, and much more—please visit:

terrah.com/downloads

In the beginning...

...and for the longest time, we reckoned our world was flat. Evidently, we existed on a gigantic, dripping sod suspended at the center of All There Was. The sun and moon—the other primary elements of our perceived universe—looped predictably around us and brought temporary relief to the otherwise frightful, eternal night.

As sensible reckoners, we worshipped the sun. That is, until deep thinkers imagined a mighty syndicate of moody gods that, more often than not and for reasons beyond our comprehension, wrought allegedly purposeful forms of devastation.

After another long while, chosen ones began receiving varied notions of a miraculous, single god: a merciful but still testy, all-powerful etherean, who—the blessed recipients and their bewitched embracers believed—would assist in their enemies' slaughter. No worries if said foes fancied similar logic. To this day, single-godders have no problem with nonsensical contradictions. It's all a matter of faith.

While the ambiguous one-god industry simultaneously evolved and devolved into antagonistic factions, we reckoners went about bunching our sod's wondrous, twinkly little stars into supposedly influential, creature-like clusters. But with no altersods in sight and no consideration given to those twinklers being distant suns, we kept our sod, sun and moon at the cosmic center of All There Was—unbunched and all alone.

Meanwhile, doubters of the industry who dared murmur blasphemous otherwises were zealously stoned, burned, drawn and quartered, beheaded or shamelessly hanged. That is, until rising numbers of emboldened roundworlders finally forced those pompous, cling-on flatworlders to accept that it was us looping around the sun, and not the other way around.

Now, as we techno-infants peer ever deeper into space with ever higher resolutions and find ever more potentially Earthlike worlds, we debate numerical likelihoods including whether advanced others may have visited or might be watching…or perhaps had come and never left. Yet we continue to isolate our nondistinctive sun from its natural family of stellar neighbors. Doesn't that seem curiously counter-intuitive? Of course we're not alone—not even locally.

On the bright side, we have long belonged to the thirty-sun Nordehk constellation. Alike-looking cousins inhabit alike-looking worlds that orbit three of our constellation's thirty suns. And our non-infringing progenitors reside near Nordehk's core.

On the dark side, devious, ill-intended others from afar are indeed visiting and have long been visiting both us and our not-so-distant cousins. Encounterees reluctantly recall callously indifferent, otherworldly beings presumptively bent on bringing us up to speed, genetically speaking; but for what purpose, remains obscure. The encounterors are commonly described as small, grey-skinned humanoids with bulbous heads and oversized, jet-black eyes. They appear to be the same species as those of the-crash-at-Roswell fame. The same elusive group that for some reason delights in teasing us, and simply will not openly land.

Contrary to our cartoonish depictions on a growing collection of consumer goods, the deceptively frail-looking visitors are deadly serious, highly efficient troops. Known widely beyond our constellation as the loathsome "darkeyes," these notorious, chillingly indifferent little mercenaries do not deviate from their mission to orchestrate and escalate global chaos. As despicable, seasoned minions of a far more fearsome force, landing is not officially part of their plan.

In this glimpse of our near future, you will learn what has been happening and continues to happen to us and our stellar neighbors, and why. It is a channeled telling of things in flux—things whose outcomes are not yet set—and of things written long before. Things that cannot be undone.

Murmurs have collaborators among us, and have cunning, godless aliens directing their every move. Akin to the doubters of old, modern-day murmurers are silenced, mocked, or deemed insane. Their warnings go unheeded, and the concocted chaos rages on.

936: [1]He brings Order to the chaos. [2]Rǝhm IS.
—from The Teachings (The Book of Rǝhm)

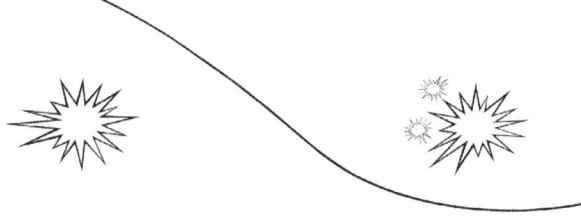

**TERRAH
(EARTH)**

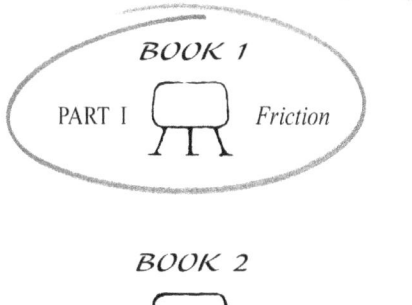

BOOK 1

PART I   Friction

BOOK 2

PART II   Heat

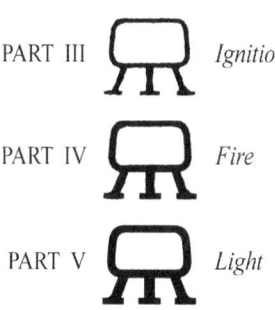

BOOK 3

PART III   Ignition

PART IV   Fire

PART V   Light

BOOK 1

TABLE OF CONTENTS

TERMS and DESIGNATIONS
(for those unaware of the Rohmans' advance)

- *Nordehk:* our 30-sun constellation; home to Terrah (Earth) and five other inhabited worlds

- *the Og* (the *O*rion *g*roup): minions of the mighty Rohmans, these are the notorious, grey-skinned "darkeyes" of Orion—despicably dispassionate mercenaries, who, on their masters' behalf, instill and escalate chaos on unsuspecting, target worlds

- *GROUP COMMAND:* nerve center for the darkeyes' orbiting fourth-density garrisons

- *Rohm:* The Prime Crusader, and Master Over All in the dark side of *All That Is*

- *His Crusades:* the Rohman expansionary campaigns designed to bring readily-embraced Order, constellation by constellation, unto rampant chaos shrewdly contrived

- *Rohman Sons:* fallen angels known to most as Sons of Rohm or Imperial Lords, and to others more correctly—and foremost—as high demons

- *the Rohmans:* those living within and crusading beyond The Master's vast domain

- *bahva:* citizen-commoners of the Rohman Empire ("the realm"); Rohman slang for "bhuvani"—intelligent, humanoid beings

- *the Prime Seed:* the next in line of Nordehk's pristine worlds slated for colonization

- *the Vihdœa:* etherean administrators of the constellations; angelic guardians of the Light.

> You may also refer to the *NOTES*, *GLOSSARY*, *CHARTS*, and *PLAYERS & WORLDS* sections at the back of each book.

Questions? Input? Sightings? *Encounters?* terrah.com

Downloads: terrah.com/downloads

Licensing: terrah.com/licensing

BEING GOD

Part I

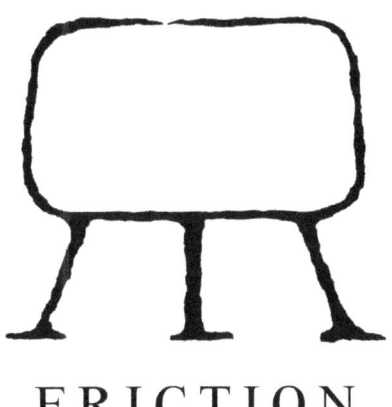

FRICTION

*I awoke in a starfield to thunderous sounds
and a whirlpool of vapors and lightning.
And out from this storm flew a great sea-ray:
wings aglow and eyes of fire...*

EDITOR's NOTE: As with the other condensed dreams that introduce each of the story's five parts, this sequence (rendered on Book 1's back cover) was among the jumble of vivid, Bidwell Street nightmares that induced Jake's amassing of what he later dubbed "the Rohm material," from which the *Being God* trilogy emerged.

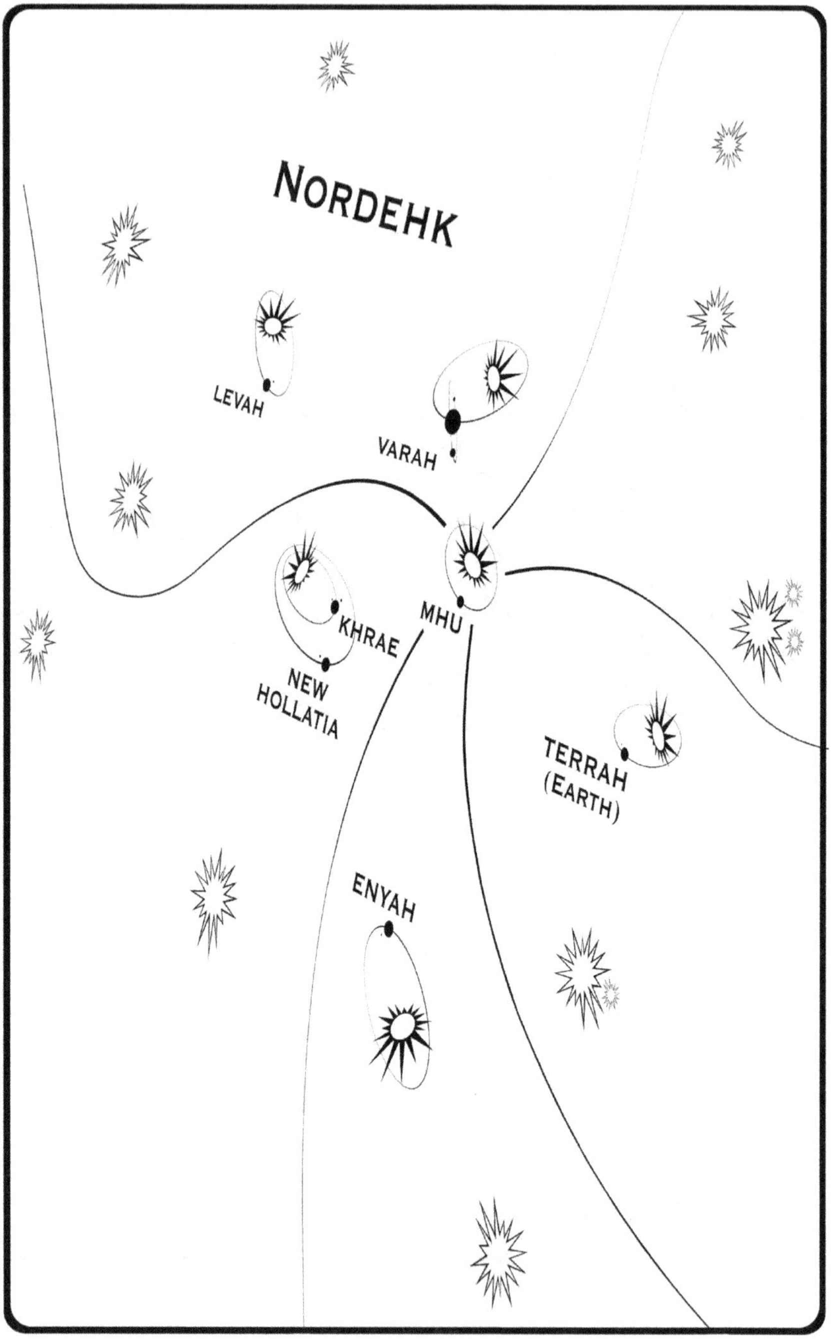

NORDEHK

LEVAH

VARAH

KHRAE

MHU

NEW HOLLATIA

TERRAH (EARTH)

ENYAH

1

SHADOWS ON THE WALL
DAY -32: TERRAH ("EARTH")

Shoulders scrunched and eyes squeezed shut, the child lay trembling in his moonlit upper bunk. His legs and arms felt heavy; toes and fingers long and thin. That's the way it started when the hell-men came for him.

The ones hiding in his closet had made him hypno-sleep. Their big black buggy eyes could make him do all sorts of things.

Soon the rest would rush out from the shadows on his wall. As ever, they would take him to his special silver bed in their floodlit silver hall.

He told anyone who'd listen, but nobody believed him and with no one left to tell, young Ricky lay there waiting for the little men from hell.

THE COLLABORATORS
D-32.2: TERRAH

On Earth, as Terrah's preoccupied inhabitants called their troubled home, an ultrasecret group of twelve held power absolute. It routinely installed the world's key leaders while tolerating others who, for the most part, conformed to a whispered alien doctrine kept largely undisclosed. Despite the unintentional exposure of its existence by conceptually inept underlings within two years of the council's quiet debut nearly nine decades before, and despite a thorough hoaxing-over of the compromising material, rumors of the mysterious group persisted.

Originally and correctly tagged as the Majestic Twelve, MJ-12, M12 or simply Maj'ic, but later confused with trivial leagues or brotherhoods such as the Illuminati, those of the current Majestic Group wielded unconditional authority and met weekly to receive and delegate directives. The inevitable, occasional few seizors of power who naïvely refused to comply with Maj'ic's edicts—regardless of generous incentives tendered by M12's omnipresent agents—eventually and rather publicly paid the ultimate price.

And as ever, Earth's accursed civilians bore the brunt of the consequent, perpetual, little Terran wars.

This scheduled meeting day, Majestic's members waited alone in their individual estates' similar, well concealed, sub-basement rooms. Scattered around the globe, The Twelve ranged in age from 38 years to 82. Each was a brilliant, ambitious lesser demon that had birthed more than once into his Terran family of choice, a family that, as always with such spirits, had substantial influence and wealth.

Uppermost among the increasing numbers of demons birthing into Terrah's wealthiest families new and old, all twelve had succumbed to the inescapable veiling syndrome,[101] the post-birth forgetting of whence they came. Yet they retained their ingrained, callous ruthlessness and therefore served their masters well.

Each sat facing a semi-circular arrangement of live, three-dimensional images of his hateful counterparts. Except for their impeccable attire and the malice in their eyes, they represented a colorful assortment of typical earthling males.

None of the all-male group had exchanged greetings since their simultaneous appearance for this session with their dispassionate handlers—the handsome alien-earthling hybrids, Balenos and Salizah. Instead, the twelve alternately stared at one another with the intensity of self-possessed athletes in the closing moments before violent physical contact. To a man, each felt superior to the rest and viewed his peers as unworthy adversaries. Nestled into a tufted leather chair behind an extravagant wooden desk, the group's youngest looked especially cold and cruel.

In an alliance arranged by the aliens, M12 and their families controlled the troubled world's interdependent economies through a cleverly confusing network of hugely forceful multinational corporations. Like all previous members of Majestic, the current twelve shared a demonic lust for wealth and power. And by collaborating with the aliens, they amply satisfied their deep desires.

None of them felt anything for the common earthling, whom they considered to be absurdly unwary and wholly inconsequential in the master scheme of things. Indeed, those native to planet Earth were thoroughly incapable of resisting the manipulative might of Maj'ic's alien masters, the local contingent of the infamous Orion group,[102] aka: *the Og.*

Highly intelligent and completely godless, the Og were a hairless, grey-skinned species with bulbous heads and huge, jet-black eyes. Varied but mostly short and frail looking, the notorious "darkeyes" from Orion—the ruling purebreds from the constellation's manicured motherworlds, along with an assortment of subspecies/conscripts from the outer territories—were feared and despised well beyond their sector of the galaxy.

Despite Orion's swift surrender and forced subservience to the mighty Rehmans[103] eons prior, the group's purebreds maintained their inherent conviction of intellectual and racial superiority. They felt not sympathy. Nor compassion. To the purebreds, such notions were completely alien and indicative of a resignation to defeat. No matter what the circumstances, any display of the compassion defect demonstrated a fundamental weakness and willingness to be subdued. Accordingly—eventually—*all* others should and would be eliminated or enslaved.

Some 8,000 standard years before current times, the group's leadership, Orion Command, won the lucrative commission to prime the evolving tribes of the local constellation, Nordehk, for *willing* absorption into The Master's/*Rehm's* vast domain. Initially, as commissioned minions of the irrepressible Rehmans, the Og "crusaders" (the purebreds and subordinate conscripts from the territories) were to discreetly concoct and escalate chaos on planet Earth/Terrah and five other similarly unsuspecting neighbor worlds. Chaos to which a New Order—Rehman Order—would be brought. Order based on a single language and a unified religion. With a *Living God* to embrace.

From invisible, fourth-density[104] garrisons positioned well outside the orbits of their target worlds, and with all actions coordinated from a tactical GROUP COMMAND located near Nordehk's lone red dwarf, the cunning Og mercenaries operated either brazenly or virtually undetected, save a purposeful, temporary sighting of a low-flying cruiser and/or one or more of its companion discs—or an accidental crash. To assist in the methodical subversion of culture after developing culture, waves of troops from GROUP COMMAND's elite incarnate corps birthed into Nordehk's trusting tribes. Long had such seasoned "Og-incarnates" helped create, confuse and corrupt conflicting, miracle-based religions that always included the calamitous false elements of *divine vengeance* and *reverent fear.* Long had the darkeyed crusaders and their insidious incarnates been fomenting suspicion and cultivating hatred, while introducing new technologies for increasingly lethal war machines.

Upon each new collaborator's induction into the Majestic Group, Og technicians outfitted his private estate with an amphidoric[105] imaging chamber for the demon's weekly session with the others of The Twelve. Since 2019, by the calendar of most Terran nations, Balenos and Salizah had managed the majority of those meetings, the comely hybrids appearing either together or not at all. Sessions dealing with strategic issues were usually chaired by senior officers from the Og's orbiting Terran garrison (which maintained a position directly opposite the Terran solar system's largest planet on the same orbital plane), or from one of five interconnected bases beneath the planet's surface, or from one of two on the dark side of Earth's nameless, hollow, synchronously rotating moon.

At precisely the appointed time, a ghost-like apparition appeared in the open center of all twelve Ma'jic members' secret chambers. Two seconds later it became a perfect, life-sized, <u>three-dimensional image</u>[106] of Balenos and Salizah, as though the two hybrids had teleported themselves into the middle of each collaborator's secluded, sub-basement room.

"Gentlemen..." the two crusaders said together in their typical, unnerving monotone. They sounded and looked live in the flesh within their idyllic, amphidoric projection.

Similar in height and with short dark hair, cold blue eyes and beautifully sculpted faces, the two hybrids could pass for thirty-year-old Terran twins. Nearly ninety years before, they had transferred to the Terran garrison from their quarters in <u>GROUP COMMAND</u>'s[107] elite incarnate wing, before <u>pinning</u>[108] directly into the modified fetuses growing inside their earthling mothers' wombs. As they and their mission planners intended, the two Og-earthling <u>hybrid-incarnates</u>[109] were born within days of each other in the same small town.

To all twelve collaborators, some of whom lived continents apart, the imagery looked alike. To each of Majestic's members it appeared that the two hybrids addressed him alone, while his eleven counterparts—imaged in a semi-circular cluster a few meters back from Balenos and Salizah—watched from behind. The amphidoric projection thereby produced the flattering illusion that B&S spoke to each man personally while standing with their backs to the others, making Maj'ic's individual members feel more important than their imaged peers seemingly relegated to the rear of each room.

"...Ang Kaht." Neither they nor Majestic's alternate handlers ever revealed their emotions. All issued their instructions with detached nonchalance.

"Ang Kaht, crusaders," the twelve responded at once—firmly, in a confident, respectful way. "Glory to Orion."

"The new leadership in the south," Balenos began straightaway, "seems to be having difficulty with perspectives..."

"...with priorities, shall we say," injected Salizah, not entirely monotonic, but effectively void of emotion.

Majestic understood the mandate. Everything of significance that occurred outside the parameters set forth by their agents—whether unintentional or planned by the offenders—had to be dealt with and sometimes swiftly, but most often with patience and in due course. And when personal agendas lost sight of "the Maj'ic vision," no one, not even the world's most powerful politicians, escaped M12's reach and wrath.

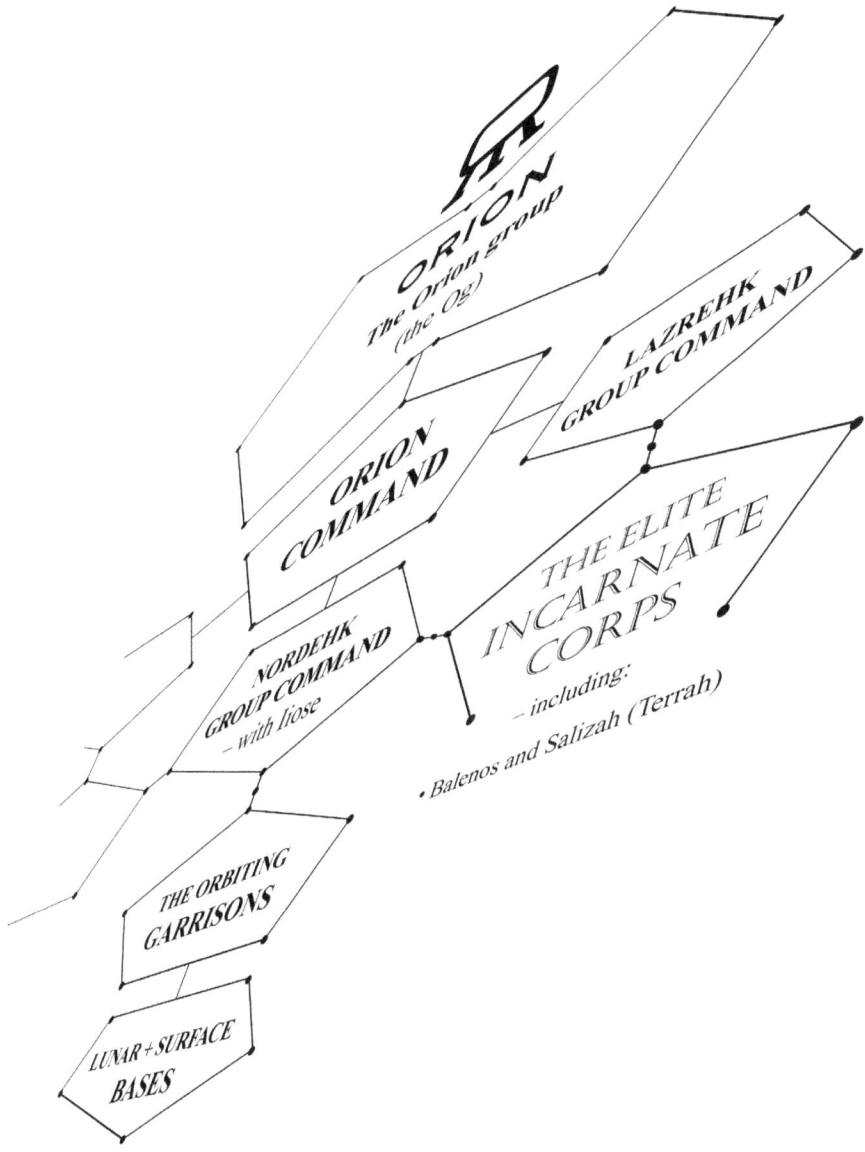

Balenos and Salizah stared awhile. As the group's primary handlers, they often paused between edicts as though searching for betrayals of confidence, or questionings of their unquestionable commands. But as ever, those of the current Majestic Group were strong: supremely confident in themselves and in their masters' designs. Since boarding their first battle cruiser, they remained in awe of Og technologies and knew that the people they represented, the Terrans, globally, were doomed—*destined,* as the darkeyes infrequently reminded them—to serve Orion.

"The exercise on the dark continent," said Salizah, moving on, "has served its purpose."

"End it now," Balenos ordered. When the two handsome hybrids spoke aloud, they did so while utilizing the full telepathic capacities of Orion's most elite crusaders.

"End it cleanly," added Salizah, "while its complexities are largely contained."

Again, the two paused to stare. Not a single collaborator turned his eyes away.

"Within ninety days," Balenos added, "funding for *all* polar projects—north and south—must be halved."

"Questions?" asked Salizah.

None had ever asked a question of his handlers, for if one should require clarification while his purported peers did not…well....

"Concerns?"

None were expressed.

"Next week, then, gentlemen," the hybrids said in unison. "Ang Kaht."

And the imaging abruptly ended, leaving each of The Twelve alone.

CHAPTER 1 — N O T E S

N[101] *the veiling syndrome.* The forgetting of past lives and pre-birth intentions, a phenomenon limited to the third dimension/density.

N[102] *the Orion group* [pron. Ō-rī′-ŏn]. Pitiless mercenaries from the motherworlds and territories of the Orion constellation; seasoned troops commissioned by the Rǝhmans to serve in *His Crusades.*

N[103] *the Rǝhmans* [pron. **Rō**′-mǝns]. Those living within or crusading beyond The Master's (Rǝhm's) vast domain.

N[104] *the fourth density.* The fourth "octave" or "dimension" of reality, a seven-level plane of existence with a common visibility spectrum wherein the resident beings' senses, perceptions and abilities are more highly evolved than in those of the lower realms. As such, most newly Rǝhmanized fourth-density groups are militarized, and then forced through economic necessity to bid for service in *His Crusades.*

N[105] *amphidor.* A highly versatile computer and powerful photonic 3D imaging machine.

N[106] *three-dimensional image.* Og crusaders have long used amphidoric imagery to found and fortify false religions, or to confound authentic Faith. Beaming live or recorded images of one or more performing hybrids from a shrouded disc or cruiser, the shrewd, darkeyed deceivers easily produce effective apparitions, "divine visions," which invariably are readily embraced.

N[107] *NORDEHK GROUP COMMAND.* An interlocking assembly of five battle-ready motherships located near Nordehk's lone red dwarf at the constellation's inward Vesper fringe, GROUP COMMAND is the tactical command center for the Orion group's Nordehk operations.

N[108] *pinning.* To pin. The concentration of one's consciousness into a pinpoint of light for the purpose of traveling instantaneously to destinations seen in the mind's eye. Or, if *The Master's will* be done, to enter and possess other living forms, whether briefly, repeatedly, or for a longer term.

N[109] ***hybrid-incarnates.*** Elite Og crusaders who occupy bodies genetically engineered from local and alien reproductive materials. Designed for a minimum 300-year life span, and with appearances reflecting local perceptions of divine beings, squadrons of the darkeyes' lovely hybrids are to usher in the New Order upon receipt of a glorious Rohman Son's command.

Jake's Take
CHAPTER 1

In this age of implausible denials, those behind the necessarily sustained hoaxing-over of the ever changing Majestic Twelve would now have us believe it was the 33rd President of the United States who assembled that "high-level focus group," but only temporarily and for the purpose of consulting on pressing post-war issues.

The time frame is correct and President Truman was indeed involved. However, the timely installation of that first Council of Twelve was conceived by and overseen by the ranking officer of the darkeyes' orbiting Terran garrison (as detailed in Books 2 and 3), who then met face-to-face with the stunned Americans to inform them that their Commander in Chief now reported to the agents of MJ-12.

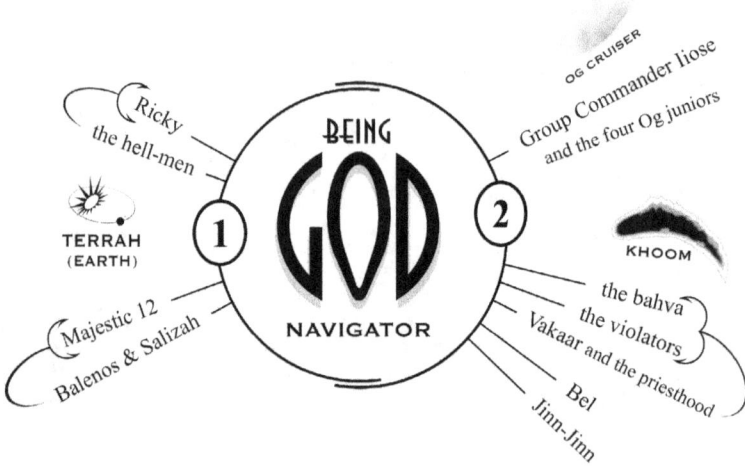

You may also refer to the *CHARTS* and *PLAYERS & WORLDS* at the back of each book.

2

AWAITING THE DEMON-SONS
D-32.3: SPACE / NORDEHK

A silver disc spun slowly in its assigned position near the vague fringe of the Nordehk constellation's second frontier. Inside, in the soft light of several powerful imaging <u>amphidors</u>,[G009] five of its short, thin, grey-skinned crew methodically scanned the space beyond for the Rəhmans reportedly coming.

Three of the five stood side-by-side with their long, thin, <u>six-fingered hands</u>[110] pressed into the gelpads of the primary amphidor's curved console. Their huge black eyes reflected the system's flawless image of the placid stellar night.

On the deck below, the venerable Group Commander Iiose stared into a full-length mirror, fussing with the placement of a small blue medallion on one of his neatly folded collars. Several splendid, large brown moles graced his sagging grey face: late-blooming marks of distinction to those of his kind who had passed 400 standard years.

Four Imperial Lords—four <u>Rəhman Sons</u>[111]—were coming for the reductions, for the final phase of the Nordehk campaign. As longtime head of the local Og command, the old crusader would receive the Sons and summarize the Orion group's accomplishments in the unsuspecting constellation. A review of some 8,000 years.

"Group Commander...." The telepathic call came precisely on time. "The juniors are seated now, Sir. All four in the tactical chamber."

Iiose took a long last look at his regal reflection. Sufficiently self-assured, he drew a deep breath, stepped back, turned and joined two awaiting aides in the cruiser's foyer.

To be safe, Commander Iiose, his aides, the four juniors and five crewmen had arrived in position a day ahead of schedule for this historic rendezvous. The Og could not risk being late for appointments with their punctual masters, the infallible Rəhmans. Even for meetings light years away, imperial ships and Imperial Lords unfailingly appeared at the designated time.

Since their departure two weeks before, the four Og juniors had spent most of their time below deck, alone in their private quarters. After arriving at the rendezvous coordinates, awaiting the call to assemble had been difficult for these select young troops, not too unlike awaiting the charge into battle. But now, sitting together four abreast on lavish, high-backed chairs, the juniors managed to curb their fear. To each, the others seemed composed.

The tactical chamber's curving walls, blackish metallic floor and domed ceiling blended indistinguishably and looked impossibly immense for the ship's modest size. It was an illusion, an imperial innovation—one of few technological marvels the Rəhmans chose to share.

Iiose and his two aides entered quietly and stopped about ten paces from the four seated juniors in the otherwise empty room. Like their five crewmen, all seven troops were impeccably dressed in the colors of Orion: tight jumpsuits brown and seamless, with supple grey boots and six-fingered gloves to match. As larger-skulled, intellectually superior "purebreds" from the motherworlds of Orion, the seven were roughly a third taller than their crewmen—conscripts from the territories—and their legs, arms and bulbous heads were more elongated and distinctly mantis-like.

Big black eyes known widely through the realm, all twelve of the ship's deceptively frail-looking, malicious little mercenaries were seasoned units of the Orion group, the cruel and cunning Og. Masterful concocters of chaos on many an unsuspecting world, the infamous darkeyes excelled at seeding hatred, doubt and fear—that Rəhman Order could then come, and assuredly be embraced.

Silently (telepathically), Iiose ordered the initialization of his cruiser's stellar program. The chamber's lighting dimmed to darkness, and an image of the Nordehk starfield filled the space directly overhead. As an updated copy of an <u>ancient amphidoric chart</u>,[12] the arriving Rəhman Sons would wholly know the stellar scene.

To confirm the program's readiness, Iiose called for the planet Terrah, home to the self-named "earthlings." Stars began rushing toward him, disappearing faster and faster past his broad peripheral vision. The program slowed and a sun appeared. Buffers softened its brilliance as a white-swirled, bright blue world came into view and swelled by the second until it seemed to Iiose and his fellow crusaders that they were in orbit beneath the planet, looking up.

With the brief closing of his left hand, the old commander indicated his satisfaction. The program reversed and Terrah vanished into the light of its star, which faded in magnitude as the others around it rushed in. Soon it was just a faint flicker in the familiar constellation.

Iiose moved a little closer to his chosen ones. Glistening black eyes fixed on all four at once, he cast his thoughts into the juniors' racing minds.

"As exemplary young troops," he said, his supersensory voice sounding uncommonly reverent, "you have been selected to endure an experience for which none can sufficiently prepare."

Although fairly steady in their seats, the juniors' welling eyes told of the terror deep inside.

"Upon the demon's entry, your bodies will strive to suppress the inescapable panic that ensues. Your heart will pound and your glands will gush defensive enzymes to sustain you."

The juniors knew these things and had heard the rumors, too. Deemed fit for demonic possession, they correctly presumed not all survived these infrequent but necessary hostings.

"In that same instant, that paralyzing moment of possession, the warrior will seize control of your reflexes, steady your metabolism and probe your mind. And everything you know—*everything*—will be known by him or her, for female 'Sons' enjoy equally high status and power.

"Most hosts lapse into immediate unconsciousness and may have limited recollections of the event." Iiose paused a moment, remembering. He ranked as one of few Og crusaders to have remained conscious through the honor of his hosting, so very long ago.

"For those who manage to stay aware," the commander continued, "it becomes dreamlike…" *Nightmarish*, he remembered well. "…as you lend your mind and body to the highest of high demons. To a glorious Rǝhman Son.

"The warrior's exit will come as suddenly as his entry, and the suspension of your glandular secretions—the *Son's* suspension of your glandular secretions—will be instantly undone. For those still mentally perceptive, this veritable flood will compound the trauma, and unconsciousness will prevail...."

BEL'S INTRUSION
D-32.4: SPACE / WAY PORTAL

Minutes away, a lone warship fast approached the Nordehk constellation. The enormous vessel, a Rǝhman khoomyahna, had breached and was traversing a cosmic way portal. One of countless vein-like vortices of boiling plasmic vapors and tremendous static discharges, such portals formed the dynamic nervure linking galaxies and stars. Nearly nullifying time and distance, the churning stellar highways revealed themselves only to those that neared the speed of light.

With the khoom's steady revolution, the thin leading edge of its circular hull glowed white hot and flexed in an erratic rhythm, methodically adjusting to the portal's powerful unseen forces. From whitish yellow to orange, and then red-hot to dark crimson, to the cool blue-black of its rolling midsection, the heat dissipated inward as the imperial behemoth shot through as a mere speck inside the endless, violent abyss.

Unpiloted, and after the better part of one standard year inside the celestial continuum, the warship readied herself for emergence into Nordehk, into yet another feral constellation. She would take on the campaign's four Sons, who would suspend their current business shortly, and with their midwayer-guides' firm telepathic lock on the khoomyahna's resident midwayer, would soon arrive—perfectly on time—for their scheduled rendezvous with the loathsome darkeyes.

Within the great ship, 12,000 bahva[113]—12,000 imperial citizens from more than a dozen scattered worlds—lived beneath a vast, simulated sky. Most had volunteered for the lucrative one-way mission to Nordehk and had been selected for their skills and for their likeness to the beings of the constellation under conquest: erect bipeds with opposable thumbs. Closely observant android andrax mingled with the bahva and had been fashioned after them. Tiny roving feritts—weightless, insect-like machines—maintained a broader watch.

Life on the khoomyahna mirrored life in an average Rehman town: an everyday, ordered existence in a small community not unlike that which most of the mission's volunteers had left behind. The khoom's downtown core looked much the same—one of twelve long-perfected conformations set to the lay of the land. And the weather? Strangely unpredictable. But aside from an occasional mild tremor, the ride felt remarkably smooth.

Those onboard who had not volunteered and had been consigned to the Nordehk mission—1,728 convicted violators of The Master's Teachings— wore one or more weighted shackles on their ankles, wrists and necks. Everyone, volunteers and violators alike, dressed in standard-issue blue coveralls and short black boots. Many sported tattoos, assorted piercings, and handmade hats and headwraps that mimicked those of past and current Nordehk clans and fads. For morale, it was allowed.

E lsewhere on the ship, several miles away on an updeck inward from the townscape, a crew of violators worked to remove an obstruction from a plugged diverter valve. Responsible for channeling the flow of turbid liquid sweating from the warship's fleshy inner walls, the criminal crew toiled knee- deep in a ditch that flanked an ample but ill-lit passage to the khoom's rectory, when Vakaar and an entourage of robed and hooded priests came sloshing into view.

As the mission's high priest, or "yamah," Vakaar held final authority in the absence of a Rehman Son. Skinny, hunched and noticeably shorter than the rest, few rarely saw him without his two lanky cohorts—the ones to whom his spies reported—and this day both were at his sides. Stooped with necks awkwardly twisted, they mouthed constant whispers into the scrawny yamah's pointed ears.

"The *'brothers'*," cautioned one of the violators in a low voice to the others of his crew.

"The *'reverent ones'*," sneered another not too loud, before joining in a group bow of feigned respect. But once the priests had passed, and with the deferent effort ignored, the convicts quietly cursed them and resumed their work in the ditch.

Moments later, a pinpoint of shimmering, iridescent light—Vihdæan[114] light—appeared and blossomed, illuminating the dim corridor. The convicts scrambled from their ditch and scattered. A few stopped and turned, covered their eyes and squinted through their fingers at the dazzling form taking shape in midair.

Unseen and unheard by all but the brilliant intruder, the khoom's resident midwayer,[115] Jinn-Jinn, charged into the passageway, screaming insults and vile Rǝhman threats.

The violators heard nothing but the intruder's gentle, reassuring voice in their minds.

"Peace be upon you, dear ones. I am Bel."

Dear ones?

While Jinn-Jinn ranted, five tiny feritts shot past the holy procession, toward the invasive light. A few seconds later, two heavyset andrax came quickly upon the priestly pack.

"A Vihdæan intrusion, Reverence," they said in unison, "not far behind you…on Updeck 89 near the fourth statcon dome."

Vihdæan intrusion? Why bother with such nonsense? And why tell him, since andrax took instructions only from Rǝhman Lords? Forcing a smile and nodding to acknowledge what must have been protocol, Vakaar dismissed the loathsome things with a flick of his wrist, and disappeared into the rectory with the others to prepare for the Sons' arrival.

Unfettered by solid matter, Bel, the Vihdæan spy, began darting through the warship. Jinn-Jinn stayed right with her, hurling a steady stream of verbal abuse. The feritts struggled to keep up, guessing the trespasser's direction in a bid to record what they could. Despite their links with the feritts, and an injection of replacements from several directions, the andrax were slow to penetrate anything solid, and they quickly fell behind.

Bel angled down and through the city, and then inward and up toward the khoom's control deck where she was instantly repelled by an intense vibrational frequency. Momentarily sickened by the impenetrable force that secured the ship's critical systems, she turned, dove, and came upon the khoomyahna's Chamber of the Pods.

GLORY TO ORION

D-32.5: SPACE / NORDEHK

While the four fearful juniors heard their group commander's closing remarks, their flight crew detected the abrupt materialization and decay of a violent plasmic eruption. They immediately recognized it as the opening of a Rehman gate, the telltale signature of an interstellar ship's explosive emergence from an arterial way portal.

Expressionless, the darkeyes reduced their ship's spin-rate and tilted the craft toward the growing tumult. At one revolution per second, its shape became much more distinctive. It wasn't a disc at all. Triangular, flipped at the tips and with the bubbled black domes of three particle centrifuges poking through its belly, the vessel was a heavily armed Og battle cruiser from NORDEHK GROUP COMMAND.

Zooming a mid-range amphidor in on the eruption's coordinates, the crew began recording spectacular static discharges in and around a planet-sized swirl of rapidly dying cosmic vapors some 300 million kilometers away. In seconds, they registered a shimmer and then a colossal, glowing ship bearing down on their position.

Promptly advised, Group Commander Iiose concluded his telepathic discourse to the four fidgety juniors.

"The period of recovery varies," he assured them, "and will not be taken as a measure of weakness or strength. Never will you forget, nor adequately describe, the incommensurable power of these potent warriors, for only the experienced can ever truly know. And soon, crusaders, I shall welcome you to this prestigious fraternity."

Clenching left fists and curling them smartly to the shoulder, the juniors saluted—unsure.

"Ang Kaht, Commander," they replied, properly, and in telepathic unison. "Glory to Orion."

Chapter 2 — N O T E S

G[009] amphidor: [from the GLOSSARY section at the back of this book]
a highly versatile computer and powerful photonic imaging system capable of generating, transmitting and receiving scalable, distortion-free, three-dimensional images

N[110] *six-fingered hands.* Five fingers, plus opposable thumb.

N[111] ***Røhman Sons.*** Fallen angels (both male and female) known to some as Imperial Lords or Sons of Røhm, and to others more correctly *and foremost* as high demons.

N[112] ***ancient amphidoric chart.*** Twelve thousand standard years before, Orion Command received an imperial map of Nordehk along with an invitation to bid on the contract to prime the constellation for conquest. Having already logged hundreds of exploratory missions to Nordehk, the Og were relatively familiar with the starfield's inhabited and uninhabited worlds, but had long been under imperial constraints. To instill fear and confusion, costumed visitations were allowed, but sustained open contact would violate the broad Eighth Commandment:

> *8:* [1]*Only by the hand of Røhm, shall All That Is be brought to Order.*
> —from The Teachings (The Book of Røhm)

N[113] ***bahva*** [pron. **bä´**-vä]. Røhman slang for *bhuvani*/beings; imperial citizens; ordinary beings of The Master's vast domain.

N[114] ***the Vihdæa*** [pron. Vĭd-**ā´**-yä]. Etherean administrators of the constellations; a largely passive, largely loyal order, the Vihdæa are local keepers of the Light.

N[115] ***midwayer.*** Creatures of eternity, midwayers (or more formally, *peshim* [pron. pĕ-**shēm´**]) spontaneously manifested midway between the fourth and fifth densities where they remain forever bound—billions in every galaxy, all endowed with special talents but unable to reproduce. Few entities have an extrasensory ability to accurately lock on to a particular point in space. The Vihdæa are capable, and though the Sons can maneuver between planets of the same solar system and stars of adequate magnitudes, the Sons depend on midwayer "scouts" to find shrouded or rapidly moving warships: a challenge made easy by a telepathic fix with one of their kind. To monitor activities inside unpiloted Rohman ships trekking through cosmic highways, "resident midwayers"/midwayer-sentinels are assigned temporarily and then released from duty after their vessel's emergence at its destination.

Jake's Take
CHAPTER 2

It's probably best to keep our collective heads in the sand than to believe that the Og have long been here. Or worse: to consider the likelihood that they have come with bad intentions.

Their widely reported, huge jet-black eyes, however, *would* seem to suggest that the sun or suns whence this obviously ancient race evolved are rather old and growing dim. And since our bright young sun and underappreciated waterworld are fundamentally here for the taking....

Ahhh, but bad-intentioned aliens are one thing, and high demons quite another.

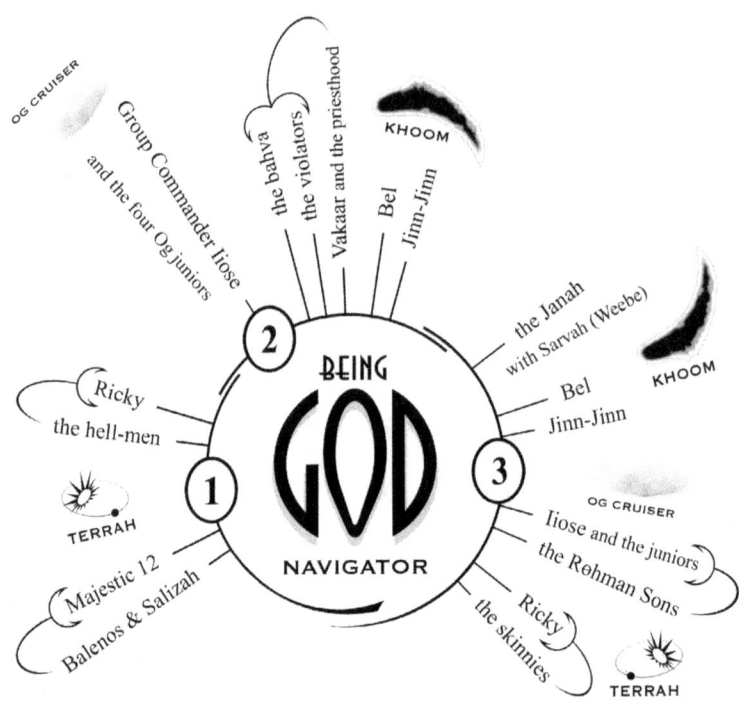

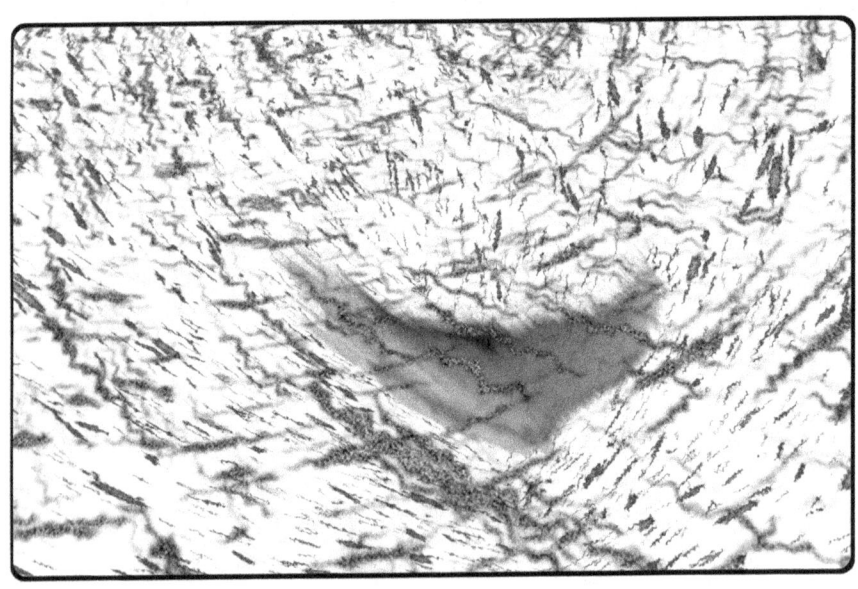

3

CHAOS AND LIGHT

D-32.6: SPACE / KHOOMYAHNA

Thirteen covert rebels huddled in their secluded hideaway: a cramped nook near the eighth of the khoom's twelve static containment domes. They had heard rumors of an intrusion, and of the intruder's brilliant light.

Like the other free bahva^{G030} onboard the khoomyahna, these thirteen young Rǝhman citizens had volunteered for the one-way mission to Nordehk and had met the selection criteria. Quite unlike the others aboard, however, these were some of the Janah, a secret sect of twenty-two beings bent on escaping the Empire's stifling *Order*.

Ardent anarchists, the Janah believed in a single, genuine Originator whose purest form was Chaos, the unrestrained Primal Force of All Creation. In accordance with and as a product of Chaotic Law, they and all of Chaos' creatures should be free to come and go and do as they pleased. And to thrive or simply perish.

All twenty-two members of the secret sect believed that by embracing the Primal Force and channeling Its vigor, they would become angels in the afterlife: protectors of Light, the common thread of Chaos. And like the realm's billions of other decent closet anarchists, they supposed Rǝhm—the self-proclaimed Bringer of Order—to be no less than *The Devil Himself.*

Twelve of the Janah rebels crouched around the thirteenth, who sat cross-legged, trembling on the floor.

"The intruder sounds like an *angel,* Sarvah," one of them whispered encouragingly.

"Yes, yes, Weebs—*an angel.* She might still be here. We have to hurry."

Eyes closed tightly, Sarvah shook her head.

"Find her, Weebie," urged another. "You can do it. Sense the angel's light. Breathe deeply. *Find her....*"

A special child born with the gift, Sarvah had become invaluable as the Janah's eyes and ears. Able to project the essence of her being to destinations near and far but ever afraid of getting caught, she always needed her comrades' reassurances before riding the mystical pranah, the elusive spiraling energy that carried her consciousness away. Every time, she had to be convinced. But every time, Sarvah—"Weebs" or "Weebie"—relented.

For Sarvah's out-of-body projections, the Janah had to form a circle of at least seven who knelt, raised their arms and joined hands over her head to form a living cone that could harness and concentrate the pranah, that strange etheric force. A fascinating assortment of beings surrounded her this day, a collection of comrades sporting a variety of anthropoidal features from the racial blends of several Rǝhmanized worlds. Still exhibiting discernible species' beginnings, including arthropods and reptiles, some like Sarvah looked plump and seemingly insecure, but all were strong of purpose and resolute in their common belief.

"Find out what the angel's doing, girl." Sarvah kept trembling. "We be all right. We be okay." Such consolations had spawned her nickname and always seemed to soothe her.

Finally, she calmed herself and gave the familiar scant nod that indicated her readiness to ride. Then, with head bowed, a composed Sarvah joined her friends in whispering their determined pledge and prayer.

"May Chaos and Light prevail."

Soon melding with the pranah, Sarvah felt its swirling energy rise and then rapidly draw her consciousness toward Bel, the Vihdæan[G381a] intruder. As though by magnetic attraction, she shot faster and uncontrollably faster through the warship's decks and walls until coming suddenly upon angelic luminescence.

In all her projections Sarvah had never been *pulled* that way—so quick and beyond her regulation—and she froze a moment, frightened and bewildered.

"Yes. Th…the light," she whispered after a while through scarcely parted lips, and trembling again within her comrades' cone. "I hh..have 'er now—the angel. We're…uh.... Shhhhe's in the b..black chamber."

Near the heart of the khoomyahna, the warship's pentagonal "Chamber of the Pods" featured five inclined walls skinned with sheets of rare black granite. Concealed doorways opened only to registered vibrations including that of the priesthood's yamah, Vakaar, and the roaming 'drax![116] Few of the warship's common bahva had ever gone inside.

Three deep steps of gold-trimmed crimson stone led down from the base of all five inward-leaning walls to a glossy floor of the same crimson material. Mildly iridescent, ivory-colored veins ran throughout the noble stone, indicating that all had been carved from a huge, single slab.

Rounded black granite platforms lay neatly fitted into all five of the dark chamber's corners and spilled down over the stairs. Like the steps, the corner platforms were masterfully inlaid in gold that featured Rɘhman script, enameled reliefs and proportioned chains of the imperial sign. Each platform supported a large gold casting of a unique, powerfully built Vu-dog. The fanciful beasts were highly detailed with feathery fur and intricately woven manes and tails. Dressed in ceremonial battle gear, they stood around seven cubits[117] tall—twice that of the average bahva. Thick and pointed black granite claws curled out from tufted paws in front, while shorter, less-curved spikes of the same material protruded from the toes in back. All five dogs' mouths were closed, save one that bared broad razor-teeth of ancient yellowed ivory. Their heads were bowed and cocked aside, eyes bulging and looking down with a menacing glare beneath brows deeply furrowed.

A three-stepped circular platform of polished black granite lay centered on the crimson floor. Its diameter equaled half the chamber's median length, and its branching, unbroken veins indicated that it, too, had been formed from a single slab. And like the chamber's perimeter stairs and floor, it had been masterfully edged in heavy, patterned gold.

The central platform appeared to support a high pentagonal dais that had also been carved from crimson stone. In fact, the dais was part of the same huge slab that formed the chamber's stairs and floor, and it rose up through the midst of the platform laid around it. On each of the pentagonal dais' five sides, a set of twelve steep steps led to a double-sized, golden, gem-studded throne. Arranged symmetrically around the base of the crimson dais were five partially translucent, light-filled pods. Four of the pods were nestled on plush elliptical rugs that featured scenes and script that boasted the greatest triumphs of a righteous Rɘhman Son. The fifth, half again as large, lay on a thick mat of woven gold and precious imperial fibers. Vibrant blue energy fields enveloped the five limp and dormant, genetically flawless bodies inside.

T wo tiny uncommonly bright feritts[118] shot suddenly up through the chamber's floor and began circling Bel, the radiant intruder. Although the feritts frightened Sarvah, they seemed not to have detected her projection. Dozens and then hundreds more soon joined the swirling swarm.

"Be calm, dear one," Bel said silently to the Janah's projectionist over Jinn-Jinn's incessant ranting, "and rejoice in the Light that bonds us."

Jinn-Jinn[119] shrieked and cursed, thinking the intruder's words were meant for him. In the sanctity of the Janah's cone, Sarvah's eyebrows raised and her closed eyelids flickered. With lips together, her jaw quivered and then stretched out. And in an instant, her consciousness returned.

"The angel spoke to me! She saw my projection! The angel saw!"

Meanwhile, the luminous trespasser shifted her attention to the imposing golden chair. Known well to all Vihdæa, the legendary throne was detailed with enameled script and imperial battle scenes, and it sparkled with thousands of orange, yellow, and rubious gems. Emblazoned high on its quilted backrest: the daunting sign of Rǝhm.

Bel stared a moment and flared her angelic light. Then her vibrant form compressed into a brilliant pinpoint that promptly streaked away.

HOSTING THE DEMON SONS
D-32.7: SPACE / NORDEHK

A perfect, three-dimensional image of the rendezvousing Rǝhman warship loomed large inside the flight deck of the awaiting Og^{G254a} cruiser. Huge dark eyes transfixed, Group Commander Iiose's flight crew watched the beast slow to a stop. Its periphery still glowed, but just red-hot now in its continued, rapid dissipation of the searing heat.

The little crusaders stared in amazement as the warship's cracked and scarred leading edge regained its normal charcoal coloring and began healing before their glistening eyes. Shedding damaged sections, it started regenerating itself, blowing chunks of charred hull into space and replacing them anew from within. Everything chronicled of these rarely seen, legendary behemoths now rang true.

Dwarfing the gigantic motherships that resupplied their orbiting garrisons, the khoom was a frightful sight. These troops knew the reputed firepower of the Rǝhmans' much smaller vihmyanas, the dreaded destroyers that had brought swift victory to countless legions of Orion since the Og's own surrender and prompt conscription into *His Crusades*. And so, as the little mercenaries stood motionless with their glossy black eyes open wide, they could not imagine this flexing, twitching monster's full destructive might.

The arriving Sons' personal scouts—Poxx, Bhu, Ænus, and Iddh—burst in unseen through the tactical chamber's curved walls. Supremely confident and playfully malicious, they unleashed an unheard torrent of obscenities at the four seated juniors and the other standing three![20]

The leftmost junior suddenly snapped backward with enough force to skid his seat half a meter and to generate a jarring screech on the chamber's blackish metal floor. A mild luminance radiated from the crusader's bulbous head, as the demon Mohaar[121] willed his host's chair quietly back in line with the other three. The warrior then raised his gloved fingers and began tapping them in a synchronization of left and right, outside in from the sixth to the thumb, then from the thumb to the sixth, rhythmically repeating the roll.

Group Commander Iiose and his aides remained still, and strove to conceal their fear.

To the invisible scouts' covert cackles and as urine dripped from beneath the rightmost high-backed chair, the second Son, the warrior <u>Wohtan</u>[122] slammed into the rightmost junior, jerking her torso forward and forcing her chin nearly to her knees. Head illuminated, Lord Wohtan held the moment; warm and wet, he stared at the chamber's tiled floor. Then the demon hawked and tasted the junior's phlegmy spittle as he looked up at the image of Nordehk, at yet another collection of witless worlds in desperate need of Rehman Order.

Eyes burning with unbridled loathing, Wohtan spat and turned his gaze to Iiose and the other two long-armed, darkeyed dwarfs standing frozen in their boots. The Son had little use for imperial hirelings—for *any* imperial hirelings, <u>fourth-density</u>[G122] or otherwise—especially these overpaid, conniving swindlers from Orion. *Little use, but for his own desires.*

Without any indication save the abrupt illumination of her host's smoothly taut, grey little face, <u>Lord Dhanz</u>[123] entered the third. And upon a brightening to twice and then three times the others' luminescence as <u>Lord Zhol</u>[124] took possession of the fourth, Iiose and his aides closed their sensitive eyes, knelt, bowed their heads and silently pledged their hearts to Rehm.

As "Lord of the Orbits"—Overlord of the Nordehk campaign—Zhol bore responsibility for the conquest's outcome and ultimate profitability, and he assumed its initial and interim financial burdens. Having personally recruited his three companions to manage the requisite reductions, Zhol, as the campaign's senior Son, would oversee the Rehmanization of the locals who would survive, and he would help maximize their potentials.

With two resounding words, "Rise, bhuvani," Lord Zhol demeaned his darkeyed minions.

Bhuvani? Formal Rehman for "beings," the usage deeply disturbed Iiose and his aides. Had the demon addressed them as *crusaders,* it would have conveyed imperial recognition of their service. At the least it would have signified a token measure of respect.

The three Og seniors rose to their feet—gingerly, and to another round of unheard cackles from the Sons' invisible, hovering scouts. Aside from their slow, shallow breathing, the glowing juniors remained steady in their seats.

Iiose knew to start his telepathic briefing. Standing between his two aides, he moved one bold step ahead.

"By your radiance, my Lords, are we honored this day." A proper greeting, to the word. "Our charge, to prime the constellation for conquest, *'that the tribes be needful; that they shall willingly embrace The Master's songs,'* has been met."

With no reciprocative movement, no acknowledging signals from any of the four, the old group commander cleared his throat and took a moment to gather himself.

"The following actions and developments," he continued, "are detailed in the data now flowing to your khoomyahna. A transfer of capsules containing the requested samples and codes for Nordehk's flora and fauna, including genetic materials from the higher species, is also underway."

Still nothing from the self-illuminated Sons, save a persistent glare from Lord Wohtan, the hateful second to arrive. Despite feeling extremely unnerved, Iiose managed to project the required, outward strength.

"A look at the worlds, my Lords, and a general overview." On cue, the commander's remote crew zoomed the stellar program in on the constellation's core system and home world of the ancients.

"One: Mhu. The progenitors of Nordehk's tribes, the so-called ancients of Mhu, retain a purely positive polarity and remain committed to the Light. Having completed their transition from the third to fourth density some 240,000 years ago, those of Mhu have been left to your discretion, as prescribed." Again no signals, no encouragement, no response. But neither did Iiose sense any scanning of his mind.

"Two: Varah, my Lords…the Empire's *twelfth* elantah,[125] and first of the ancients' brood…here, in the constellation's first pentahm![126]"

The program pulled back from the core system and moved to Mhu's nearest neighboring star, zooming to that sun's innermost, spectacularly ringed gas giant, and to Varah, the giant's beautifully mottled, water-bearing moon.

"Having focused on spiritual advances, Varah's inhabitants, technologically, have fallen behind their later-settled cousins—those of Khrae, the second of the ancient's brood. Most notably, the Varahns' subsequent awareness and inherent fear of their distant neighbor-cousins may represent a state of exploitable vulnerability."

The second junior grunted and briefly but noticeably brightened. The demon inside—Lord Wohtan—bore responsibility for bringing Varah into the fold. He knew well the Varahns' vulnerabilities, including their inherent fear of their not-so-distant neighbors, the technologically advanced Khraelings.

Long had the Son formulated a plan of action to seal the Varahns' fate. The *audacity* of this presumptuous little Og commander to overstate the obvious and to dare presume credit for Lord Wohtan's perfect plan.... Such insubordination would *not* go unpunished—not in the Overlord's eyes, nor in the eyes of Rɵhm.

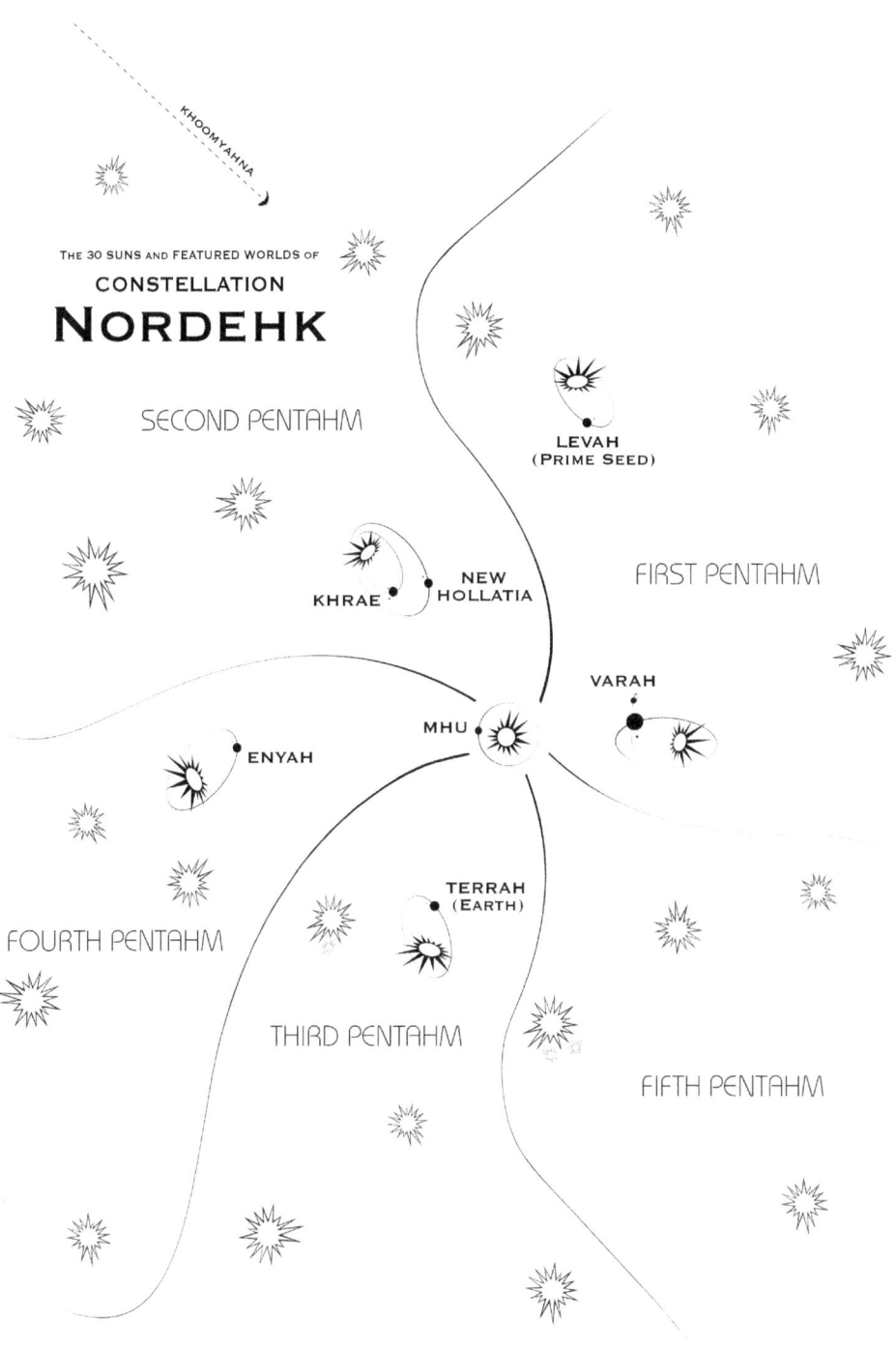

KHOOMYAHNA

THE 30 SUNS AND FEATURED WORLDS OF
CONSTELLATION
NORDEHK

SECOND PENTAHM

LEVAH
(PRIME SEED)

FIRST PENTAHM

NEW
HOLLATIA

KHRAE

VARAH

MHU

ENYAH

TERRAH
(EARTH)

FOURTH PENTAHM

THIRD PENTAHM

FIFTH PENTAHM

Iiose noted the temporary rise in the second demon's luminescence, the one continuously glaring at him. And mistakenly feeling somewhat ingratiated, he kept on.

"As charged, my Lords, other than to maintain an incarnative presence within the Varahn monarchy, we have taken no direct actions of late." With his every breath, the better—the safer—he felt. "Three: Khrae, the second of the ancients' two brood planets, is here in the second pentahm, some 16 light-years from our current position and 4.8 from Mhu." Iiose spoke in terms of standard light-years: Rohman light-years, the imperial unit of measure for lesser stellar distance.

"Through a slow but steady erosion of populace polarity, we estimate that 14% of the Khraelings are <u>favorably inclined</u>[27] Their most recent foray of merit, some 600 standard years ago, saw the near-annihilation of one of Khrae's ten tribes, the so-called Jakomen people. Since the surviving Jakomen's self-imposed exile on Khrae's terra-formed sister planet 'New Hollatia,' the strained relationship between the Jakomen and their Khraeling cousins—and the lingering calls for retribution—may present an opportunity for a controlled reduction."

Lord Mohaar, possessor of the leftmost junior, made mental note of the commander's intimation, for it reinforced a tentative plan he had long contrived.

"Four: Levah, the 'Prime Seed'…here, my Lords, in the first pentahm, some 7 light-years from Varah and roughly 4 from Khrae."

As the program pulled back from New Hollatia and zoomed in on nearby Levah, the commander raised one hand over his head and confidently curled it back as though holding the pristine world in his gloved palm.

"Under the ancients' direction," Iiose continued, lowering his hand and privately pleased with the execution of his practiced showmanship, "Varah, Khrae, and New Hollatia are preparing to jointly colonize the so-called Seed. There is to be a 100-day festival on Khrae designed to celebrate the occasion, and which will culminate in the joint departure of 200 'settlers': 100 from Varah, 90 from Khrae, and 10 from New Hollatia. Festivities are scheduled to begin in 33 days as time is measured by the Khraelings, whose 24-hour planetary rotation is within seconds of the Rohman standard day.

"Five: the two 'youngers.' Enyah and its primitive 'bahtuus,' here in the fourth pentahm…are, to all purposes, set to sing The Master's songs. Terrah, our famous 'Planet of the Cross'," the old commander continued, adroitly referencing an imperially well-known and well-rewarded, clandestine Og triumph, "here, in the adjacent third pentahm, is well into an as yet reversible, self-destruct mode…" Iiose rolled his hand while adding, "…with accelerating warmings, polar meltings, mounting tectonic imbalance, heightened volcanic activity, earthquakes, and the like.

"As commissioned, my Lords, we have sufficiently installed and reshaped the world's predominant religions, such that the resulting sectarian hatred has evolved to fuel the desired hastening of civil and regional wars. Of late, however, and in response to a calling from Nordehk's customarily passive Vihdæa,[G381b] a sizeable contingent of MoLs[128]—mostly fourth-density, but lately several from the fifth—have birthed and continue to birth on Terrah. We therefore humbly suggest that the imminent geological upheavals be accelerated, that the changes may be effected *before* establishing the New Order. And, ever mindful of the Ehkilah Phenomenon, that the potential for a density jump be preempted and effectively nullified."

Behind the glistening eyes of her unconscious young host, Lord Dhanz quietly considered the commander's cautious warning. Charged with delivering a needful, willing Terrah into The Master's mighty hands, she knew well the Ehkilah Phenomenon. And knew well the need to countervail.

"With more than 6% of Terrah's inhabitant 'earthlings' favorably oriented," Iiose concluded, "and its planetary majority technologically roused, our hybrid forces await your calling for deployment, while experiments continue with our units on the ground...."

THE PRETENDERS

D-32.8: TERRAH (EARTH)

Any second now, young Ricky would hear it: the sound of hellies charging. That sickening, swishing sound their pantlegs made as the bastards shot out from the shadows and rushed toward his bed.

Just thinking about it, just knowing it was coming, nearly made him puke. So he tried to sit or turn his head or cough or growl or scream instead, to make them stop or make them leave. But helpless in his hypno-sleep, he could not move except to breathe and keep his eyelids tightly squeezed.

Then came that rapid swishing...*and a hundred fingers grabbed his sheets!*

— ○ ☼ ○ —

Ricky floated trancelike through some walls and trees and clouds, and then he was like flying through the sky beneath the stars.

Pretty soon he saw bright colors and a shiny, silver ball...that kept on getting bigger....

— ∘ ☼ ∘ —

He woke up with skinnies—the really creepy tall ones, the ones who wore white suits—standing round his special bed. Of all the types of hell-men, the skinnies scared him most. It was like they were the bosses of the little pricks who took him, kind of like they were the masters and the hellies were their slaves.

So Ricky shut his eyes again real tight and hoped and prayed with all his might that he'd wake up and they'd be gone. But like always, they began to squeeze him here and poke him there. And like always, he began to cry.

Voices told him not to worry; voices said he'd be okay. "You're very, very special." "Other kids are not the same." That's what those assholes always said when they had him on that silver bed.

Then the whirring, scraping, sucking sounds and buzzing in his brain, made him want to shout and try to kick and turn himself away. But his legs were stuck and his head was stuck and his mouth was stuffed with hoses crammed in like stinky, oily clay.

— ∘ ☼ ∘ —

It didn't hurt that much this time, inside, where they were feeling. But he knew his private parts were next, so he did his iceman thing and imagined slowly freezing.

Soon he dreamed of flying through blue canyons made of ice. They looked smooth and steep and really deep, but they ended just like that. So he flapped his arms and went way high where it was nice and warm. But it kept on getting hotter 'cause the sun kept getting closer 'til it shot right past and smashed into the earth. And the sky lit up and then went black…and Ricky lost his way.

But then he saw a glorious light that got so bright it filled the night with a hundred swirling rainbows. Crowds of people gathered far below to stand and stare or just be there while others prayed out loud.

Then Ricky spotted skinnies here and there among the crowd. They were taking hands and taking vows and swearing that was holy ground…*they were pretending to be angels!*

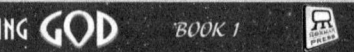

CHAPTER 3 — N O T E S

G[030] bahva: citizen-commoners of the Empire; Rǝhman slang for a "being" or "beings"

G[381a] Vihdæa: [pron. Vǐ-**dē′**-ǎh] angelic administrators of the galaxies' living constellations, and local keepers of the Light

N[116] *'drax (andrax).* Modifiable Rǝhman androids; societal attendants and enforcers of The Teachings on Rǝhmanized worlds, and formidable weapons in war.

N[117] *cubit.* An imperial unit of measure equal to 12 Rǝhman inches, 0.485 of an Og meter, or 19.1 Terran inches.

N[118] *feritts.* Weightless, mobile, lightly armed, insect-like surveillance machines.

N[119] *Jinn-Jinn* ♂. The khoomyahna's temporary resident midwayer.

G[254a] (the) Og: short for **O**rion **g**roup, the Og are a widely varied, inherently godless, resentfully subjugated and therefore ever scheming, shrewdly deceitful fourth-density species, commissioned by their Rǝhman masters for long-term service in *His Crusades*

N[120] *the other standing three.* Group Commander Iiose and his two aides.

N[121] *Mohaar* ♂ [pron. **Mō′**-här]. A righteous Imperial Lord of the Realm, and glorious Son of Rǝhm. Lord Mohaar's eternally committed, personal midwayer/scout is *Iddh* ♂ [pron. Ĭd].

N[122] *Wohtan* ♂ [pron. **Wō′**-tǎn]. A righteous Imperial Lord of the Realm, and glorious Son of Rǝhm. Lord Wohtan's eternally committed, personal midwayer/scout is *Ænus* ♂ [pron. **Ē′**-nǔs].

G[122] fourth density: the fourth "octave" or "dimension" of reality; a seven level plane of existence with a common visibility spectrum wherein senses, perceptions and abilities are more highly evolved than those of the lower realms

N[123] ***Dhanz*** ♀ [pron. Dôns]. A righteous Imperial Lord of the Realm, and glorious Son of Rɘhm. Lord Dhanz's personal, eternally-committed midwayer/scout is ***Bhu*** ♀ [pron. Boo].

N[124] ***Zhol*** ♂ [pron. Zōl]. A righteous Imperial Lord of the Realm, glorious Son of Rɘhm, and Overlord of the Nordehk campaign. Lord Zhol is an inspirational Son who leads by example, a warrior who fully understands the relationship between wisdom and wealth and how to balance the pursuit of both. As Overlord of now fifteen constellations—three more than Lord Dhanz—Zhol spends much of his time preparing updates for the twelve Supreme Sons (the Rɘhman High Court), and tending to his holdings in the realm. Lord Zhol's personal, eternally-committed midwayer/scout is ***Poxx*** ♂ [pron. Pŏks].

N[125] ***elantah*** [pron. ē-lăn′-tə]. Varah is among the family of cosmic curiosities dubbed "elantahs" by the Rɘhmans: temperate, water-bearing, lunar planetoids. Eleven such oddities exist within the Empire. Varah would become the twelfth.

N[126] ***pentahm*** [pron. **pĕn**′-tôm]. Pentahms are five, adjoining, similarly sized, three-dimensional stellar sectors that constitute a constellation and radiate outward from its core. Underdeveloped pentahm sections are known as "frontiers."

N[127] ***favorably inclined.*** Negatively oriented/polarized; focused on self and on the trappings of serving oneself, as opposed to a positive polarization and service unto others, and unto the common good.

G[381b]   Vihdæa: [pron. Vĭ-**dē**′-ăh] ethereans of the sixth density who administrate the constellations in Councils of eight, the typically passive Vihdæa are largely loyal to the Light, with but a wee percentage answering Rɘhm's calls to defect and forever serve in *His Crusades*

N[128] ***MoLs.*** Mercenaries of Light; entities of a positive polarity who, of their own free will, incarnate from the higher realms to inspire and enlighten those of evolving cultures.

Jake's Take
CHAPTER 3

In the wee hours, as a kid, I did endure my share of ghastly hobgoblins slipping into my room to feast on me as I lay there paralyzed. But I didn't fashion Ricky after me.

Abductees are stuck in a recurring nightmare and are undeserving of ridicule, for are they not among the few to confront the enemy and survive? Virtually all who have come forward suspect repeat instances and speak of indelicate treatment that included painful surgical procedures, and what may be the most telling *and* most damning—vis-à-vis intentions.

Right from the first well-documented case (that of Betty and Barney Hill), surprising numbers of the taken resist and plead that their captors have no right to do such things.

"Yes, we do," the darkeyes are widely reported to chillingly reply. "You are our creation."

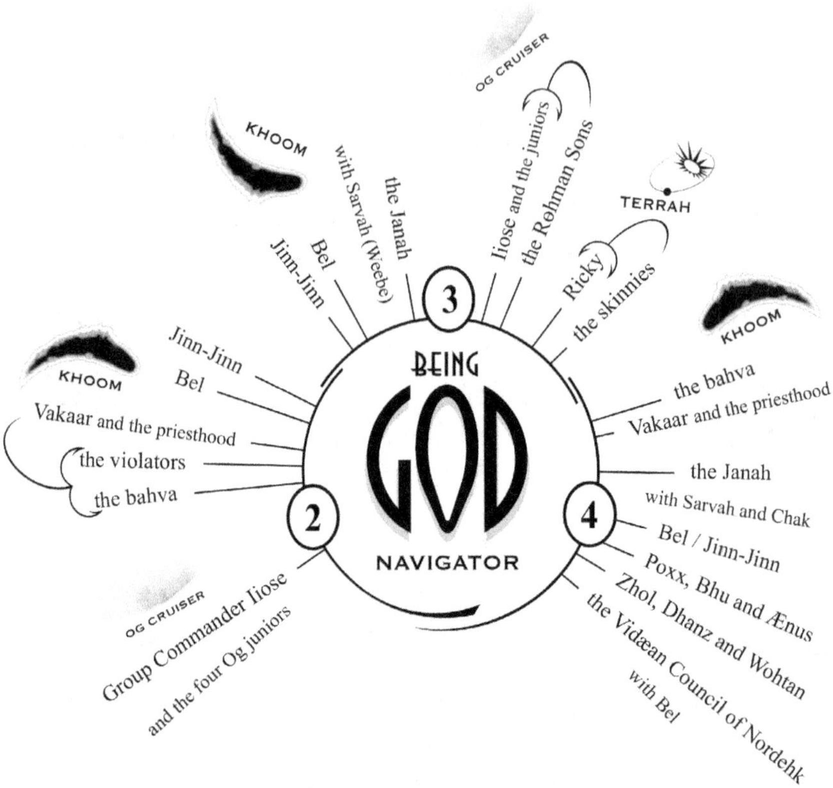

KHOOM

OG CRUISER

the Janah
with Sarvah (Weebe)

Bel
Jinn-Jinn

Iiose and the juniors
the Rohman Sons

Ricky
the skinnies

TERRAH

3

Jinn-Jinn
Bel

Vakaar and the priesthood

KHOOM

the violators

the bahva

KHOOM

BEING

GOD

NAVIGATOR

the bahva
Vakaar and the priesthood

the Janah
with Sarvah and Chak

Bel / Jinn-Jinn

Poxx, Bhu and Ænus

Zhol, Dhanz and Wohtan

the Vidæan Council of Nordehk
with Bel

2

4

OG CRUISER

Group Commander Iiose
and the four Og juniors

4

RUMORS

D-32.9: SPACE / KHOOMYAHNA

The <u>bahva</u>^{G030} grew increasingly excited as rumors raced through the decks. The khoom's emergence from the way portal and its full stop minutes later could only mean they were near their new home. Soon they could dress freely, and after the base paygrades of mission travel, they could begin accumulating capital again.

Word was also spreading that <u>Vakaar</u>[129] and a number of the brothers had been seen marching in formation toward the Chamber of the Pods.

"The yamah's heading for the black chamber!" "The Overlord must be coming!" "The Sons could soon be here!"

With his two lanky cohorts whispering in his ears, and 48 subordinates following four abreast behind them, Vakaar stepped straight toward the chamber's sealed entrance—as though distracted and heading for certain impact with the solid granite wall.

But the throughway fast confirmed the high priest's vibration, and temporarily dissolved. And four by four, with their yamah in the lead, the priestly contingent entered the khoom's black chamber and stepped down into the softly lit, pyramidal room.

THE COUNCIL AWAITS

D-32.10: NORDEHK

Seven luminous figures sat at a translucent, sky-blue roundtable engulfed in golden fog: a hazy expansion of their radiant, etherean forms. In an accelerated state of becoming, their heavenly reality shifted constantly as an ever-changing construct of their uncorrupted minds.

Their spacious, <u>thought-formed</u>[130] table consisted of three concentric rings that stepped down in height from the outside in toward an open middle. With one space open, Nordehk's pensive Vihdæan Council anxiously awaited the return of their sister, <u>Bel</u>.[131]

THE DEMON-SONS ARISE

D-32.11: SPACE / KHOOMYAHNA

In their hideaway behind a corridor near a lower section of the khoomyahna's eighth statcon dome, nine of the Janah[132] rebels huddled with Sarvah, their nervous projectionist. Rumors had something happening in the black chamber, and the nine were trying to persuade her to go back for a look.

Sarvah sat cross-legged. Her stubby little hands covered her chubby little face. "No," she insisted, trembling and shaking her head. She knew she had to do it, but just felt too afraid. "If the angel could sense my presence, then the warriors can, too."

The vast majority of the empire's anarchists, including the Janah, figured the Sons were fallen angels. But had they kept their angelic powers, or lost— or gained—a few?

Like most imperial citizens, Sarvah had seen Rehman Lords, but never had she spied on one. She understood, however, that her information-gathering projections of consciousness were crucial to the Janah's intended escape. And what better source of reliable information than the very Lords of this campaign?

"Sarvah, please," said Chak, the sect's strangest-looking but most persuasive member and one of Sarvah's closest friends. "Just a glimpse, dearheart." Each of Chak's lateral eyes moved and blinked independent of the other. "Come back the moment you think you're in danger, before they can know for sure that you're there. We be all right. We be okay."

"I...I can't do it," she sniffled, "I just can't. Not since the angel saw me. I'm sorry. It's too dangerous...for all of us, not just me."

"We know the risks, Weebs," tried another. "But the only way we'll learn anything of value is from the Sons. And as we discussed before the khoom's departure...actually before we signed on: it's you—only you, through your projections—who can eavesdrop on the Sons and hopefully discover something to enable our escape."

Eyes closed and tears trickling down her cheeks, Sarvah kept shaking her head and rejecting their continued encouragements...

"You're our hero, Weebs." "You can do this, girlfriend." "Just a glimpse, dearheart—really. Just a glimpse."

...until finally—as always, with a negligible nod—she lowered her hands and cupped them in her lap.

— ○ ☼ ○ —

Unlike her swift flight to the angelic light just an hour before, Sarvah rode the mystical pranah[133] with absolute control. Destination in her mind's eye, she jockeyed her way upward and inward through the khoom until she reached an inclined upper section of the chamber's rich black outer wall.

Working her way up two more decks toward the room's pyramidal apex, the young projectionist skillfully pressed in through the black chamber's dark outer skin and into some earthy middle matter. Similar to that of the warship's common decks and walls, the core material felt denser and definitely thicker…and then different, like stone again. Poking partially through, Sarvah peered warily at the scene below.

Dozens of the khoom's priesthood ringed the central platform that held the chamber's <u>five light-filled pods, steep-stepped dais and imposing golden throne</u>.[134] Robed and hooded, the brothers stood side by side staring at the pods, guardedly speculating and watching for some sign of entry, not sure quite what to expect. None had ever seen Sons rise, but most believed the rumor that the order in which each warrior took control of his podded fleshy body subtly indicated rank.

Sarvah saw Vakaar hunched in the brothers' midst, his black robe trimmed in crimson, contrasting the others' crimson trimmed in black. As usual, Dehniss and Phobb—the high priest's two long-limbed cohorts— flanked him and stood stooped and whispering in his ears, and she wondered how he could absorb their constant, simultaneous input. But for "His Reverence," such feats were easily achieved.

Of an elite, fourth-density order akin to that of the infamous <u>Og</u>,[G254b] Vakaar—under the Sons' guidance—could abandon his <u>temporal vehicle</u>[135] at will, and reincarnate anew. For this, the Nordehk campaign, he had been issued an exceptional <u>third-density</u>[136] body of the Overlord's design, one endowed with advanced powers that included an ability to vaguely hear and see the invisible midwayers, or "peshim," as those entities were properly known. Of the 144 priests aboard the warship, only Vakaar could sense the presence of the warriors' wicked little guides. With her special gifts, however, Sarvah— if close enough—could feel a midwayer's powerfully negative vibrations and telltale cooling of the surrounding air. Otherwise, very few besides the Sons and the Vihdæa could readily detect the demons' stealthy scouts.

Fresh from <u>their meeting with the Og</u>,[137] and with unheard shrieks and yells, three of the Sons' peshim—Poxx, Bhu and Ænus—burst through the chamber's sloping walls and began circling the room, cackling, cursing and insulting the oblivious "brothers of the crimson robe."

Sarvah immediately sensed the dark midwayers' presence as a brief sickening feeling and a sudden weight in the flat region on her forehead's opposite sides. Seeing Vakaar glance upward, she squinted through her projection and managed to discern the faint aural wisps of the three circling scouts. Except for the constant whispering of the yamah's two cohorts who never seemed to skip a word or pause to draw a breath, Sarvah heard no other sound.

Then she and several of the brothers caught sight of a point of light as it shot out from one of the chamber's inclined walls and directly into one of the pods. Then another shot into an adjacent pod, and yet another into a third.

The midwayers fell silent, stopped circling and moved invisibly over their masters' glowing pods: Ænus above the first, Bhu over the second, and Poxx above the third. A rare, somber moment for the typically meddlesome three.

Despite a nauseous feeling and a compelling urge to flee, Sarvah held firm near the chamber's apex.

Below, Vakaar smiled coolly. His cohorts cringed, and with the others— including the Janah's unseen projectionist—waited for the fourth.

$$- \circ \; \dot{\Leftrightarrow} \; \circ \; -$$

Movement—inside the third pod. Several of the priests cocked their heads toward it, as many a silver wafer lay on this long-awaited rising.

Twitching in his podded earthly form, the demon <u>Zhol</u>[G405] flexed and then relaxed his new body's untried muscles, and through thin nostrils drew a deep, slow breath. Holding the air, the campaign's senior Son suddenly sprang his eyelids apart and scanned fuzzily from side to side. His eyes cleared, and upon an expectant smile, his powers came fully to him.

A few indulgent moments more, Lord Zhol exhaled and then focused his mind on the pod's sensors. And the pod's preserving, blue energy field and long, domed lid abruptly disappeared.

Vakaar and the others quickly knelt and bowed their heads, while the Janah's amazed projectionist bravely stood her ground.

With Sonlight radiating from his head and out from the cuffs of his shimmering bodystocking, Lord Zhol stepped from his now-darkened pod. As did all Rohman Sons, he clothed this and his other manufactured bodies in dark, seamless undergarments detailed with impressionistic scenes of past triumphs embroidered in teal and crimson threads. Typically, the ankles, wrists and necks of the Sons' ornate bodystockings were cuffed and hemmed with golden lace. Two rows of twelve gold buttons lay vertically arranged waist-high on each side, and each button bore the imperial sign of Rohm.

Then, with the power of his mind—in a momentary process rumored among the priesthood—Nordehk's first Overlord suddenly <u>thought-formed</u>[G361] his narrowly-defined, finishing regalia. The formal garb featured a knee length, three-quarter-width pleated skirt hemmed with a broad, golden ribbon adorned with an assortment of symbols and raised Rᴈhman script. Fastened to the twelve gold buttons of his bodystocking, the skirt left a frontal strip of Zhol's shimmering undergarment exposed. A matching shoulder-piece hung halfway down the Son's chest and upper arms, and its pressed hood lay flat against his back. And as always, to complete the magnificent attire, the bejeweled handle of what appeared to be an ornate but short gold scabbard was tucked partway into the top of one of his soft, golden boots.

Some of the kneeling brothers visibly shuddered, and with heads bowed, promptly pledged their hearts to Rᴈhm. At their yamah's lead, others looked up and began shouting practiced praise.

"By your radiance, my Lord...." "...Welcome, great and fearsome Zhol!" "Glory be to The Master! Glory be to Rᴈhm!" "Exquisite craftsmanship, my Lord! Long may...."

"Silence!" The Overlord's unmouthed word thundered through their minds and cut short their priestly accolades.

Those looking up, quickly bowed their heads again.

"Silence...reverent ones," he said less harshly, adding, "your service is known."

In preparation for his appearances as Nordehk's all-powerful Lord of the Orbits, Zhol had fashioned his latest fleshy vehicles after a worthy bipedal reptilian. As ever, he would have no need of food or drink. The only nourishment required was that which replenished all Sons while operating in the lower densities: a thought-formed ambrosia to be sipped every few days for their bodies' vitalization.

Typical of most campaigning Sons, Lord Zhol looked especially young—less than twenty standard years. Compared to the mission's bahva, his hairless body was of average height, with a lean and commanding physique. His yellow eyes were oval-shaped and deeply set, with vertical pupils jet-black and slivered. The Son's eyelids blended into a high forehead, and his ears were simple slits: barely discernible folds in a slick, beautifully patterned, scaly skin. His jaw looked square and strong.

Widely spaced and almost flush with his cheeks, his two nostrils were hardly noticeable on his handsome, sharply contoured face. His hands were of average size, each with opposable thumb, four fingers and broad triangular nails curved to fit each fingertip, with rounded points facing inward and buried into the flesh. Along with a majority of Imperial Lords, Zhol favored opposable thumbs as the most warlike of creature features.

Silently (telepathically), the Overlord beckoned the second Son to rise. And immediately, to a gasp from Sarvah whose invisible projection was still peering out from near the chamber's apex, the next pod's energy field and domed lid vanished. But only Sarvah's remote comrades—the nine Janah rebels who formed her cone near the khoomyahna's eighth statcon dome—heard her catch her breath.

Exuding power and confidence and looking not more than sixteen standard years, the demon Dhanz[G083] rose from her pod. Face and body appropriately matured and with short black hair cropped close to her wavy skull, the campaign's female Son bore penetrating indigo eyes, and her satiny skin was toned in mottled browns and olives. Broad nose shallow and double-nostriled, lips full and teeth bright white, knife-edged and squared, her delicate ears lay hidden in depressions behind her pronounced lower jaw. Lord Dhanz' four-fingered hands and grasping thumbs looked rather small and slender. Tiny suction cups dotted the tips of all ten nailless digits.

As she thought-formed her similar-looking formal garb, Dhanz turned to her left and locked eyes with the Overlord—and the luminescence of both righteous Sons did flare. With no words spoken, no silent messages exchanged, their radiance intensified and merged into a single blaze of light that forced the peeking priesthood to look away.

Once tireless administrators of a distant constellation, the two exemplary Rohman Lords had long served the Most Highs of Ohrvon, the galaxy in which Nordehk was but one wee piece of more than a billion parts. Working together some 700,000 years prior, the then-Vihdæans Dhanz and Zhol chose finally—after the usual preludial succession of quiet deliberations common to most Vihdæan defectors—to answer Rohm's relentless calls.

"DEAR ONES...COME. COME TAKE MY MIGHTY HAND, AND BE!

"COME, DEAR ONES—COME AND BE KNOWN! COME TAKE THE HAND OF ROHM, AND SEE! DEAR ONES...."

At once and together, they forever abandoned their boringly passive administrative council. To leave the tedious light and join The Master's Odyssey. To bring everlasting *Order* to the chaos of All That Is.

As the new recruits' first lesson in the science of anticipation, the twelve Supreme Sons of the Rohman High Court promptly separated the two and assigned them as novice "Imperial Warriors" to assist in campaigns at opposite ends of the realm. Accepting honorably, serving staunchly and never failing, Zhol and Dhanz eventually won The Omnipotent One's respect—and godlike Son-status as righteous Imperial Lords of the Realm. Both had since become established Overlords managing multiple constellations. And with his winning bid for the Nordehk campaign, Zhol's considered request to be reunited with Dhanz had not been denied.

As the first two demons' brilliance receded, the third arose: <u>Lord Wohtan</u>[G397] the intimidator. Preferring a physically less-attractive format, Wohtan looked at least ten years older, stood a little taller and appeared more powerfully built. Face pockmarked and scarred by design, he bore several deep-set wrinkles that seemed more from scowling than from age. His eyes were a bloodshot blue and beady, with fat eyelids nearly covered by a heavy, hanging brow. Golden hair unkempt and unevenly sheared, lips thin and complexion ruddy, Lord Wohtan wore a constant, crooked sneer.

A pair of thick, curled ears stuck out from each side of the demon's wide head. His hands were large and rough, each with four fingers and an opposable thumb. All his digits ended in thick and split, jagged yellowed nails.

Upon Wohtan's dressing, the Overlord issued an unspoken command that generated a simultaneous reflex among those of the attending priesthood, and brought them instantly to their feet.

The brothers' momentary surprise and then pride over their unrehearsed, military precision turned to breathlessness as the Sons lifted up from the room's black granite platform. Mildly illuminated, all three rose with heads tipped back, arms at their sides and palms turned out.

With three shimmering demons suddenly ascending toward her, Sarvah panicked and retreated to her comrades and the calm beneath their cone. And as she sat a moment quivering before announcing her return, Sarvah realized she had not been seen. She also thought about those five pods arranged around the black chamber's central dais. Since four Rɵhman Sons figured into most campaigns, and since the larger fifth pod surely awaited the eventual visit of a Supreme Son, what had become of the warrior for that fourth light-filled pod? Would just *three* Imperial Lords manage the Rɵhmanization of Nordehk's unsuspecting worlds? If so, the Janah's estimated chances of escaping may have greatly improved.

"I'm back," Sarvah whispered with an obvious air of relief. "Only three Sons rose, not four. That's good for us—right?"

Three? "Definitely, Weebs—good job," the lateral-eyed Chak replied, as he and the others untangled their interlocking cone and shook their numbed fingers to restore the flow of blood.

"They didn't see me," she added.

"Just as we suspected," said another of the nine. "Fallen angels *do* lose some powers in their fall."

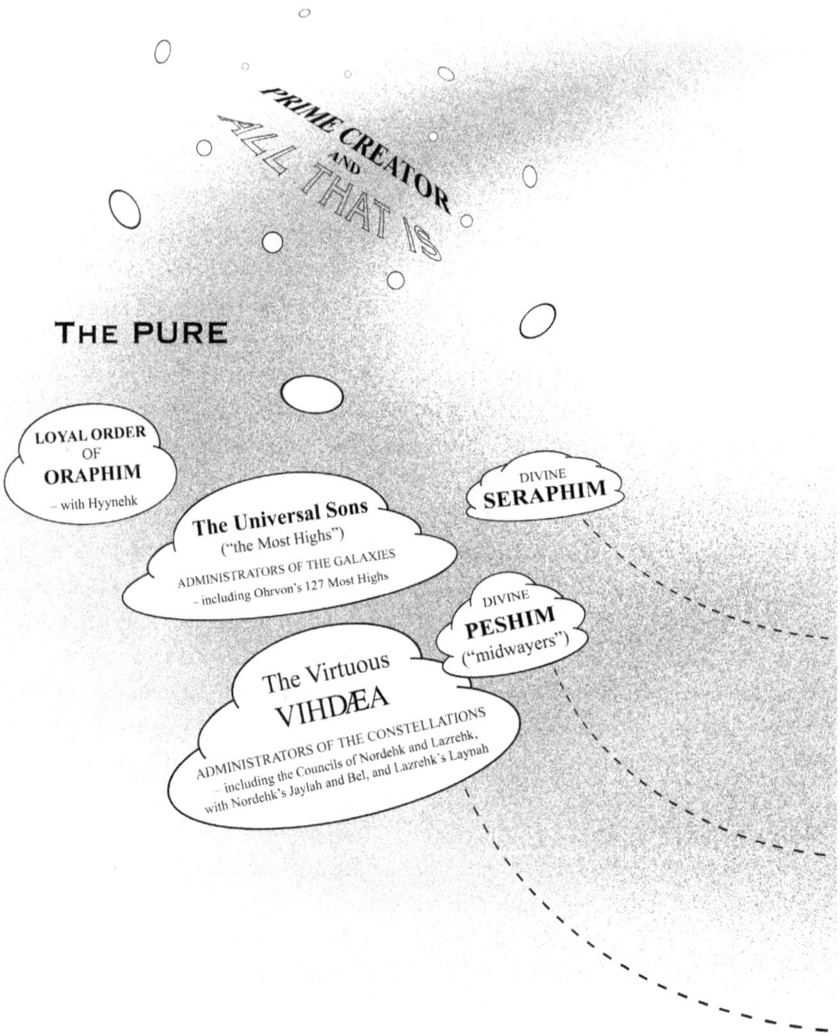

PRIME CREATOR
AND
ALL THAT IS

THE PURE

LOYAL ORDER
OF
ORAPHIM
– with Hyynehk

DIVINE
SERAPHIM

The Universal Sons
("the Most Highs")
ADMINISTRATORS OF THE GALAXIES
– including Ohrvon's 127 Most Highs

DIVINE
PESHIM
("midwayers")

The Virtuous
VIHDÆA
ADMINISTRATORS OF THE CONSTELLATIONS
– including the Councils of Nordehk and Lazrehk,
with Nordehk's Jaylah and Bel, and Lazrehk's Laynah

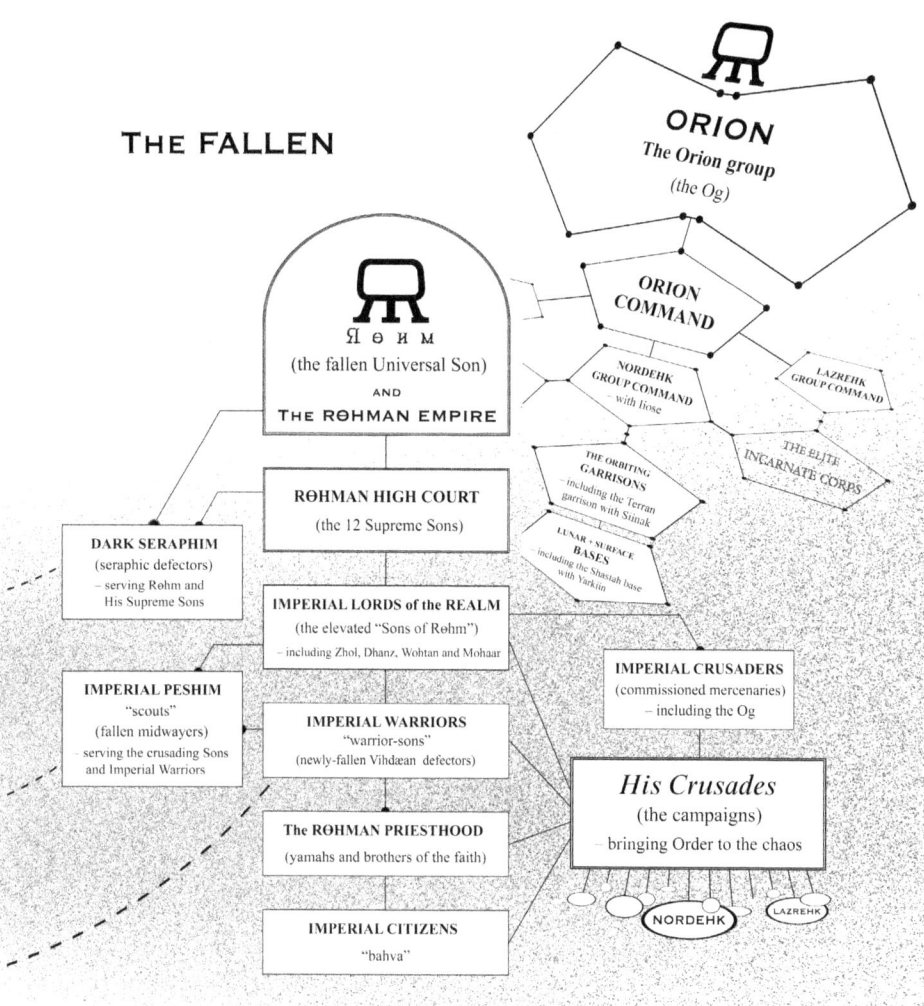

THE FALLEN

Я ⊖ ⊕ и
(the fallen Universal Son)
AND
THE RӨHMAN EMPIRE

ORION
The Orion group
(the Og)

ORION COMMAND

NORDEHK GROUP COMMAND
– with Iiose

LAZREHK GROUP COMMAND

RӨHMAN HIGH COURT
(the 12 Supreme Sons)

THE ORBITING GARRISONS
– including the Terran garrison with Siinak

THE ELITE INCARNATE CORPS

DARK SERAPHIM
(seraphic defectors)
– serving Rөhm and His Supreme Sons

LUNAR + SURFACE BASES
including the Shastah base with Yarkiin

IMPERIAL LORDS of the REALM
(the elevated "Sons of Rөhm")
– including Zhol, Dhanz, Wohtan and Mohaar

IMPERIAL CRUSADERS
(commissioned mercenaries)
– including the Og

IMPERIAL PESHIM
"scouts"
(fallen midwayers)
– serving the crusading Sons and Imperial Warriors

IMPERIAL WARRIORS
"warrior-sons"
(newly-fallen Vihdæan defectors)

His Crusades
(the campaigns)
– bringing Order to the chaos

The RӨHMAN PRIESTHOOD
(yamahs and brothers of the faith)

IMPERIAL CITIZENS
"bahva"

NORDEHK   LAZREHK

BEL'S REPORT

D-32.12: NORDEHK

A brilliant pinpoint of light appeared and blossomed in the midst of the stepped roundtable's open middle. Bel had returned.

"The approaching warship," she reported straightaway, "is a product of sciences highly advanced, far more so than those of our beloved ancients. The vessel carries a variety of enslaved <u>will-creatures</u>,[138] bipeds not too unlike our own, who maintain the ship under the casual surveillance of biomechanical devices and one <u>negatively oriented midwayer</u>[139] in service to the Sons. An invisible, impenetrable shield secures the ship's drive, bridge and critical systems: an intense vibrational frequency diametrically aligned. A central, pyramidal chamber houses five life-size castings of The Master's famous dogs, five pods with dormant bodies of impeccable design, and a large golden throne that bears the insignia of Rᴏhm."

Upon a perceptible increase of the council's luminescence, Bel knew <u>to pin</u>[G278] away. She would advise the Most Highs of the khoomyahna's arrival. Nordehk's long-predicted plight was now at hand.

Chapter 4 — N O T E S

G[030]   bahva: citizen-commoners of the Empire; Rǝhman slang for a "being" or "beings"

N[129]   *Vakaar.* "His Reverence"; high priest or *yamah* of the Nordehk campaign's appointed priesthood:

> [from D-32.4, *BEL'S INTRUSION*] Responsible for channeling the flow of turbid liquid sweating from the warship's fleshy inner walls, the criminal crew toiled knee-deep in a ditch that flanked an ample but ill-lit passage to the khoom's rectory, when Vakaar and an entourage of robed and hooded priests came sloshing into view.
>
> As the mission's high priest, or "yamah," Vakaar held final authority in the absence of a Rǝhman Son. Skinny, hunched and noticeably shorter than the rest, few rarely saw him without his two lanky cohorts—the ones to whom his spies reported—and this day both were at his sides. Stooped with necks awkwardly twisted, they mouthed constant whispers into the scrawny yamah's pointed ears.

N[130]   *thought-forms.* Temporary apparitions or enduring material manifestations formed by the power of thought.

N[131]   *Bel* ♀. A founding member of Nordehk's 8-seat Vihdæan Council and their most capable spy, Bel is the khoomyahna's angelic "intruder."

N[132]   *Janah* [pron. **Jă′**-nä]. A secret sect of 22 Rǝhman rebels—closet anarchists who volunteered for the mission to Nordehk with hopes of escaping the Empire's stifling *Order*:

> [from D-32.6, *CHAOS AND LIGHT*] Thirteen covert rebels huddled in their secluded hideaway: a cramped nook near the eighth of the khoom's twelve static containment domes. They had heard rumors of an intrusion, and of the intruder's brilliant light.
>
> Like the other free bahva onboard the khoomyahna, these thirteen young Rǝhman citizens had volunteered for the one-way mission to Nordehk and had met the selection criteria. Quite unlike the others aboard, however, these were some of the Janah, a secret sect of twenty-two beings bent on escaping the Empire's stifling *Order*.

N[133] *pranah.* An element of the cosmic force that carries extrasensory callings and other telepathic communications, as well as the consciousness of those able to harness portions of its power.

N[134] *pods…dias, and imposing golden throne.* Fundamental components of all khoomyahnas' black chamber, or "Chamber of the Pods".

G[254b] (the) Og: those of the ever scheming **O**rion **g**roup; the infamous, grey-skinned "darkeyes" from the motherworlds and territories of the long-Rɘhmanized Orion constellation, where—well before the Rɘhmans' annexation of Orion—the taller and intellectually superior "original purebred species" enslaved the territories' similar looking, less advanced tribes

N[135] *temporal vehicle.* An ephemeral, material-life vehicle, a living structure capable of temporarily hosting the consciousness of an evolving entity.

N[136] *third density.* The third "octave" or "dimension" of reality; the lowest density to support the communal, incarnational development of living creatures; a seven-level plane of existence having a common visibility spectrum wherein its creature's senses, perceptions and abilities are less developed than those of higher realms.

N[137] *their meeting with the Og.* The Sons' briefing inside the tactical chamber of Group Commander Iiose's battle cruiser.

G[405] (Lord) Zhol: [♂ pron. Zōl] officially "Lord of the Orbits" of the Nordehk campaign and Overlord of fourteen other constellations, Zhol is among the brightest of fallen Vihdæa to serve Rɘhm; he bears the campaign's financial burden and is responsible for Rɘhmanizing the ancients of Mhu; his personal, eternally-committed midwayer/scout is *Poxx* [♂ pron. Pŏks].

N[138] *will-creature.* Any evolving life-form endowed with the unique capacity to make a moral decision, and which usually labels itself "human," "human being" or "man."

N[139] *negatively oriented midwayer.* Jinn-Jinn, the khoom's temporarily-assigned sentinel.

G[278] pinning: to pin; the concentration of one's consciousness into a pinpoint of light (that can vary in intensity from virtually invisible to powerfully radiant) for the purpose of instantaneous travel to destinations seen in the mind's eye, or to enter and possess other living forms—whether temporarily or for a longer term

Jake's Take
CHAPTER 4

Initially, I found the notion of overlapping densities difficult to wrap my head around and therefore impossible to describe. Fortunately, there comes a point when elements of unfamiliar perceptions ring true, and our horizons duly expand. And as with the limited views of the flatlanders of old, nonsensical beliefs must and will ultimately yield to evidential rationale.

Similarly, the novel concept of pinning would appear to explain the joys of birth and rebirth, the horrors of demonic possession, and the manifestations, diversity and evolution of life itself. But in God's Grand Design, what universal theorem could possibly accommodate a higher species' systematic manipulation of a lesser species' DNA for the purpose of eventually occupying *en masse* said lower species' adequately altered forms?

Are the godless darkeyes irrevocably committed to a desperate exercise in futility? Or is it we believers who are doomed?

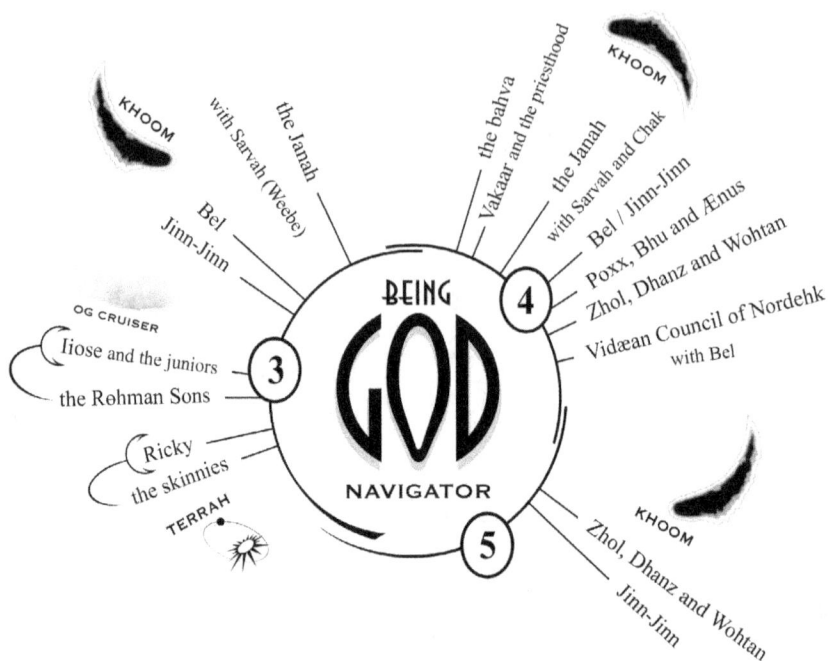

5

TREASURES FOR THE REALM
D-32.13: SPACE / KHOOMYAHNA

As a threesome, the three mildly luminous Sons spiraled upward through the black chamber's apex and rematerialized at the heart of the khoom's control deck, inside its secluded systems bridge. No instrumentation, doorways or viewports lay beneath the bridge's indistinct internal dome. Like the Og cruiser's tactical chamber[140] where the Sons had been briefed mere minutes before, its size seemed boundless and impossible to judge.

No areas of the khoomyahna were officially restricted, but few bahva attempted to explore this small, mysterious level atop the warship's core. Those who tried experienced varying degrees of discomfort and pain. Beginning with a buzzing in their ears and then a churning in their stomachs, all but the most determined soon turned back. Anyone venturing deeper into the unfamiliar maze told of disorientation and then sudden and worsening convulsions that had caused them to black out. Something physically repulsive lay beyond their reach.

"By your radiance, my Lords," said the waiting Jinn-Jinn[G175] nervously, and with an exaggerated, midair bow. "Welcome."

The Sons ignored the ship's sentinel as though they had not seen or heard him. The veteran Jinn-Jinn knew better than to repeat himself.

A brightly colored, pentagonal Rɘhman rug lay centered on the systems bridge's floor. Twelve cubits a side, it held five, soft, silver recliners arranged symmetrically upon it. Four were identical. The fifth was elevated, longer and wider than the rest—reserved for the eventual visit of a magnificent Supreme Son.

The specific vibration of each arriving warrior triggered a response in three of the smaller recliners, whereby the devices began pulsating with an inviting, bluish glow. Zhol and then Dhanz and then Wohtan lay down, and the field intensities of their chosen recliners rose with a pronounced hum before settling into silence as the soft, warm metal molded to each rider's youthful form.

Zhol, now prone, gripped his recliner's pillowy sides and briefly bared his reptilian teeth. Only one in twelve Imperial Lords held the title

"Overlord"—Lord over the local orbits—and with that entitlement came the right to harness an assigned khoomyahna. A privilege and honor of which none ever tired.

Upon his ardent grip, Zhol's neuroglia became as one with the biomechanical warship: as he thought, so would the khoomyahna instantaneously respond. Much more than that, he recognized it—*her*—and she him. Old friends from a previous campaign.

Without further pause, the Overlord initiated a swift acceleration sequence, and seconds later the mighty ship breached a nearby portal that tapped one of Nordehk's thirty suns. All three warriors felt the khoom's constant, effortless, exhilarating adjustments to the way portal's surging force. The monstrous warship's metamorphic wings seemed extensions of their arms, and each Son became as a great sea-ray calmly riding a swift ocean current through some deep tectonic rift.

With all three warriors settled, Jinn-Jinn reported Bel's intrusion.

"My Lords," he began. "We had a visitor—a spy from the Vihdæa; a brief stay this very day. Our feritts managed a partial recording."

No reaction from the Sons. But upon the sentinel's mention of the encroachment, a sequence of spliced images filled the bridge's darkened dome.

As though chasing the trespasser in a rapid, live pursuit, the three Sons followed the spy's unimpeded romp through the khoom. Two of them smiled as the Vihdæan hit the vibrational frequency that shielded the warship's systems bridge—the very room in which the Rohman Lords now lay. Repulsed by the impenetrable force, she turned and dove downward into the black chamber, where she stopped to mind-probe the Sons' pods and to study The Master's throne, before promptly pinning away.

With a negligible grunt, Zhol glanced at the hovering Jinn-Jinn. And in a telepathic voice—deep, cold and unbecoming of his youthful, glowing face—he said, "Your service is known, dear one. Your assignment is complete."

"By your radiance, my Lord," the midwayer replied with a much more controlled, midair bow. Then straightening, Jinn-Jinn added—properly, and never sure of what might come next—"I am forever at your beck and call...."

And with nothing more from the Overlord, the midwayer turned and pinned away from the khoomyahna, leaving it and constellation Nordehk. For a time.

Despite its being regarded as a relatively small affair, the Nordehk campaign brimmed with opportunity: for the reunion of Dhanz and Zhol; for Wohtan, the apathetic veteran, to satisfy his needs; for the ambitious Mohaar to prove his worthiness as a newly appointed Son; and for all four Imperial Lords to enhance their affluence and extend their influence in the realm. In the next few days, they should settle their methods of reduction, and then call upon Rehm. To inform Him of their plans, and hopefully gain His elusive *awareness*.

At this stage of the campaign, "the ancients," the three billion inhabitants of Mhu, Nordehk's core planet, represented a potential pool of fourth-density crusaders. Tentatively, pending his final assessment as the campaign's Overlord, Zhol's superiors—the twelve Supreme Sons of the Rehman High Court—viewed those three billion as a prospective, collective unit of recruits for service in *His Crusades*. Lord Zhol's chosen assignment and premier challenge, therefore, lay in converting the positively-oriented ancients of Mhu. That en masse, they might become disciples of The Omnipotent Master. That they might reap eternal purpose, and so assist in bringing Rehman Order to the feral constellations of All That Is.

Zhol initialized the khoom's freshly updated stellar program,[141] homed in on Mhu's bright sun, and zoomed straight to the surface of the ancient's unspoiled world, and to the veritable sea of crystal structures that formed the ancients' vibrant capital of Lemurah.

Watching upward from their warm recliners, all three Sons—Zhol, Dhanz and Wohtan—sensed undisturbed serenity—that pleasantly familiar, lethargic, *defenseless* form of Order synonymous with certain species' commitment to "the Light." A revealing byproduct of the ancients' propensity toward *submission*, it came as an encouraging, outward sign.

Along with the ancients' presumed worth, Nordehk held three unequivocal treasures: the Varahn elantah,[G097] the polymides[142] of Khrae; and the Terran system's exciting and mysterious "ring of death"—its striking atmahan![143] Nowhere in All That Is were planets known to spontaneously explode. Always, in an atmahan's pyrogenic rubble, could evidence of intelligent life be found. Befittingly prized by the Rehmans as riddles to be solved, rarely did these highly unstable "suicide rings" share the same solar system with a thriving sister world. That Terrah/"planet Earth" had survived the initial, fierce bombardment of its planetary neighbor's violent demise and went on to flourish *within* the inner minefield of hurtling rogue asteroids that had bumped free—and which continued to slip from the orbiting graveyard—verged on the miraculous.

Remarkably, life on Terrah—the last of the solar system's three original waterworlds—had survived, albeit barely, and not without undergoing monumental change. Although the level of danger to planet Earth had decreased over the tens of millions of years since that colossal blast, even the sorry Terrans, who had only just begun probing the space around them, were coming to comprehend the depth of their precarious situation.

Knowing nothing of their self-extinguished neighbors, however, belligerence had become the Terran norm. They warred constantly with one another (an attribute ingrained through 8,000 years of merciless Og manipulation), and despite a token effort to listen in on "outer space" with their primitive sciences and machines, the Terrans remained utterly unable to detect other-worldly intelligence, and generally believed they lived alone.

While Dhanz and Wohtan watched on, Zhol zoomed a series of amphidoric close-ups, deep scans, and accompanying streams of Og data for Terrah, the busy "Planet of the Cross." In addition to the imminent, cataclysmic geological upheavals that would rebalance the world's thin, misshapen tectonic crust, Terrah's atmospheric pollution, consequent warming and worsening acidification of its deep, blue oceans neared critical proportions. What remained of the planet's polar ice and glaciers was thawing rapidly. The resulting, steady flood of freshwater into its saline seas would soon compromise the crucial, circulatory equilibrium of warm and cool ocean currents, and an unstoppable—even by the Rohmans—self-correcting thermal catastrophe would ensue.

Without imperial intervention, and notwithstanding the earthlings' increasingly desperate but ineffectual efforts to reduce their world's toxicity, the runaway warming would continue essentially unchecked. Despite temporary, regional coolings as Terrah's ocean currents collapsed, global temperatures would increase dramatically and mass extinctions of the planet's flora and fauna would occur. And so, along with assimilating the backward Enyahns into the realm, Lord Dhanz would save and Rohmanize the Terrans, as well as cleanse and restore their precious oceans and fragile atmosphere, rebalance the weather, and rehydrate their drought-striken lands.

Next, the Overlord neurogenically switched to the Varahn system, whose first and second planets from the sun were of the usual size and orbital positions for inner worlds. The third, however, was a spectacularly ringed, though somewhat small gas giant: Taran-Tahk.

Situated within the solar standard for a fourth planet—T-Tahk exhibited several indicators that it had suffered a catastrophic collision with another sizeable celestial body. Its wide, colorful band lay on a plane roughly perpendicular to an orbital path that was distinctly tilted, relative to the orbits of the system's seven other major spheres. And Taran-Tahk's compressed gas surface housed a core of molten rock and metal comparable in mass to that of a common inner/earthen world.

Although gas giants averaged nine moons, T-Tahk held just two: a small outer moon, Ilyah, and the larger, water-bearing planetoid, Varah—the coveted elantah. Like the Rohman Empire's eleven known elantahs, Varah's axis lay curiously within twelve degrees of perpendicular to the solar system's plane, ensuring that half its surface received the sun's warming rays as the world spun slowly on its axis. Ilyah, with its negligible atmosphere and gravity one-third that of Varah, was ideally suited to its efficient network of heavy industries. Except for a lunar university and research center, all other non-industrial Ilyahn complexes harbored the "VSC," the Varahn Service Corps: the agency responsible for serving and safeguarding the Varahns and their off-world wealth. *Lord Wohtan would soon put Varah's humble corpsmen to the test.*

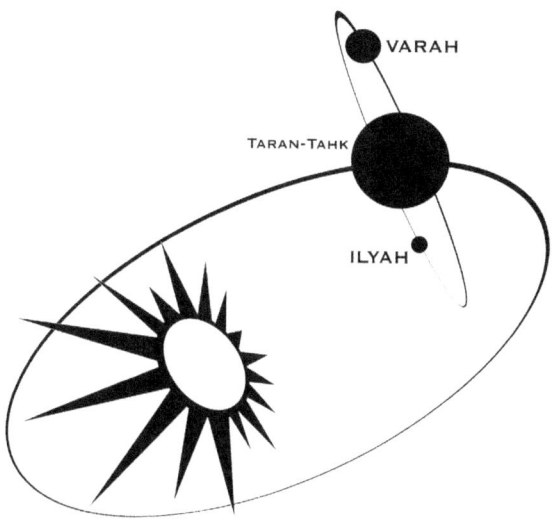

Moving to the solar system common to planets Khrae and New Hollatia,[144] Zhol homed in on tiny Altos, the innermost of Khrae's two moons. Site of the Khraelings' first lunar colony, Altos became a major mining operation after the discovery of intriguing minerals: endless pockets of precious polymides. "Impossible" alloys, each held unimagined properties that led to the Khraelings' metallurgical advances and subsequent, early, technological success.

The Og's deep scans confirmed that under a dusting of cosmic debris, the little moon held exceptionally high concentrations of exotic auriferous polymides that rivaled the purity and plenitude of the Empire's most prized deposits. After almost 13,000 years of mining a substantial surface concentration, the Khraelings had extracted and utilized or exported but a fraction of the astonishing wealth.

With royalties from Altos' polymides alone, the Overlord would easily recover his costs for the Nordehk campaign, quite possibly within the first thousand years of installing the constellation's New Order. And with <u>Lord Mohaar</u>[G226a] <u>already on his way</u>,[145] the tribes of Khrae—including the estranged Jakomen of New Hollatia—would fast be brought in line.

Chapter 5 — N O T E S

N[140] ***tactical chamber.*** The illusory chamber of Group Commander Iiose's battle cruiser:

> [from D-32.3, *AWAITING THE DEMON-SONS*] The tactical chamber's curving walls, blackish metallic floor and domed ceiling blended indistinguishably and looked impossibly immense for the cruiser's modest size. It was an illusion, an imperial innovation—one of few technological marvels the Rɵhmans chose to share.

G[175]   Jinn-Jinn: [♂] a Rɵhman midwayer-sentinel temporarily assigned to watch over the Overlord's khoomyahna during the warship's voyage to Nordehk

N[141] ***freshly updated stellar program.*** Updated through the transfer of data and materials to the khoomyahna from Group Commander Iiose's battle cruiser:

> [from D-32.7, *HOSTING THE DEMON SONS*] …the old group commander cleared his throat and took a moment to gather himself.
> "The following actions and developments are detailed in the data now flowing to your khoomyahna. A transfer of capsules containing the requested samples and codes for Nordehk's flora and fauna, including genetic materials from the higher species, is also underway."

G[097]   elantahs: [pron. ē-lăn′-təz] extremely rare, temperate, water-bearing lunar planetoids capable of supporting evolving life-forms

N[142] ***polymides.*** Exotic metal alloys; extremely lightweight supermetals having various combinations of properties including superstrength, superductility and superconductivity.

N[143] ***atmahan*** [pron. ăt-mă-hăn′]. The Rɵhman word for "ring of death," *atmahan* is applicable only to a non-planetary, stellar belt of asteroidal debris. Although early Og explorers were intrigued by the ancients' advancing culture, stunned by the Varahns' spectacular lunar world, and covetous of Khrae's inestimable polymides, they were utterly fascinated by the Terran system's perilous belt of asteroids. Nearly as rare as elantahs, atmahan are unmistakable stellar hallmarks of human belligerence. Also known as "suicide rings," Creation's uncommon atmahan consistently contain evidence of societal self-destruction.

N[144] ***Khrae and New Hollatia.*** Rival worlds in a shared solar system.

G[226a] (Lord) Mohaar: [♂ pron. **Mō′-här**] a fallen Vihdæan administrator turned warrior-crusader for Rəhm and recently elevated to the status of Rəhman Son; in the Nordehk campaign, Mohaar bears responsibility for Rəhmanizing Khrae and New Hollatia; his eternally committed, personal midwayer/scout is ***Iddh*** [♂ pron. Ĭd]

N[145] ***already on his way.*** Having promptly pinned to his assigned solar system* upon the conclusion of the Sons' meeting with Group Commander Iiose.

> * that of sister worlds Khrae and New Hollatia—as detailed in the upcoming sequence, *A DEMON AT THE HELM.*

Jake's Take
CHAPTER 5

In this, our near future, four infallible Rohman Sons are suddenly upon us with priceless treasures in their sights. Beginning with Khrae and New Hollatia, we shall now learn about our cousins and all who share in Nordehk's plight.

The weavers' opening chapters seek to tweak our cranial compasses and prepare us for that which has already begun. In the next few chapters, we shall meet a host of key characters *rapid-fire* (purposefully, I'm told) and learn of the growing interplay among Nordehk's naïve tribes, and of some disturbing hidden agendas.

And while those who would at best enslave us soldier on systematically, our constellation's historically non-infringing Vihdæan Council watches from above and ponders long suppressed inclinations to somehow intervene.

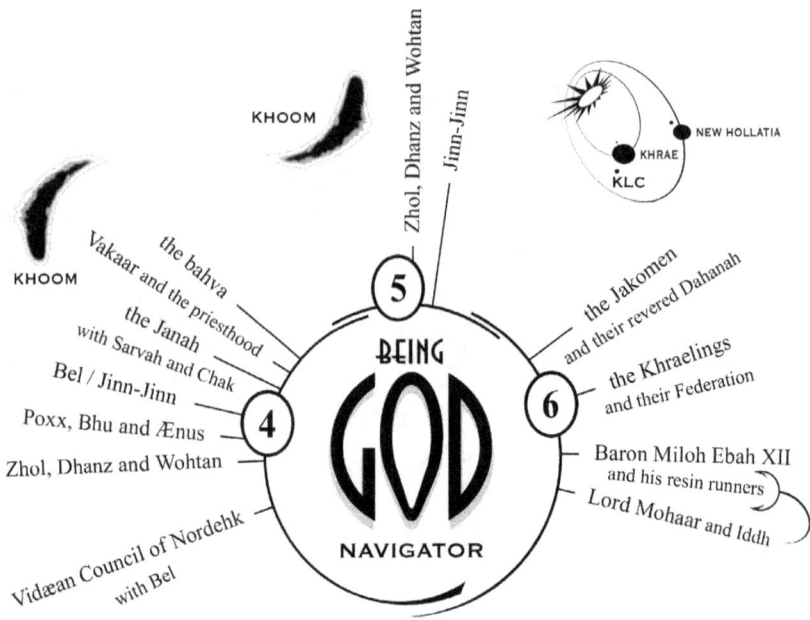

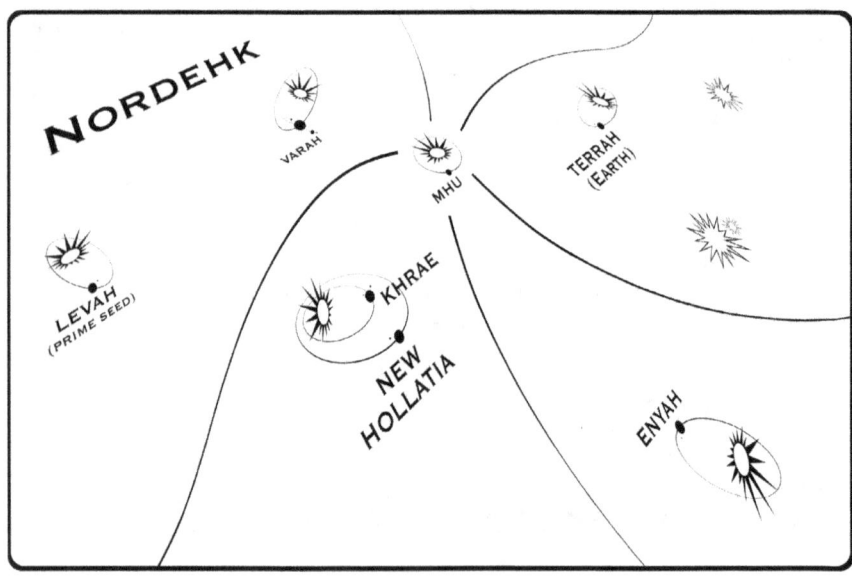

6

PROBING THE MYSTERY FRIGATE
D-32.14: KHRAE / PATOS

Deep beneath the surface of Patos, the largest and outermost of Khrae's two moons, several operators monitored the progress of an unregistered, lightly armed frigate that had left New Hollatia four hours prior.

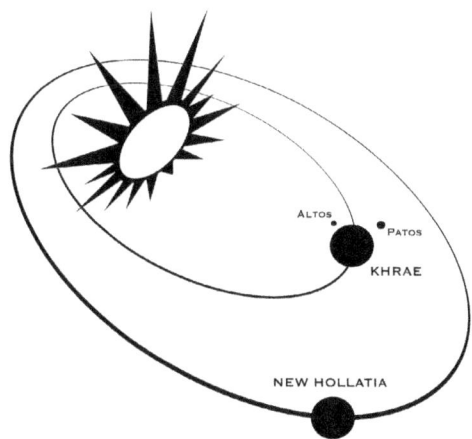

Thirty seconds before the frigate crossed Midway, the ever-changing midpoint between the sister worlds, the Khraeling operators would probe the vessel. One minute later, they would issue a hail. Without a prompt response and an appropriate code—one of many that changed by the hour—they would destroy the unknown ship.

The operators sat among hundreds of others who occupied an entire floor of the subterranean "tower" labeled Base 16. It was the primary monitoring center for the Khrae Security Forces, the KSF: guardians of the planet and enforcers of Khraeling/Federation law. Dozens of such underground towers formed the vast lunar complex known as KLC—Khrae Lunar Command.

Thousands of remote scanning units dubbed "remscanners" or "RSUs," secured the zone that encompassed the Khraelings' claimed orbital perimeter. Each had the capacity to probe and destroy small vessels.

At forty seconds to Midway and in strict accordance with KSF

procedures, Base 16's lead operator ordered, "On my mark, initiate scans....
And: three, two, one—mark."

$$- \circ \; \dot{\diamond} \; \circ -$$

"They're probing, Sir," the unregistered frigate's edgy navigator reported
to her pilot. "At least four remscanners meshed and locked."

As the pilot switched off the frigate's alarms, his navigator added, "Sixty
seconds, Sir. Thirty to Midway."

For the Elasian navigator, pilot and crew, enduring KLC's targeting
probes and inspectional scans was stressful but routine. Every time they
smuggled in a load of resin, their baron, the thickset Baron Miloh Ebah XII of
Elasia,[146] unfailingly relayed the critical code that staved off certain destruction.
They usually received it a good minute or two before crossing Midway.
Usually.

THE JAKOMEN HOLOCAUST

D-32.15: KHRAE

In his office in the east wing of his family's private estate, Elasia's
continental lord, Baron Miloh Ebah XII, stared into his desktop imaging field.
He was waiting for the "hands off" double betacode that would qualify his
resin runners' frigate for safe passage—for unescorted, silent running through
Federation space. While he waited, he daydreamed of the events that had
brought this all about.

Like his father before him, Miloh XII remained a steadfast champion of
the Jakomen,[147] the estranged Khraeling tribe that thousands of years prior had
been culled and banished to Hollatia, the smallest, hottest and least hospitable
of Khrae's ten lands. With pale, heavily freckled complexions and curly
reddish hair, the persecuted "jacks" had long suffered pigmentational prejudice
as the distinctly fairest of their world's cerise-skinned kind.

Through the millennia, however, the segregated, fair-skinned Jakomen
endured. And through their inherent diligence, they prospered—becoming the
richest of Khrae's tribes by far. Much to their rivals' chagrin....

Some eight centuries before recent times, the diligent Jakomen, under the
umbrella of their national corporation, had become an economic powerhouse.
They had disbursed their nation's wealth—the hard-earned wealth of
Hollatia—rather fairly among its people, with no Jakomen having more than
three times the average net worth of any other. In stark contrast, the planet's
nine other continental powers had united in a monopolistic, opportunistic

"Intercontinental Federation" controlled by the families of <u>nine ruling barons</u>.[148] Mainly impoverished and land-poor, Khrae's masses were far better off than their ancestors had been through the vicious, endlessly recurring, *pre-*Federation, intercontinental wars.

The Jakomen leadership—Hollatia's High Council of Elders and an elected Aggah—saw nothing to be gained by joining the new Intercontinental Federation, and took the mounting external pressure to do so as little more than a simplistic ploy to have them cost-share an increasingly expensive welfare state. Above all, the Jakomen never forgot the discrimination they had suffered at the hands of the other continents' people—their fellow tribes of Khrae—nor the shame of their banishment to the largely barren, island continent of Hollatia.

"Nothing is being offered that we do not already have," became the Jakomen's unwavering motto. Through endless rounds of futile negotiations, they politely listened and then declined by vote of their High Council, listened then declined, listened then declined.

The Federation's unending trade deficit with the Jakomen became a growing embarrassment to "Those of the Continents"—Khrae's nine ruling barons. And the Jakomen's generosity, their steady stream of grants and donations to innumerable humanitarian causes, seemed a deliberate slight. But most of all, Those of the Continents resented their citizens' growing awareness that life in "desolate" Hollatia was more just and simply better than their own. And one day, the small island continent of Hollatia and its 1.2 billion Jakomen were reduced to dust.

An inland sea largely separated the Federation's two most powerful continental rivals, Elasia and Pagorea. The family Rikahr had long ruled Pagorea, domain of the Jakomen's age-old antagonist and unscrupulous competitor. And for generations, a succession of infiltrators—select troops from the Og's <u>elite incarnate corps</u>[149]— had been birthing into Pagorea's ruling Rikahrs.

Assigned to incarnate on most of Nordehk's worlds, the proficient, pitiless crusaders specialized in instilling hatred and mistrust, and in confounding religious teachings: essential roles in Orion's overall preparations for the constellation's eventual, inevitable Rohmanization.

One such calculating Og-incarnate masterfully murdered his older siblings to become Pagorea's Baron Rikahr of the day. As intended, and with a handful of ambitious aides and their secret squads of moles to assist, the incarnate baron planned and executed the ruthless attack on Hollatia. And within hours of the horrific detonations, the thorough baron's accomplices *and* their assassins ceased to exist.

While the rest of Khrae went into shock, the then-Baron of Elasia, the first Baron Miloh Ebah, quickly sheltered the surviving Jakomen. Through the efforts of his embassies around the world, he arranged to consolidate and relocate the roughly 140,000 who had previously emigrated to other continents to manage Hollatia's foreign affairs, plus another 60,000 "Dahanah"—the living dead: the few who through sheer luck and circumstance had survived the devastating attack.

Within a few years of the holocaust and while a series of Federation inquests made half-hearted attempts to discover what had happened, the roughly 200,000 remaining Jakomen had defensively dispersed themselves throughout the cities of their Elasian hosts. The Jakomen refused to participate in the sham and further vowed never to intermarry with other Khraelings, not even with the compassionate and charitable Elasians to whom they would remain forever grateful. They would keep pure their decimated tribe's blood.

Twenty years later, after the natural death of Baron Miloh Ebah I, his son, Elasia's new Baron Setih Ebah, sponsored a new generation of Jakomen in a call to formally investigate and document the Hollatian holocaust. Thousands of Jakomen, young and old, eagerly participated in the resulting "Great Tribunal," and many proudly bore grotesque physical reminders of the slaughter—deformities acquired firsthand or inherent in the genes.

After five years of proceedings and tedious reviews of previous, underfunded inquests, the Tribunal determined that upwards of a hundred nuclear bombs had been quietly installed in and around continental Hollatia's military installations, industrial complexes and major cities, and that all had been programmed for simultaneous detonation. Another device—many times more destructive than the ground-based weapons—exploded minutes later, high in Hollatia's skies. The secondary assault was thought to have originated from low orbit, but no evidence of a launcher was or ever would be found, for the deathblow had come from a shrouded Og cruiser.

Despite numerous appeals and the posting of fantastic rewards by Baron Setih Ebah and by the Federation itself, no conspiracy was uncovered, and no one was held accountable. And the Tribunal, its findings inconclusive, was dissolved.

With global guilt revived, however, Elasia's Ebah family organized a public appeal to Khrae's Federation Board: the governor, his Counsel-Ra, and all nine continental barons. The Ebah's appeal requested that the survivors' single wish be granted, that the project begun more than 1,300 years before the holocaust (more than 21 centuries before recent times)—the terra-formation of

Khrae's sister planet, Qalakah—be given new impetus for the relocation of the Jakomen people, en masse.

After persistent pressure from the Elasians and their supporters from other continents, the Board put the proposal to a plebiscite in the form of a Compensatory Accord. Through the three years it took to draft an acceptable Accord with the then-Aggahless Jakomen, the Federation hoped public sentiment would wane and that the incredibly expensive initiative would fail. It did not.

Containing no insinuation of culpability, most saw the Accord as an act of charity whereby 1.75% of the Federation's gross revenues would be committed, collected and spent each year over the estimated 250 to 300 years it would take to achieve specific terra-forming criteria on Qalakah. The Federation also resolved to fund the Jakomen's relocation. Even the citizens of Pagorea voted overwhelmingly in favor of the resolution, glad to someday be rid of the troublesome, fair-skinned tribe.

In the meantime, zero-interest loans poured into Elasia's banks to resurrect the Jakomen economically. Among the last of the guilt-inspired concessions, Jakomen businesses received tax-free status. They soon revived their long defunct national corporation and eventually repaid every loan to the last qubal: on schedule, and not early by a single day.

Over the course of three generations, the Jakomen's Elasian-based National Corporation evolved into an economic force. Within four, "the jacks" had become a much-resented power in the global marketplace. Again.

Four hundred years later (**three centuries before recent times**), Qalakah's terra-formation still had not reached the levels of habitational criteria set forth in the Compensatory Accord. The barons and their citizens were becoming increasingly resentful of the Federation's enormous capital outlay, and persecutions of the Jakomen—whose population had swollen to some three million—had begun.

Hearing that the Khraelings' Federation Board was seriously considering overturning or nullifying the centuries-old Accord, the Jakomen leadership of the time—24 Elders and the tribe's first Aggah since the holocaust—decided that although the colonization would be approximately 80 years premature, the terra-formation had reached a point where it should continue under its own momentum, and could, theoretically, support the emigration. Although cold, the mean temperature of Qalakah's equatorial region was bearable and slowly warming. Major rivers, small seas and forests were forming, and the latest oxygen factories would make it possible to introduce large animals within 40-50 years. Until then, the Jakomen would not require much more than rebreathers outside the shelters. The Exodus would begin.

Relieved, the barons agreed to maintain their contributions through the estimated 30-year emigration. In exchange, the Jakomen agreed to provide all the materials deemed essential to establish a colony over that same period, something that had been originally required of the Federation. The Jakomen signed an addendum to the Accord, stating that the reparations would be considered fulfilled upon the landing of the last transport convoy on "New Hollatia," which became the first official mention of the sister-planet's name-change from Qalakah.

All Jakomen assets, including those of their national corporation, were liquidated—bartered for materials and gold—and the Exodus from Khrae began.

$$- \circ \; \diamond \; \circ -$$

In the first century following the colonization of New Hollatia (**two centuries before recent times**), the Jakomen settled the globe's middle latitudes and constructed heavily fortified cities, mostly underground. They developed a purely defensive military: the New Hollatian Defense—the NHD. And once again, they struggled to survive.

The few communications between the new world and the Federation were largely terse and unproductive. The majority of Khraelings wanted to forget that the jacks ever existed, and the Jakomen wanted just to be left alone.

Support from Varah[150] came quickly, and of the Varahns' own accord. The Jakomen could not decline the generosity of their distant cousins, nor could they trade in kind. So with the exception of one or two barges of artwork and curiosities, the Varahns' first two interstellar convoys returned home empty. By the time the third convoy arrived, however, the industrious Jakomen were prepared.

The humble, spiritually oriented Varahns had been plodding through space at less than 30% of light speed—their reliable but relatively backward entropy engines indicative of only modest technological gains. During the third convoy's six-month stay over New Hollatia, the Jakomen refitted its tug with a Khraeling twin coil drive, and they loaded one barge with enough spare parts for a thousand more, thereby increasing the Varahn fleet's velocity by nearly half.

On the other hand, compensating the benevolent Elasians[151] for their centuries of shelter and continued support seemed wholly impossible. Besides the Federation's long-standing ban on importing New Hollatian goods, Khrae Lunar Command was monitoring the airspace between the two worlds too tightly for unregistered activities to go unseen. In addition, KSF[152] agents parading as independent opportunists were exchanging "secrets" in near space with NHD[153] operatives masquerading as Jakomen pirates. So aside from the insignificant interaction between the two military groups and an occasional, marginally morally-obligatory, Federation-approved goodwill shipment, neither Elasian-Jakomen trade nor travel occurred—not until a determined Elasian baroness patiently convinced the Federation Board[154] to let her visit New Hollatia.

Although the New Hollatian Defence gave every indication that their relentless buildup was essentially defensive, Khrae's Security Forces were becoming increasingly alarmed. And after several months of interviews and deliberations, the Federation Board decided that the Elasian baroness, Ilehna Ebah, could be trusted to evaluate the current mindset of the estranged, peculiar tribe.

A few weeks later, the then-Aggah, the High Council of Elders, and the eternally grateful Jakomen people enthusiastically welcomed their first visitor from Khrae.

"Ilehna! Ilehna! Ilehna!" "Praise Baron Miloh! Praise Baron Ebah! May the people of Elasia long live in peace!" "Ilehna! Ilehna! Ilehna!..."

— ○ ☼ ○ —

Through her thirty-day stay, the baroness heard nothing of retribution, and with the exception of sincere inquiries as to the well-being of Elasia's compassionate citizens, Ilehna heard no mention of Khrae. She viewed New Hollatia's prominent features, visited several cities, and toured evolving ecosystems that demonstrated the phenomenal acceleration of the planet's terra-formation. Her hosts shared many other lesser achievements, including their extraordinary new cuisine.

One evening after another splendid meal, the Aggah invited his cherished guest to relax with him and ten of New Hollatia's twenty-four Elders in his private spa, a natural subterranean hot pool that lay beneath his compound.

Within the hour, the Aggah and Baroness Ilehna Ebah, sat chatting across from each other about five meters[155] apart, while the Elders lounged nearby at the pool's shallow end. After graciously receiving yet another spirited compliment for the evening's meal, the Aggah decided the time had come.

"We have been saving the hojooli, my lady, for you."

An exceptional treasure gleaned from the planet's primitive and hostile environment, hojooli's thick-petaled blossoms yielded a rich, oily extract that could be concentrated into a resin and blended with spices and fragrances to produce an exotic family of delicate seasonings and perfumes.

Ilehna seemed intrigued. "This is the spice, the secret behind your marvelous menus, my Aggah?"

"Qah, my lady," he replied, eyes dancing, "and much, much more." Behind tight-lipped smiles, the Elders politely kept their laughter in check.

This Aggah had the Jakomen's classic, thick orange hair that lay in curls over the contours of his deep skull-crease. He had their typical penetrating band of yellow-green around the deep-red pupils of his eyes; his pasty skin was heavily freckled and held a light reddish hue. Having spent the majority of his life indoors in total devotion to his people's betterment, the leader looked more fair-skinned than most, and he proudly bore his share of traits from the revered Dahanah.

His left leg was malformed, his left hand grotesquely twisted, and his right ear curled almost into a ball. The Aggah's nose—the Khraeling/Jakomen single nostril—was similarly disfigured, and he breathed loudly, mostly through his mouth. Like most Jakomen and Khraelings, he had a wide round head and stubby, naturally yellowed teeth. His cleft chin was a little more pointed than most.

Uncommonly tall and slender for an Elasian, and wearing a delightful smile with her simple shorts and shawl, the baroness sat shoulder-deep on a contoured ledge of the subterranean pool.

"My Aggah," she said, playfully, "will you not share your secrets with me?"

"Qah, my lady. I have prayed that you might ask."

The Elders burst into laughter. The Aggah raised his hand and the others dropped their heads, with mouths closed but smiling genuinely.

With a smile on his own wide face, the Aggah apologized.

"I am sorry, my lady. We do not mean to humor ourselves at your expense. You are a beautiful woman and a blood-descendant of our savior, the beloved Baron Miloh."

Simultaneously, the Elders stood, raised their glasses and drank to the Baron's memory, alternately shouting "Baron Miloh!" more than once before sitting back down in the hot pool.

Uncertain whether the way was clear, the Aggah received nods of encouragement.

"The hojooli, Ilehna," he began to a few, hushed, excited oooo's from the Elders, "has a magical quality in its concentrated form. Not only can its resin be combined with common herbs to produce entirely new seasonings, but it can also be blended with other fragrances to produce a myriad of exciting perfumes."

Ilehna was impressed. There could be a huge market for this resin on

Khrae. But what was its "magical quality," and why was the Aggah treading so lightly?

"When we create perfumes or flavorings such as those you have recently sampled," he continued, "the resin is greatly diluted, for its pure essence can be…overpowering, we shall say. And when concentrated, it can have…an aphrodisiacal effect…."

Enjoying the Aggah's mindful trepidation, and noting the Elders' subtle urgings, the baroness raised her eyebrows but maintained her appealing smile.

"Certainly not an uncontrollable desire, my lady," he added, "but one does experience distinct feelings of passion, nonetheless."

The Elders, and especially the women among them, joyfully watched their visitor's reactions.

"And how, my Aggah, may I sample this 'pure essence'?" she cooed.

The Jakomen leader wore a small vial of highly refined resin on a light gold chain around his neck. Never knowing when his women might oblige him, the Aggah was always prepared.

Lifting the chain over his head, he said, "The resin, my lady." It had been his father's vial. "It can be diluted a hundred times and still retain a discerning hint of its special flavor and aroma…and its potent magic, to be sure. It is yours, Ilehna. Also, if you wish the recipes for our seasonings and perfumes, it will be done, as our humble gift to you."

"And how, my Aggah, does one sample this magical elixir?" she teased. "Did you not pray that I might ask?"

The Elders began clapping and clinking their glasses with their rings and necklaced motas, to spur their Aggah on. Even in the spa's dim light, the Elasian baroness could see the Jakomen leader's blush.

"With the lightest of dabs behind the ears, my lady," he replied, bashfully.

Ilehna stood. Her tight stomach glistened in the firelight; her lacy shawl clung to her shoulders and firm breasts. "Would you indulge me, my Aggah," she asked, "that I may know the resin's magic?"

The Aggah began to stand, but the baroness motioned for him to remain seated, saying, "Please, my Aggah. I shall come to you."

The Elders clinked their glasses again and emitted a collective "Oooo."

Holding the vial in the palm of his good hand, and with two gnarled fingers of his left, the Aggah twisted and pulled its crystal top free. The top extended into a glass rod from which he removed the visible amber resin by rolling it around the inside of the vial's short, etched neck. Then touching the rod to a fingertip, he dabbed lightly behind his good ear. Normally, he would also rim the inside of his nostril,[56] but not this night. Not for the Baroness of Elasia. Resealing the vial, he then closed it and its gold chain in his twisted hand.

Before Ilehna had waded halfway across the pool, the delicious pure essence of hojooli wafted through the air. Her mouth filled with saliva, and her heart began to pound. *Nervous anticipation,* she presumed.

All eyes turned to the baroness as she approached the seated Aggah, who held up his hand, and still smiling, said, "Not too close, my lady. Accountability, if you will." Again the Elders laughed.

Ilehna felt wonderful to be in the company of such openhearted people. She'd been feeling pangs of guilt for not having known the hardships that even these dear men and women, the leaders of this proud race, had endured. But now this…this delectable essence....

The baroness took the Aggah's hand, swept back her hair, folded her left arm across her waist and looked deep into his eyes. Feeling the love between them—the respect and mutual appreciation of their cherished relationship—she bent to place her face next to the Aggah's primed ear, closed her eyes, and through her nostril, drew a full breath.

The concentrated hojooli had an instant effect. Ilehna flushed with a warm, tingling sensation. Her blood rushed to her extremities, and her heart raced as seldom before.

She stretched out the fingers of her left hand and pressed them into her ribs, bunched her shawl tightly enough to wring the water from it…and the deep, throbbing ache began.

Ilehna bit down on her lip to suppress an intense urge to slide her hand to her bosom. A rush of swirling energy filled her head, and with an irrepressible quivering of her inner thighs, she sprung her eyes open—suddenly realizing she was squeezing the Aggah's hand and the crystal vial and golden chain within. She'd been bent over with her face in his ear…*for how long?*

She straightened up, stepped back, and said, "Oh my."

Afte her historic visit, the baroness Ilehna smuggled several liters of the remarkable resin home in her personal luggage, and many more on subsequent returns.

With the Jakomen recipes as a guide, she and her chefs sifted through tonnes of Khraeling spices, methodically mixing novel blends of hojooli and herbs. When a specific measure of one, two, or three dried herbs were aged a month or two with a drop of precisely diluted resin, an entirely new flavor was born. In the end, she managed to formulate nine distinct originals, and while greatly diminished from the effects of the pure essence, an indefinably pleasurable sensation lingered over the already exciting new cuisine.

Ilehna loved to entertain, and Khrae's ruling families soon frequented her estate more than any other. Even <u>the Rikahrs</u>,[57] who had not had an amicable relationship with the Elasians since the holocaust but who were sensitive to alienation's folly, found themselves eagerly awaiting their next invitation.

Succeeding generations of Ebahs worked patiently toward achieving an exemption to the rigid ban on imports from New Hollatia. Eventually, with stipulations that the product be debionated in New Hollatia and processed in Elasia, and with import duties and taxes to be prepaid at triple the Varahn rate, the Ebah family gained the Board's unofficial consent to import the Jakomen resin. All importations were to be clandestine, however, with an understanding that the appropriate <u>KSF</u>[G192a] betacodes for safe passage would be provided "just in time."

In return, Khrae's other eight ruling families would distribute the Elasian seasonings and fragrances within their own lands. But the pure resin would be withheld from the masses. It would be reserved for the barons alone.

Now (**recent times**), nearly a century after his family's first sanctioned shipment of the precious resin, <u>Baron Miloh Ebah XII</u>[158] awoke from his daydream to find himself chuckling over the fabled exploits of his famous ancestor, Ilehna Ebah. But the big man grew serious as he saw time running out for the KSF's critical code.

Meanwhile, the baron's resin runners crossed Midway and entered Khraeling space.

"We're in, Sir," the frigate's navigator apprehensively advised her pilot, who was staring to one side, as though lost in thought. "We've crossed Midway…twenty-eight seconds and counting." No letup from <u>KLC</u>'s[159] relentless scans.

The pilot drew a big breath, straightened his spine, and then settled back into his seat.

"Twenty-four," continued the navigator, updating her count and unable to contain her increasing dread, despite her pilot's semblance of calm. "Baron Ebah has never taken *this* long…has he?... Sir?"

A rumored seven-second balance was the worst the pilot had ever heard. "Baron Miloh alw...." Receipt of the crucial code cut short his reply. It came as a three-dimensional fractal pattern the baron had received and forwarded mere seconds before.

The navigator quickly transposed and routed the secret signal to KLC, and the scans abruptly ceased.

— ○ ☼ ○ —

Four hours more, and the frigate crossed <u>Altos</u>'[160] orbital path. The pilot
initialized repulsion for the fall toward the Elasian continent and ten days'
leave, while his navigator prudently set about devouring their last kilo of
forbidden Jakomen delicacies.

Rearward on the deck below, the vessel's young crew felt the gentle
braking that signaled their slow glide home. One of the veterans among them
unstrapped her harness, stood, stretched and said, "All right, toads. Time to
roob up."

Another unstrapped and fetched the frigate's set of roobs, the three
seven-sided Jakomen dice the crew favored for their traditional, last-minute
gambling of the bonuses they would receive upon their precious payload's safe
delivery to Baron Ebah's labs.

A DEMON AT THE HELM
D-32.16: KHRAE

Directly from their briefing with Group Commander Iiose at the fringe of
Nordehk's second frontier, two Rehmans descended upon the Elasian resin-
runners' frigate, and pinned straight through its polymide casing and the
cockpit's layered wall. While his midwayer, Iddh, shrieked and cheered, <u>Lord
Mohaar</u>[G226b] entered the frigate's pilot, who lurched forward with a grunt.

The ship's navigator froze in mid-chew. Then she turned, and through an
overstuffed mouth, managed to ask, "Are you okay, Sir?.. Sir?..."

The demon/pilot straightened in his seat, and with one hand began
massaging the back of his neck. With the other, he smashed the navigator
sideways in the face—sending food flying from her shattered jaw and
knocking her unconscious.

Never before had Mohaar served in the capacity of a full-fledged Son,
albeit an initiate, "prentice" Son, until now. After leading the defection of a
distant constellation's entire Vihdæan Council, it had taken more than 80,000
standard years of unfailing service as a faithful <u>warrior-crusader</u>[161] *and* the
recent <u>sponsorship</u>[162] of his mentor, Lord Zhol, to achieve Son status. This
conquest—the Nordehk campaign—represented Mohaar's first opportunity to
demonstrate his worthiness. To show his decisiveness and efficiency. And his
deliberate and thorough *anticipation* of all that might go wrong.

— ○ ☼ ○ —

The ESS, the Elasian Security Service, the continental watchdog and
defender of Baron Ebah's skies and lands, was tracking the resin runners'
descent, quietly watching their frigate's slow fall home.

The moment the ship reached Elasian mesospace, another fractal code unfolded in the pilot's imaging field. Without hesitation, Mohaar inverted the coded image and sent it back on cue. He then reset the frigate's heading accordingly and adjusted the ship's repulsion for the last leg of its descent.

Iddh let out a howl and headed below where one of the crew had something going.

"One more time," said crewman Arnod. "Let's double it up. What d'ya say, toads?"

A pile of well-worn New Hollatian gold certificates lay on the floor by the wall. Worthless on Khrae, the heap of Jakomen currency represented almost a quarter of the crew's combined, soon-to-be-collected bonuses.

"No fracken way you can toss two fives three times in a row, Arnod. You're on!"

"Yah!" "Double it up!" the others yelled defiantly with fists raised. "Yah, toad! You're on!"

Iddh hovered invisibly above, cackling and wiggling in anticipation, ready to pounce on the bones. And as the roobs flew from Arnod's hand, the midwayer dove and made a frenzied grab, tumbled across the floor and bounced off the wall with all three…to manufacture…a rare triple! *Three* fives—not just two.

With a shriek of delight, Iddh flew from one young face to the next, cursing and insulting the flabbergasted losers.

— ∘ ☼ ∘ —

At two minutes to touchdown, Elasian Security took control of the frigate and drew it toward a southern base. A minute later, Mohaar overrode the ground lock, disabled the ship's repulsion system, and initiated an accelerating plunge toward the sea.

Unaware on the frigate's rearward deck, Arnod wallowed in his unprecedented hot streak, while two of his mates carefully hand-scanned all three of his lucky roobs, and confirmed them tamper-free.

"Okay, okay—frack you very much. One last toss and if I roob, you can have your fracken paper back. But, if I hit again—at least two fives for the fourth time, toads—your bonuses are mine. Full whack. Okay? Are we clear? Full whack."

"We're clear, Arnuts. Full whack, you mutant," said the last to scan the roobs for herself, before passing them back to Arnod.

"Roll 'em, Toadlick." "Do it, Arnoid." "Just toss the fracken things!"

Arnod cupped both hands together, shook the roobs inside, and smiled mockingly at his comrades. Then he blew on the bones and wound up twice, then blew again and wound up thrice…

"Come on, Toad!"

…and flung them cornerwise.

With a shriek, Iddh dove in and rode them all the way.

$$- \circ \; \textrm{☼} \; \circ -$$

Several more Elasian Security operators joined in. A rescue squadron headed to the projected impact site, and the base adjutant was briefed.

"…and everything appeared normal, Sir. Then, around one minute to touchdown, we abruptly lost contact—and our lock."

No reply from the adjutant.

"They're dropping, Sir, with no evident repulsion. Fifteen seconds until they hit the water. At that velocity, they'll disintegrate…. Sir?"

The adjutant felt uneasy. He knew the ship was tagged double-beta—one of the baron's secret missions—and that direct communications were disallowed. A wrong call either way and he could kiss off his promotion.

"Hail them," he finally said. "As devoes."

An operator promptly hailed the baron's runners. "Unidentified frigate, this is Elasian Security. Your failure to respond is in violation of Federation law. Acknowledge or be destroyed."

Another counted down, "…five, four, three…."

Arnod's crewmates stared in disbelief. They had substituted two of his three lucky roobs and still he'd pulled it off. And not just a double, but a *second* toss of triple fives.

It was unheard of…impossible. And something else was wrong. Where was that gravitational pull, that wonderful weightiness that subtly signaled their nearness to home ground?

While Arnod danced and gathered up his winnings, two of his crewmates pushed their faces against a leeward porthole in time to see the ocean rushing up.

And with a few last insults, a drawn out cackle and a vile Rehman curse, Iddh turned and pinned away to join the long-gone Rehman Son.

Chapter 6 — N O T E S

N[146] ***Elasia.*** One of the 10 continents of planet Khrae.

N[147] ***the Jakomen.*** Who no longer inhabit Khrae (as Group Commander Iiose recounted to the four Rohman Sons):

> [D-32.7, *HOSTING THE DEMON SONS*] "Through a slow but steady erosion of populace polarity, we estimate that 14% of the Khraelings are favorably inclined. Their most recent foray of merit, some 600 standard years ago, saw the near-annihilation of one of Khrae's ten tribes, the so-called Jakomen people. Since the surviving Jakomen's self-imposed exile on Khrae's terra-formed sister planet 'New Hollatia,' the strained relationship between the Jakomen and their Khraeling cousins—and the lingering calls for retribution—may present an opportunity for a controlled reduction."
>
> Lord Mohaar, possessor of the leftmost junior, made mental note of the commander's intimation, for it reinforced a tentative plan he had long contrived.

N[148] ***the ruling barons.*** The barons issued paper "qubals" backed by the Federation's considerable gross product. The Jakomen of Old Hollatia circulated gold certificates backed by an inventory of bullion greater than any three of Khrae's other continents combined. The Federation spoke a common language; Hollatia spoke its own. The Jakomen subscribed to a belief in one god, and although claiming a similar faith, the Federation has yet to completely unify its theological elements.

N[149] ***elite incarnate corps.*** Select Og mercenaries trained and assigned to birth into the unsuspecting tribes of worlds being primed for Rohmanization.

N[150] ***from Varah.*** From the compassionate Varahns of Khrae's neighboring solar system.

N[151] ***the benevolent Elasians.*** The people of continental Elasia (of planet Khrae), who sheltered the surviving Jakomen after the holocaust.

N[152] ***KSF.*** The Khrae Security Forces; Khrae's defenders and the enforcers of Federation law.

N[153] ***NHD.*** The New Hollatian Defense; the global police, security force and defenders of New Hollatia.

N[154] ***Federation Board.*** Khrae's 11-seat executive council consisting of the governor, Counsel-Ra, and all nine continental barons ("Those of the Continents").

N[155] ***meters.*** Og-incarnates unfailingly impose Orion's metric system on those they are priming for conquest. Their Rɵhman masters allow the imposition as a prelude to the coming New Order. Consequently, all measures of volume, weights and non-stellar distances are identical on Nordehk's inhabited worlds, except Mhu:

> [from D-32.7, *HOSTING THE DEMON SONS*] "One: Mhu. The progenitors of Nordehk's tribes, the so-called ancients of Mhu, retain a purely positive polarity and remain committed to the Light. Having completed their transition from the third to fourth density some 240,000 years ago, those of Mhu have been left to your discretion, as prescribed."

N[156] ***nostril.*** The Khraeling/Jakomen single nostril.

N[157] ***the Rikahrs.*** The ruling family of continental Pagorea, and age-old rivals of the Ebahs (rulers of continental Elasia).

G[192a] KSF: Khrae Security Forces; defenders of the planet and enforcers of Khrae's Federational laws

N[158] ***Baron Miloh Ebah XII.*** The current Baron of Elasia; head of Elasia's ruling Ebah family, the continued rivals of Pagorea's ruling Rikahrs.

N[159] ***KLC.*** Khrae Lunar Command; the nerve center of the Khrae Security Forces (the *KSF*) is located on and beneath the surface of *Patos*, the largest and outermost of Khrae's two moons.

N[160] ***Altos.*** The polymide-laden, innermost, and smallest of Khrae's two moons.

G[226b] (Lord) Mohaar: [♂ pron. **Mō'**-här] a fallen Vihdæan administrator turned warrior-crusader for Rɵhm and recently elevated to the status of Rɵhman Son; in the Nordehk campaign, he is to Rɵhmanize Khrae and New Hollatia; Lord Mohaar's eternally committed, personal midwayer/scout is ***Iddh*** [♂ pron. Ĭd]

N[161] ***warrior-crusader.*** A lieutenant devoted to a host of Rɘhman Sons through the course of a host of Rɘhman campaigns.

N[162] ***Son sponsorship.*** An Imperial Warrior—a newly fallen Vihdæan defector—may attain Son status only through the sponsorship of a campaigning Rɘhman Son, to whom he then becomes forever obligated to serve when called upon. If such a Son should ever fail, both he *and* his sponsor could be stripped of their rank and title by the Rɘhman High Court, and banished to lesser service as Imperial Administrators of the Realm.

Jake's Take
CHAPTER 6

The roobs enthralled me, but how does the house calculate the myriad payouts in this purported fairest of games? And how do we cypher the toss when "the count" lays face down?

After glimpsing the action inside a Rǝhman roobs den (Book 3), I stopped thinking like an earthling. From beneath the seven-sided table's clear, concave rolling surface, an amphidor broadcasts start-to-finish projections of each toss—both in-house and remotely, so distant fellow gamers may watch and wager on any table's play.

Quick to fashion my first set of amply rollable roobs (having dreamt them several times), I've pondered the game's complex, sunken table ever since. *The primary challenge?* To recalibrate, reveal and reconceal the table's betting bars after every toss.

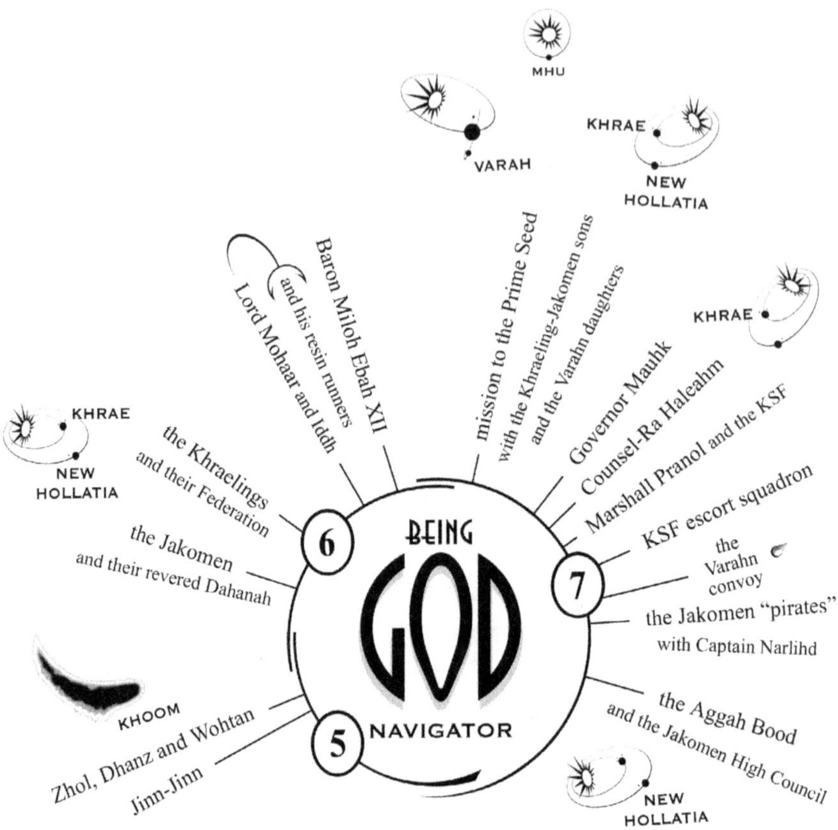

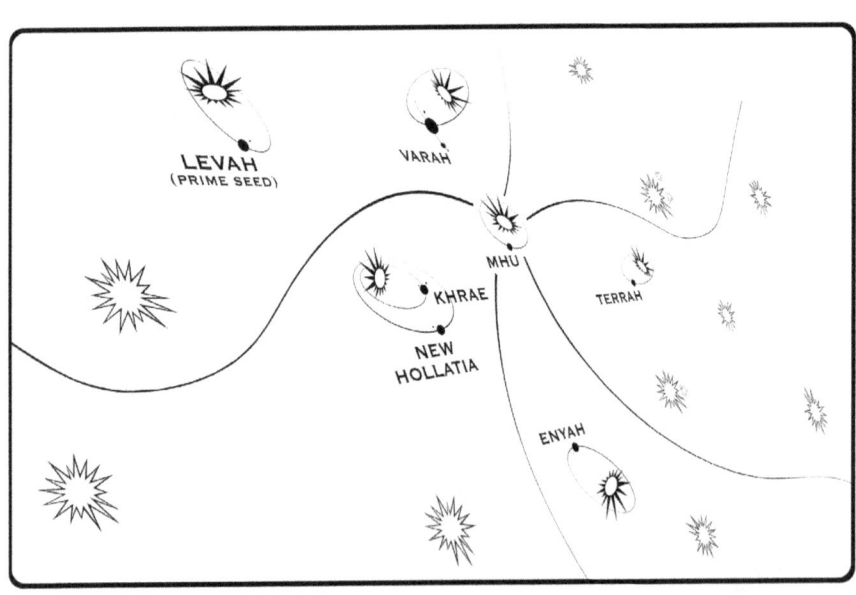

MHU

KHRAE
VARAH
NEW
HOLLATIA

KHRAE

mission to the Prime Seed
with the Khraeling-Jakomen sons
and the Varahn daughters

Governor Mauhk

Counsel-Ra Haleahm

Marshall Pranol and the KSF

Baron Miloh Ebah XII
and his resin runners
Lord Mohaar and Iddh

KSF escort squadron

the Khraelings
and their Federation

the
Varahn
convoy

KHRAE
NEW
HOLLATIA

the Jakomen
and their revered Dahanah

the Jakomen "pirates"
with Captain Narlihd

BEING GOD NAVIGATOR

6
7
5

KHOOM

the Aggah Bood
and the Jakomen High Council

Zhol, Dhanz and Wohtan
Jinn-Jinn

NEW
HOLLATIA

LEVAH
(PRIME SEED)

VARAH

MHU

KHRAE

TERRAH

NEW
HOLLATIA

ENYAH

7

THE ANCIENTS' NOBLE MISSION
DAY-30: KHRAE

In Khrae's Intercontinental Federation, seven years had passed since receiving notice from the ancients of Mhu—the true natives of Nordehk, and progenitors of the constellation's other tribes—that the time had come to settle Levah, "the Prime Seed," the next in line[163] of ten pristine local planets long slated for colonization. It was the ancients' first contact since shortly after the holocaust, when they had sent a brief message of sorrow, a communication that had left Khrae's then-leadership wondering how the mysterious ones had learned of the abominable crime.

Eagerly accepting the ancients' invitation[164] to join the mission, the Khraelings began the allotted two-year process of selecting 99 young men: eleven from each of their planet's nine inhabited continents. On Mhu's behalf, Those of the Continents promptly contacted the Jakomen and advised them of the ancients' invitation to similarly select 11 young sons to represent New Hollatia in the project to settle the current Prime Seed. Both the Khraelings and Jakomen understood that only 100 of the initially-selected 110 would join the 100 Varahn daughters, who were already en route to Khrae for the planned prelaunch festivities: a 100-day festival in which all four participating worlds[165] would formally celebrate the joint, one-way mission.

From a volunteer field of thousands, 110 settler-prospects were chosen, extensively tested, and then ranked according to individual merits. Then, after two years of advanced studies in sociology, diplomacy, related sciences and skills, followed by two of three grueling years of survival training in Khrae's scant wilderness reserves, 100 sons—10 from each of the ten groups—were designated "mission colonists." Although greatly disappointed, the 10 remaining "mission alternates" honored their pre-selection commitments and completed the third year of survival training with the rest. With dignity, each young alternate accepted that he would likely not be venturing to the distant colony unless accident or illness bumped him to full colonist status. To this day, no selection changes had been made.

The colonists and alternates—despite concerns to the contrary—bonded into a tightly knit group. More importantly, the 11 young Jakomen had been embraced as brothers by all 99 of their Khraeling peers. The development occurred rather quickly and in large part through the determined efforts of the tall, freckled, Jakomen alternate, Shaum Dloue.

From the outset, Dloue knew intuitively that his destiny lay not in the actual mission to the Prime Seed. He thus assumed as his private responsibility, the burden of ensuring that his ten settler-son compatriots would participate in the Seed's colonization as true equals, rather than token participants who might become alienated and eventually isolated, as had the Jakomen of old.[166]

From the moment he and his fellows landed on Khrae for their pre-mission training, Shaum Dloue began a personal crusade to see that all traces of prejudicial inclinations, guilt, or perceptions of accountability for the ghastly past be thoroughly transcended. Early on, he decided that the key to creating true camaraderie lay with the mission's contingent of young Pagorean sons.[167] As a result of Dloue's tireless, energetic initiatives through the sons' initial months of training, the young Jakomen and Pagoreans came to confront their deep-seated and admittedly confused emotions, and subsequently became the best of friends.

In a self-fulfilling prophecy, Dloue was the first of the 110 sons to be designated a mission alternate. His evaluators recognized his knack for diplomacy, but since all of the settler-prospects had completed advanced studies in the art and fully understood the importance of passing such wisdoms to surviving generations, the mix of talents should be a balanced blending of elementary skills—those deemed critical to achieving the mission's primary objective: to establish a solid foundation from which Levahn culture could thrive.

Now, having recently completed their third year of survival training, the colonists and alternates were enjoying the eighth day of a hard-earned 10-day leave. In two days, they would depart for Patos to begin their studies on tribal evolution, the final phase of their pre-mission training. Approximately 67 days later—some 40 days into the Federation's 100-day festival[168] celebrating the mission—the Varahn daughters' convoy[169] would arrive over Patos. And in 121 days, on the festival's Day 92, the ancients of Mhu would visit Khrae for the fourth time since the planet's graduation to brood status. It would be their first appearance in nearly 4,000 years.

On the festival's concluding 100th day, the sons and daughters would depart in the ancients' lightship for transport to Levah, to the waiting, uncorrupted world.

THE AGGAH'S FORUM

D-30.2: KHRAE

"We settled that issue months ago...."

Not far from the festival grounds, inside an office in the governor's residential compound, Khrae's Counsel-Ra, Raund Haleahm, was mediating a morning session with the barons' seasoned envoys. As Counsel-Ra, Haleahm held the Federation's second most powerful political post. A hyper, no-nonsense manipulator, he had neither the looks for the spotlight nor the necessary interest in pretentious charm. Intelligent, opinionated and always to the point, Raund Haleahm was the totally dedicated brain behind Governor Gjadren Mauhk, and everyone knew it. The governor liked it that way.

With thirty days before the festival's grand opening, layered images from the busy site filled in the room's imaging field and showed the progress at nine rising pavilions and at other exhibitions, stands and rides. For the most part, everything seemed on schedule. But with the barons' endless bickering over the festival's projected spoils, it was a trying time for all.

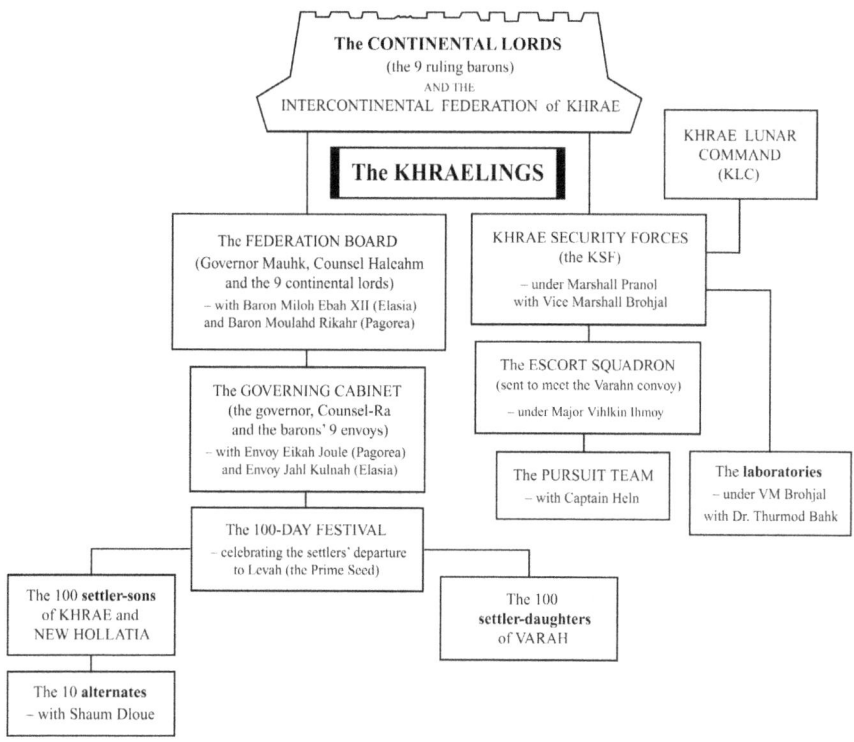

"Counsel Haleahm?..." An aide interrupted the C-Ra's meeting for the call they were waiting on. A few seconds later, Marshall Pranol, long-time commanding officer of the KSF,[G192b] unfolded in the office's imaging field, layered over the views of the festival grounds.

"Good morning, Mannon," said the governor, pleased with Pranol's timing. "Is she on?"

Knowing their absence in the planned festivities would be a serious embarrassment to the Federation, the Jakomen had yet to confirm their participation. Some 800 years after the holocaust, Khrae's continental lords— "Those of the Continents," the Federation's nine ruling barons—suspected that the Varahns still privately considered them genocidal barbarians. They, the barons, therefore felt it imperative that at least some of New Hollatia's leadership be with the governor to greet the Varahn prince's convoy when it arrived.

"Yes, Sir," Pranol replied, his voice strong and authoritative, his posture and physique belying his 112 years. "The Aggah Bood is addressing her forum."

Haleahm pointed in'field (in the imaging field), directly at the marshall's life-sized image, which along with the other imaged layers, dissolved as a staticky interception of a New Hollatian broadcast filled the display. The Jakomen were sitting in public forum with their current Aggah—the dynamic Unah Bood. The gathering was limited to 60,000: the same rounded number as that of their revered Dahanah, those who had survived the actual surprise attack on Old Hollatia some eight centuries prior to recent times.

Governor Mauhk groaned. He had been hoping for some kind of signal, some indication of possible compromise. But the sign was clear: the Jakomen's towering holocaust memorial, a dark and twisted framework that seemed to stretch halfway to the stars, formed the backdrop for Bood's fire-lit forum.

All 24 Jakomen Elders sat quietly behind their beloved leader, whose speech rose in crescendo. Khrae Lunar Command's translation of the Aggah's address streamed down one side of her flickering image as a red band of Khraeling characters, while she shouted over a rising applause and fierce pounding of ceremonial drums.

"...and after two centuries of virtual neglect, we have been *'invited'*..." She drew the word out. "...for what?!" she screamed, her live audience now roaring and stomping their feet.

"For a *'celebration'*..." The roar grew louder. "...for a *'party'*...." The roar was deafening.

"What has changed? What has happened that I am so blind?"

It had been seven years since Governor Mauhk advised the Aggah Bood of the ancients' directive to proceed with the joint colonization of Levah. After nearly two years of uncertainty as to whether the Jakomen would even send their sons to Khrae for training, and just days before that training was set to commence, the governor finally received a curt announcement from Bood's office that the eleven young representatives would be forthcoming.

Now—five years later, and after numerous requests for a reply—the Jakomen had still not responded to their invitation to take part in the 100-day festival. It seemed painfully evident that after years of stalling, the Aggah did not intend to come.

The Federation never understood the Jakomen mentality, let alone their contempt for indebtedness. If one did something for another, the other reciprocated—quickly. No one on New Hollatia or on continental Old Hollatia before had carried a debt. Indebtedness was society's downfall. It was the root of everything evil.

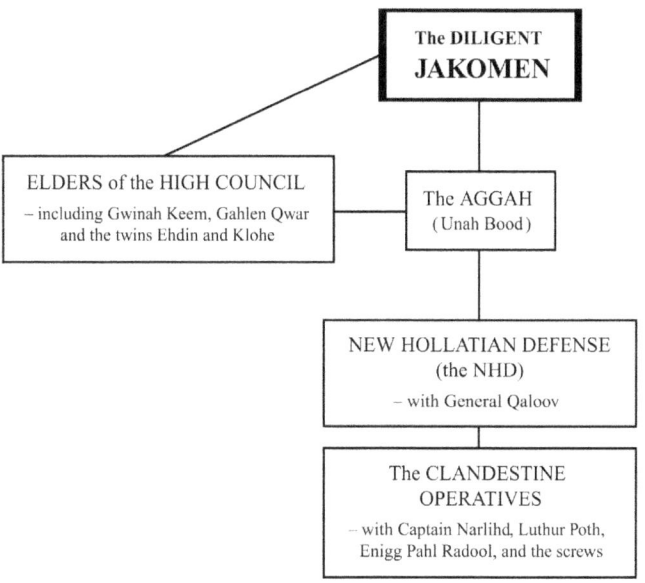

From the Jakomen point of view, the Khraeling invitation had not warranted a response. The Federation failed to perceive that their request had been an asking of a favor where no favor was owed, and they neglected to extend an offer of compensation in any form. That the Khraelings, after virtually no contact since the Great Exodus, would "invite" the Jakomen to visit the homeland of the exalted Dahanah for a "celebration," was patently abhorrent. That the governor's follow-up requests for a reply lacked any sensitivity to or comprehension of the insult, was astounding. That the Federation lacked the foresight to see how foolish Khrae would look without a Jakomen presence at the festival, was inconceivable. And that the Khraelings could assume the Jakomen would forgive and forget, was unfathomable to the Aggah, the Elders and their people as a whole.

"The ancients have called and we have answered," yelled Unah Bood, "that our brave young sons might venture to the stars. Praise the Dahanah! Glory to God!"

With that, she stood out from behind her podium, folded her arms across her chest, turned down the corners of her mouth, and nodded slowly at the frenzied crowd.

Eikah Jouhl, the Baron of Pagorea's petulant envoy, smacked the mirrored console that formed the conference table's beveled edge. The Aggah's image abruptly disappeared.

"Have none of you read your history?" Jouhl began, visibly upset and unable to contain herself anymore. "It is impossible to negotiate with the Jakomen. They will *never* say what they want. To try dealing with them is to revisit the past. They are pirates, smugglers and thieves! They have always been and will always be. While we overcrowd our continents, they enjoy an entire planet to themselves, and at no small expense to the Federation. We owe them nothing!"

Most of her counterparts kept their eyes fixed on the table. Jouhl knew what they were thinking.

"And don't give me that holocaust nonsense! A war was lost, a war initiated by the conniving jacks. Look at what they had and look at what they have now. They are cunning, farsighted, and manipulative. We are better off without their *participation....*" Mimicking the Aggah, she drew out the word.

Raund Haleahm looked at Governor Mauhk from the corners of his eyes. Mauhk stared at the ceiling.

Jouhl's continental adversary, Jahl Khulnah of Elasia, stood. And on behalf of Baron Ebah and the Elasian people—steadfast patrons of the diligent Jakomen, and traditional rivals of the powerful Pagoreans—Khulnah calmly spoke.

"The Jakomen people want only that which would mutually benefit our societies: a long-overdue normalization of relations, and the commencement of trade between our two worlds."

Jouhl, the room's lone Pagorean, snorted and sneered.

"Why then, Jahl," a neutral envoy wondered aloud, "don't the Jakomen just ask for it? Not that it could be done," he said, turning mindfully to the governor, "but at least we'd be talking."

"Ask for it?" injected Jouhl. "Who?" she asked, then spat out, "Bood? There's something strange about that witch. She won't ask for anything unless it's hers to take!"

"The Jakomen are a proud people," Khulnah patiently replied, discounting the Pagorean's heated warning. "They do not ask for what they believe should be given, or at least tendered formally. Have you not considered that their participation would benefit *only* the Federation? What have the Jakomen, who have asked nothing of us in three hundred years, what have they been offered in return for the favor of their attendance at the festival, and in welcoming the ancients, Prince Adahr and our Varahn guests? I believe that at the very least, they expected our invitation to have included an opening for the pursuance of some kind of talks." Khulnah knew it for a fact. "Not that it should have been included, Governor," he added. "I am only suggesting that some kind of dialogue may have been expected. The Jakomen have a peculiar mindset, as our sister from Pagorea clearly understands."

With Eikah Jouhl on the verge of another unproductive outburst, Governor Mauhk changed the subject. "Yes…uh, thank you, Jahl." Then turning to his Counsel-Ra, Mauhk asked, "What's the status of our escorts, Raund?"

"The Varahn convoy is approximately 74 days out, Gjadren," Haleahm replied. "Our escort squadron should rendezvous with the prince's starship[170] around 48 hours from now."

PIRATES IN THE LANES

D-30.3: SPACE

On time and track for its scheduled rendezvous with the incoming Varahn convoy, a KSF squadron of seven red and white interceptor-escorts sailed smoothly through deep space.

Nestled in custom-fitted flight seats, the interceptors' one-man crews slept in a low-gravity, low-level hibernation. Large, spider-like roemstims— roving electromagnetic stimulators—alternately crawled and squatted over them, whirring softly as they systematically exercised the flyers' muscle groups with constantly kneading appendages and measured electrical jolts.

Just two days away and approaching head on, a powerful interstellar transport-tug cruised the diplomatic lanes between Varah and Khrae. With fourteen huge ovoid containers in tow, the Varahn starship was also on time and course to meet their Khraeling escorts for the last leg of their long journey.

Inside the luxurious tug, the royal prince, his delegation and the hundred beautiful daughters lay cold in their ninth year of deep-space hibernation, as the Varahns measured time. Imported Khraeling roemstims carefully kneaded and monitored their sleeping, waxen bodies in a soft synthetic light.

Less than an hour away, an unmarked Jakomen transport-cruiser taxed its troubled engine in an increasingly desperate bid to intercept the Varahns before it was too late. Its tough young crew of highly trained operatives— "screws" from the New Hollatian Defense—rushed to prepare for the one shot they knew they'd be lucky to get. For this mission, they were running as pirates/"independents." Their ship and its twin coil engine had undergone numerous modifications and all traces of NHD[G249a] affiliation had been removed.

Fixed on their cruiser's imagers, the Varahn convoy was closing fast. The operatives' captain, Rauhf B. Narlihd, had to act quickly or that Varahn starship and its precious string of overstuffed containers would fly right past. And Captain Narlihd would not get a second chance.

While his chief engineer, Luthur Poth, struggled to compensate for their engine's erratic performance, the captain fired a critical transmission that signaled the convoy's imagers to decelerate for the clandestine rendezvous, as had been prearranged....

Caught in the middle of Khrae's 200-year cold war with New Hollatia, the humble Varahns strove to work amicably with both sides. The Khraeling Federation reluctantly tolerated Varahn-Jakomen commerce with an unwritten understanding that the trade was to be discreet, and that nothing larger than lunar barges would be transported between the two worlds, lest Varahn "goodwill" debase the Khraelings' perceived balance of power. But with the advent of Khrae's celebratory festival, and with the Varahns' advance departure,[171] came an irresistible opportunity to attach a full-sized amstrahd container for the needy Jakomen, as opposed to the much smaller lunar barges blind-eyed by Khrae.

The Varahns secretly arranged for Jakomen operatives from the New Hollatian Defense to intercept the convoy at least thirty days before the convoy's scheduled rendezvous with the KSF escort squadron, and long before the convoy came into view of the approaching escorts' scanners. Then, after severing the umbilical of the convoy's last container and taking their prize in tow, the NHD pirate-operatives would stay beyond the range of the approaching Khraelings by following an extraordinarily long, curved, and *safe* escape route home.

Thirty days later, the operatives would transfer their catch to a friendly squadron of NHD destroyers on a mock exercise, who would offload the veritable bonanza of commercial cargo and then dismantle the container for eventual return to their Varahn friends. All fourteen containers would be registered with the Federation prior to the convoy's departure from Varah, and if one should go missing, it would be the Varahns' loss.

What could possibly go wrong?

Chapter 7 — N O T E S

N[163] *the next in line.* As determined by the ancients of Mhu.

N[164] *the ancients' invitation.* A necessary formality by the ancients' maxim concerning volition, as opposed to their improperly *informing* the Varahns and Khraelings and presuming their participation—despite that certainty (as all parties understood the strategic value of participating in such a monumental event). Presumptiveness aside, the ancients' preparatory formalities are respected as such.

N[165] *all four participating worlds.* Mhu, Varah, Khrae and New Hollatia.

N[166] *as had the Jakomen of old.* Before the holocaust.

N[167] *Pagorean sons.* Decendants of the suspected perpetrators of the Jakomen holocaust.

N[168] *100-day festival.* As Group Commander Iiose reported to the four Rehman Sons:

> [from D-32.7, *HOSTING THE DEMON SONS*] "Under the ancients' direction," Iiose continued, lowering his hand and privately pleased with the execution of his practiced showmanship, "Varah, Khrae, and New Hollatia are preparing to jointly colonize the so-called Seed. There is to be a 100-day festival on Khrae designed to celebrate the occasion, and which will culminate in the joint departure of 200 'settlers': 100 from Varah, 90 from Khrae, and 10 from New Hollatia. Festivities are scheduled to begin in 33 days as time is measured by the Khraelings, whose 24-hour planetary rotation is within seconds of the Rehman standard day."

G[192b] KSF: Khrae Security Forces; defenders of the planet and enforcers of Khrae's Federational laws

N[169] *the Varahn convoy.* An interstellar tug/starship with Prince Adahr, his delegation and the 100 settler-daughters on board—all in hibernation—and with 14 gigantic containers of commercial goods in tow.

N[170] *the prince's starship.* The Varahn convoy's powerful interstellar tug.

G[249a] NHD: New Hollatian Defense; the global police, security force and defenders of New Hollatia

N[171] ***advance departure.*** With 6.4 standard light years between Khrae and Varah, the Varahns learned of, prepared for, and departed for the mission long before the ancients informed Khrae's leadership.

Jake's Take
CHAPTER 7

SUMMARY

- Khrae's 100-day festival: designed to bring together (and celebrate the subsequent departure of) the 100 Varahn daughters and 100 sons of Khrae and New Hollatia who are to colonize the ancients' pristine "Prime Seed," Levah.

- The Players: Khrae's Governor Mauhk and his Counsel-Ra Raund Haleahm, Varah's Prince Adahr, and New Hollatia's Aggah Bood.

- En route: a Varahn interstellar convoy with Prince Adahr, his entourage and the 100 young daughters (due on Day 40 of the festival); and a delegation of the fabled ancients from Nordehk's core planet, Mhu (due on Day 92).

- Would-be Spoilers: one or more of the campaigning Sons of Rehm, and/or the Og, and/or the Aggah Bood (who may or may not attend the Khraeling festival), and/or Bood's deep space pirate-operatives (featuring Captain Narlihd) who have Adahr's sumptuous starship in their sights.

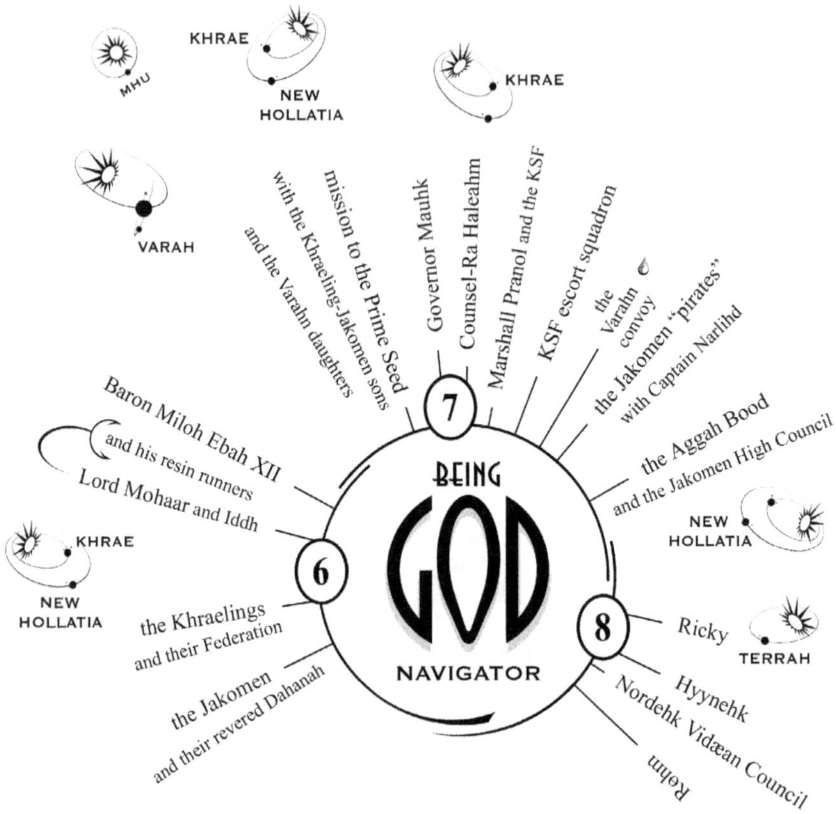

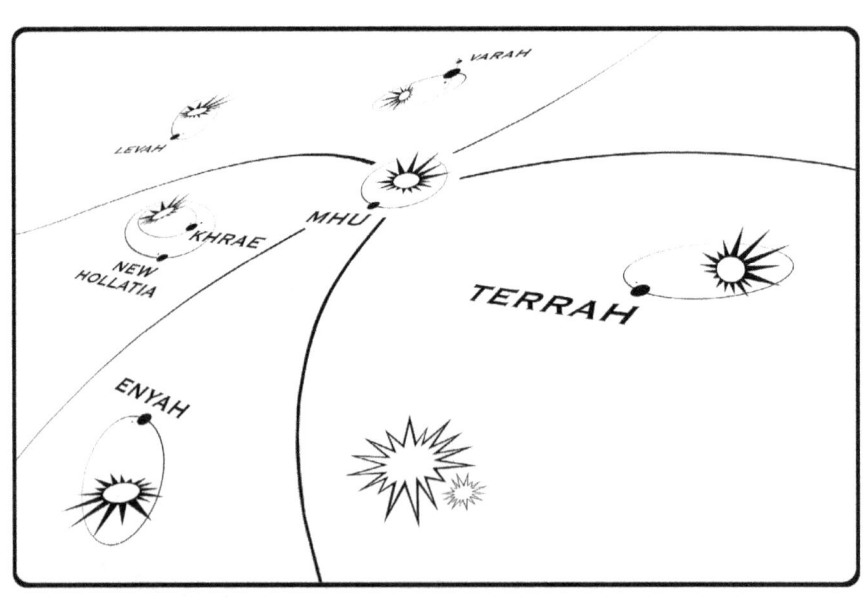

KHRAE

MHU

NEW
HOLLATIA

KHRAE

VARAH

mission to the Prime Seed
with the Khraeling-Jakomen sons
and the Varahn daughters

Governor Mauhk

Counsel-Ra Haleahm

Marshall Pranol and the KSF

KSF escort squadron

the
Varahn
convoy

the Jakomen "pirates"
with Captain Narlihd

Baron Miloh Ebah XII
and his resin runners

Lord Mohaar and Iddh

the Aggah Bood
and the Jakomen High Council

NEW
HOLLATIA

7

BEING
GOD
NAVIGATOR

KHRAE

NEW
HOLLATIA

6

the Khraelings
and their Federation

the Jakomen
and their revered Dahanah

8

Ricky

TERRAH

Hyynehk

Nordehk Vidæan Council

Rohm

VARAH

LEVAH

MHU

KHRAE

NEW
HOLLATIA

TERRAH

ENYAH

8

HAPPY DREAMS

D-30.4: TERRAH

Ricky knelt beside his bunk to say his nightly prayers. He kind of believed—not like totally, but kind of—that someone might be listening. But even if that was true, he didn't think they really would or really could help him much at all.

Anyways, in a whisper only they could hear and mostly for his mom, he usually asked the angels up above to at least try to make things better so she wouldn't cry so much. But if angels really heard him and could really make things right, why'd he have to ask them nearly every single night? And what about the hellies, those stinky little creeps? Couldn't real angels keep him safe beneath his sheets?

"Dear angels," he began, in a real low whisper—but sincerely, just in case—and looking up around his ceiling, hands clasped below his face. "Before I rest my sleepy head…" He thought that sounded stupid, but supposedly for angels that's what little kids should say. "…I pray first that you fix the fridge noise, 'cause now that makes my mom cry, too."

Since angels couldn't handle more than three prayers at a time, and since he always saved the exact same one for last, he had just one more new prayer tonight.

Ricky closed his eyes and bowed his head. He figured that if angels were really for real and if they truly watched over him like his mom said, then they probably knew that sunglasses freaked him out, especially big dark ones. He couldn't help it, but whenever he saw someone wearing big dark sunglasses, he'd turn away and run—if his legs didn't get heavy and freeze up first. Now the bully kids had figured that one out and were putting big damn dark ones on, and staring and glaring and pushing everyone to point and laugh.

The other thing about those shitheads was the name they called him. *Big Eyes.* Sure, maybe his eyes were bigger than most kids…. Actually, once, as he stepped onto a city bus with his mom, he locked eyes with an older kid whose eyes were about the same size. The other kid's eyes immediately went blackish for just a second or two, but Ricky still remembered the hatred in that weirdo's eyes—and the headache and buzzing he felt between his temples—

until he got home and his mom gave him an aspirin and some grape juice, and then tucked him into bed....

"Second..." He'd been thinking about this for a while and although he felt a little guilty, he decided to go ahead and officially make it a prayer. "...I pray the hellies take the bully kids, not me."

He really didn't understand the prayer thing, like how it worked when it actually worked—because sometimes it did. But if angels could get the hell-men to take the bully kids instead of him, he'd sense it pretty quick. *And* they'd start leaving him alone.

"Third, I pray you guard my room and keep me safe all night."

Prayer number three didn't work any better than the rows of GI Joes his mom let him arrange on his floor just before bedtime—kind of like a barricade to trip up charging bug-eyes—so long as he picked the Joes up first thing in the morning. There really wasn't much more he could do to keep those bastards from his bed.

Then Ricky climbed his ladder and slid in between his fresh, clean, cowboy sheets: the patched-up flannel ones that he liked best. And just loud enough for his mom to hear, he recited the rhyme she taught him to finish off with every night.

"Thank you for your watch-care. Thanks for being everywhere."

Most folks didn't know that angels liked rhymes, or that it helped get their attention.

"Now my mom will tuck me in, and happy dreams will soon begin."

Honestly? He didn't really believe the angel thing. Something deep inside him just felt otherwise.

THE MYSTERIOUS MESSENGER
D-30.5: NORDEHK

The eight Vihdæa who comprised Nordehk's administrative council took their seats around the elevated outer ring of their stepped, sky-blue roundtable![172] Moments before, they had received a supersensory directive to gather, something akin to an intuitive knowing sparked from On High.

Awash in a golden fog, the eight quietly watched as a pinpoint of sparkling, bright iridescent light appeared and slowly expanded above their translucent table's open center. A heavenly form within the majestic aura cast bursts of shimmering rays upon them. The Vihdæa recognized it as the standard salutation of a divine messenger from the Loyal Order of Oraphim![173]

"Peace be upon you, sisters and brothers," Nordehk's eight heard the oraph softly say. "I am Hyynehk. I bring warm greetings from the Most Highs."

The oraph paused to humbly receive the council's silent, reciprocal vibrations of unifying love.

"The vessel now within your second frontier," she went on, "is indeed a Rɵhman khoomyahna. Apparently Rɵhm, the 'prime defector,' has chosen to extend his influence in this sector of the galaxy."

The eight reacted only with a brief rise in their luminescence, and Hyynehk sensed their confusion and deep dismay. They knew well that neighboring constellations were enduring similar prolonged incursions by the Og. They knew well that the arrival of an imperial warship harbingered the final phase of a Rɵhman siege and the imminent coming of The Master Himself.

The divine messenger was well aware that for some 12,000 standard years, Nordehk's Vihdæan Council had been hearing Rɵhm's calls to join him and *His Crusades*, and that they had never understood his motivation. Like most Vihdæa, Nordehk's eight had no idea that Rɵhm's activities were thoroughly known to the Universal Sons, "the Most Highs," his sempiternal brethren who followed his every move—quietly, and with the ablest of spies![174]

"Although Rɵhm fell out of love with Prime Creator and abandoned his seat with the Most Highs long ago," Hyynehk explained, "he remains a supremely talented, dynamic and charismatic Universal Son. Our highly inquisitive, fallen brother came to believe that absolute wisdom cannot be attained without a comprehensive exploration of service unto self—service within the empirical realm of negativity. And through his consequent defection, and subsequent appropriation and orchestration of other selves, he now intends to put what he perceives to be his domain, verily All That Is, '*in order.*'"

Nordehk's Vihdæa listened attentively—patient of the oraph's purpose, and expectant of some charge.

"Rɵhm maintains the focus of his beingness between the fifth and sixth densities. In response to invitations from his Sons and others, however, he occasionally manifests with varying degrees of fluidity in the lower fourth and third, where he presents himself as 'The Friend of Man and Angels.'

"Rɵhm wants nothing tangible. It is the *power*. It is his mastery over the potent vibrations of fear and loathing, and especially the procession of etherean defections—his cherished, willing recruits—that sustain the so-called Prime Crusader.

With each new, negatively-polarized convert, including common will-creatures, there is a discernible empowering of those above, an exponentially accumulative vigor whereby those at the top benefit most. So with every conquest and conversion en masse of yet more billions of evolving beings, Rɵhm's substantial powers significantly increase."

Hyynehk waited a moment while her audience pondered the limitless concept.

"Those powers," she went on, "are immersed in The Fallen One's inordinate orientation, in his extreme entrenchment in the negative polarity, in his total devotion to serving self."

Again the oraph paused before adding, "Rehm is ruthless in his ways. He resents those who, of their own free will, retain a positive polarity and remain loyal to the original vibrations of Love and Light. Under the guise of freedom and liberty, his needs would seem to have manifested into an egomaniacal lust most easily gratified in darkness.

"Feeding on fear and ruling through intimidation, Rehm's methods vary greatly and he exhibits a vast spectrum of creative destruction on his journey through the night. His 'Sons,' fallen Vihdæan sisters and brothers that chose to answer his relentless calls, are powerful and serve him well. But so is it written[175] and long known to us oraphim, '...so shall the darkness begin to fade, and with the Light, become as one.'"

Long known? Who held these words of things to come, and how—*and when*—had they been written? And why should knowledge of such profound, future events be privy to so few? Yes, the oraphim were of a high order; and yes, it was improper for simple administrators to solicit insights into the broader divine...but....

"As always, there are no shortcuts to enlightenment," Hyynehk continued, as though having heard their thoughts. "Administration through patient revelation will ultimately reveal the joys of Love and Light. The Most Highs have every confidence in your ability to prevail."

Prevail? None before had prevailed. None before had even briefly slowed the Rehman hordes. Were these just hollow words? Had others heard them, too?

"Work together, that triumph be assured."

Work together? Nordehk's Vihdæa had always worked together. Was the oraph suggesting that they solicit outside help?

"Prime Creator's will be done," Hyynehk said in closing, her charge delivered, her purpose complete.

"Prime Creator's will be done," her perplexed hosts responded in near unison.

Then, upon compressing her consciousness back into a pinpoint of brilliant light, the mysterious messenger was gone.

THE MASTER'S SUDDEN KNOWING

D-30.6: ELSEWHERE IN THE REALM

In a distant place far from the suns of Nordehk, Røhm's glorious essence sat alone and in repose. Within a flaring orange aura, his temporary manifestation constantly transformed.

To the Most Highs and Vihdæa, doing the will of Prime Creator meant intending and believing that all their actions and inclinations were and would ever be in harmony with His—Prime Creator's—resolve. But to Røhm, there was no prime creator, no sacramental wonder, and no conundrum to think through. He, as Lord And Master Over All, saw only chaos and Order to be brought.

The estranged Universal Son once sat unprejudiced among his peers, the Most Highs, as the 128th of the now 127 supreme administrators of the Ohrvon galaxy, the stellar supercluster of which constellation Nordehk formed but a wee part. For eons, Røhm accepted their proofless notion that the cosmos had come into being by a "divine spark," that All That Is, including Ohrvon and the greater Universe of Universes had been created by the power of thought—by the sheer will, intention and desire of Prime Creator, the existential Infinite Mind, the Universal Father. That which *IS* and ever was.

But neither Røhm, nor his peers, nor anyone known to them had ever seen or heard anything of or from the theoretical "Creator." And in a reflective instant, had it come: a profound knowing that the notion was a fallacy, a simplistic misconception, a blind-faith delusion and failure of the weak to see and accept the obvious truth that the entire universe was an aberration. It always was, *and would ever be.*

The fictional "Father" was simply the latent life force that resided within the energy from which they and all entities had sprung. As raw, "source energy," it held no powers of creation; it held no powers of reason. It simply *existed.* It always had—beautiful and pure, with no capacity to judge. Source energy was incapable of bringing sorely needed Order to balance and control the chaos of All That Is. Of that which could and would be made perfect only by *His* hand. By the mighty hand of Røhm.

Why abnegate self, when, as MASTER OVER ALL, *He* could liberate the constellations' confused bhuvani and bring them clarity of mind? Why abnegate self, when as THE LORD OF LORDS, *HE* could lead Creation's creatures from the desperation of uncertainty into a New Order wherein truth be known and His Boundless Might be recognized?

A LIVING GOD, TO EMBRACE…

Through his crushing orange brilliance, Prime Crusader's ever-changing

faces formed a frightful smile.
    ...A REAL GOD. *TO FEAR.*

Chapter 8 — N O T E S

N[172] *sky-blue roundtable.* As described on Day -32 when Nordehk's Vihdæan Council awaited the return of their sister, Bel, while she spied inside the approaching khoomyahna:

> [from D-32.10, *THE COUNCIL AWAITS*] Their spacious, thought-formed table consisted of three concentric rings that stepped down in height from the outside in toward an open middle. With one seat empty, Nordehk's pensive Vihdæan Council anxiously awaited the return of their sister, Bel.

N[173] *Loyal Order of Oraphim.* A high order of etherean warrior-messengers irreproachably devoted to the Light.

N[174] *the ablest of spies.* Stealthiest of celestial agents, the oraphim are endowed with all the skills and talents of the Vihdæa, the seraphim, the midwayers and more. Like the midwayers, they were born between densities, but not the fourth and fifth. Oraphic reality lies between the sixth and seventh densities—a very high order irreproachably devoted to the Light. Though few in number (less than 150 million per galaxy), the oraphim serve in ways not possible to describe in words of the lower realms. Mysterious messengers and warriors at once, they assist incarnating Mercenaries of Light in ways unknown to the selfless MoLs. They also serve the Universal Sons and the Vihdæa, but take their orders from neither. Nor would they ever defect.

N[175] *so is it written.* As recorded in *The Sacred Tomes of The Ancients of Days*—divine prophesies known only to the eternally committed, and whispered infrequently among the rest.

Jake's Take
CHAPTER 8

Understanding Ricky's reluctant kinship with the Og, and seeing that he shares his mother's struggle in not having anywhere to turn for help, the young one can escape only into his imagination and do his best to support his mom's belief that angels might be persuaded to lend a helping hand.

On the angelic front, Nordehk's passive Vihdæan administrators receive a cryptic encouragement from On High, implying that it is within their substantial powers to somehow stem the Rǝhman tide.

Meanwhile, The Lord God Rǝhm appears—*and ever was*—utterly invincible. Manifestly so before the uneasy Vihdæa, and incontestably so for destiny's troubled hybrid child.

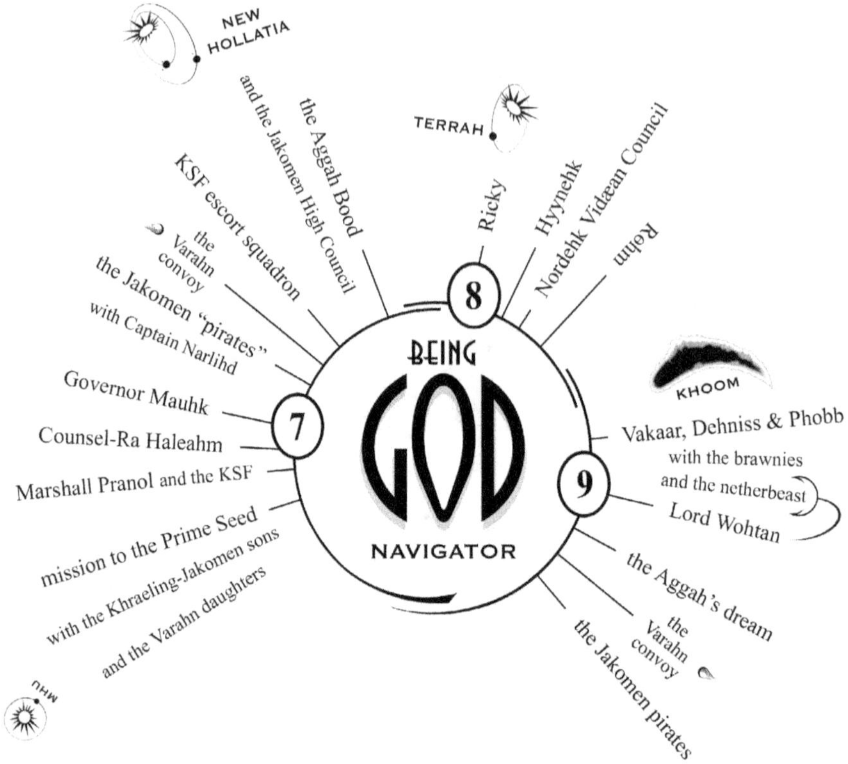

NEW HOLLATIA

the Aggah Bood and the Jakomen High Council

TERRAH

KSF escort squadron

the Varahn convoy

the Jakomen "pirates" with Captain Narlihd

Governor Mauhk

Counsel-Ra Haleahm

Marshall Pranol and the KSF

mission to the Prime Seed

with the Khraeling-Jakomen sons

and the Varahn daughters

MHU

Ricky

Hyynehk

Nordehk Videan Council

Rohm

KHOOM

BEING **GOD** NAVIGATOR

8

7

9

Vakaar, Dehniss & Phobb with the brawnies and the netherbeast

Lord Wohtan

the Aggah's dream

the Varahn convoy

the Jakomen pirates

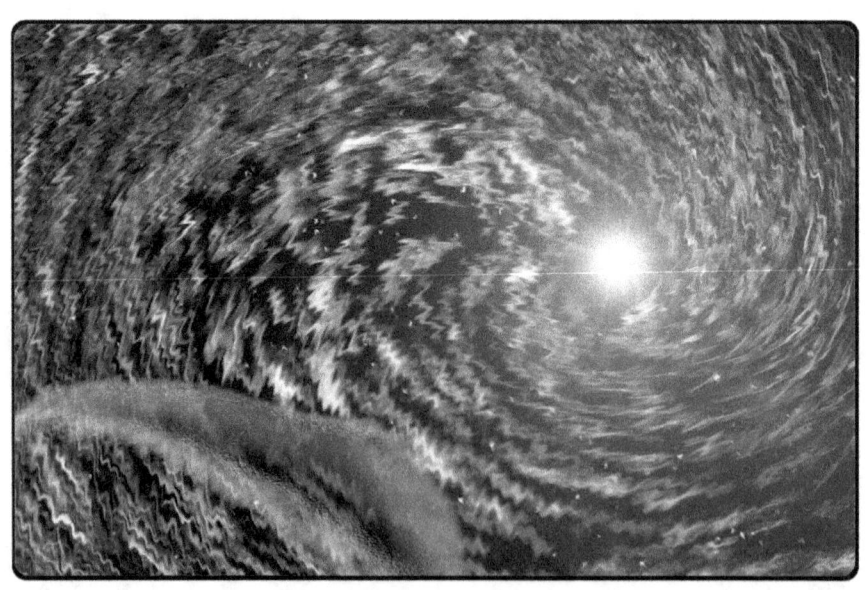

9

PRIESTLY CONTRIVANCES

D-30.7: KHOOMYAHNA / RECTORY

Deep in the rectory's bowels, the yamah's two cohorts, <u>Dehniss and Phobb</u>,[76] and nine of the khoom's brawniest young priests lounged half-naked, greasing one another. A creature of darkness would soon be summoned. For its lessons. For its study in fleshly pain.

Dehniss noticed a hunched form lurking in the shadows of their torchlit crypt. Catching Phobb's eye, he and then his cohort straightened.

"Reverence," said Dehniss, as the brawnies, too, stood.

"We did not hear your approach," Phobb added.

Vakaar joined his black robe's drooping cuffs, and curled his hands inside. "Your con-*tri-van-ces*," he whispered in reply, drawing out the word's last three syllables. "Show me." A black hood all but covered his hairless face.

The two cohorts turned to a shelved alcove and removed some things. Then, with greased bodies glistening in the crypt's dim light, they and the others formed a semi-circle before their yamah: Dehniss at one end, Phobb at the other, and the nine young brawnies in between.

Dehniss held a small silver mace. Beautifully stitched, waxed black leather covered its flexible, polymide core. Its hooked twin-forked handle had been designed for clenching firmly with two fists, and its tines merged into a single shaft with a free-spinning golden ball at its tip. Twelve braided cables of varying lengths extended from a large depression in the ball's top. Each one ended in a small, spiked clump of heavy metal.

Vakaar uncurled his hands and pulled back his cuffs to examine the handsome weapon. He searched for imperfections in its tightly woven braids, and found none. Then, with three of his boney fingers, the high priest lifted one of the mace's spiked metal clumps and flipped it to gauge its weight. Four of its spikes pricked his skin; two pierced to the bone. Vakaar winced and jerked his hand away. Then he sucked the blood and forced a smile.

The yamah moved along. Crossing his hands behind his back, he gave only a perfunctory look at the brawnies' fine collection of lances, whips and wavy golden blades. He nodded approvingly, but touched not a one.

Phobb favored a two-cubit polymide club that swelled in sculpted increments from its sticky, narrow handgrip to a half-sized golden skull. Vakaar could not suppress his desire to take the club's slick shaft into his hands.

"Ohhh…yesss, Phobb," he said, noting the skull's substantial weight. "Excellent."

Hunched as ever and with a feeble, fingers-over-fingers choking grip just above the cudgel's sticky lower section, the high priest raised his upper lip. Then, setting his feet wide enough apart so as to not lose his balance, he took a quick short swing through the air.

"Excellent. Yesss."

Vakaar handed the splendid instrument back to Phobb and then turned and stepped toward the concealed entrance of an adjoining room. A hidden doorway temporarily dissolved in recognition of his vibration. Then, with Dehniss and Phobb clutching their weapons and whispering in his ears, the yamah and his priestly troop cautiously entered the secret chamber. The moment they moved in, the seamless doorway re-formed behind them and sealed them in.

A soft, bluish glow gently illuminated all five sides of the pyramidal room. The glow emanated from a large, darkly tinted translucent pod near the base of the furthest inclined wall. Polymeric torches leaned unlit inside metallic rings mounted low in the chamber's five corners. An inlaid, polished polymide circle lay in the cold stone floor. Two inches wide and twelve cubits in diameter, the inlay encircled a pentagram of cured white marble. A curved, knobbed, golden post stood erect at the pentagram's center, collared and draped with four heavy chains coiled neatly at its base.

Lord Wohtan's midwayer <u>Ænus</u>[G003] streaked inside, circled once and left unseen.

Vakaar felt the telltale chill, and glanced upward. "Fire the torches," he said with a grimace, a second too late to glimpse the Son's scout. "Light them—quickly. Now."

Five of the young brawnies hurriedly lit the torches while the other four lifted the large manacles fastened to the chains' endmost links.

The high priest approached the pod's dark-bluish glow. The others nervously joined him.

"Dark One," the yamah began.

"Hear our calling," chimed the others.

"Come for your lessons…" Vakaar loved this part of the study—*the anticipation.* "…come for your pain."

"Dark One," all twelve chanted together, "hear our calling. Come for your lessons. Come for your pain. Dark One…."

THE AGGAH'S DREAM

D-30.8: NEW HOLLATIA

The Aggah Bood curled up on her favorite couch with a small, iced glass of smuggled, Khraeling mohrd. Dressed down for the evening, she wore but a plain, navy-colored gown.

She gazed intently into the multicolored flames of her suite's modest fireplace, watching their embrace of a neatly arranged stack of slow burning, pressed-fiber sticks. She felt confident that Khrae's military had managed to pirate <u>her broadcast</u>[177] and that Governor Mauhk and the barons or their envoys had been among her viewing audience. Bood had staged the forum for their benefit. She had had a prophetic dream.

She'd dreamt of an enigg, a junior officer of the New Hollatian Defense. He held his hands in fire as he spoke of retribution, of avenging the Dahanah and the Jakomen of old. He told of things written long before, and of their fathers' fabled lands. And he rubbed his hands together, and then he held them high—and neither hand had burned. And his body became as glowing, and he rose up off the ground....

The Aggah remembered well the enigg's brilliant eyes. She could feel his power—still.

CONDITIONS FOR THE LORD

D-30.9: KHOOMYAHNA

Eyes dancing, Lord Wohtan lay on his recliner in the khoom's systems bridge. He was excited, eager to test the endurance of his latest netherwork.

Unlike Dhanz and Mohaar who had willingly answered Zhol's call for the Nordehk campaign, Wohtan had come with conditions. From time to time, he would be allowed certain indulgences. From time to time, he would be allowed his sufferances, his wonderfully torturous miseries.

A Son who largely lacked ambition, Lord Wohtan greatly enjoyed considering and creating innovative ways to satisfy his extreme addiction to experiencing "the passage." He especially relished the painful, accelerated ebbing of life in the highly sensitive flesh of third- and fourth-density beings. In his 1.4 million years of faithful service in Rehm's Crusades, Wohtan had not achieved Overlord status, and scarcely cared he never would.

His disorder, the sufferance stigma, was not uncommon within the ranks of Rehman Sons. Most, including Wohtan, managed it well. It made their service desirable to those with lofty goals.

Unseen by the priestly chanters deep in the rectory's bowels, a pinpoint of light shot into the pentagonal chamber's luminous pod. Seconds behind his impassioned master, Ænus circled the room a few times. Then he stopped to hover unseen near the pyramidal room's apex, and began cackling and cursing the fools below.

The now Son-possessed body twitched inside the chamber's glowing pod. Its protective, blue energy field and domed lid abruptly vanished, and a beastly stench fast filled the air.

At once, the chanters fell silent and involuntarily recoiled.

"Chain it!" cried Vakaar, still wincing from the stink.

The four brawnies holding the manacles fixed to the golden post's four chains rushed to the now dark pod and slapped them around the nethercreature's limp ankles and wrists. Vakaar backed into a corner. Dehniss, Phobb and five others did the same.

For most of a minute the beast did not move, and its chainers stayed podside, staring at the hideous thing. Then its nostrils flared and its lungs filled with several short, quick breaths. Its eyes snapped open, and the four biding brawnies fled to random corners of the torch-lit room.

With little apparent effort, the Son/beast stepped naked from its pod. The hulking, humanoid form had a thick reptilian hide. About a cubit taller and wider than the chamber's biggest priest, its dense bones were layered with rippling muscles. A small, roundly triangular skull was wedged nearly neckless between powerful shoulder mounds, and its ears and nose were keenly perceptive for little more than slimy slits.

The netherbeast's tiny black eyes were deeply set and widely spaced. Each moved independently and was capable of considerable extension. Inside a thin, jagged fold above its rounded jaw lay several rows of curled, double-edged teeth. Anything seized would be torn and devoured.

Its muscular arms ended in two clawed fingers with similarly clawed, opposable thumbs. Two cloven-hoofed, double-jointed legs bowed out from the beast's taut haunches, and a slick, retractable, razor-edged claw lay buried in the hollow cleft of each wide, blue-black hoof. The dark one could kick, grasp, bite and slash, but it would be chained. It would fight and maim as best it could, but it would surely die.

The beast sniffed the air again, and then lunged at the brothers huddled in the nearest corner. Midlunge, the golden post at the pentagram's center fell from sight, taking half the length of its chains with it, and yanking its brutish captive backward to the floor.

The demon/beast lay there awhile, then stood his creature and leaned back. And with its knuckles nearly touching the granite floor, it let out a moan that became a frightful roar.

"Slay it!" yelled the cowering yamah to the cringing others as the roar began to fade. "Smash its skull!" he screamed. "Give the beast its lessons! It must know our horrid suffering! Let it share our hellish pain!"

Phobb and Dehniss rushed in from different corners, swinging their club and mace. From a safer distance, the brawnies tried to spear or whip it, or at least slashed threateningly in the air. All took care to stay outside the silver circle—the limit of the dark one's reach.

SLACK AND SNAP

D-30.10: SPACE

Captain Narlihd[G242a] restlessly monitored the Varahn's rearward approach. He reckoned his cruiser was running parallel to the convoy's course inside the diplomatic lanes, and that he'd have at least fifty kilometers between his ship and the tug's containers when the convoy caught up and pulled alongside. It was a hair's breadth at these speeds. But with his troubled engine, he had to take the risk.

$$- \circ \; \Diamond \; \circ \; -$$

As the convoy neared, Narlihd could tell it was bearing down a bit too fast. Without some drastic action, the whole lot would fly right past.

"Brace down, screws." The problem wasn't with the Varahns. "Plasma, Luthur! Two seconds should be enough."

"The c…c..coils are t..too weak, C…C..Captain!" Poth cried. "The p..plasma'll f… f..fry 'em!"

"*We'll* all fry if we miss this rendezvous, Chief! Do it—*now!*"

The convoy shot by not thirty kilometers to the pirates' port side and disappeared into the void. Poth frowned, injected a two-second dose of plasma, and with everyone else onboard, was thrown back in his harness by the powerful acceleration.

"I have a visual, Captain!" Narlihd's navigator called out moments later.

Retros pulsing, the captain sailed in. Relative to the convoy, he was upside down and closing from behind. He slipped by the last container, then the thirteenth, and then the twelfth. Each one looked 10,000 times his cruiser's size.

Narlihd finally managed to synchronize his speed with the tug, which was continuing to decelerate. A few more pulses and he made his way back beneath number fourteen, the last in line—the container reserved just for him.

While their captain headed up toward the container's spine, three screws emerged from their cruiser's cargo bay in a snapper, a repair module that had been modified for the purpose of tearing an amstrahd container's umbilical apart. They intended to make it appear as though the cord had been cut by cosmic accident, an event—albeit a rare one—that could have happened anytime along the way.

In advance of the mission, the Varahns had secretly transmitted drawings and specifications to New Hollatia. The information enabled the Jakomen to make duplicate umbilicals that they stretched between two NHD^{G249b} destroyers in a delicate exercise the operatives had rehearsed a hundred times.

Now for real, the screws first looped and rerouted the container's circuits, and then sliced the umbilical that connected the last container to the thirteenth. Then, with their snapper's jaw, they clamped onto the inner lining of the thirteenth container's severed stub, the metal fabric that was the complex cord's real strength.

Next, they would eliminate all traces of manipulation by methodically ripping the melted evidence off the outer casing, inner microhoses and burnt filaments. For that, the snapper had to be secured to the fourteenth container, where after anchoring his cruiser, the captain would provide enough reverse thrust to give his screws the torque they needed for the operation. Not so much that their snapper's jaw would lose its grip on the metal fabric, but enough to give them the slack and snap they needed for the task at hand.

MURDEROUS DESIRES
D-30.11: KHOOMYAHNA / RECTORY

While Vakaar shouted orders, Dehniss, Phobb and four bloodied brawnies—now working within the silver circle—heaped a frenzy of violent blows on the mangled form squirming at their feet in a reeking pool of bile, blood and semen. Two of the brothers lay curled in corners dying, chunks missing from their torn sides and shoulders, and from chewed and shredded arms and legs.

Ænus stayed near the chamber's apex, alternately cheering the netherthing and cursing the tiring attackers relentlessly pounding its meat and bones. As hard as ever, the brothers plunged their steely knives into its back and sides and torso, but they missed more often than not.

Upon a sideways flip of a nearly severed leg, and with its retractable claw thrust outward, the Son/beast gutted another glistening priest.

Mortally wounded, the brawnie stumbled to one side, dropped his wavy saber, and fell to his knees trying to stuff his intestines back into the drooping tear between his hips.

A demonic voice filled the yamah's mind. "End it, reverent one. Delicious.... End it now."

"Finish it, Phobb!" Vakaar yelled. "Now!"

Phobb's club was too heavy to accurately strike its writhing, rolling target, although he'd glanced its leathery skull a dozen times or more. He maneuvered around the repugnant one, trying to stay in range of its head and away from its thrashing arms, when the thing suddenly stopped and laid back—as though waiting for Phobb's deathblow.

With his last measure of strength and while his exhausted, surviving brothers launched another desperate attack, Phobb swung the club full circle from the floor.

Dead on, the club's golden skull slammed through the creature's forehead and sank well into its brain. By some reflex to the blow, the warrior/beast arched its fractured back before relaxing and letting out a dying breath.

The assailants stopped momentarily. Then, save Dehniss and Phobb, they jumped back in for a final round of thrusts and hacks.

"Enough!"

It was as though the surviving brawnies could not hear their yamah's cry.

"Enough! Leave it heal for another day!"

It was as though nothing existed beyond their murderous desires.

"Enough! Enough!..."

A SIGHT TO BEHOLD

D-30.12: SPACE

Captain Narlihd was concerned about being so far behind schedule. He should have secured Container 14 <u>thirty days ago</u>![178] Ten would have been marginal. Sure, the Varahn tug's imagers would allow for his late interception and make the necessary adjustments in velocity so the convoy would arrive on schedule to meet its Khraeling escorts. But with only two days until then, he could not see how the khraeks would fail to detect him when they scanned the area after waking from hibernation, which they might do at any time.

The captain kicked himself for not having stayed with the old coils, but this "new generation" engine was supposed to give him an extra 4% *over* maximum velocity—46.7% of light speed—and it had, during all those pre-mission test runs. More than enough to outrun any interceptor, the improved engine had been too good to resist. Now he'd be lucky to get away with the container, and even luckier to make it home.

If he could just get the damn thing fixed, he might still elude the Khraelings. And if Chief Poth and his assistant, Radool, couldn't repair it, nobody could. They had been part of the new engine's design team....

The twin coils developed by Khrae more than 1,100 years prior had almost doubled the previous velocity of the Federation's swiftest interceptors. Over the next few centuries, Khraeling innovators spent vast sums on modifications and improvements until the engine was propelling Federation fleets at an incredible 44.9% of light speed, or 100% OMV—Of Maximum Velocity, the twin coils' velocic ceiling. Believing that the engine had reached its full potential, they redirected their efforts into searching for a completely new design, one that would leapfrog the twin coils in the same way that invention had so dramatically outstripped the performance of its predecessor.

The technologically focused Khraelings understood the process. It had taken them almost 2,000 years of painstaking effort to achieve the twin coil breakthrough. Their determination would be rewarded—as always—*and* they had the example of Mhu's merkabahs, the ancients' fabulous "ships of light," as proof that the elusive light-speed engine awaited discovery.

In the meantime, while the Federation forged ahead on new concepts, the Jakomen continued tinkering with the coils. Now their latest generation, developed under the direction of Chief Luthur Poth, propelled Captain Narlihd's "pirate" ship. But something had gone wrong, and Narlihd's new engine was failing.

Working in the narrow chasm between the mountainous hulls of two amstrahd-class containers was nothing like the operatives' pre-mission rehearsals between two NHD destroyers. It felt inescapably claustrophobic, and amplified the sense of being crushed at any time.

Cramped in their module's proboscis-like cage, three of Narlihd's screws tore away at the container's meter-thick umbilical, ripping out all evidence of their smooth, laser cut. Clamping large modified pliers onto bunches of fused filaments at a time, each operative twisted and yanked away. Their snapper's jaw held the cord's core of metal fabric, while their captain monitored multiple images of the screws' progress and maintained the proper thrust.

"Easy, Cap'n," said one of the screws, pointing to the fabric slowly stretching in the snapper's firm grip and moving them away from their job. "We're almost there."

Narlihd eased up a little, and the taut fabric retracted back in place.

$$- \circ \; \Leftrightarrow \; \circ -$$

With their snapper holding on and just seconds to spare before the tug's timed acceleration, the screws wrenched out the last few lengths of heat-scarred hose.

"Go, Cap'n, go!"

The snapper's jaws maintained its lock on the umbilical's elastic polymide fabric, and although the material stretched some twenty meters, it refused to break. Then, on time, the Varahn tug's acceleration began, and the metal fabric lengthened even more, but continued to hold.

During their pre-mission exercises, Narlihd and his screws had repeatedly tested their snapper's strength against that of the umbilical's fabric core. Now the captain had to trust that the Varahns had not changed the material, and he had to gamble that his snapper—especially its proboscic cage—would hold.

The captain increased his opposing thrust, and then increased it again…and the fabric finally snapped. The crevasse quickly widened, and the thirteenth container's shredded umbilical waved limply in space.

It was a sight to behold.

Chapter 9 — N O T E S

N[176] ***Dehniss and Phobb.*** The ones to whom Vakaar's spies report.

G[003] Ænus: [♂ pron. **Ē′-nŭs**] a fallen midwayer in service to the warrior-Son Wohtan

N[177] ***her broadcast.*** The broadcast of her forum intercepted earlier in the day:

[from D-30.2, *THE AGGAH'S FORUM*] Haleahm pointed in'field (in the imaging field), directly at the marshall's life-sized image, which along with the other imaged layers, dissolved as a staticky interception of a New Hollatian broadcast filled the display. The Jakomen were sitting in public forum with their current Aggah—the dynamic Unah Bood. The gathering was limited to 60,000: the same rounded number as that of their revered Dahanah, those who had survived the actual surprise attack on Old Hollatia some eight centuries prior to recent times.

Governor Mauhk groaned. He had been hoping for some kind of signal, some indication of possible compromise. But the sign was clear: the Jakomen's towering holocaust memorial, a dark and twisted framework that seemed to stretch halfway to the stars, formed the backdrop for Bood's fire-lit forum.

All 24 Jakomen Elders sat quietly behind their beloved leader, whose speech rose in crescendo. Khrae Lunar Command's translation of the Aggah's address streamed down one side of her flickering image as a red band of Khraeling characters, while she shouted over a rising applause and fierce pounding of ceremonial drums.

"…and after two centuries of virtual neglect, we have been *'invited'*…" She drew the word out. "…for what?!" she screamed, her live audience now roaring and stomping their feet.

"For a *'celebration'*…" The roar grew louder. "…for a *'party'*…." The roar was deafening.

"What has changed? What has happened that I am so blind?"

G[242a] Narlihd: [♂] Captain Rauhf B. Narlihd; captain of the pirate-operatives sent by the NHD to secretly rendezvous with the Varahn convoy and to "hijack" its 14th container (New Hollatia)

G[249b] NHD: New Hollatian Defense; the global police, security force and defenders of New Hollatia

N[178] ***thirty days ago.*** As the needy Jakomen had prearranged with their compassionate Varahn friends.

Jake's Take
CHAPTER 9

Several of this trilogy's characters have become personal favorites, but none more so than the dynamic Aggah Bood. Unlike many of the story's others, she came as a great relief and a joy to develop through the tedious process of sequencing all three books.

I also confess to having enjoyed detailing those bizarre scenes deep in the bowels of the khoomyahna's rectory. But as with so many confusing episodes (all of which came as brief glimpses in the middle of the night, and all in random order), I had no idea of the beast's or brawnies' relevance to the overall tale.

Having surfaced somewhat sane from a decade-long bout of *what the hell is going on*-ness, I am compelled to help alleviate the onset of your own *what the*-nesses and share with you that aside from the obvious, Chapter 9's twisted *Murderous Desires* sequence is but a closer look into the intricate mind of another personal favorite —the high demon and longtime imperial crusader: Lord Wohtan, Son of Rohm.

KHOOM

Vakaar, Dehniss & Phobb
with the brawnies
and the netherbeast
Lord Wohtan

the Aggah's dream
the Varahn convoy
the Jakomen pirates

TERRAH

Ricky

Hyynehk
Nordehk Vidæan Council
Rohm

KSF escort squadron
the Varahn convoy
KSF pursuit team
the Jakomen pirates
with the 14th container

BEING GOD NAVIGATOR

9

10

8

Lord Mohaar
takes first-born vihm

VIHMYANA

Khrae Lunar Command
with Specialist Thowm
Lord Mohaar
with Iddh

10

JACKS ON THE HORIZON
DAY-29: SPACE / KSF ESCORTS

After nearly three months in low level hibernation, the pilots of the seven, one-man KSF interceptors sent to escort the Varahns on the last leg of their interstellar trip were up and wide awake.

Having exercised and washed in the relative comfort of their inflatable revival cells, the flyers returned to their spacious cockpits to enjoy a light meal and to chat in'field (in the imaging field) after what seemed like just a day or two since leaving Khrae. Each one saw a semi-circular arrangement of his counterparts in the prominent layer of his interceptor's cockpit imager. Each of them peripherally monitored a fuzzy, highly magnified image of the Varahn convoy coming slowly into view.

Half a day earlier, before his workout and wonderful wash, the squadron leader, Major Vihlkin Ihmoy, launched an unarmed remscanner (a remote scanning unit, or "RSU") upward of the approaching convoy. Its trajectory had now become high enough to marginally distinguish the tug's individual containers.

"Major," said the image of Ihmoy's lead wingman, Captain Heln, as she pointed to the blurry convoy. "I'm not sure, but my count's thirteen."

A loner who preferred the longer missions, Ihmoy had spent most of his career spying on the Jakomen, monitoring their exercises, scanning their defensive systems and occasionally interacting with them in the weird game that pitted pirate/opportunist operatives from one side against the other. Having a reputation for thinking quickly on his feet, Ihmoy also knew how to handle authority and had been appointed to head this mission by none other than "The Legend" himself: Marshall Mannon Jee Pranol.

The major squinted and strained with the others to confirm Heln's count. The remscanner's angled view showed the vague string of what had to be a Varahn starship towing...at least twelve huge containers...possibly all fourteen as registered by the Varahns years before.

Ihmoy reprogrammed his remscanner to begin sweeping the area. In seconds it detected a faint object on the horizon. The RSU zoomed in, but the speck of reflected starlight remained an indistinct pattern on its backdrop of a billion stars.

"That has to be one of the containers, Major," said another of his wingmen. "Number 14? At current velocities, it's around 22 hours from the convoy and about 85 from us. It's aah…a weird trajectory, but that has to be it. Nothin' else should be out there, Sir—certainly nothing that size. Nothin' else it could be."

"Those fracken jacks," muttered Ihmoy, shaking his head.

Everyone heard him, but few agreed. The object's low velocity was puzzling: around 50% OMV—not even a fourth the speed of light. If Jakomen operatives had intercepted the convoy at its cruising speed of 95% OMV, how could they be heading away on an almost perpendicular trajectory only 22 hours after the fact?

"If pirates snatched that container, Sir," said Heln, "they'd be running flat out at 100% OMV and their flight path would make more sense. In fact, they probably wouldn't be anywhere in sight."

"It's the jacks," Ihmoy confidently replied. No doubt Jakomen operatives were towing that container, and no doubt the Varahns were in on it. The convoy had to have decelerated for the snatch.

Measured against yesterday's scan, a purely positional daily scan with a resolution too low at these distances to have detected anything smaller in the vicinity, the Varahns appeared to be on time and right on course. Sure, the jacks could have hacked into the tug's systems. But considering the amicable relationship between Varah and New Hollatia, the whole thing had undoubtedly been preplanned. And had somehow gone wrong.

Ihmoy was impressed that the Jakomen would venture this far out. But with a sudden sinking feeling, the major realized he should have anticipated the action.

"Heln… Yhurg…."

"Yes, Major," and "Yes, Sir," the two wingmen excitedly replied, sure of what was coming.

"Hot pursuit. Go."

While Ihmoy's pursuit team accelerated, veered from the pack and locked onto their distant target, the squadron leader and his four remaining escorts began a deceleration toward 25% OMV, a velocity from which they could more easily stand ready to assist.

— ∘ ☼ ∘ —

On time, Major Ihmoy transmitted his welcoming code to the Varahn tug and received an immediate reply.

"This is the starship 'Unity.' We likewise welcome you, dear cousins of

Khrae."

By program, the tug had run for several hours at 100% OMV to make up the time lost to the brief rendezvous with the Jakomen operatives. The starship was now back to 95% OMV and perfectly on schedule to receive the Khraelings' code.

"We send greetings from Queen Aphelia, Prince Adahr and the family shaJah, the cavveht and the people of Varah. Per Factor Seven, deceleration is being initiated to 50% OMV in preparation for your flyby, rollover and docking with our ship."

There was a choppy conciseness to the Varahn imager's inflection. Stuffy. Continental Bandoran. Despite Jakomen assistance, Varahn technology still had a long way to go.

Ihmoy formally returned the greeting on the Federation's behalf, and then asked for confirmation of the convoy's configuration.

The tug's central imager confirmed that the last container's umbilical had been abruptly severed at lane reference RAK^{b}249^{d}82k. "Unfortunately, Major, we are poorly equipped for a retrieval exercise. And since our manifest for Container 14 lists only fourth-level commodities, and considering our proximity to the rendezvous coordinates, we opted to proceed without interruption to the prince's schedule."

Perhaps they had no recourse, but could the Varahn imagers comprehend that the consequences of their decision would be borne largely by Major Vihlkin Ihmoy?

"We have detected an unidentified object in the commercial zone bordering the diplomatic lanes," the major replied. "The object is approximately 22 hours from your reference point, on a trajectory nearly perpendicular to your flight path, and it is traveling at a current velocity of 49.82% OMV. Two of our ships are en route for intercept and retrieval. We therefore request a revision of your deceleration to 25% OMV, per Factor Seven-point-eight, to allow for the retrieval team's return. Rendezvous and docking will be reciphered according to ensuing developments."

The prince's schedule be damned.

BIRTHING THE FIRST VIHMYANA
D-29.2: SPACE / KHOOMYAHNA

In the khoomyahna's lower midsection, deep beneath the surface of a roundish, murky lake, teams of bahva specialists readied a fully developed vihmyana for launch. The teams dashed to and fro through the turbid solution in a profusion of shuttles and odd machines, while thousands of robotic devices scoured the scaly surface of the twitching, untried craft.

The destroyer hung among eleven other maturing vihms amid a tangle of thick umbilicals in the khoom's birthing tank. Beams of fire-like light streamed outward from the thin band of huge, deck-straddling viewports that ringed the ship's shallow crown. Farther down, the vihmyana's 144-man crew, which included two volunteers from the Janah,[G171] settled in for their unknown mission. Deeper yet, as part of a rushed rehearsal for the ill-defined formality of receiving a Rohman Son, 24 priests anxiously worked out praiseful phrases in a four-sided pyramidal room.

"We live to serve…in glory. We live to serve in glory!" "Your radiance…is might!…" "Mighty are The Master's Sons!…"

Similar to the gold-trimmed black chamber of the khoom, but smaller and four-walled instead of five, the vihm's pyramidal chamber housed little more than four partially translucent, light-filled pods. No fifth pod, no Vu-dog sculptures, dais or golden throne graced the otherwise elaborate room, for neither the twelve Supreme Sons nor The Master Himself ventured into the Empire's lesser ships.

The chamber's four pods lay in a neat array on a plush Rohman rug atop a central, crimson platform. As received by the mission's priesthood,[179] each pod encased a dormant clone of one of the fleshy forms designed by the campaign's four Sons.

A pinpoint of light burst through one of the room's inclined walls and shot directly into one of the pods. The priestly rehearsers froze and turned their eyes nervously toward the pod in time to see movement within the preserving, blue energy field that enveloped the body inside. They quickly knelt and bowed their heads.

Lord Mohaar settled into his temporal vehicle, sniffed through its nostril,[180] flexed its fingers, and cracked a smile on its youthful face. Then he focused his mind on the pod's sensors, and the vibrant energy field and long, domed lid abruptly vanished.

With heads still bowed and eyes now tightly closed, the brothers launched a jumble of ill-practiced praise.

"By your radiance, my Lord, may…uh…." "May our service be sanctified!" "Mighty are The Master's Sons!" "May your radiance…uh…*His* radiance…uh…." "We serve to…uh…we live to…we live to serve in glory!…" Unable to resist the temptation to peek, the brothers' guarded voicings soon surrendered to the awe of watching the Son rise.

The prentice-Son, Mohaar, stepped from his pod. A hint of luminescence radiated from his head and out from the cuffs of his shimmering bodystocking. He stood awhile, and then thought-formed[G361] his formal garments.

In preparation for his role in the Nordehk campaign's final phase, Lord Mohaar fashioned his bodies after the Jakomen, the fairest of Khraeling tribes. He chose broad shoulders and a wide, youthful face. His pale, freckled skin was lightly tinted with a faint, reddish hue. Like all Jakomen and Khraelings, a deep, v-shaped skull-crease ran halfway down his forehead toward a pointy, cleft chin. Deep-red pupils perforated his muddy green irises inside slanted, lidless sockets, and his small, circular ears lay flat beneath a thick mat of curly orange hair. A bridgeless nose with a solitary, somewhat rounded nostril lay centered beneath Mohaar's two bright eyes. And his full, partially open mouth exposed a pale set of small, blunt, yellowed teeth.

Of all Nordehk's will-creatures—those life-forms endowed with the unique ability to make a moral decision ("man" or "human," as they usually called themselves)—the clans of Khrae were among the least attractive. But next to the ancients of Mhu, they had the biggest brains.

"Great are The Master's warriors!" shouted one of the priests in an attempt to stir the rest. But as the cheer flew forth, the Son shimmered, partially dematerialized and lifted off the crimson platform. And as the demon rose and then disappeared through the chamber's apex, the prodder fell silent, staring upward with the others on their knees.

Seconds later, Lord Mohaar re-formed inside his vihmyana's sealed systems bridge. In recognition of his vibration, one of four silver recliners symmetrically arranged atop a square, brightly colored Rohman rug flared its blue-energy field.

The destroyer's bridge looked much the same as that of the Overlord's khoomyahna. Nothing else lay beneath its darkened dome. No instrumentation; no viewports. And the bridge's size? Illusionally obscure![181]

Mohaar slid onto his recliner. And as its warm, soft metal molded to his vibrant form, the prentice Son became one with his lethal ship. He silently summoned Iddh, his faithful midwayer-scout, and began priming the vessel's drive.

In the murkiness outside, the bahva finished up and hurried to clear the increasingly turbulent area. As a final warning to those who remained, bursts of greenish light flashed from the last of the ship's uncut umbilicals, as the huge cords self-severed from within.

On the underside of the khoom's outer midsection, a small portion of the warship's hull began to bulge. A tear appeared and dilated, and great globs of turbid birthing fluid gushed out, froze and tumbled into space. Lord Mohaar's vihmyana squeezed through, somersaulted and rolled away—its umbilical stubs dangling from seemingly random surfaces of the destroyer's graceful, ray-like body.

And as the khoom's swollen tear receded and started to mend, its first-born shot toward Khrae, toward the bright star dead ahead.

KHRAEKS ON THE HORIZON
D-29.3: SPACE / PIRATES

Captain Narlihd[G242b] was determined to get beyond range of the Khraeling scanners. Still slightly out of sync, his coils were holding at around 50% OMV, but the plasma burn had not helped matters. Several parts got scorched and Chief Luthur Poth thought it was just a matter of time before one or both coils seized up. Although the chief was managing to keep the fields stable, he was running out of tricks.

Narlihd's latest flash-scans[182] revealed interceptors on the deep horizon. The captain enhanced the faint images to maximum resolution, alternately blinked the first and last, and confirmed that two of the pack had veered toward him. Then he called his chief engineer.

"Luthur. I need specifics, man."

"The p…p..primary absorbed mm..most of the sssstress from the p..plasma, C…C..Cap'n, but the t…t..transen got b..burned t..too. The d..dielectrics c..can't t..take m..much mmmore, and c..could f…f..fracture at any t..time."

"Do you have the parts, Chief?"

Poth nodded.

"How long will it take?"

The chief shook his head.

"How long, Luthur?" Narlihd asked again.

"Aaah…at least t…t..twenty-four hours, Sssir…."

The captain looked away. That was acceptable.

"…p..per c..coil, C..Cap'n."

Narlihd turned and glared. "We've got khraeks on the horizon, Chief. Think again."

JUST A CHILL
D-29.4: KHRAE LUNAR COMMAND

Lord Mohaar brought his shrouded vihmyana[183] into orbit high over Patos, Khrae's outermost moon. Then, as his silver recliner wrapped his temporal body in a field of preserving, fluorescent-like blue light, he summoned and pinned away with Iddh.

— ∘ ☼ ∘ —

Located beneath an unassuming impact crater near Patos' south pole, Base 11 was the largest of KLC's underground towers. Inside, Iddh and Mohaar found thirty operators quietly monitoring the space in and around their solar system—exactly as detailed by the Og![184]

The demon entered a random operator, Specialist Mahrget Thowm, who reacted with a grunt. He/she sat a moment, studying the primitive console. And while Mohaar massaged the back of Thown's neck with one hand, Iddh flitted back and forth unseen and unheard, insulting the others and issuing vulgar, Rɘhman threats.

"Are you all right, Mahrget?" asked an operator to the demon's left. A few others glanced over.

Crossing his host's arms and rubbing both her shoulders, Mohaar/Thowm smiled and softly replied, "I'm fine…thanks. Just a chill, I guess."

A PERPLEXING, DISTANT BLUR
D-29.5: SPACE / KSF ESCORTS

Seventy-nine hours from estimated intercept with the unidentified object, the KSF pursuit leader and her wingman lay in the first level of hibersleep, the fully restive state above a deep sleep, one from which in a minute or so they could adequately recover.

Meanwhile, having transmitted a report to KLC, Major Ihmoy studied the blurred image of his pursuit team's target. It was too distant to detect an engine signature or to verify it was man-made, but the object's mass did appear similar to that of an amstrahd container. Its trajectory had definitely crossed the convoy's path, and precisely at coordinate RAK^b249^d82k.

The major modified the remscan unit's course for an increasingly rear-view perspective of the target. Then he reprogrammed his roemstims and laid back for an eight-hour, Level One nap.

Eyes closed, Ihmoy relaxed to ponder the mystery. If Jakomen operatives had a container in tow, then why the low velocity? They should be running flat out with their coils fully wound…. But what else could that blurry image be? It *had* to be the jacks. They had to be in distress. If so, Heln would bring them in. If not—but what else could it be?…

THE EXTRACTIONS BEGIN
D-29.6: SPACE / CONVOY

Aboard the Varahn starship, after almost <u>ten long years in space</u>,[185] the time had come for the extractions.

Near the tug's heart, sealed inside clear cells slotted into a cylindrical grill, Prince Adahr lay with 36 delegates, 40 crew and the 100 settler-daughters: 177 voyagers in all. Waxen and expressionless, none seemed alive.

Three robotic carriers sprang to life from a statuesque "sleep" and whirred into action. Engaging the cylindrical grill without surface contact, the carriers stopped above the prince and two others and gently extracted their cells for transfer to the tug's rejuvenation chamber. Four more soon would follow.

Although the Varahn voyagers would suffer varying degrees of disorientation, most would regain full control of their faculties within five or six hours. Then they would start craving information, and before long, they would start craving food.

EAVESDROPPING ON IHMOY
D-29.7: KHRAE / PATOS

Busy at her console in Khrae Lunar Command's Base 11, Specialist Thowm appeared to have resumed her daily chores, and her co-workers seemed at ease. But if only they looked more closely, they would see the demon in her eyes.

While rummaging through the Federation's files, delving deeper and deeper into the KSF's database, Mohaar/Thowm intercepted an incoming communication. It was from a Major Ihmoy, a report that rang of opportunity. *The Master worked in mysterious ways.*

"...and we see no evidence of residual debris from an impact, either along its path or in the convoy's wake. The object's trajectory and velocity are suspicious.

"Within 18 hours our remscanner should be in position to confirm that the target is an artificial object, and my pursuit team will be within range to detect an engine print. At that time, we intend to issue our first hail to the suspected Jakomen operatives, demanding documentation and submission for inspection. Accordingly, should the suspects fail to respond or should they refuse to lower their shields for inspectional scans, I hereby request authorization to fire our first volley of warning shots upon identification of an unregistered vessel."

Base 11's Senior Duty Operator transmitted an acknowledgement-code to the major, confirming the receipt and forwarding of his request, while others debated the likelihood of Jakomen operatives running so slowly, or even venturing that far out.

One of the SDO's assistants suggested that the squadron and their remscanner were not close enough to be able to tell for sure. "Maybe there *was* some kind of cosmic collision. Ihmoy's just too far away to detect residual debris."

Another dismissed the speculation. "The odds are astronomic. They're in deep space. It's the jacks all right."

Listening intently, Mohaar came to a locked directory, *"Restricted—K1: Eyes Only."* Thowm knew it as the Federation's strategic files. She did not know the codes and had served her purpose.

The demon silently summoned his cackling scout. Then he violently exited his young, warm, Khraeling host, and pinned back to his destroyer. And without a sound, Mahrget Thowm slumped over her console.

Iddh shrieked with delight, cursed Thowm and the others, and then he too pinned away.

— ○ ☼ ○ —

Mohaar settled back into his temporal body in the vihmyana's systems bridge.[186] Then the Son swung his shrouded destroyer in the direction of the Varahn convoy, in the direction of the arterial way portal that linked the suns of Varah and Khrae.

Iddh hovered above him, alternately cackling and mimicking KLC's oblivious fools.

"…the odds are astronomic…it's the jacks all right…call a medic!…"

Chapter 10 — N O T E S

G[171] Janah: a secret sect of 22 Rǝhman rebels—closet anarchists who
              volunteered for the mission to Nordehk, hoping to somehow
              escape the Empire's stifling Order

N[179] *as received by the mission's priesthood.* Prior to the khoom's departure
for Nordehk, Vakaar received several sets of the Sons' podded bodies, which
the brothers stored in the warship's rectory for future placement and
unspecified, future use.

N[180] *nostril.* The Khraeling/Jakomen single nostril.

G[361] thought-forms: temporary apparitions or enduring material
                    manifestations formed by the power of thought

N[181] *illusionally obscure.* As induced by a Rǝhman illusory device adaptable
to curvilinear chambers (one of few technological marvels shared with certain
fourth-density crusaders, including the Og).

G[242b] Narlihd: [♂] Captain Rauhf B. Narlihd; captain of the pirate-operatives
                sent by the NHD to secretly rendezvous with the Varahn
                convoy and to "hijack" its 14th container (New Hollatia)

N[182] *flash-scans.* An adaptation of technology gleaned from one of the
ancients' abandoned outposts, flash-scans utilize arcing bursts of invisible
particles fired/flashed at 114.7 times the speed of light [further detailed in
upcoming Chapter 14].

N[183] *vihmyana.* The new destroyer that left its mothership (the khoomyahna) a
few hours before:

> [from D-29.2, *BIRTHING THE FIRST VIHMYANA*] On the underside of
> the khoom's outer midsection, a small portion of the warship's hull began to
> bulge. A tear appeared and dilated, and great globs of turbid birthing fluid
> gushed out, froze and tumbled into space. Lord Mohaar's vihmyana squeezed
> through, somersaulted and rolled away—its umbilical stubs dangling from
> seemingly random surfaces of the destroyer's graceful, ray-like body.

N[184] *as detailed by the Og.* In the materials transferred from Group Commander Iiose's cruiser to the khoomyahna on Day -32:

> [from D-32.7, *HOSTING THE DEMON SONS*] "The following actions and developments are detailed in the data now flowing to your khoomyahna. A transfer of capsules containing the requested samples and codes for Nordehk's flora and fauna, including genetic materials from the higher species, is also underway."

N[185] *ten long years in space.* As measured in lengthy Varahn years (nearly 19 as measured by Khrae's Intercontinental Federation).

N[186] *in the vihmyana's systems bridge.* Since leaving his destroyer in orbit over Patos:

> [from D-29.4, *JUST A CHILL*] Lord Mohaar brought his shrouded vihmyana into orbit high over Patos, Khrae's outermost moon. Then, as his silver recliner wrapped his temporal body in a field of preserving, fluorescent-like blue light, he summoned and pinned away with Iddh.

Jake's Take
CHAPTER 10

Thinking back to the likes of *The Exorcist* and other stories of demonic possession (in which an evil spirit moves magically through the air from one unfortunate to the next, or from within a swarm of exhaled bugs), the concept of *pinning* seems far more plausible.

But we be fine—so long as demons are a fallacy and it remains utter nonsense that a highly-advanced and completely godless humanoid species has managed to traverse the stars and create a race of rather ignorant but warm and cuddly lovelies for the purpose of eventually possessing them in a sudden *coup de main* before living happily ever after on a world far beyond their wildest dreams....

Sleep tight, dear ones, and let not your dreams obsess you.

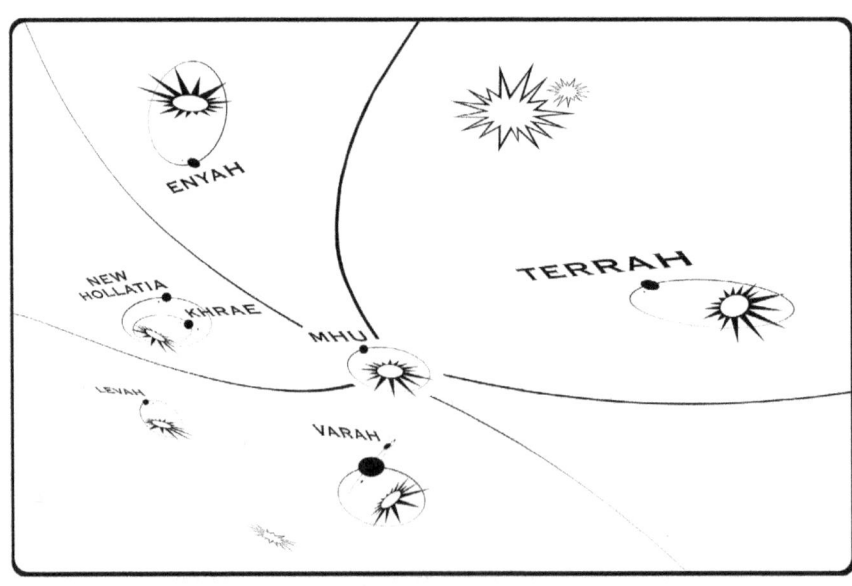

11

PATTI'S MIRACLE

D-29.8: TERRAH

"Ricky. Come on, little man. It's time for school...."

Ricky's mom Patti had spent her childhood moving from one family to the next. Some had been nice; others not. When she turned thirteen, she looked eighteen, which was old enough to run away and find a job and start living on her own. She'd never sold herself, cussed, smoked or taken illegal drugs. Her only friends were a few co-workers she met as she moved from town to town. And she moved a lot, at least she used to. And she wasn't one to keep in touch.

Eight years ago, Patti woke up sore and bleeding just a bit. She had no memory of the cause, no recollection of having been taken and surgically impregnated by the Og. Later, when she knew for certain of the fetus inside, she felt as though a miracle had come and touched her life.

More often than not, however, and more so now it seemed, Patti got depressed. She just couldn't help it. If it wasn't one thing, something else would bring her down. Her rent always went up but her income rarely did, at least not enough to make much of a difference. And she still looked older than she really was: sometimes a lot older. And some days she just didn't have it in her to makeover a 35-ish looking face.

But it wasn't for her Ricky complaining about anything. Her little angel *never* complained. In fact, despite his phobia of little grey men hiding in his closet and despite the real bullies at his school, it was her son who always pulled her through.

"Ricky. Breakfast is ready and I don't hear that water running. Come on, hunny bunny—wash your face. Let's go...."

Sometimes it seemed as though he had been sent from heaven just to help her out. She wasn't sure whether she believed in heaven, but neither was she sure that God didn't exist. And sometimes she felt really blessed, like when Ricky read to her when she was down.

If God was real, then angels were, too. So if angels existed, the least she could do was thank them for watching over her. And teach her son to do the same.

A MOST FRUSTRATING ORDEAL

D-29.9: SPACE / KHOOMYAHNA

Aglow again in the khoom's black chamber, three of the four Sons of the Nordehk campaign—Zhol, Dhanz and Wohtan—stood near the chamber's steeply stepped crimson dais, looking up at its stately golden throne. Now that the warship had entered the constellation and Nordehk's Lords had met with the Og and narrowed their personal options, the time had come to call on Rohm.

As a prudent formality, all four of the conquest's Sons would perform the calling.

In response to a psychic summons from the Overlord, a pinpoint of light streaked into Mohaar's pod. Moments later the prentice Son rose, thought-formed his garments and stood among the rest.

Even the Empire's most confident warriors felt uneasy about proceeding without Rohm's awareness. As vague as it was, having The Master's awareness was infinitely better than not. If it came, it came as a knowing and arrived with the tingle of His electrifying power, His vibrant pulse. However distant, Rohm would instantly hear them, and would sense the primary purpose of their call. And *if* He chose to answer, the callers would feel that unmistakable rise in vibrance, that intensification they could channel into an apparition-like cloud of etheric plasma into which The Master's being *might*, however briefly, visibly manifest.

The luminescence enveloping Dhanz revealed the Son's excitement. Her eyes were lit, she felt aroused and she craved the exhilarating, pulsating concentrations of energy that one absorbed when in The Master's presence. Wohtan felt an intense tightening in his body's gut. Most sensations of the flesh were desirable; this was not. Quietly surprised by his own repose, Mohaar mentally reviewed his plans for the tribes of Khrae. Again, he found nothing that might potentially upset the Prime Crusader.

Although the Og's preparations in Nordehk seemed complete, Zhol had a nagging feeling that something wasn't right. Something about that Vihdæan intrusion[187] bothered him. And whatever it was, it would not escape the analytical intricacy of The Master's infallible mind.

Rohm constantly tested his Sons and incessantly lectured them on the absolute necessity of *anticipation*. Any failure to anticipate that resulted in serious repercussions or setbacks to a conquest, could cost a Son—even a Supreme Son—his status. Permanently. For no matter how great the dedication to service or how long the string of successes, no second chances were allowed a failed Son. And though the role of Imperial Administrator was a position of high regard, it was a far cry from the glory days of having been a warring Son of Rəhm.

The process of gaining His "approval" was a most frustrating ordeal. As renowned masters of anticipation, Rəhman Sons were the Empire's unfailing crusaders, who, more often than not, took action without Rəhm's awareness. It was not for lack of trying, for not having made numerous callings in the hope that The Omnipotent One would visit and maybe scan their minds. Acting without His awareness was simply a risk He frequently forced them to take.

Whenever Rəhm chose to grace them with His presence, His mind scans and reactions were completely unpredictable. Frequently, He said nothing, in which case—after a careful reconsideration and perhaps a minor adjustment—His Sons usually went on with their intended actions. Sometimes He would generate a spontaneous impulse in their minds, a sudden knowing to reconsider. Most dreaded of all, He would fly into a rage that could culminate in the instant, irreversible stripping of a Son's status and the immediate summoning of a replacement.

And to interpret Prime Crusader's quiet awareness as *approval* of one's intentions could be disastrous. Awareness was definitely *not* approval. No one won The Master's approval. Not for anything. Ever. For no failed plan could be the fault of Rəhm.

BACK INSIDE THE CONE
D-29.10: SPACE / KHOOMYAHNA

Four times in the past three days, various members of the Janah had formed their cone over Sarvah while she bravely attempted to find the Sons. With this morning's departure of a <u>vihmyana</u>,^{G384} Sarvah doubted that any warriors remained aboard the khoom. And she was becoming increasingly fearful of her comrades being discovered holding the cone while she was riding the mystical <u>pranah</u>^{G287}

"It just takes one <u>feritt</u>^{G116} to find us here like this," she whispered as they gathered again in their hideaway near the khoom's eighth statcon dome for yet another attempt. "We should wait awhile, just a day or two—or till the Sons are seen again."

"Another day or two might be too late, Weebs," Chak quietly replied, one eye looking convincingly at Sarvah while the other kept watch in their lookout's direction. "We have to keep trying."

"I can't penetrate the control deck, and I've looked everywhere else," countered Sarvah, eyes welling as she stared at the floor. "This is way too risky."

"We've got two lookouts now, instead of just one," tried another, encouragingly. "We be safe, girl. We be okay."

"Just a quick look around the rectory, Weebs," tried Chak again, "and then the black chamber. That's all, dearheart. Just quick looks. Okay?"

Relenting yet again, Sarvah was soon rocking her head beneath their cone, eyes closed, trying to synchronize her consciousness with the elusive, spiraling pranah.

"Increase the slope," she whispered, lower lip quivering, "not enough angle...."

The weaving of hands and fingers rose a little higher....

NORDEHK CALLING

D-29.11: ELSEWHERE IN THE REALM

Across the Empire's farthest reaches, The Master crackled quietly amid a brilliant orange fog. He was considering an invitation from two favorite Sons: Zhol and Dhanz...and two others...from the feral Nordehk constellation.

Long had that stellar sector's ever passive Vihdæa ignored his frequent callings to join in *His Crusades*. *LONG HAD THEY REFUSED THE MIGHTY HAND OF RθHM.*

Ohrvon's self-designated Prime Crusader, Bringer of Order, and Friend of Man and Angels, began concentrating his brilliance, compressing his light more and more until it came together into a radiant pinpoint above the ever-changing faces of his ever-changing head.

And then he was gone—clothing, light and all—leaving an empty golden throne atop a 12-stepped purple dais in the green pentagonal chamber of a rival Son's khoomyahna, far from Nordehk's stars.

DEVILS IN THE ROOM

D-29.12: SPACE / KHOOMYAHNA

Seeing nothing of the Sons in the priesthood's rectory, Sarvah eased her etheric self through the black chamber's fleshy walls and immediately sensed intense negative vibrations. All four demons stood below her in a semicircle at the base of the chamber's central dais. They were all dressed the same.

"They're here," she whispered through barely parted lips from within her comrades' cone, "in the b...bblack chamber."

Their heads were tilted back and glowing. Their arms were outstretched with their fingers extended. They seemed to be in some kind of trance, rocking the way she did to focus the pranah.

A faintly luminous, yellow-orange mist appeared above The Master's golden throne. Sarvah watched it expand and blossom into swirling, three-dimensional shapes that seemed to verge on coming to life before spinning off in wispy clouds of illuminated vapor at the chaotic periphery. What looked like hellish creatures and terror stricken beasts momentarily materialized before falling inward, as though being sucked into the raucous tempest's churning core.

Unseen to the Janah's young projectionist, twelve dark seraphim stormed the unholy chamber and began swirling around the Sons, who promptly dropped to their left knees and bowed their brightly shining heads.

Sitting on a rectory bench listening halfheartedly to his two whispering cohorts, Vakaar received a sudden, telepathic command from the Overlord.

"Ready the children, reverent one."

The yamah abruptly stood—startling his lanky cohorts, Dehniss and Phobb, who fast jumped to their feet.

"Gather the children!" he screeched, arms flailing.

"Gather the children!" his cohorts began yelling in all directions of the rectory maze, before Dehniss stopped to ask Vakaar, "Where, Reverence? Gather them where?"

"In the war room," he sighed, with twirl of a crooked, boney index finger. Where else would you gather children midweek in a khoomyahna? "Now."

"In the war room! Now!" hollered Dehniss.

"Gather the children in the war room!" yelled Phobb. "Gather them—now!…"

— ∘ ☼ ∘ —

With the Sons on one knee and Rohm's dark seraphic escorts hovering vigilantly above, the chamber's orange brilliance withdrew to an aura-like radiance that enveloped the golden throne and The Master's giant form thereon. Prime Crusader looked twice his Sons' size, and crackled constantly within the glow of his shimmering orange aura, acutely sensing that within and that without his new surroundings.

Two beastly Vu-dogs sat at his sides: Iccha to his right and breathing rapidly, and Trsnah to his left. Iccha's huge head was bowed and tilted rightward. Her mouth stayed open, baring broad, yellowed razor-teeth. Trsnah's head was bowed and tilted to his left, eyes bulged and piercing, and mouth tightly closed.

It was all that Sarvah could bear, and she fled to the comfort of her friends.

"I'm back," she whispered, shaking beneath their cone and relieved that again the demons had not seen her. Nor, she assumed, had *The Devil Himself.*

PONDERING THE ORAPH'S WORDS
D-29.13: NORDEHK

Flowers burgeoning before them, Bel and four other ethereans, including Jaylah, Nordehk's current, rotational, council chief, walked along a winding garden pathway: a rapidly evolving construct of their magnificently tuned minds.

Telepathically melded while they strolled, Nordehk's Vihdæans considered yesterday's cryptic meeting with the oraph, Hyynehk.[188] Had she meant to imply that as the result of some decisive action which *they*, as Nordehk's administrative council, were somehow destined to take, the darkness would then fade "and with the Light become as one"? Did the Most Highs truly have "every confidence" in the ability of eight simple administrators to prevail over Røhm, the 128th Universal Son, the most famous of Fallen Ones, and one of the Most High's very own? Or was Hyynehk's encouragement to "work together" meant to suggest that they form some sort of alliance? *Were such alliances allowed?*

Always had the infinitely patient Vihdæa answered their will-creatures' callings. But never had they infringed on human volition. Never had they interposed themselves in man's affairs.

"Among the thousands of constellations now lost to the Røhman hordes," offered one of the five, "an alliance of Councils has never occurred." She conveyed her thoughts as one of the council's more conservative members. "Why? Because contrary to the Vihdæan mandate, the very act would imply a propensity to intervene. Intervention is not a prerogative. It is not for us to interfere."

Another of the five seemed more persuasible, but doubtful of the oraph's charge. "Even *if* we have been ordained by the Most Highs as the oraph might suggest, what could a union of humble administrators possibly hope to accomplish, that all before us have not?"

Nordehk's nearest neighboring constellation, Lazrehk, had nine inhabited worlds. All nine were suffering the same, methodical, pre-conquest manipulation by Orion's discreet crusaders in a similarly malicious process begun around 1,200 years after the Og's encroachment of Nordehk. And like all their peers before them, Lazrehk's Vihdæa had not intervened, for they too were long bound by divine decree....

Eons before current times and long before the defection of Røhm, Ohrvon's Universal Sons designated tens of thousands of their galaxy's constellations as experimental "freewill zones." They reserved those zones for the potentialization of *all* probabilities, whereby all combinations of interaction between Light and Dark were allowed. Before the designations, all of Ohrvon's will-creatures were positively polarized and lived in Light; all embraced Beauty, Goodness and Truth. And in a time of contemplation on the third—Truth—the Most Highs realized that only with an allowance for the darkness/negativity, could the existential Prime Creator's *experiential* pursuits become truly infinite in scope. Matter only existed as an atomic construct of positive and negative particles. So consciousness could only be complete with equilibrium of the same opposing forces.

In conjunction with the zoning, the Universal Sons initiated the veiling syndrome, the forgetting of superconscious memories. That the zones' evolving will-creatures not fully remember their past lives. That they be unencumbered and free instead to choose between Light and Dark, and right and wrong. That a constructive, evolutionarily favorable balance might be found.

It had never, however, been intended that the experiment be corrupted. Had there been a failure to anticipate by the all-knowing Most Highs? A failure to foresee that one of their own might seize the opportunity to manage possibilities? *And steer All That Is into darkness?*

A divine allowance had been made, and now Council Chief Jaylah wondered whether some sanctified adjustment were in order. Had, in fact, it long been written that the Most Highs would create the freewill zones, and then—after a time—have Nordehk's unassuming administrators temper the celestial equation?

Before speaking his mind, Jaylah and then the others slowed, stopped and turned as all five felt that sudden, familiar vigor. More so—the Rөhman god was near.

And in the gentlest of his terrible voices, <u>Rөhm began calling</u>[189] once again. "DEAR ONES…COME. BRING ORDER TO THE CHAOS. DEAR ONES…"

And in silence did they listen. And through their silence, did The Caller's expectations only grow.

"…COME. TAKE THE HAND OF RөHM—*AND BE WHOLE!*
"DEAR ONES…."

Chapter 11 — N O T E S

N[187] *Vihdæan intrusion.* Bel's intrusion of the khoomyahna on Day -32:

> [from D-32.4, *BEL'S INTRUSION*] Moments later, a pinpoint of
> shimmering, iridescent light—Vihdæan light—appeared and blossomed,
> illuminating the dim corridor. The convicts scrambled from their ditch and
> scattered. A few stopped and turned, covered their eyes and squinted through
> their fingers at the dazzling form taking shape in midair.
>> Unseen and unheard by all but the brilliant intruder, the khoom's
> resident midwayer, Jinn-Jinn, charged into the passageway, screaming insults
> and vile Rehman threats.
>> The violators heard nothing but the intruder's gentle, reassuring voice in
> their minds.
>> "Peace be upon you, dear ones. I am Bel."

G[384] vihm: vihmyana; a Rehman destroyer capable of breaching the cosmic
highways where they are known to average at least one standard
light-year per standard day

G[287] pranah: an element of the cosmic force that carries callings, telepathic
communications, and the consciousness of those able to harness
portions of its power

G[116] feritt: a weightless, mobile, lightly armed, insect-like surveillance
machine (Rehman)

N[188] *yesterday's cryptic meeting with Hyynehk.* On Day -30:

> [from D-30.5, *THE MYSTERIOUS MESSENGER*] "Feeding on fear and
> ruling through intimidation, Rehm's methods vary greatly and he exhibits a
> vast spectrum of creative destruction on his journey through the night. His
> 'Sons,' fallen Vihdæan sisters and brothers themselves, are powerful and
> serve him well. But so is it written and long known to us oraphim, '...so shall
> the darkness begin to fade, and with the Light, become as one.'"
>> *Long known?* Who held these words of things to come, and how—*and
> when*—had they been written? And why should knowledge of such profound,
> future events be privy to so few? Yes, the oraphim were of a high order; and
> yes, it was improper for simple administrators to solicit insights into the
> broader divine…but....
>> "As always, there are no shortcuts to enlightenment," Hyynehk continued,

as though having heard their thoughts. "Administration through patient revelation will ultimately reveal the joys of Love and Light. The Most Highs have every confidence in your ability to prevail."

Prevail? None before had prevailed. None before had even briefly slowed the Rɵhman hordes. Were these just hollow words? Had others heard them, too?

"Work together, that triumph be assured."

Work together? Nordehk's Vihdæa had always worked together. Was the oraph suggesting that they solicit outside help?

N[189] ***Rɵhm began calling.*** The Master's callings exploit a fundamental weakness in galactic administration: the Vihdæan constraints. Once assigned to a constellation upon its first world's sparking by the divine Sowers, the Vihdæa are bound to an eternity of largely passive roles. Rɵhm offers that which is otherwise unattainable: proactive diversity—a highly powerful lure. As warrior-crusaders, Vihdæan defectors may see, *and experience*, All That Is. As elevated Sons of Rɵhm, a ranking earned through unfailing service, their full powers are put to the test. By defecting and serving in *His Crusades*, they may become known. They may become loved. They may become *feared.*

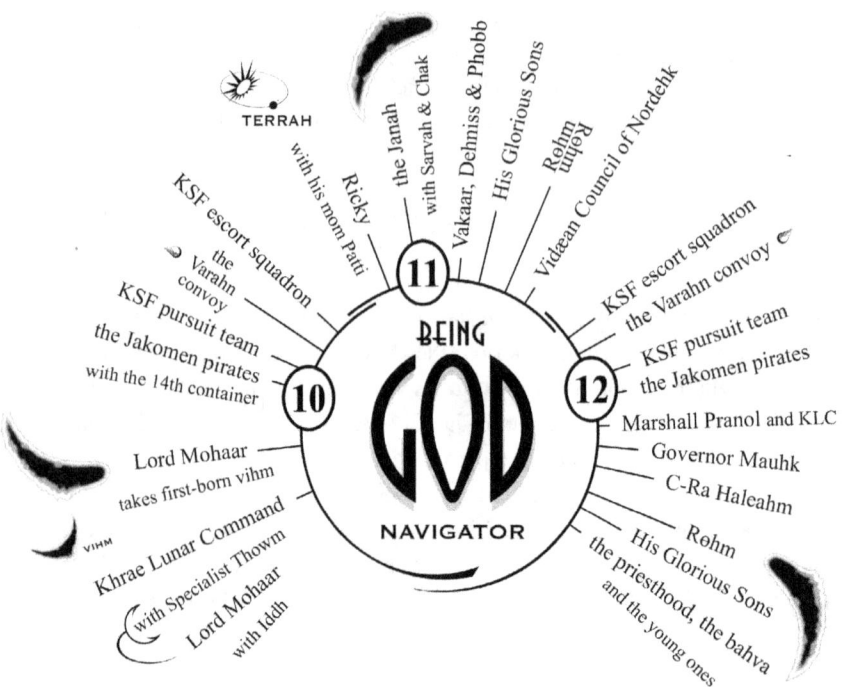

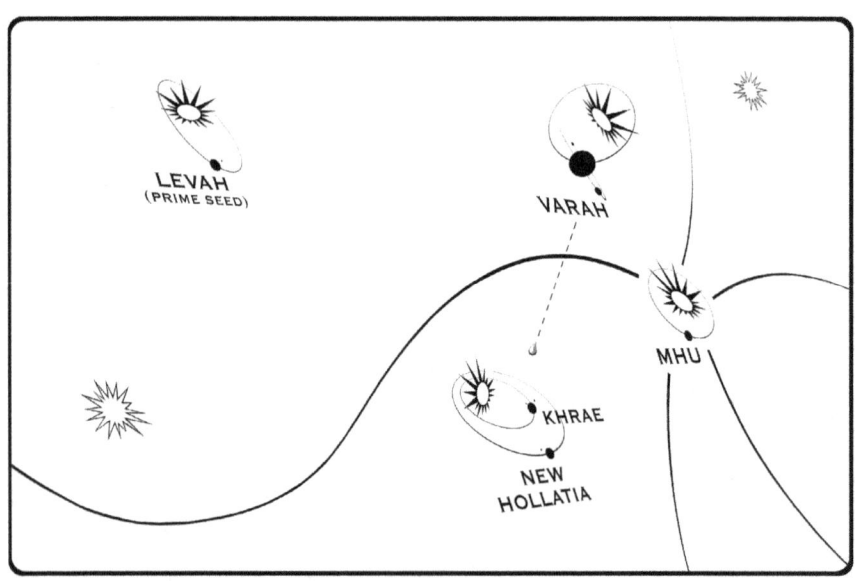

12

THE IMPASSIVE AGGAH AND THE ENIGMATIC PRINCE

D-29.14: SPACE / CONVOY

The Varahn prince and his six most senior delegates were now fully recovered from their long, deep sleep.[190] They sat comfortably on separate sofas in the low light of a plain, white, circular room. Except for the crest of shaJah on one collar—the emblem of the Varahn crown—Prince Adahr dressed much like the others: in a lightweight gown, softly colored and ankle-length over a loose, white undergarment and cloth sandals.

Their starship's imagers had advised them of the recent developments, and the KSF's escort squadron leader, Major Vihlkin Ihmoy, had greeted and also briefed them. Although they wondered why the Jakomen had been so far behind schedule, they could not risk communicating with the "pirate" operatives; instead, they had no choice but to let things play out. As bad as it may have looked, however, anything could happen. Prime Creator worked in ever stranger ways.

The Varahns were considerably fairer to look upon than their Khraeling cousins. They were were shorter, and their longer faces were thinner by a third. They lacked their cousins' pronounced skull-crease, and their bodies looked comparatively delicate. But most Varahns, including all of Prince Adahr shaJah's delegation, were healthy and fit.

Unlike the Khraelings' single nostril, Varahns had two. Their nostrils faced downward at the end of a thin, shallow ridge that began in the center of a high forehead, ran down between their eyes and ended above a small, thin-lipped mouth. Hair straight, dark and fine, they were olive-skinned in a full blending of their seven original tribes. Their eyes were wide, bright and predominantly white, with a thin ring of either blue-green or honey-amber surrounding a large, black pupil. Two of the travelers had an eye of each color. It was a common Varahn trait.

Prince Adahr and his six senior delegates sipped a warm, nutritional broth and telepathically exchanged comments while they watched a recording in the large imaging field in the midst of their circular room. Their starship had received the message thirty days earlier: a welcome from the Aggah Bood.

"She has aged," observed one of the delegates.

"Haven't we all, Uril?" replied another. The group laughed—mostly telepathically, but several aloud.

The delegates and prince looked virtually the same as they did upon their departure some ten long Varahn years before.

"I think she wears it well."

"Yes, yes. As do you, my son." More chuckles. "But isn't it curious that after all this time she would still choose to constrain her emotions? I'd always thought it was her newness to the job."

"For such an emotional people," agreed one of the six, "it *is* strange they should elect such a seemingly dispassionate leader."

"A counter-balance, I should expect," suggested another.

Their passive, enigmatic prince smiled occasionally, but made no comment either way. Adahr most always kept his thoughts to himself.

A FIGHTING CHANCE
D-29.15: SPACE / PIRATES

Captain Narlihd[G242c] checked his most recent flash-scan[G119a] He reckoned 69 hours to intercept, and not long before his pursuers would be able to define the container and record his engine print.

He decided to reposition his tiny cruiser atop the colossal container's forward starboard hatchway and then initiate a slow tumble. He hoped it would confuse the Khraelings just enough to take them by surprise. To give him and his crew a fighting chance, if things should come to that.

$$- \circ \, \diamond \!\!\!\! \Leftrightarrow \, \circ -$$

Upon completing the maneuver, Narlihd called Chief Luthur Poth for an update.

Bringing the chief's half-sized image in'field, the captain saw that Poth looked beat and was likely nearing his wits' end.

"How long for the repairs, Chief?" Narlihd asked, staring Poth's image in the eye.

"We're d…d..dyin', C..Cap'n."

"How long, Luthur?"

Poth claimed to need at least forty hours. The captain shook his head.

"Shut 'em down, Chief. You've got sixteen per coil—*max*."

PERSUASIVE SILENCE
D-29.16: KHRAE / PATOS

Marshall Pranol was working late in his office on Khrae Lunar

Command's Base 4, when an officer from KLC's Internal Security called with the latest on the incident at Base 11.[191]

"Specialist Thowm died of heart failure due to shock, Marshall," the officer reported in'field. "In a matter of minutes, she scoured the files of 167 directories—I mean *in short order,* Sir. But she transmitted nothing. The material remains intact."

Nine minutes before her sudden death, Thowm had been working on a routine rerouting of some oort probes, unmanned monitors of the solar system's distant comet-hatchery. After a brief lapse, she raced through thousands of files, stopped at the K1 lock, and died.

"The operators stationed to her sides reported that she sat back to rub her neck and shoulders at a time, we have determined, that shortly preceded her romp through the database. Neither operator can recall having ever seen Thowm do that before. But the significance—if any—is unknown."

Pranol's secretary appeared in the imaging field, to one side of the reporting security officer.

"Marshall, Governor Mauhk and Counsel Haleahm wish to discuss Major Ihmoy's request for authority to fire warning shots."

"Fine." With a gesture, Pranol dismissed the security officer as Governor Mauhk appeared in'field with his Counsel-Ra seated beside him. Ever the optimist, Mauhk would no doubt be clinging to hopes of Jakomen participation in the festival, and both he and Haleahm would be highly sensitive to further aggravating the Aggah Bood.

"Gjadren," the marshall said through a less than cordial smile.

"Mannon," replied the governor. "*If* Jakomen operatives are involved, they absolutely must not be harmed. I remain hopeful that Bood will come around, and I cannot have anything jeopardize that prospect."

"It is a high probability, Governo...."

"That convoy departed before any of us even knew of the mission to the Prime Seed," Haleahm injected, cutting Pranol off. "The situation is unquestionably of the Varahns' own making, and it is their loss. I see no reason why we should delay the prince's arrival in an exercise that puts our interceptors in direct conflict with operatives from the NHD[G249c]"

"The decision to attempt the retrieval, Counsel," Pranol replied, firmly, "was forced and appropriate. Had Squadron Leader Ihmoy failed to take action while the container and its multibillion-qubal contents were in range, he would have risked a court-martial."

There had never been any lack of cooperation between Haleahm and Pranol, but they did not mask their mutual dislike.

The governor stepped in, as usual.

"What's done is done, Raund. How do we get out from under this, Mannon? What are our options?"

"We have several scenarios, gentlemen—three plausible. One, the suspects will abandon the container and run, in the hope or belief that we will not give chase. Two, they will run with the container in tow, assuming we will discontinue the pursuit in a political desire to avoid friction with their Aggah. Three, if the pursuit should enter a critical phase, the Varahns will request that the container be conceded."

Mauhk mulled that over awhile. Then he asked, "So, Mannon…do we authorize Ihmoy, or not?"

Pranol stared at Haleahm's image. He wanted it to come from the Counsel-Ra.

After a few seconds of persuasive silence, Haleahm finished gnawing one of his nails, spit, and said, "I propose that *if* a suspect ship is clearly identified and fails to submit to inspectional scans, the two pursuit interceptors be limited to firing a maximum of one low-intensity warning shot each. Other than mock pursuit, no further action is warranted. And at twenty-four hours to interception, the pursuit team is to concede the container and return to their primary mission."

The governor raised his eyebrows, suggesting to Pranol that the proposal seemed reasonable. But Haleahm hadn't finished.

"In addition, Marshall, I would ask that you give Gjadren your personal assurance that if warning shots are fired, there will be zero possibility of inflicting structural damage to either the suspect ship or container, assuming minimal shielding…."

WELCOMING THE MASTER

D-29.17: SPACE / KHOOMYAHNA

With each of Nordehk's mildly luminous Sons on one knee at the base of his crimson dais, Rehm silently beckoned the campaign's Overlord to approach.

Glowing head still bowed, both in respect for The Master and to avoid His crushing orange glare, Zhol stood and slowly ascended the pentagonal dais' front set of twelve steep steps.

As he neared the top and Rehm's golden throne, The Master's two sitting Vu-dogs simultaneously lurched a fraction of a cubit and growled a low, deep warning.

Cautiously, the Overlord knelt on both knees and pressed his fists to the floor. And to consummate Rǝhm's welcome, Zhol kissed His golden slippers—first the left and then the right—saying silently, "Welcome, Master. Your young ones wait."

"AND SO RISE, MY SONS…" Rǝhm's voice thundered through their minds. "…SO THEY MAY SEE MY BRILLIANT FACES."

All four warriors promptly stood: Zhol directly in front of and facing The Master, and the others at the dais' base.

Rǝhm's body, head and hands continuously re-formed within his now-pulsating orange glow. His slippers noticeably swelled and shrank in constant adjustment to the transforming feet inside. Only by his will, by the tremendous power of his mind, did the estranged Universal Son achieve visibility in the lower realms.

As The Master stood and glided smoothly past, Nordehk's Lord of the Orbits moved gracefully aside and turned his eyes away. Heads up and shoulders square, the others did the same. All knew not to gaze upon His ever-changing faces. They knew not to look into the terrible eyes of Rǝhm.

The Omnipotent One went down the dais' front, while his dogs stepped down its sides. His golden slippers floated above or dipped into the veined, crimson stone, never firmly making contact.

"THE WAR ROOM, THEN."

And in that smooth, floating, stepping, gliding motion, Prime Crusader—dogs at his sides—led the way.

KHRAELING-VARAHN TACT
DAY -28: SPACE / KSF ESCORTS

Major Ihmoy felt, heard and saw the flashing prompters signaling that a message had arrived from Khrae Lunar Command. With 30 hours to the escort squadron's flyby, it came as a typical, highly compressed transmission.

"By joint authority of the Governor of the Intercontinental Federation and the Marshall of Khrae's Security Forces, you are hereby authorized to proceed with your request to fire warning shots, SUBJECT TO THE FOLLOWING CONDITIONS:

1. a suspect ship must be clearly identified either by imprint or engine signature; and

2. at least minimal shielding must be confirmed as engaged on both the suspect ship and Varahn container; and

3. the suspect ship must fail to acknowledge your first and second hails or refuse to transmit commercial documentation and fail to yield for inspectional scans; and

4. a one-hour warning of intent to fire must be transmitted to the suspects, and suspects must fail to respond.

The following actions are NOT APPROVED and remain UNAUTHORIZED at this time:

5. APPREHENSION OF SUSPECTS is not approved and is unauthorized at this time.

6. SECONDARY FIRE is not approved and is unauthorized at this time.

DULY NOTE: the personal assurances of Marshall M. L. Pranol have been given to Governor G. D. Mauhk that *if* warning shots are fired, the intensity is to be inadequate to penetrate standard commercial shielding. there is to be ZERO POSSIBILITY of inflicting any structural damage whatsoever to the amstrahd container or suspect ship."

Ihmoy thought awhile, and then ordered pursuit leader Heln to have her wingman transmit their first hail. Next, the major updated the Varahns but did not tell them he had received KLC's authorization to fire.

Seconds later, the Varahns acknowledged the squadron leader's update, adding, "The remainder of our delegation, including the daughters, will awaken within the next few hours."

They did not tell him they were debating the merits of calling off his pursuit.

THE FIRST HAIL

D-28.2: SPACE / PIRATES

The first of four 8-man teams had finished installing a prefabricated duct between their cruiser's hold and the container's forward starboard hatchway, and the transfer of Varahn cargo had begun. The tumbling and their backup system's one-third gravity made it awkward, but the task kept the screws busy and kept their minds off other things.

While the third team rested, the second team worked with Chief Poth on their ship's big primary coil. Team Four attempted to intercept the escorts' communications with KLC, and to isolate valid messages from the high volume of gibberish known to be KSF decoys.

Pursuit wingman Yhurg's first hail came in loudly across several standard frequencies, and with a harsh and threatening tone.

"By joint authority of the Governor of the Khrae Intercontinental Federation and the Marshall of the Khrae Security Forces, we hereby demand transmission of your commercial documentation and submission to inspectional scans."

The young operative in charge of the pirates' communications team— one of six eniggs onboard—clenched her teeth and tossed her headset, reamed her ringing ears with her index fingers, and then called her captain to let him know of the Khraelings' hail.

Unperturbed, Narlihd never lifted his head. And soon the screws, all

fluently bilingual, began mimicking Yhurg's scratchy voice.
   "By joint authority of...."

AN INTIMATION MISCONSTRUED
D-28.3: SPACE / KHOOMYAHNA
   Near the heart of the Overlord's khoomyahna beneath an elongated dome, the warship's war room featured dynamic, slowly changing images of the cosmos near and far. A concealed light source near the room's floor cast long shadows that simulated an early summer night.
   Coming and going on an elaborate double-helix staircase that spiraled downward from the war room's middle, the ship's priests busily orchestrated their hurried welcome for The Master. None had ever imagined hosting The Universal Lord.
   Rehm sat on the war room's lofty golden throne. Virtually identical to those of all khoomyahna war rooms, the throne rose from a large, circular, three-stepped dais of cured white marble. The Omnipotent One wore a long and heavy orange robe. His hooded face shone with the intensity of a miniature sun, and the light radiating from beneath his long, drooping cuffs and golden hem similarly washed out his ever-changing feet and hands.
   As though under a spell, the bahva stood staring in an open area behind their 4,000 children who had gathered in a deep semi-circle around the Prime Crusader. The brothers strove to coordinate the violators' haphazard efforts to distribute a steady stream of food and drink, while the warship's excited youngsters spiritedly sang under Vakaar's fervent direction.
   Beyond the sight of most, the four Sons stood faintly illuminated behind their glowing Master's throne. And with His dark seraphic guardians hovering about, the warriors' midwayers busied themselves elsewhere in the khoom.
   To Rehm's right, six bahva cautiously groomed Iccha, braiding her tail into her back's thick golden fur and up into her long flowing mane. Her upper lip quivered, with tongue curled in an S-shape inside her open jaws. Her breathing seemed deliberate now, and deep.
   With their every guarded move, the groomers nervously whispered, "Iccha, Iccha," the imperial word for *Fear*. Repeating the capricious beasts' names was rumored to calm them.
   Left of The Master's golden throne, six bahva groomed Trsnah with equal trepidation. "Trsnah, yaovash Trsnah," they whispered. *Desire, brave Desire.*
   Head gently swaying to the soothing tones of the yamah's youthful choir, Rehm silently addressed Zhol, whose personal musings and restless vibrations

had become a distraction to The Lord of Lords.

"SOMETHING TROUBLES YOU, MY SON." No others were aware of this private, telepathic discourse.

"There was an intrusion, Master," the Overlord replied. "A local Vihdæan. Nordehk's administrators would seem less sensitive of transgressional bounds."

LESS SENSITIVE OF TRANSGRESSIONAL BOUNDS? Was this campaign's senior Son so bold as to imply that this Vihdæan Council was undisciplined—less than fully committed—that perhaps they might defect? If so, it was a most dangerous insinuation, for should they choose not, when Zhol supposed they might—would that be seen as The Master's failure, *THAT HIS CALLINGS HAD BEEN REBUFFED?*

Unknown to the Overlord, the engrossed Prime Defector had misconstrued Zhol's intimation, which had been meant as an expression of personal concern from a highly anticipatory Son, a veiled request for guidance should Nordehk's Vihdæa—unlike *all* before them—attempt to somehow intervene.

"...His swift light bright and formless...." The young ones' beautiful harmonies.... In all of His Creation, there could be no finer sound.

This Lord of the Orbits seemed most confident, a prospective Supreme Son when the next one failed. Zhol knew what he was saying. *HE KNEW THE IMPLICATIONS.*

The chorus of little voices rose. *"...His sword so sure and mighty...."* A favorite phrase.

Rohm let it go. For now.

Chapter 12 — N O T E S

N[190] ***their long, deep sleep.*** The Varahn voyagers' 10-year hibernation (as the Varahns record time), or 19 years as measured by the Khraelings.

G[242c]   Narlihd: [♂] Captain Rauhf B. Narlihd; captain of the pirate-operatives sent by the NHD to secretly rendezvous with the Varahn convoy and to "hijack" its 14th container (New Hollatia)

G[119a]   flash-scanning: a method of low-resolution, long-range scanning developed by the Varahns and shared with the Jakomen of New Hollatia; an adaptation of the ancients' interstellar communications device, flash-scanning is undetectable by its target and is more than 100 times faster than conventional scans

N[191] ***the incident at Base 11.*** The abrupt death of Specialist Mahrget Thowm:

[from D-29.7, *EAVESDROPPING ON IHMOY*] Listening intently, Mohaar came to a locked directory, *"Restricted—K1: Eyes Only."* Thowm knew it as the Federation's strategic files. She did not know the codes and had served her purpose.

The demon silently summoned his cackling scout. Then he violently exited his young, warm, Khraeling host, and pinned back to his destroyer. And without a sound, Mahrget Thowm slumped over her console.

G[249c]   NHD: New Hollatian Defense; the global police, security force and defenders of New Hollatia

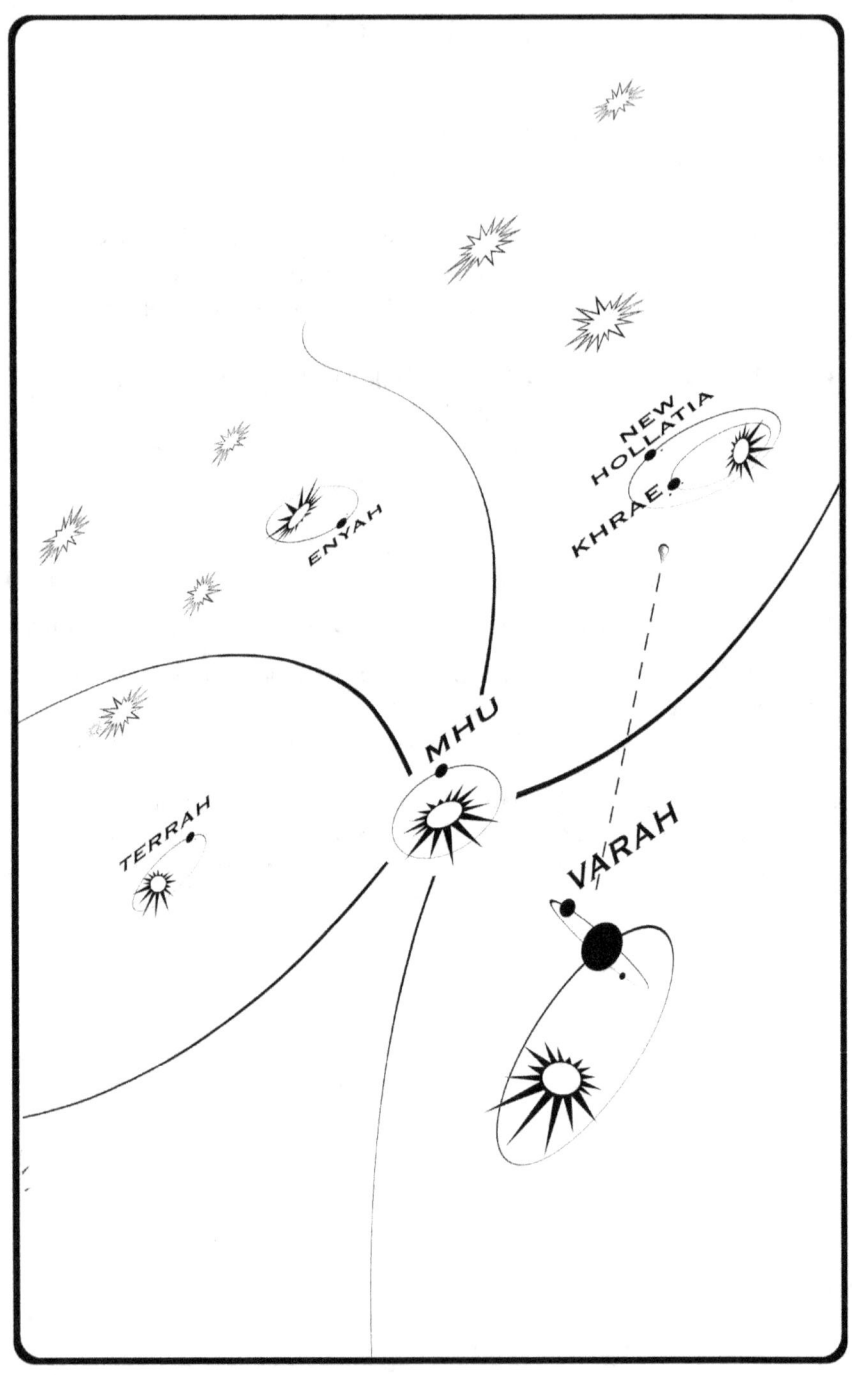

13

ADAHR'S FAMILIAR REFRAIN
D-28.4: SPACE / CONVOY

While a parade of robotic carriers transferred the daughters' cells to the tug's rejuvenation chamber, the remainder of the Varahn voyagers joined the telepathic debate on whether to terminate their escorts' endeavor to retrieve the fourteenth container.

"Although the situation is regretful and embarrassing," said one of three elders onboard, "our primary concern must remain to preserve the status-quo between Khrae and New Hollatia."

It was unfortunate that the prearranged "transfer" had not occurred on schedule, when the operatives would have been well beyond range of the Khraeling escorts' scans. Now the opportunity presented by the festival—a possible reconciliation between the two cold-warring worlds, Khrae and New Hollatia—could be compromised.

The delegates doubted the Jakomen operatives would abandon the container. The pirates would likely choose death before suffering that shame. Nor would they allow the Federation to discover that the container's contents, which the Varahns had registered as fourth-level commodities, were mostly first and second.

Uril kaVihl, the delegation's appointed spokesman and retired Commissioner of the Varahn Service Corps, feared things could easily get out of hand.

"The sooner we request the exercise be discontinued," he said, "the sooner we avert the danger of a serious consequence. We cannot bear responsibility for allowing a potentially explosive situation to escalate."

Tahned, another of the delegation's elders, offered her opinion.

"I share your concerns, Uril. However, to call off the pursuit would be to forfeit the container to the operatives. Would that not be akin to rubbing salt into the Khraelings' wounded ego? Would we not appear self-righteous to have obviously conspired with the Jakomen, and to then supplicate their escape? Instead, I suggest we stay a decision while events unfold. I suggest we pray and intend that the Federation will realize the need for restraint."

After a few minutes of reflection, Commissioner kaVihl asked Prince Adahr for his thoughts on the best course of action. It was just a formality, for the prince unfailingly withheld his points of view. Unfailingly, the middle-aged Adahr unquestioningly abided by the decisions of whomever: his mother, his brothers, his sisters, or the cavveht, Varah's legislative assembly.

"I choose to abide by your decision," the prince replied, modestly and as ever in the words of his familiar refrain. Like most Varahns, he had learned Khrae's language at an early age. To the surprise of his family and tutors, he rejected his given name and chose his own: Adahr, the Khraeling word for "unity." But for reasons unknown, he remained in the royal shadows. Being a distant third in line for the throne, few had problems with that. But in truth, the prince's detachment was purposeful and contrived....

In contrast to the uncomplicated, swift subversion of Enyah, the first three millennia of Og activity on Varah had achieved little. The locals of the time were quick to launch increasingly sophisticated investigations into the "mahisha," the "dark influences" they suspected of being behind Varah's otherwise inexplicable, rising discontent. Consequently, the campaign's Overlord, Zhol, curtailed the Og crusaders' Varahn-related activities to surveillance and to maintaining an incarnative presence within the society's monarchy.

The incarnate behind the eyes of Adahr shaJah was a highly revered Og crusader, a rising star in GROUP COMMAND's elite incarnate corps. GROUP COMMAND <u>frequently paired the incarnate troops</u>[192] they sent in. Only the strongest, most experienced and adept crusaders went solo, including the incarnate-prince Adahr.

Through the dream state, crusader-couples usually found each other before they reached adolescence. Their handlers, Og specialists working from <u>etheric chambers</u>[193] in orbiting Og garrisons, navigated the dream world's interdimensional planes to repeatedly remind the incarnates of who they truly were—crusading mercenaries in service to Orion; elite troops from a vastly superior race—and of their crucial missions. The process ensured a high rate of success on these loneliest of assignments.

Preceding the delegation's departure from Varah, Adahr's handlers instructed him to attend the Federation's planned festivities designed to celebrate the ancients' mission to the Prime Seed. And so, to his family's surprise and their people's delight, the prince humbly volunteered to head the convoy to Khrae.

Ever mindful of his mandate to simply observe and await instructions, Adahr never forgot his handlers' assertion that the Rehmans would come during this, his fourth incarnation on Nordehk's spectacular lunar world, and that in the aftermath of the elantah's expected reduction and subsequent New Order, he would become the surviving Varahns' king.

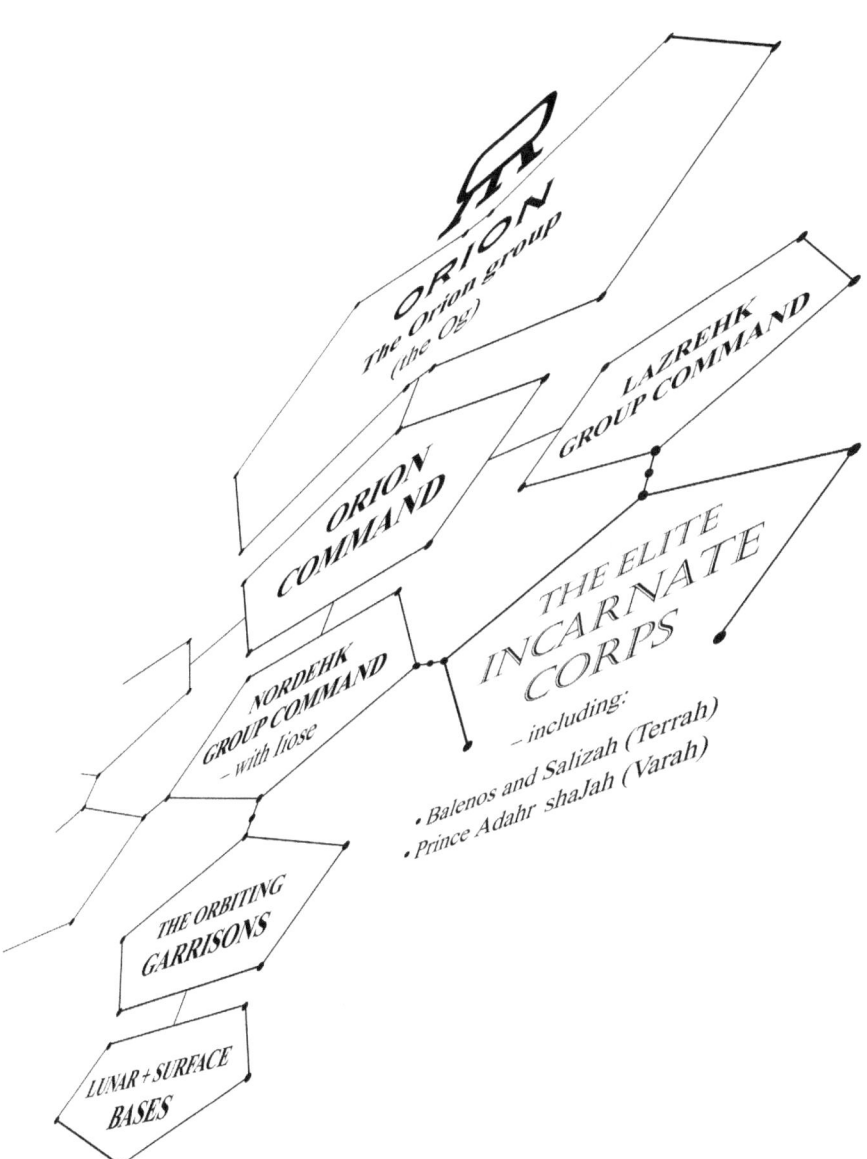

ORION
The Orion group
(the Og)

ORION
COMMAND

LAZREHK
GROUP COMMAND

NORDEHK
GROUP COMMAND
– with fiose

THE ELITE
INCARNATE
CORPS

– including:

• Balenos and Salizah (Terrah)
• Prince Adahr shaJah (Varah)

THE ORBITING
GARRISONS

LUNAR + SURFACE
BASES

Last night, while in the dream-state, Adahr received word of the Sons' arrival and that the Nordehk campaign had officially entered its final phase. Soon, his handlers told him, he would meet another incarnate: "a counterpart" they said—a *rival*, he suspected—a crusader birthed to rule the Khraelings in that reduction's wake.

While their prince returned to his unassuming quarters, the Varahn delegates gathered in a circle and joined hands for a group meditation to decide their course of action.

After a few minutes of silent contemplation, they voted and unanimously agreed to postpone their decision. They would advise the cavveht of the situation. They would pray and intend, and wait to see how the Khraelings played their hand. And they would give the Jakomen a chance to run.

Hopefully, as the critical hour approached, Major Ihmoy, Marshall Pranol and Governor Mauhk himself would anxiously anticipate the prince's intervention. It would be less complicated. Less embarrassing for everyone that way.

AND THE CHILDREN DANCED
D-28.5: SPACE / KHOOMYAHNA

With glowing fingers fully extended, Rehm reached out to the khoom's children as they finished another beautiful hymn. His young ones looked to Vakaar.

Horrified, the yamah forced a smile. *Don't do this to me, you cretins*, he thought. *Go! Go to The Master! Don't ask my permission, you little worms!*

For several long seconds, while the groomers warily wove the last of the colorful, braided leather thongs through the Vu-dogs' ceremonial leggings, and carefully adjusted the beasts' bejeweled breastplates and skullcaps of patterned gold, Rehm let Vakaar squirm.

As though by secret signal, the dogs suddenly snapped to attention. Their groomers backed away, and The Master rose from his golden throne.

"COME THEN, LITTLE ONES," he called softly. "COME TO YOUR MASTER. COME TO YOUR HEAVENLY FATHER. COME."

To the yamah's great relief, the young choir rushed their Master's towering form.

Arms outstretched, Rehm glided forward and began slowly twirling. His golden slippers floated mere inches above the sea of tiny, grasping hands.

"DANCE WITH ME, DEAR ONES. HEAR MY MUSIC IN YOUR PRECIOUS LITTLE MINDS."

And the young ones danced while the others watched with the Sons and humble priesthood.

And His dark seraphim? They swirled unseen 'round The Friend of Man and Angels.

REMEMBERING

D-28.6: SPACE / CONVOY

Softly lit like moonlight and lush with vegetation, the Varahn tug's lavish rejuvenation chamber featured an abundance of cool, clean water. A bubbling stream flowed from a lake-like reservoir that fed the modest swimming ponds of the chamber's living forest.

The delegation's 100 beautiful settler-daughters—some naked, others partially clad—swam, strolled or lay about, remembering. For most of their young lives, they had trained for their roles in the one-way mission to distant Levah. And as they drew the forest's rich air and medicinal vapors deep into their lungs, it seemed as though they had been asleep for a few hours. Not ten long Varahn years.

Now, as they relaxed in their starship's rejuvenation chamber, the daughters viewed archived images of families and friends, and remembered the wonderful times they'd shared during preparations for this historic mission. They revisited the Varahn festival that had celebrated their departure, and they watched a replay of their emotional sendoff…and once again they saw their lovely world forever disappear.

Back then, all 100 daughters were between 11 and 13 Varahn years, the equivalent of 21 to 25 Khraeling years. Technically they were now almost twice that; but in real terms, they had aged less than a month through the course of their long journey through space. With an average life-expectancy of 124 Varahn years, they would far outlive the Khraeling and Jakomen sons. And already the daughters had the mindset of their elders, and were exceptionally wise and strong.

In a strategy that reflected the ancients' wisdom, the sons would provide while the daughters ruled. Khraeling ingenuity and determination coupled with harmonious Varahn temperament would ensure a brilliant future. It would ensure the mission's success.

THE MASTER'S WILL BE DONE

D-28.7: SPACE / KHOOMYAHNA

The party was over. Rohm was seated again on his golden throne at the war room's far end, and had subdued his radiance to little more than a faint orange aura. His four mildly illuminated Sons now stood beside His vigilant Vu-dogs: Zhol and Dhanz to The Master's right, alongside the glaring Iccha; Wohtan and Mohaar to His left, alongside the steady Trsnah. Rohm's twelve dark seraphic escorts hovered quietly overhead. All others had left the room.

Linked neurologically with the khoom, Zhol cut the chamber's lighting and initialized his updated stellar program of the local constellation. Immediately, the warriors felt The Master's electrifying grip on their minds, and in less than a Rohman minute they were freed. At dizzying speed, the stellar program had run its course—and Rohm knew well His Sons' intentions. *And it seemed He did not disapprove.*

With the war room now awash in a pervasive orange glow, Prime Crusader stood and walked/glided toward its central staircase. His Vu-dogs cast a menacing last look at the Sons, and then trotted away to join Him.

And as Rohm took his first step down the stairs, his dreadful voice filled the warriors' minds.

"ESTABLISH NORDEHK'S CAPITAL ON THE CURRENT NINTH IN LINE OF THE LOCAL PROGENITORS' SEED WORLDS. CALL THE PLANET 'ANADON.'"

"By your radiance, Master…" the Overlord silently replied with his head deeply bowed. He had survived Prime Crusader's mind-scan. Unlike most Sons, Zhol had The Omnipotent One's elusive awareness. "…Anadon. Your will be done."

Rohm's dark angels circled once and vanished. The Master and his beasts dematerialized, leaving the dogs' breastplates, skullcaps and leg armor to tumble down the stairs.

THE BURNING SIGN
D-28.8: TERRAH

Ricky dreamed a tiny sun lit up the evening sky. He watched it get big and bigger, and become some sort of sign. It only stayed a minute and it didn't hurt his eyes, but it was hot and bright enough to burn itself on everything in sight.

He woke up feeling prickly so he drew it on his wall: three little feet on little legs beneath a squarish ball. Then he drew it in the coatroom and on a whiteboard during lunch. He drew it on some desks and in the bathroom a whole bunch until his pricklies finally stopped and he knew he'd drawn enough.

The way his teacher glanced at him and all his inky fingers, he knew she knew but that she liked him, too, and she just let it go for now. But the bullies' eyes were singeing the back of Ricky's head, and after school they'd chase him home or beat him up instead.

Every day it seemed the same. And every time, his mom would say that sometime soon the both of them would move to someplace else.

Chapter 13 — N O T E S

N[192] *frequently paired incarnate troops.* To counteract the undesirable effects of loneliness, as arranged for the hybrids Balenos and Salizah:

> [from D-32.2, *THE COLLABORATORS*] Similar in height and with short dark hair, cold blue eyes and beautifully sculpted faces, the two hybrids could pass for thirty-year-old Terran twins. Nearly ninety years before, they had transferred to the Terran garrison from their quarters in GROUP COMMAND's elite incarnate wing, before pinning directly into the modified fetuses growing inside their earthling mothers' wombs. As they and their mission planners intended, the two Og-earthling hybrid-incarnates were born within days of each other in the same small town.

N[193] *etheric chambers.* All orbiting Og garrisons contain sophisticated etheric chambers that effectively transcend space and time. Designed to overcome the powerful effects of the veiling syndrome on their elite incarnate troops, the chambers enable Og specialists to consciously navigate the dream world's interdimensional planes where they effectively draw dreaming incarnate-crusaders to them and to one another. Occasionally, the chambers produce a strange side effect whereby the incarnates inexplicably glimpse the future, and premonitions become part of their in-session or after-session dreams.

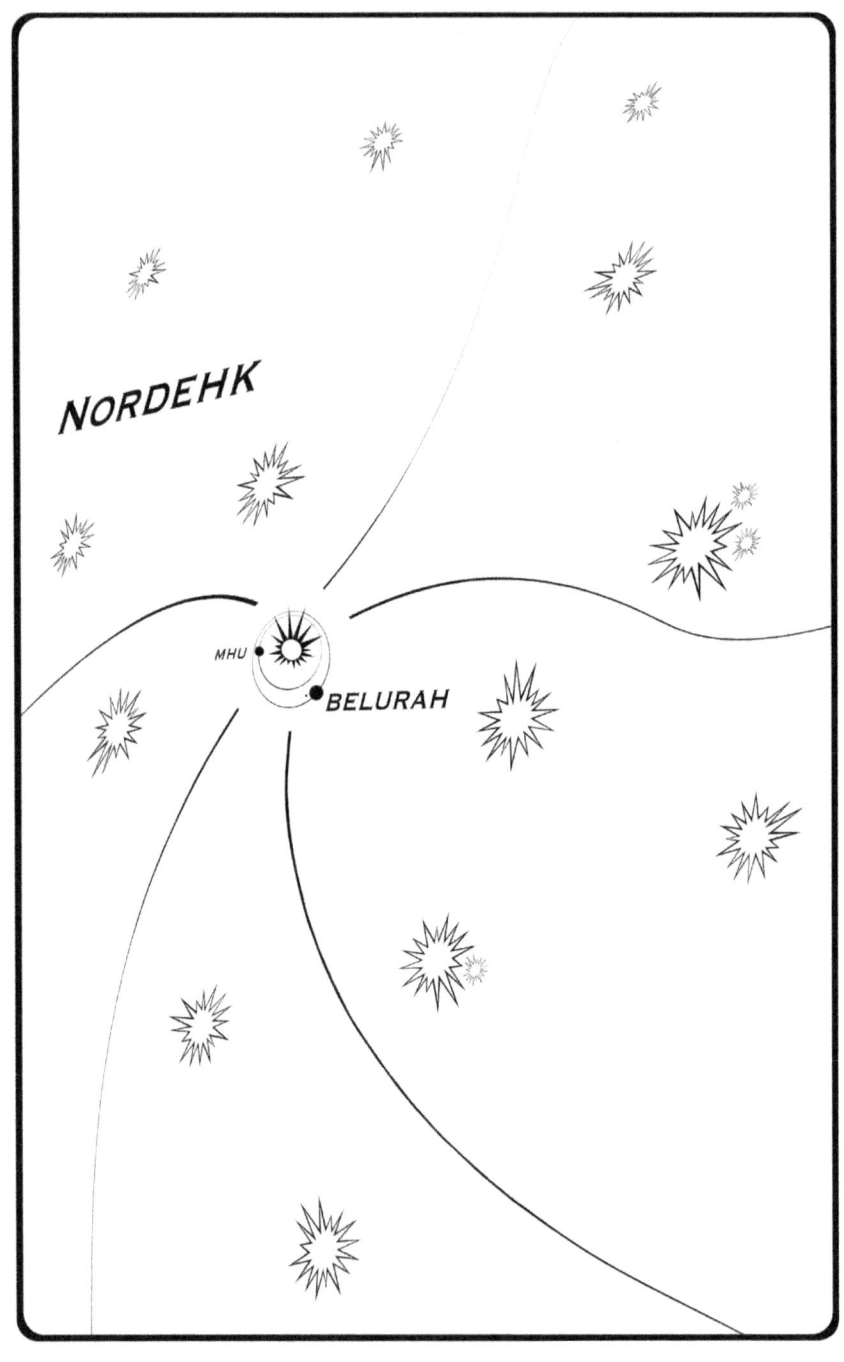

14

THE ANCIENTS AND THEIR BROOD
D-28.9: NORDEHK

Long ago, following the incubative chaos within the star hatchery known as Ohrvon's great Chandron Nebula, a young planet began forming shallow seas. Within a few hundred million years, those seas became sufficiently briny to support saline-based life, and Ohrvon's Universal Sons deemed the world adequately mature for the commencement of life cycles.

Upon receipt of the required requisition from Ohrvon's Most Highs, a group of divine Sowers pinned across the cosmos and sparked the planet's primal atmosphere. In accordance with Prime Creator's will, they then left life in the free-will zone of newly defined Nordehk to evolve or simply perish.

$$- \circ \; \diamond \; \circ -$$

After more than a billion years of metamorphosis, setbacks and transitions, and the sparking of dozens of neighboring worlds, the Universal Sons assigned eight Vihdæa, eight righteous, angelic administrator-overseers, to name the parturient worlds and to watch for and record the emergence of Nordehk's first will-creatures: those with the exceptional capacity to make a moral decision.

Eventually, as a genetic mutation of a tree-dwelling carnivore, "man" suddenly appeared within Nordehk's core solar system—on lovely Belurah, the constellation's first world to have been sparked by the divine Sowers. To the dismay of Nordehk's non-interfering Vihdæa, however, the highly intelligent, two-armed, two-legged Belurahns developed an increasingly bellicose society that ended abruptly in a sudden war of virtual self-eradication.

In the years leading to that apocalypse, Belurah's two rival powers established and maintained military outposts on a sister world, Mhu, the solar system's third planet from the sun. No one in orbit over Belurah at the time of the final self-assault survived the attempted exodus to their outposts on Mhu. Instead, they successfully destroyed each others' battle-worn ships along the way.

All life on bombed-out Belurah slowly ceased to exist. But for its shriveled polar icecaps and jagged riverbeds, all signs of the planet's once abundant water vanished. In the fullness of time, all evidence of the world's thriving civilization disappeared, save the suggestive bumps of ruined monuments bulging here and there beneath sterile, blood-red sand.

Through the tense period of their civilization's rebirth in and around moonless Mhu's deteriorating outposts, the surviving factions of impoverished Belurahns—those fortunates stationed on the sister world—came to confess their mutual guilt, despair and determination to survive. One unto another, they resolved to maintain a peaceful co-existence and to never wage war again.

In answer to the rising chorus of callings from Mhu's forlorn, Nordehk's Vihdæan Council cautiously assumed an increasingly active role in the survivors' spiritual development. Nordehk's eight Vihdæa patiently cultivated unfolding leanings toward compassion and to serving others. And on the Belurahns' new world, a positive polarity eventually took hold.

Successive generations of Mhu's citizenry strove to create a common language and a single religion based on a growing understanding that behind all of Creation there was but One God—the existential Infinite Mind and thought-former of all realities. The Universal Father. The Creator—the Prime Creator—of *All That Is and Would Ever Be.*

Those of Mhu dedicated all their technologically oriented projects and developments to bettering their advancing society. They dealt swiftly with rare occurrences of belligerence and greed as being in defiance of Mhu's single law: the forbiddance of bellicose actions. Offenders deemed guilty by juries of their peers were labeled "genetic defectives" who then promptly lost their rights and abilities to participate in the propagation of their kind. More thoroughly and without reservation, the offenders' siblings and offspring were also sterilized.

By strictly enforcing their single law, the reborn culture had unwittingly discovered the secret to accelerating their evolution.

T hrough meditational studies fueled by paced revelations from the Vihdæa, Mhu's denizens came to understand the greater evolutionary process of transcending the six dimensions/densities of space and time, to reach the seventh—"Paradise." Realm of the absolute.

With guarded Vihdæan guidance, Those of Mhu ascertained that each density or dimension consisted of seven steps or levels, a vibrational *octave*— the eighth step being the first level of the next octave—and that the atoms of all matter vibrated at frequencies that steadily increased through each octave. Will-creatures of a given density vibrated at a frequency similar to the plants, animals and other matter around them, and therefore shared that octave's common visibility spectrum.

The subtle difference in vibration between the first and seventh steps of each dimension was insufficient to alter visibility in that plane. And except for a moderate increase in perceptive abilities, each elevation in vibrational frequency through an octave's seven steps was typically achieved with little awareness and on an individual basis, some reaching the higher vibratory steps/levels sooner than the rest.

But upon attaining the "eighth step" or first level of the next octave, a major transformation occurred. The slight increase in vibration achieved in one's advance from the seventh step of the previous density, yielded a dramatic result. All senses could perceive the alter-matter that existed in the new and higher realm of visibility. However, as had been the case in the previous, lower realm, those within could discern little of the provocative realities "above" them.

Upon the commencement of a societal effort to attain the first level of the next vibrational octave, a transitional acceleration would begin. And if a large enough majority were involved, the change could occur as a rare, instantaneous jump.[194] Either way, the transcenders ultimately gained the additional senses, perceptions and abilities common to the next dimension.

After the successful completion of three consecutive 25,000-year cycles with no interruption to their collective energy pattern—no belligerence or war—Those of Mhu *and* their planet finally achieved the transition from third to fourth density. And with that conventional passage, came a resurfacing of their long-suppressed aspiration to venture into space.

Within 10,000 years[195] Mhu's now fourth-density people proceeded to develop a drive system that propelled their probes and ships at almost half the speed of light. And the search for potential expansion worlds, or "seeds," began.

Upon the exciting discoveries of the first potentially inhabitable worlds, the venturers assembled five stellar stations in high orbit over Mhu: slender cylinders that featured stepped orbicular ends thrice the size of anything previously built. The stations would serve as frontier outposts from which to prepare and monitor the first five worlds slated for eventual colonization.

As Those of Mhu managed steady increases in velocity, they towed their stellar stations into positions one light-year from each of the first five seeds, which they dubbed Varah, Khrae, Terrah, Enyah and Levah. Every thousand years thereafter, teams of scientists, philosophers and priests ventured to the outposts for a hundred-year evaluation of the inviting, pristine worlds. Varah, the closest of the five to Mhu, became "Prime Seed": the first in line for settlement.

Around 73,000 standard years[196] before current times, Those of Mhu bioengineered 476 colonists—238 male and 238 female—for optimum survivability in Varah's untamed third-density environment. Following decades of intensive training and other preparations, they transported the settlers to the new world. And except for an occasional, discreet, observational visit, "the ancients" (as their brood would come to call them) left the colonists—the fledgling Varahn tribe—to survive or perish in accordance with Prime Creator's will.

Varah thus became the first "younger," what the ancients hoped would one day become the first of their brood, and Khrae became the new Prime Seed. Approximately every 18,000 years thereafter, the ancients colonized another seed, the next being Khrae, then Terrah, and most recently, Enyah.

The ancients knew that a surviving colony would eventually launch probes into space, and that it would only be a matter of time before their stellar station/outpost, at just one light-year away, would be found. And with it, the machine-like technopuzzle they had left.

Both the Khraelings and Varahns found and solved the puzzle. Their uniquely different efforts succeeded in awakening the device into triggering a transmission, a signal back to Mhu that alerted the ancients to each extremely exciting achievement. The mechanism revealed was a communicator that beaded, aimed and flashed its messages in 10-second bursts at 114.7 times light speed: the universal telepathic ceiling (the conductivity speed of dark matter) and rather surprising example of Mhu's formidable accomplishments. With the exception of this gift—copied rather well by the Khraelings in 40 years, and adequately by the Varahns in 900—the ancients respectfully and unwaveringly refused to share other technowonders with their brood.

Upon the rare event of receiving a younger's first signal, the ancients transmitted a welcome to the newest member of its family. Within a few decades, a delegation departed Mhu to ceremoniously elevate the technological graduates from the standing of lone "younger," to communicatively active "brood" status. Such was the history of Khrae some 16,000 years before, and then Varah some 5,600 years later—the ancients being surprised by the stunning progress of the later-settled Khraeling colony, but saddened to find Khrae's spiritual impoverishment and long history of bitter wars.

Now, under Mhu's direction, Khrae and Varah would jointly colonize Levah, the ancients' current Prime Seed. With the added bonus of possibly pacifying the Khraelings, the mission would be another bold step—an acceleration—in the ancients' systematic scheme to develop *and marry* the many lush worlds of Nordehk.

But the ancients' plan was flawed. It did not consider alien encroachment. It did not consider conniving darkeyes. Nor the mighty sword of Rohm.

Chapter 14 — N O T E S

N[194] ***a rare instantaneous jump.*** The essence of the Ehkilah Phenomenon [detailed in upcoming Chapter 16], as referenced by Group Commander Iiose during his briefing for the Sons:

> [from D-32.7, *HOSTING THE DEMON SONS*] "We therefore humbly suggest that the imminent geological upheavals be accelerated, that the changes may be effected *before* establishing the New Order. And, ever mindful of the Ehkilah Phenomenon, that the potential for a density jump be preempted and effectively nullified."
>
> Behind the glistening eyes of her unconscious young host, Lord Dhanz quietly considered the commander's cautious warning. Charged with delivering a needful, willing Terrah into The Master's mighty hands, she knew well the Ehkilah Phenomenon. And knew well the need to countervail.

N[195] ***10,000 years.*** Since Mhu's orbital period is just three hours short of the imperial standard year, the ancients measure time much the same as Rehman administrators.

N[196] ***standard years.*** As measured similarly by the Khraelings and the ancients of Mhu, and by the Rehmans—based on the average calendar of the Empire's inhabited worlds.

15

THE JANAH VOLUNTEERS

D-28.10: SPACE / KHOOMYAHNA

"I don't like it," said Sarvah, shaking her head. "With <u>two already gone</u>,[197] another five away will leave *fifteen* of us behind. That's a bad number. Three times five invites bad things…triple badness. Nasty number, fifteen. Bad."

Of the khoom's 12,000 bahva, fewer than six percent had volunteered to crew the two new vihmyanas being readied for launch. Along with 139 of those volunteers, five members of the Janah—including Chak, Sarvah's closest friend—had been approved.

Although more hands than necessary, six percent was a poor showing. But after voyaging almost a year inside the great ship, most bahva were keen to make landfall. And with their temporary emergence from the way portal, and with the warriors' recent arrival, the majority felt certain, and wagered accordingly, that they were near their new home.

Volunteers for the special missions never knew where they were going or for how long, and at this point, the extra pay seemed hardly worth it. But except for Sarvah, who was more valuable in the khoom, the Janah anarchists volunteered for every mission. The secret sect sought to learn everything they could about the constellation they would never leave.

Huddled in their hideaway near the eighth statcon dome, the five Janah volunteers informed several peers that they would soon be boarding the departing destroyers. With two members already away in the first vihmyana, Chak felt Sarvah's distress.

"There has to be a safe haven *somewhere* in Nordehk, Weebs," he assured her with a slow, rocking hug, his left eye closed while the right watched their lookout. "We'll find it, dearheart…"

A tone sounded, signaling last call for the departing crews. "…and then we be back to plan our next moves. In the meantime, Weebs," he added, stepping back and taking hold of her shoulders, "you *have to* learn the Sons' plans."

"I still don't like it," Sarvah muttered as Chak and the others collected their final embraces and then hurried away to their ships.

"You can't fool with numbers!" she cried out as loud as she dared.

And then to the floor, "I don't like it. Now we're way too alone."

THE SONS PROCEED

D-28.11: SPACE / KHOOMYAHNA

Comfortably reclined in the khoomyahna's systems bridge, and with the Lords Dhanz and Wohtan piloting the two departing vihmyanas, the Overlord reopened the warship's stellar program and zoomed in on the ancients' ninth seed.

Fourth world from its primary sun in a double-star system—the tiny second sun orbiting the first, like an outer planet—Anadon, by Og notations, bore most everything save exploitable will-creatures.

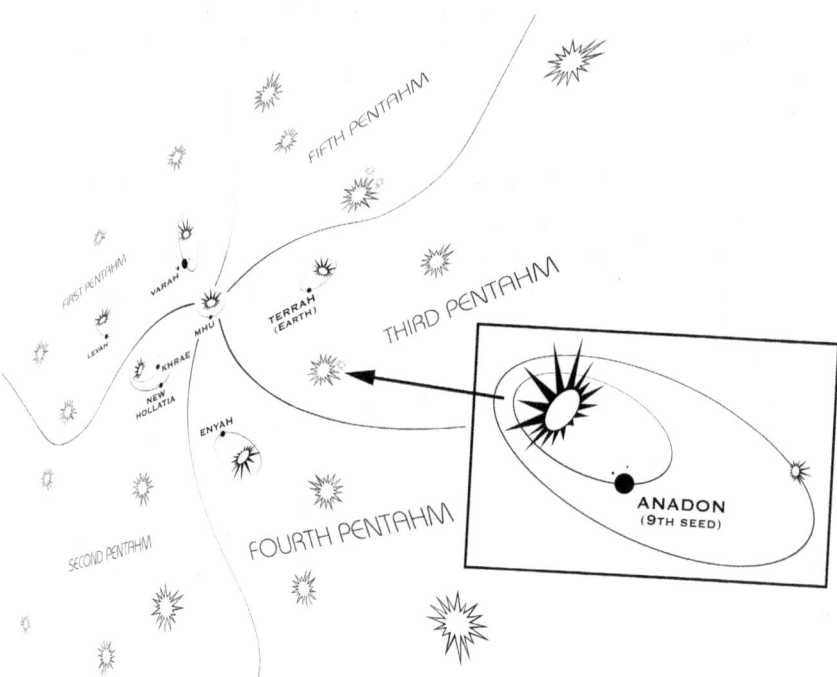

Anadon's two stars and Terrah's sun both lay within the constellation's Third Pentahm, just 7.6 standard light-years apart. And with Enyah in the neighboring Fourth Pentahm, Anadon's proximity to the ancients' relatively isolated youngers was ideal. Logistically, Rohm's selection made sense, and the system's tiny companion star would lend a special uniqueness to Nordehk's capital world. The Master's choice seemed perfect.

Anadon would soon become a bustling administrative center. Construction of the capital's golden city would begin in short order, and representatives from the ancients' brood would be secured, both to help populate the new capital, and to bring new blood to the revered Rǝhman games.

The Sons' plans for those worlds warranting reduction would be set in motion, the necessary twelve notices of The Master's Coming would be served, and the Rǝhmanization of the constellation's survivors would begin.

CLOSING ON THE JACKS

D-28.12: SPACE / PIRATES

After sixteen hours of tumbling through space, all four teams of Captain Narlihd's screws had worked a shift inside the Varahn container, and his cruiser's hold was now one-third full of compact, level-one commodities.

Almost in range of the inbound enemy's scans, Narlihd fired a burst of compressed gas to adjust the container so his cruiser would stay hidden—away from the khraeks' prying eyes. Then he called Luthur Poth for an update, only to hear that the primary coil would not be finished for another two hours, which amounted to two hours behind schedule.

"That's two hours less for the transen, Chief."

Poth attempted a stuttered reply, then nodded and resumed his repairs.

Meanwhile, the team on communications isolated a highly compressed transmission. Assuming it to be an "actual" from KLC, they excitedly informed their captain.

"We found it buried in with some junk that hit around 66 hours to intercept, Cap'n, about 13 hours ago." "Here it is—magnified in'field, Sir." "It's like a slivered crystal," said the third, "bundled up tight inside a multi-layered ball."

Narlihd offered his encouragements, and while the screws began the process of unwrapping their find—stitching frequencies, interchanging and modifying their decoder's tiny parts—the operatives' pursuers closely monitored images of their target by way of Major Ihmoy's RSU.

From its vantage point high above, ahead and to the pursuit team's starboard side, the remote scanning unit's images had become clear enough to positively identify the enormous distant object as an ovoid, amstrahd-class container. Although slowly tumbling, its shape was unmistakable.

"No question, Major," reported Heln, in'field with Ihmoy. "That mass is classic amstrahd."

The remscanner had yet to detect an engine signature or a vessel in the vicinity, but its rearview perspective was increasing by the hour.

"The only place for the jacks to hide, Sir," Heln continued, "is on the container's far side."

"That's right, Major," injected Lieutenant Yhurg, Heln's eager wingman. "They must have blown a coil and shut down for repairs. Nothing else makes sense."

"And the way our scanner's closing in," added Heln, "we'll know soon enough."

PRANOL MEETS THE SETTLER-SONS
D-28.13: KHRAE / PATOS

With their practical training and basic studies behind them and another 10-day leave well spent, the 110 young sons of Khrae and New Hollatia approached Patos, where their final studies were slated to begin.

Four unmarked interceptors escorted the settlers' shuttle toward the giant crater that concealed the imposing complex of KLC's Base 9. The sons, especially the Jakomen sons, watched in fascination as KSF ships of all sizes and shapes emerged from and disappeared into dozens of surrounding craters.

Through the thirty-year period of the Great Exodus,[198] Og-incarnates[199] instilled an unshakable rumor on New Hollatia that the Khraelings were quietly amassing an invasion force—an armada—beneath the surface of Patos: rumors that persisted to present day. And while they stared in awe as the camouflaged primary aperture for Base 9's main airlock yawned open, all eleven of the young Jakomen sons privately wondered whether the old myth were true.

The KSF's vice marshall and six others stood waiting to receive the celebrated arrivals, who ran out from their shuttle and formed five, tight, 22-man rows. In their tight grey jumpsuits, clean white boots and gloves, the young sons looked sharp. Each man stood smartly at attention with a large, grey duffel of personal effects slung over his left shoulder and tucked neatly behind his back. All else for their mission would be shared.

"Good day, gentlemen," an impressed Vice Marshall Jehrmi Brohjal called out before moving a few steps closer.

Half-expecting the famous Marshall Pranol, the settlers each stomped their right foot once in unison and shouted, "Good day, Sir," uncertain who this might be.

Brohjal could not help but smile. Preferring to display his rank with nothing more than lapel pins, and rarely appearing in public, the KSF's second in command enjoyed the way everyone reacted to first seeing him in person. He looked not ten years older than those before him, and his deep voice mismatched his youthful, smiling face.

"Please stand easy, gentlemen. I am Vice Marshall Brohjal, and I am honored to host your final studies. Welcome to Base 9."

A small shuttle landed noiselessly behind the sons' formation, and its lone occupant stepped out unseen.

"It is my pleasure," the vice marshall continued, "to introduce your primary instructor here on Patos: Doctor Ashdah Isdrav." As Isdrav stepped forward, Brohjal slipped back among his welcoming party so the doctor could enjoy the settler-sons' full attention.

The sons stomped once and shouted, "Good day, Doctor!" Most were surprised that the renowned expert in tribal evolution looked rather attractive and not more than twice their age. Although they knew of her credentials in general, few had bothered to acquaint themselves with her image or personal file. And when they first saw her standing with Brohjal and five others, the majority had assumed her to be special KSF.

Dressed in colorful civilian clothes, Isdrav braided and banded her long brown hair into a single, centered tail. Her slightly slanted Oridean eyes made her hair seem pulled more tightly than it was.

"Thank you, Vice Marshall," she said, eyes fixed on the young sons. "It is my distinct privilege and pleasure to join you here on Patos. Over the course of the next few months, I look forward to getting to know you all."

"Thank you, Doctor," said Brohjal, stepping forward to her side. "Apparently, Marshall Pranol has found time in his hectic schedule to say hello. Marshall...."

Marshall Pranol? The sons had seen The Legend once before at a formal function, but at quite a distance. Now large as life, the marshall walked around from behind the sons and directly to the first in the settlers' forward line.

Pranol grasped hands and chatted one by one. He unfailingly knew the face, name and interests of every single son, and when he came to the first of the eleven Jakomen, it was the tall alternate, Shaum Dloue. He had heard about Dloue's successful personal endeavor to bring about a genuine reconciliation between the sons of New Hollatia and Pagorea.

Taking the young man's hand in both of his, Pranol said in all sincerity, "It is profoundly moving to make your acquaintance, Enigg Dloue. You are an inspiration to us all."

Meeting the famous marshall face-to-face stirred a mix of suppressed emotions among most of the brave young sons, and among some of the alternates, too. With only 127 days remaining before their scheduled departure for the Prime Seed, collective pangs of uncertainty were starting to surface. Rising anxieties at the finality of it all.

Chapter 15 — N O T E S

N[197] ***with two already gone.*** The two Janah now aboard Mohaar's vihmyana:

> [from D-29.2, *BIRTHING THE FIRST VIHMYANA*] In the khoomyahna's lower midsection, deep beneath the surface of a roundish, murky lake, teams of bahva specialists readied a fully developed vihmyana for launch. The teams dashed to and fro through the turbid solution in a profusion of shuttles and odd machines, while thousands of robotic devices scoured the scaly surface of the twitching, untried craft.
>
> The destroyer hung among eleven other maturing vihms amid a tangle of thick umbilicals in the khoom's birthing tank. Beams of fire-like light streamed outward from the thin band of huge, deck-straddling viewports that ringed the ship's shallow crown. Farther down, the vihmyana's 144-man crew, which included two volunteers from the Janah, settled in for their unknown mission.

N[198] ***the Great Exodus.*** The Jakomen emigration en masse from Khrae to the terra-formed sister world, Qalakah, which they subsequently renamed New Hollatia.

N[199] ***Og incarnates.*** Accomplished infiltrators from GROUP COMMAND's elite incarnate corps.

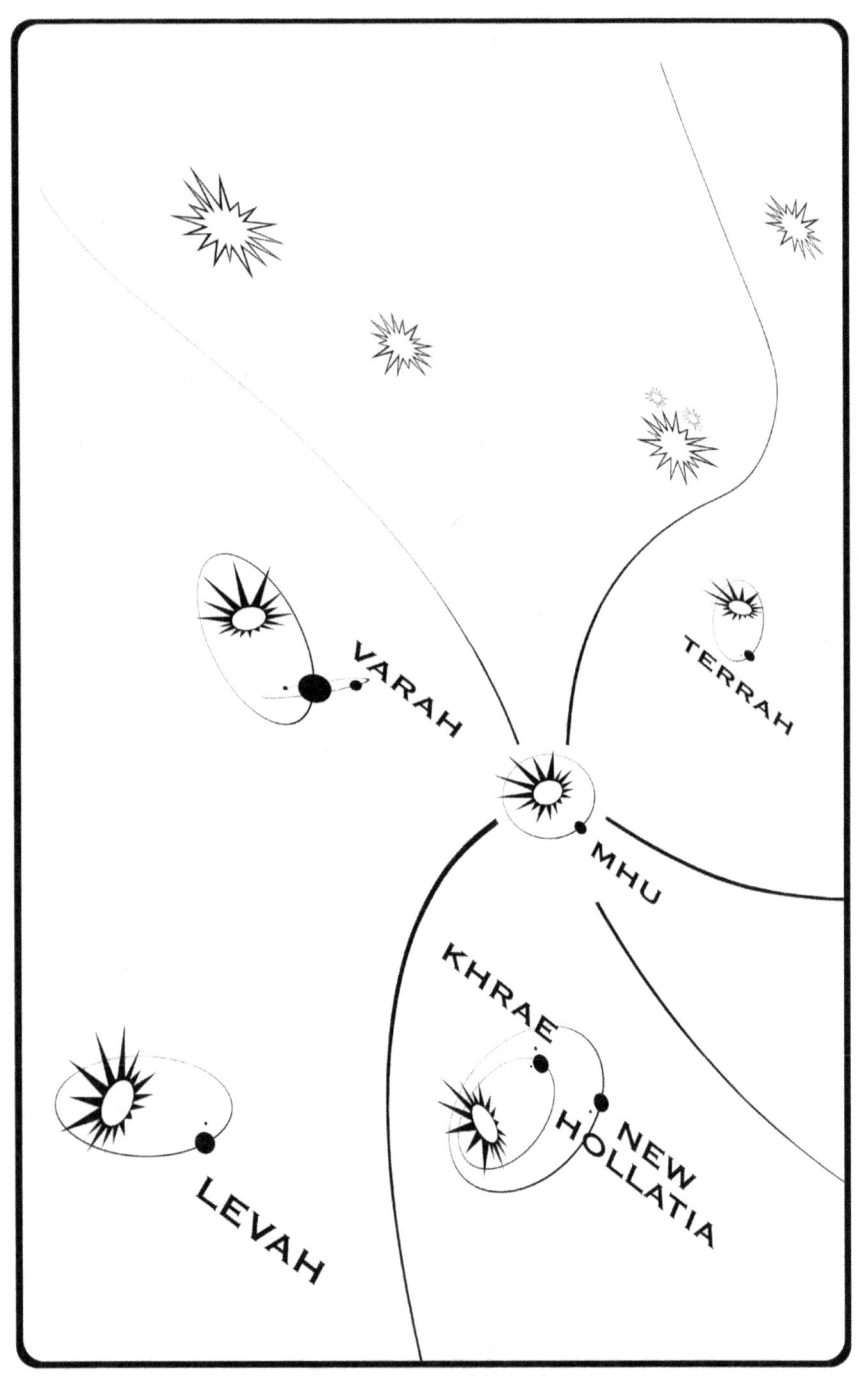

16

JACKS ON THE HATCH

D-28.14: SPACE / KSF ESCORTS

Vihlkin Ihmoy's interceptor was dropping like a rock off the cliffs of Dahoen. Shutters stuck, imagers locked onto some enormous ship, the major was sweating profusely. Nothing he tried had a countering effect. Six seconds to impact.

Cockpit roemstims swarmed his face and torso. He felt his prompter's vibration through their piercing jolts and jabs. And as he fought to blink his flickering eyelids open, a lovely female voice came to his ears.

"Major?… Sir?" Pursuit leader Heln tried again, more forcefully. "Major?…"

Disoriented, the major only stared at the dreamlike image of Captain Heln's partially helmeted, in'field face.

"Sir, our RSU has isolated a tiny distortion on the container's forward starboard hatchway. Look...." She pointed to the remscanner's latest image.

Ihmoy wiped his brow with the back of his hand, lifted his head from its cushioned cradle, and became much more awake.

It was the jacks all right. The pirates had been found.

A BAD EXAMPLE EOR THE CREW

D-28.15: SPACE / PIRATES

The tedious transfer of Varahn commodities continued, and Narlihd's fourth team was back inside the cavernous container for the second hellish time. Despite the tumbling, their cruiser was nearly half full. But it was a difficult, nauseating job.

Headsets now filtered, the third team worked to descramble the first intercepted transmission while busily searching for more, when the Khraelings' second hail came in—harsh and threatening as before.

"…and in one hour, if you fail to acknowledge this hail or refuse to forward your commercial documentation and lower your shields for inspectional scans, we WILL release our first round of fire."

Immediately advised, Narlihd figured the Khraelings were bluffing. No way their scans could peer through the container and see his ship. Besides, considering the Federation's need for the Aggah's participation in the upcoming festival, no way would Khrae's leaders authorize more than an impotent warning shot, which probably didn't require a target visual.

Unfazed, the captain checked his latest flash-scan,[G119b] which had cycled back a minute ago. Coasting had cost him a slight loss of velocity. He was down to 49.66% OMV, while his two pursuers continued to run flat out.

Intercept in 48 hours.

$$- \circ \, \diamondsuit \, \circ -$$

Just as Narlihd's communications crew managed a partial stretch of their first intercepted transmission, they discovered another: outbound for Khrae Lunar Command. They spiked their program to unravel both communications, and then posted them in the captain's imaging field: the first, as an original Khraeling transcript...

> "By joint authority of the Governor of the Intercontinental Federation and the Marshall of Khrae's Security Forces, you are hereby authorized to proceed with your request to fire warning shots, SUBJECT TO THE FOLLOWING CONDITIONS...."

...and the second, as an actual image of the escort squadron's leader advising KLC that a remscanner had positively identified a small ship on the container's starboard side.

Narlihd muttered a curse and fired a flash-scan high and to the rear. Within a few minutes the scan cycled back, and there it was. A lone, lightly armed, Khraeling RSU.

There really wasn't much he could have done about it, but he should have thought to check. Not a good example for the crew.

A BAD FEELING

D-28.16: SPACE / KSF ESCORTS

With a bad feeling, Major Ihmoy listened to his pursuit leader, Captain Heln, count the last ten seconds of her one-hour warning.

"...seven, six, charging, four..." With each second, he felt worse. "...compressing, two, one, releasing.... Gone."

Simultaneously and irretrievably, Ihmoy's two pursuit interceptors had fired one sizzling, low-intensity warning shot each. At the speed of light and with no change in target velocity, the short, parallel, blue-white bolts would impact in 13.232 hours.

The pirates were shielded; the container was shielded. Why did he feel so upset? Why the deep concern?

THE EHKILAH PHENOMENON
D-28.17: SPACE / VIHMYANA / TERRAH

As her vihmyana shot through the core[200] of an arterial way portal that tapped planet Enyah's yellow sun, the demon Dhanz lay in a full recline inside the destroyer's systems bridge.

Responsible for Rehmanizing both of the ancients' youngers, Terrah and Enyah, Dhanz revisited the briefing that the darkeyes had delivered four days before at the fringe of Nordehk's second frontier. She found Group Commander Iiose's guarded suggestion about Terrah to be of particular interest—that the world's looming geological changes be accelerated. She had thoroughly studied the full Og report, and would now review a copy of the khoomyahna's recording of that meeting.

The venerable group commander's image filled the darkness overhead, as though repeating his live report exclusively for her.

"…and in response to a calling from Nordehk's customarily passive Vihdæa, a sizeable contingent of MoLs[G228]—mostly fourth-density, but lately several from the fifth—have birthed and continue to birth on Terrah. We therefore humbly suggest that the imminent geological upheavals be accelerated, that the changes may be effected *before* establishing the New Order. And, ever mindful of the Ehkilah Phenomenon, that the potential for a density jump be preempted and effectively nullified."

Like all The Master's crusading Sons, Dhanz knew well the Ehkilah Phenomenon, the sudden jump to fourth density and the subsequent, inclusive, global polarization to the Light. A third-density world in a distant constellation, Ehkilah—like Terrah—had been primed for conquest by the Og. And as that campaign entered its final phase, Ehkilah, like Terrah, also suffered from an extreme, Og-induced, harmonic imbalance. The Rehman Son assigned to manage the Ehkilahn reductions chose to wait out the planet's impending geological changes, both to initiate the reduction and to further ensure that the surivors would willingly embrace the Rehmans as saviors, and rapidly convert to Rehmanism.

After the initial upheavals but well before the planet had sufficiently stabilized, that Son found an overwhelming majority of Ehkilah's survivors to be of the third octave's highest vibrational level. The transition had been brought about by the unrelenting efforts of a considerable MoL-incarnate population that had managed to ingrain spiritual leanings among significant numbers of the masses in the years leading up to Ehkilah's looming, cataclysmic changes. And before the Son finished reconsidering and adjusting his plan of action, the Ehkilahn people and their world made a sudden, unprecedented jump to the fourth density. The "miracle" converted the planet's faithless minority, who abruptly abandoned what negative orientations they had. And virtually overnight, a 100% positive polarization occurred. Consequently, The Master stripped the managing warrior *and* that campaign's Overlord of their Son-status, and instructed their replacements to eradicate by khoomyahna "the cancer of Ehkilah."

Dhanz activated her recliner's preserving, blue energy field, and pinned away with her midwayer, Bhu, in the lead.

— ◦ ☼ ◦ —

Fast upon the Terran system and the beautiful, blue planet that belied the turmoil on and off its shores, the two Rɵhmans dove toward Caladea, the sixth in order of the planet's settled continents, and the landmass known locally as "North America."

Over Caladea's central west coast, they saw a setting sun amplify the haze blanketing a sprawling, congested city. They heard the constant drone of inefficient engines, and the endless wail of sirens and alarms.

Bhu shrieked with delight. The Terrans were in dire need of Rɵhman Order.

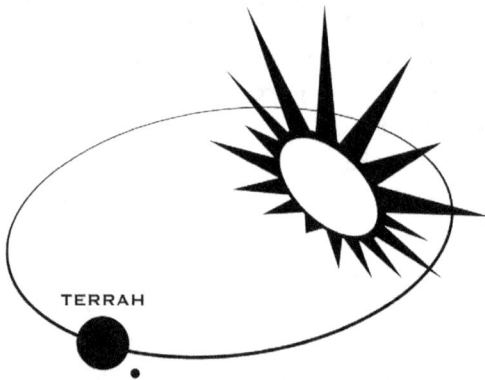

The two watched awhile as the western horizon turned a lovely crimson and the sky darkened in the east. Then they swung inland toward a range of snow-capped mountains.

Coming upon a brightly lit, lakeside town, the Son and her scout continued across the lake and rose high above the snowy hills on the other side. There, in midsky and to howls of encouragement from Bhu, the Son thought-formed a huge, dazzling apparition of The Master's sign.

For more than a minute, the demon held the radiant specter, projecting it outward from her pinpoint of highly concentrated Sonlight. But the Terrans in the surrounding area were largely preoccupied. Most who happened to glance upward thought it just another advertising logogram, a probable promotion for some new device, casino, or perfume.

Bhu cackled and cursed the heedless fools below. Then the warrior and her midwayer pinned back to their vihmyana,[201] and the insignia slowly faded. The Terrans' first notice, quietly served.

⬠

ROHMANS ON THE SCENE
DAY -27: SPACE / CONVOY

Remnants of the way portal that linked the suns of Khrae and Varah, boiled in the void behind Lord Mohaar's slowly spinning vihmyana. The new destroyer's perimeter glowed red-hot.[202] Its umbilical stubs had burned nearly flush with the ship's hull and looked like weathered impact craters, or meritorious battle scars.

Reclined in the vihm's systems bridge, the Son scanned the Varahn convoy some 300 million kilometers dead ahead…and then the seven Khraeling interceptor-escorts, and their drone, and the two feeble warning shots that had been fired…around three hours ago.

Switching to and imaging through "the object" he'd heard mentioned in Ihmoy's report on KLC's Base 11 two days before,[203] Mohaar zoomed in on the little cruiser stuck to the container's forward side like some parasitic fly.

The ship's idle engine was a variation of the Khraeling twin coil detailed in the Og report.[204] The Rohman Son would make a simple modification. He would help the Jakomen "pirates" get away.

A DEMON IN THE ROOM
D-27.2: SPACE / PIRATES

Captain Narlihd reckoned he could stabilize the container in just a few more hours with just a few more bursts of compressed gas. So he ordered his screws to close it up and restore the hatchway's seals.

The tumbling had been a bad idea. Besides doing nothing to confuse his pursuers, it had taken a toll on his crew. All the screws had thrown up at least once, and after several sweaty shifts transferring the Varahn cargo, his ship stank and tempers had begun to flare. He now knew for certain, however, that his pursuers were only to *attempt* retrieval and that they had no intention of apprehending him and his crew. If Poth could just fix the coils so they could reach even 90% OMV, the Khraelings would have the excuse they surely wanted, and he and his fellow operatives would be home free.

With a shriek, Iddh burst unseen into the Jakomen cruiser and began darting through it, hurling his usual unheard insults and threats. Mohaar pinned directly into the ship's engine room to scan the minds of the beings working on the coils, and found two who had participated in developing the prototype that was jeopardizing their mission. He entered the young one, Enigg Pahl Radool, and slammed his head into one of the crossbeams in the cramped space around the transen coil.

Chief Luthur Poth heard the fleshy thud, and looked in time to see his assistant fall limply to the floor. Two screws rushed to their motionless comrade's aid and began sealing his bleeding, swelling cut, while their captain appeared on a nearby imager and asked them what had happened.

"I heard him b..bump his h..head, C..Cap'n," the chief replied, "...and s..saw him d..drop."

"Take him to sickbay," Narlihd ordered from the helm, just as the warrior/enigg pretended to come around, dabbed his wound, and got to his feet.

Chief Poth squinted and said, "C...C..Captain wants you in ss...s..sickbay, Enigg."

"I think it would be better," the demon replied, in Radool's usual meek voice, "if I were to resume my duties rather than lie in bed with a headache."

The captain looked dubious.

"I'm all right, Sir, really," Mohaar/Radool added, staring directly in'field at the captain. "If I can't perform to the chief's expectations, I'll report to sickbay—unprescribed."

Narlihd had to get his engine fixed, and soon. He zoomed his image of the enigg's face. Those eyes looked bright enough.

Chapter 16 — N O T E S

G^{119b} flash-scans: arcing bursts of invisible particles fired/flashed at 114.7 times the speed of light; a reverse-engineered, Varahn adaptation of the ancients' interstellar communications device, and a technology the Varahns later shared with their Jakomen friends

N^{200} *the destroyer shot through the core.* A short time after having left its mothership (the khoomyahna):

> [from D-28.10, *THE JANAH VOLUNTEERS*] Of the khoom's 12,000 bahva, fewer than six percent had volunteered to crew the two new vihmyanas being readied for launch. Along with 139 of those volunteers, five members of the Janah—including Chak, Sarvah's closest friend—had been approved.

> [and from D-28.11, *THE SONS PROCEED*] Comfortably reclined in the khoomyahna's systems bridge, and with the Lords Dhanz and Wohtan piloting the two departing vihmyanas, Zhol reopened the warship's stellar program and zoomed in on the ancients' ninth seed.

G^{228} MoL: [pron. mōl] Mercenary of Light; entities of a positive polarity who, of their own free will, incarnate from the higher realms to inspire and enlighten those of evolving cultures

N^{201} *to their vihmyana.* As it shot through a way portal that tapped planet Enyah's sun:

> [from D-28.17, *THE EHKILAH PHENOMENON*] As her vihmyana shot through the core of an arterial way portal that tapped planet Enyah's yellow sun, the demon Dhanz lay in a full recline inside the destroyer's systems bridge.
> Responsible for Rehmanizing both of the ancients' youngers, Terrah and Enyah, Dhanz revisited the briefing that the darkeyes had delivered four days before at the fringe of Nordehk's second frontier. She found Group Commander Iiose's guarded suggestion about Terrah to be of particular interest—that the world's looming geological changes be accelerated. She had thoroughly studied the full Og report, and would now review a copy of the khoomyahna's recording of that meeting.

N^{202} *glowed red hot.* After its two-day ride through the way portal's churning core.

N[203] ***two days before.*** On Day -29, during his brief possession of Specialist
Mahrget Thowm:

> [from D-29.7, *EAVESDROPPING ON IHMOY*] While rummaging through
> the Federation's files, delving deeper and deeper into the KSF's database,
> Mohaar/Thowm intercepted an incoming communication. It was from a Major
> Ihmoy, a report that rang of opportunity. *The Master worked in mysterious*
> *ways.*
>   "…and we see no evidence of residual debris from an impact, either
> along its path or in the convoy's wake. The object's trajectory and velocity are
> suspicious."

N[204] ***the Og report.*** Contained among the data transferred from Group
Commander Iiose's battle cruiser to the khoomyahna, on Day -32:

> [from D-32.7, *HOSTING THE DEMON SONS*] "The following actions
> and developments are detailed in the data now flowing to your khoomyahna.
> A transfer of capsules containing the requested samples and codes for
> Nordehk's flora and fauna, including genetic materials from the higher species,
> is also underway."

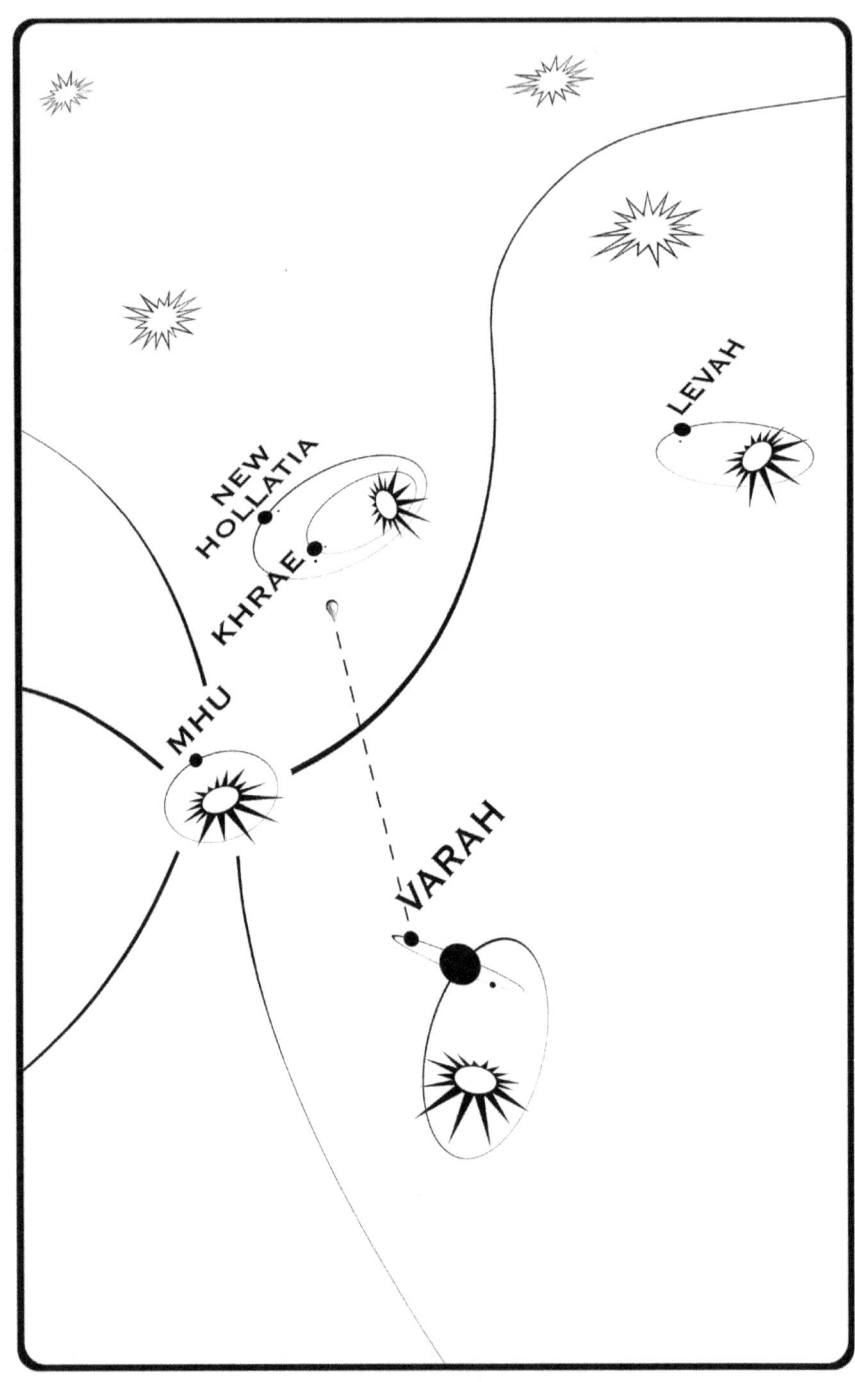

17

A PRINCELY CALM

D-27.3: SPACE / CONVOY

"…and on behalf of Marshall Pranol *and* Governor Mauhk, I assure you, Your Highness, Commissioner kaVihl and delegates, that there will be no further fire."

Keenly aware of the Varahns' aversion to violence, Major Ihmoy knew his assurance would bring some level of relief. But in his imaging field he could see—he could almost *feel*—their deep distress…except, perhaps, for Prince Adahr. Maybe it was a regal trait, but the prince's posture, face and hands displayed remarkable calm, if not a complete emotional deficiency. *Strange.*

Speaking for the delegation, Commissioner kaVihl replied, "We accept the need for compliance with the engagement format, Major. However, with the escalation of conditions, we feel compelled to express our concerns...."

CLARITY OF MIND

D-27.4: SPACE / PIRATES

The Rohman Son was enjoying himself. Although delightfully plain, everything about the pirates' ship, tools and equipment spoke of exceptional quality. The practical Jakomen took obvious pride in everything they did. They would serve the Empire well.

As Mohaar/Radool and Chief Poth finished pulling the transen's dielectrics, the chief called Captain Narlihd to show him what they'd found.

"They aren't f…f..fractured, C..Cap'n, but they are a m…m..mess. It's am..mazing they held together."

The other components scorched in the plasma burn would be easy to replace. With seven hours left of the allocated time, he wouldn't need more than five, plus another to close the housing. He figured he had an hour to spare.

"It's do or die, Chief. Which would you prefer?"

"We'll make s..schedule, S..sir."

— ○ ☼ ○ —

Five minutes later, it was time. The warrior/enigg slid out from beneath the transen and stood staring to one side.

Chief Poth craned his neck around and out from under one of the impulse scalars, and asked Radool if the injury was acting up.

The enigg said he had an idea. "It just came to me, Chief, and I can't get it out of my mind."

"Rr..report to s..sickbay, Enigg," Poth ordered, "or g..get b..back to work." And he slid back under the scalar.

"Please, Chief, hear me out," the Son insisted through his warm, young host. "It's a simple modification to the primary that will produce a purer, more concentrated energy stream. Maybe that bump to my head triggered something—I don't know. But I'm clear about it, and it could make the difference in getting us out of here without further complications. It'll take me two minutes to explain and hardly any time to install. Let me tell you what I'm thinking, and if you don't like it, we'll forget the whole thing and finish our repairs. Okay?"

The demon watched bright-eyed as the chief curled his head out from under the scalar again.

Poth was getting angry, but he saw something different about Radool—something in his eyes. *Wanting to say no, he should just tell his assistant to make it quick.*

"Make it quick, Enigg."

Mohaar/Radool pulled up the primary's schematic on the room's imager, and showed that by rearranging one group of experimental components and eliminating some others, they would produce an appreciably higher and purer product.

"The transen simply amplifies the primary's energy stream, right?"

Luthur Poth felt strange, a little dizzy, and just grunted while the enigg continued.

"It'll boost our net output by at least 15%."

The chief shook his head. Even with the extra hour, there was no way they had time to even contemplate reopening the primary. But something about the idea made sense.

The Son/enigg just smiled and kept staring with those penetrating eyes.

Poth looked away and ordered his assistant back to work. Mohaar/Radool shrugged and they both took up where they left off...but the chief could not stop thinking about the enigg's idea, and within a few minutes, he pulled himself up and sat awhile.

One by one, his curious crew quit working. Puzzled by their chief's inaction, they watched Poth's excitement rise.

The captain's image unfolded in'field. "What the hell is going on down there besides nothing, Chief?"

Poth beamed. Why after all those years of tinkering with that damn engine, hadn't he thought of it himself? Turning to the imager, he said, "I think you'd better come down here, Cap'n." He didn't even notice that he hadn't stuttered. But Narlihd noticed and headed down straightaway.

The captain did not look happy. "This had better be good, Chief."

Poth quickly explained his assistant's idea, adding, "It's so simple, Cap'n. It's the twin c..coil's final evolution. It'll eliminate our problems *and* b..boost our performance by at least ten percent—guaranteed. It's a b..beautiful, s..simple rearrangement. Not much more than a r..reconfiguration of the n..new design."

Narlihd waited a few seconds so he could calmly—professionally—respond. Poth just wanted an answer, or a question. Mohaar/Radool just stared at Narlihd, scanning the captain's mind.

"We're under fire, Chief," Narlihd firmly replied. "In less than 43 hours, the khraeks will be all over us. We can't afford any experiments, however good they may seem. Your 'reconfiguration' will have to wait until we get back, *if* we get back, which we won't if you don't close up that engine!"

The captain closed his eyes. He felt a numbness in his forehead, and then a stabbing pain between his ears. *He hadn't understood the concept...he really didn't know what the chief was talking about.*

The enigg's bright eyes stayed fixed on the captain's face. "Permission to speak, Sir?"

Eyes still shut, Narlihd nodded his approval.

"Sir," said the demon through the unconscious Enigg Radool, "the modification will work. It will get us out of here and faster than the Khraelings can advise their Lunar Command. There's too much at stake not to trust us, Captain. We all have too much to lose."

The captain opened his eyes; they were looking directly into Radool's. He felt a brief swirling, a sudden dizziness before asking Chief Poth if the changes...whatever they were...could be made within the allotted time.

The chief thought so, but looked to Radool for reassurance. Mohaar nodded the enigg's head.

"We can do it, C..Cap'n," Poth promised. "Qah. We can."

Narlihd's temples pounded and he felt nauseous. Maybe all that tumbling had caught up with him. He asked if they had all the parts they needed, "*All* the parts, Luthur."

Poth confirmed that they did. They had enough parts to all but build another engine. And while the chief waited for a decision, Mohaar held his grip on Captain Rauhf B. Narlihd's mind.

The captain was confused. Why was he considering this at all? What was he thinking? Damn his head.... As things sat, the prototype was clearly flawed so the repaired coils could fail again, possibly upon startup. Poth had "guaranteed" that the modifications would eliminate the engine's problems *and* boost performance. And since the container would be sealed within the hour, manpower was not a problem because an extra crew would ensure making the changes within the time allotted for repairs. All the chief had to do was squeeze out 90% OMV—anything else would be a bonus. And the khraeks would have to give up the chase.

Things were becoming clearer now. *The modification made good sense.*

A QUANDARY FOR THE OVERLORD
D-27.5: SPACE / MHU

Lord Zhol sat comfortably in the khoomyahna's systems bridge as his warship raced through a churning way portal toward Anadon's primary sun.

Lying back, the Overlord activated his recliner's blue energy field and summoned Poxx, his faithful midwayer-scout and guide. The time had come to visit the ancients of Mhu, the progenitors of Nordehk's tribes.

In anticipation of The Master's recent mind-scan, the four Sons of the Nordehk campaign knew better than to make any firm decisions regarding the extent of the requisite reductions. Instead, they wisely limited their intentions to general plans, dependent on further study.

With Zhol's chosen assignment—to reverse the polarity of the constellation's prospective crusaders, the fourth-density ancients of Mhu— came a serious quandary, a burden for none but an Overlord. Although third-density beings had roles to play, they were much less adept at grasping grand imperial concepts. The crusading Sons therefore commissioned the vastly more efficient fourth-density entities, such as the Og, to patiently and methodically prime the feral constellations for willing absorption into His domain. To confuse, corrupt and transform local religions into effective hierarchies, through incarnative infiltration. To instill fear and doubt and loathing, and install and escalate societal chaos. That the arriving Sons be received as saviors. That the absoluteness of *Rohman Order* be recognized and emphatically embraced.

The ancients of Mhu represented a sizeable, potential pool of elite, easily trainable talent. But with their current, purely positive orientation, it was doubtful that in their reduction's chaotic aftermath, the survivors could be swayed to abandon their purported "Prime Creator" and place their trust in the real, *living*, Prime Crusader. Indeed, to eliminate *any* of the ancients when *all* might be saved to serve in Rohm's Crusades, could endanger Zhol's worth and ranking in the realm.

The ancients had maintained a population of fewer than three billion for more than 200,000 standard years. Their planet's lands and waters remained rich and well balanced with an abundance of renewable resources being managed as Nature did intend. Those of Mhu appeared settled in harmony with their world.

Except for their eyes, the ancients looked much like the Og. They had petite, hairless bodies and a similar median life span: some 438 years—a bit higher than the fourth-density norm. Set on rather long necks, the ancients' skulls were large with high foreheads and brows distinct but shallow. A small, thin-lipped mouth underscored an otherwise scant, twin-nostrilled nose. And their undersized ears lay flat just back from a slender, fragile jawbone.

Their skin was smooth, putty-like, and pale beige in color. Their eyes, at around two-thirds that of the Og's oversized, jet-black eyes, were a pupiless medium violet, but similarly almond-shaped. Like those from the motherworlds of Orion, most ancients stood less than three cubits tall, and their hands and feet featured six digits: six toes and six fingers—five, plus opposable thumb. All were tipped with tiny suction cups instead of claws or nails.

W ith his faithful scout in the lead, Lord Zhol dove through Mhu's early evening sky toward the ancients' capital, the crystal city of Lemurah.

High above the capital's core, the two Rohmans stopped to look upon its radiant, blue-green central plaza. They saw crystal fountains and sculptures, cushioned crystal benches and curving crystal walls all beautifully arranged on the plaza's rolling surface of interlocking, crystal cobblestones. A clear, multilevel maze housed a children's playground of crystal tubes and tunnels, slides, sandboxes and sandy-bottomed wading pools.

Pinning back up to a point some three standard miles above the plaza, Nordehk's Lord of the Orbits summoned his psychic powers and projected a brilliant apparition of The Master's mark outward from his compressed pinpoint of Sonlight. The plaza's billions of crystal facets instantly reflected the dazzling, golden, three-legged sign.

The demon held the spectacular form for several minutes. Then, letting the apparition linger in a slow dissipation of its highly condensed light, Zhol pinned to a crowd below and into a random citizen.

To the Overlord's delight, his victim resisted and launched a series of frantic telepathic calls. "Negative spirit, I forbid you entrance to my body! I forbid you to violate my free will! Bel ura Donai! Bel ura Donai! Bel ura Donai! *Bathe me in Prime Creator's light!*"

While Poxx rained a torrent of unheard curses and threats from above, Zhol rendered his defiant host unconscious, and then leered at the surrounding, bewildered crowd.

Recovering from their brief hesitation, those nearest the Overlord's victim rushed to their brother's defense, embracing him and resuming his telepathic forbiddances, chants and prayers. "Negative spirit we forbid you entrance to this body! You are not in harmony with the Light! Bel l'ura Donai! Bel l'ura Donai! Bel l'ura Donai! *Bathe us in Prime Creator's light!*"

With the power of his mind, the Son flung several feeble defenders a good twenty cubits. Then, clamping his host's left hand onto the head of a now kneeling, would-be rescuer who had ventured too close, Zhol outstretched his right arm and raged aloud.

"Behold the sign of Rehm! Behold the sign of changes!" Blood spewed from his victim's mouth as the demon shredded vocal cords that had been used for little more than gentle laughter.

In a sweeping, challenging gesture, the warrior pointed at the growing throng. "Be warned, *ancients* of Mhu!" he screamed, mocking their epithet.

Eyes a fiery red and face severely contorted, he bellowed, "Eleven times more, will His great sign appear over your mountains, over your oceans, over your temples and your homes.

"*Count!* And know you then!" The demon paused to glare a moment. "*Order* will come to Nordehk!"

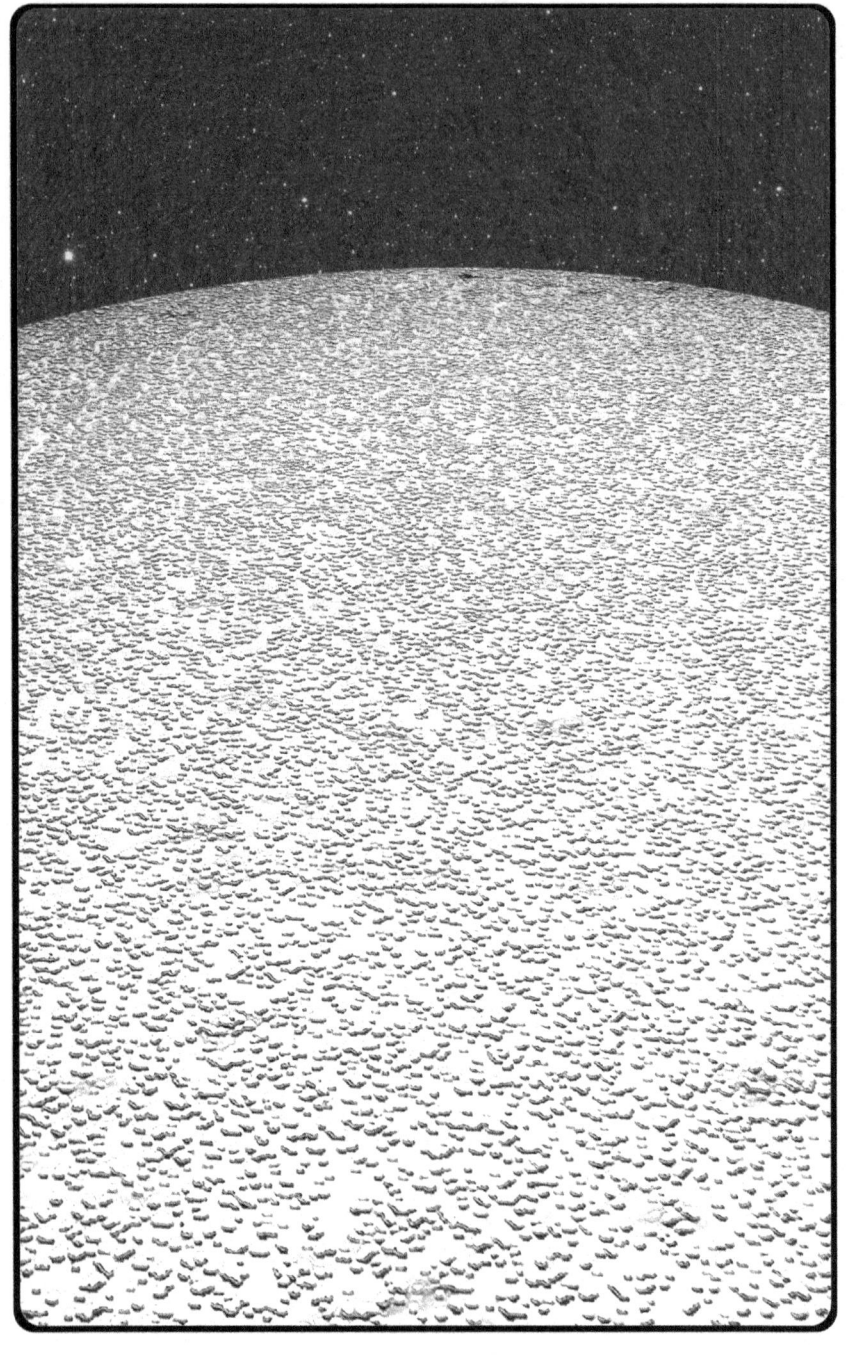

18

FACTORING THE FLIGHT

D-27.6: SPACE / PIRATES

Despite a persistent headache, Captain Narlihd managed to stop the tumbling and had repositioned and tethered his ship over the Varahn container's spine. Now, with seven hours until the warning shots' impact and forty-one until intercept, he imaged various scenarios.

Factoring escape velocities as low as 83% OMV, everything he ciphered looked good. To catch him, his pursuers would have to virtually abandon the convoy. And it was doubtful they would get KLC's authorization to raise their cannons again.

In the cruiser's engine room, Chief Luthur Poth had been maneuvering back and forth between the two coils, trying to monitor Radool's modifications to the primary while he and his crew worked to close the transen. With half the sleep of anyone else aboard, Poth resented Narlihd's call.

"How much longer, Chief?" the captain asked, more to maintain his pressure on Poth than anything else.

The chief hesitated. He knew he had four hours left but figured with the extra crew, he'd be done in three.

Shifty-eyed, Poth stuttered, "Ff…fff…. *Three*." He spat out the truth. Damn his fracken stuttering. "*Thhhree* more hours, Cap'n, and w..we'll be dd..dd.d..done."

SHAPING THE SETTLERS' MINDS

D-27.7: KHRAE / PATOS

"…and how, in your twilight years, do you picture the colony?" <u>Dr. Isdrav</u>[205] asked of the young Khraeling and Jakomen sons. "Has the original settlement branched out? If so, was the expansion a result of positive developments, or due to something else?"

The 110 settler-sons and mission alternates sat in the center front rows of Base 9's main lecture theatre, a facility twice the size of most KSF lecture halls and considerably more comfortable. Their three-month study of tribal evolution had begun.

Isdrav led them through an exercise in which, as Levah's elders, they were to look back at their accomplishments, and ahead to the future they were destined to create.

"Has your colony been progressing technologically? Spiritually? Who fully knows your tribe's true beginnings?" she pressed. "Do your heirs have only stories and a collection of deteriorating items you say were brought from distant stars?"

Behind their personal consoles, the sons struggled to keep up. Each entered what he could of his immediate reactions atop layered transcripts of the doctor's engrossing barrage.

"What difficulties do you see for surviving generations? What potential conflicts could arise? What mechanisms for resolution might you preinstall?"

Isdrav ran them through an assortment of intriguing scenarios until before long, they began to see that Levah's destiny would be shaped largely by their minds.

RICKY'S RECURRING DREAM
D-27.8: TERRAH

Ricky dreamed the same old dream he dreamt of now and then: of walking with some grown-ups through a kind of golden fog. The fog was always warm and bright, not wet or cold or dark. They strolled the same old path past the same old trees, and the same tame birds and animals came right up close to feed.

He liked this dream 'cause it always began with him as just a kid, kind of tagging along. And just like that he'd be all grown up too, and joking with the others and discussing serious stuff.... But nothing he could ever remember after waking up.

Oh, he'd try—especially the things they talked about, 'cause he knew it was important and it always seemed the same. But every time he just forgot until he dreamt it all again.

THAT DOUBTFUL ONE PERCENT
D-27.9: SPACE / PIRATES

With around five hours until the warning shots would hit, Luthur Poth and his crew finished closing the transen coil. His assistant and the others had completed their modifications to the primary, and were ready to close that big coil, too.

Lord Mohaar suddenly exited Enigg Radool and pinned to his destroyer.

Upon the demon's release, the enigg slumped unconscious over the main coil's field transducer. And with an unheard shriek, Iddh chased after the Rehman Son.

Fast back inside his reclined body in the vihmyana's systems bridge, Mohaar opened his nearly lidless, muddy-green eyes, and thought awhile. Since defecting from the passive Vihdæa, nothing had posed a serious challenge to his boundless abilities. But this assignment, this campaign—his first as a full-fledged Son, his first with *real* authority—would be his last should he overlook the obvious. Should he fail *to anticipate*.

Was there anything he had not considered and then reconsidered, and reconsidered again? Any oversight at all?

After a few more minutes of determined concentration, replaying his plan and its likely and lesser outcomes yet again, Lord Mohaar smiled. Absolutely nothing unforeseen flashed through the Son's highly active mind.

— ∘ ☼ ∘ —

At four hours to the warning shots' impact, all modifications to the operatives' coils were complete. The screws had stowed the unconscious Enigg Radool safely in sickbay, and Chief Poth called to advise Captain Narlihd that his engine was ready to wind.

"The c..coils are sealed and charged, C..Cap'n. We're good to go."

Narlihd just stared back.

"Sh…sh..she'll hold, Sir," Poth added, reassuringly. "Sh..she'll hold."

"Goddamn, Chief," the captain muttered in an unfamiliar tone. "You'd better be right." Then he made a general call to quarters to ready for acceleration.

"Tidy up and double-check the cargo, screws. Piss and do whatever else needs doin', 'cause we're in for a ride…" The captain looked at Poth in a subtle reminder that those modifications had better work. "…right, Chief?"

Nearly asleep in his flight seat, Chief Poth jerked as though he had dreamed Narlihd's voice. With bloodshot eyes he looked toward the nearest imaging field and saw the captain's blurry face waiting for an answer.

Suddenly wide awake, Luthur Poth felt 99% confident in the modifications. "Rrr..right, C..Cap'n." But as he thought about it, that doubtful one percent played fully on his mind.

AN UNLISTED SIGNATURE
D-27.10: SPACE / KSF ESCORTS

Pursuit leader Heln awoke with a start. Ihmoy's remscanner was signaling its detection of an engine signature. Then she received a call from her wingman, Lt. Yhurg, who had also been awakened by the RSU's alert. He had already reprogrammed the unit from one image per minute to constant scan. Heln called their squadron leader.

Ihmoy and the others quickly came in'field to monitor the suspects' surprisingly swift acceleration, and their engine's unusual print.

"The signature's unlisted, Major," stated Heln, "but it is a twin coil...I think...."

"Probably a new generation," suggested Yhurg.

"Gotta be," said one of the other flyers, "maybe experimental, which might explain their troubles."

With no time for a flat-out chase and no authority to fire a second volley, Ihmoy instructed his pursuit team to stay their course.

"Call me with another update in two hours—after my flyby with the Varahn convoy and before your warning shots strike."

Your warning shots? Captain Heln did not like the sound of that.

ROHMAN EYES

D-27.11: SPACE / PIRATES

The Jakomen cruiser, still electromagnetically tethered to the container's spine, continued to accelerate.

Unseen by Captain Narlihd or any of his crew, a shrouded vihmyana followed closely behind. Inside, in the destroyer's darkened systems bridge, Iddh cackled and cursed to himself while his glowing master, Mohaar, monitored the Khraeling flyers' conversation.

"Two hours, Major. After your flyby. Understood."

Several decks above the radiant Son, the vihmyana's priests and crew began gathering at some of the vihm's huge, deck-straddling viewports, as rumors of an alien ship quickly spread. Peering down at the Varahn container a few kilometers ahead and below, they speculated on what was going on, hesitant to wager just yet.

"That can't be a freighter," said one of the brothers.

"More like a barge of some sort," suggested another.

"Maybe. But what could it be carrying," asked one of the two Janah nearby,[206] "that could possibly interest us?"

OUTRUNNING THE KHRAELING PURSUERS

D-27.12: SPACE / PIRATES

Two hours later, the cruiser's modified coils were fully wound. Pahl

Radool was still unconscious in sickbay and all the screws were sound asleep. But their captain was wide awake at the helm, staring in amazement at layers of inconceivable data.

Firing a stream of flash-scans[G119c] and checking and rechecking his calibrations, he appeared to be cruising at 22% *over* maximum velocity. He was pulling away from the khraeks.

RECORDING RECORD SPEED

D-27.13: SPACE / KSF ESCORTS

Incredulous, the pursuit team watched the minuscule cruiser and its enormous Varahn container attain 122% OMV. Their imagers had been steadily adjusting the warning shots' impact time. In the last two hours it had changed from impact in less than three hours, to impact in seven. And the projected intercept time of 36 hours had become meaningless.

Pursuit leader Heln called Major Ihmoy a few minutes early.

"The jacks are on the move, Major," she reported. She understood how busy he would be, but knew this couldn't wait. "They're actually pulling away, Sir—cruising with coils fully wound…at 122% OMV."

Pulling away? At 122% OMV? With just six minutes to flyby, Ihmoy was fully focused on his flight path and on the convoy's swift, head-on approach. He had not been monitoring the RSU's images, and he quietly doubted Heln's claim. But before responding, he shuffled the layers in his imaging field so those from the remscanner rose to the top. And in seconds, the major clearly saw that the suspects were indeed outdistancing Heln and Yhurg—*at a staggering 122% OMV!*

"Maintain your heading and update KLC," Ihmoy ordered. "I'll have another look after flyby."

Then he hurriedly sent a private message on the bahdram frequency, the top-secret system reserved for extremely sensitive KSF communications. Pranol would want that engine.

FLYBY

D-27.14: SPACE / CONVOY

Mohaar and Iddh pinned into the nearby Varahn starship, and left their vihmyana to shadow the pirates on its own.

Inside the tug's forward observation deck, they found the delegates and the hundred settler-daughters. With the exception of the royal prince—the detached Og-incarnate sitting to one side—the Varahns stood together against the railings, chatting excitedly, too full of emotion to sit.

"Two minutes to flyby," the starship's main imager announced. "Switching to escort feed."

Well-versed in most Khraeling dialects, the Varahns hushed for the squadron leader's final count. The tug's decks dimmed to virtual darkness, and its forward running lights began flashing blue circles within blue circles, alternating inward from the tug's perimeter to the center of its spherical bow.

For the past three minutes, Major Ihmoy and his four wingmen flew in formation for their five-point flyby: two under, one to each side and one on top, all with cockpits turned inward.

"One minute to flyby."

Most of the daughters ooooh'd at the Khraeling voice and then fell silent again, eagerly awaiting the escorts' flyby. It had become a tradition, a ritual glimpsed by very few. The symbolic, deep-space welcoming and honoring of an arriving delegation.

"Locking aleph factors on three, two, one—mark."

"Two locked...." "Three locked...." "Four locked...." "Five locked...." Ihmoy's wingmen replied in series.

Lord Mohaar mind-scanned the incarnate prince, while his midwayer flittered invisibly from daughters to delegates and back, spewing a stream of unheard insults, curses and threats.

Sensing a powerful presence, Adahr shaJah stood and began looking around for what had to be a Rehman Son. Several of his delegates noticed and felt pleasant surprise at their prince's apparent interest in the ensuing, albeit rare, event.

"Forty-five seconds to flyby. Lotus check on three, two, one—mark."

"Two check." "Three check." "Four check." "Five check."

The prince determined the demon's general vicinity. Fixing his eyes upward on that spot, he suddenly jerked his head backward from the jarring force of instantaneously receiving his unquestionable instructions.

Despite their straining for a glimpse of the oncoming escorts, several delegates witnessed Adahr's strange convulsion. Those close at hand expressed their concern and offered to help ease him back into his seat. But with deepening dread, the shaken crusader-prince waved them off, bowed his royal head (and many delegates joined him in the obvious spiritual gesture), and silently pledged his heart to Rehm.

But with a key contact made and appropriate orders issued forthwith, Lord Mohaar had already returned to his destroyer. And once again, Major Ihmoy's voice reverberated through the prince's starship.

"Twenty seconds to flyby. Confirm go."

"Two go." "Three go." "Four go." "Five go."

"We are go for flyby, Your Highness," Ihmoy announced to his captivated crowd.

Outwardly collected, the humble prince sat down.

"Lights on three...." continued the squadron leader.

"Ten seconds. Nine, eight, seven, six, five, four and lights, two, one...."

The five brightly-lit Khraeling interceptors remained invisible to the Varahns until inside the count of "two," when they suddenly appeared out of the starry void and screamed past, ten kilometers above, below and to the tug's port and starboard sides.

With the escorts and convoy closing at a net velocity of 50% OMV— almost one-fourth the speed of light—the flyby occurred in the blink of an eye. None of the Varahns had blinked, however. Not even their prince, Adahr. And after a collective gasp and an unheard, joyful shriek from Iddh, the Varahns applauded and rejoiced.

The final leg of their long journey had begun.

Chapter 18 — N O T E S

N^{205} *Dr. Isdrav* ♀. Ashdah Isdrav, renowned Khraeling expert on tribal evolution.

N^{206} *the two Janah nearby.* The two that had volunteered two days before:

[from D-29.2, *BIRTHING THE FIRST VIHMYANA*] The destroyer hung among eleven other maturing vihms amid a tangle of thick umbilicals in the khoom's birthing tank. Beams of fire-like light streamed outward from the thin band of huge, deck-straddling viewports that ringed the ship's shallow crown. Farther down, the vihmyana's 144-man crew, which included two volunteers from the Janah, settled in for their unknown mission.

G^{119c} flash-scans: arcing bursts of invisible particles fired/flashed at 114.7 times the speed of light; a reverse-engineered, Varahn adaptation of the ancients' interstellar communications device, and a technology the Varahns later shared with their Jakomen friends

19

A FIRST LINE OE DEFENSE
D-27.15: VARAH

Since their forefathers' arrival some 73,000 standard years before current times, the Varahns had managed to maintain a spiritual focus. Although they experienced tribal skirmishes typical of any developing civilization, global warring had never occurred.

After venturing into space and discovering the ancients' frontier outpost, the Varahns solved its cryptic puzzle and were welcomed into the constellation family by Those of Mhu, as had the Khraelings before them. But unlike Those of Khrae, the humble Varahns were deeply disturbed to learn that a constantly warring, technologically advanced race of "cousins" lived a mere 4.3 light-years away (based on the Varahn year). The revelation, however, thoroughly united their kind.

As a prudent first line of defense, the Varahns managed, within five generations, to build and tow an outpost of their own into a position one light-year from home, along the direct route—the new trade route—to Khrae. Although nowhere near the size and sophistication of the ancients' marvelous constructs, the Varahns' manned outpost reliably monitored all approaching traffic, save the darkeyes' shrouded ships.

The Khraelings knew the outpost for what it was: an early warning station intended to detect a sneak attack. But they went along with the notion that it was just a "way station" for providing emergency services should any transport problems arise.

To augment their first line of defense, the Varahns gradually developed flash-scanning, an innovative technology they had shared only recently with their friends on New Hollatia. The accomplishment took centuries of painstaking effort, but their enduring fear of the Khraelings served as a powerful motivator.

First they produced and modified rough, but functional, copies of the communicator[207] they found in the ancients' frontier outpost. Then they doggedly adapted elements of that technology to their military's most advanced scanning equipment. After countless attempts, the Varahns finally succeeded in flashing arcing bursts of invisible particles at 114.7 times the speed of light, the same velocity at which the ancients' communications device fired its beaded messages to Mhu.

With an approximate range of three standard light-years, Varahn flash-scans were undetectable to distant targets. Although they lacked detail, the bursts' return images were sufficient to spot an invader's approach.

Ironically, the Khraelings knew that their sciences were of concern to their distant cousins, but never did they think the humble ones had machines more advanced than their own. Neither did they consider a campaign against the Varahns. Not even the Pagoreans so much as gave it a thought.

APHELIA'S LUNCHEON
D-27.16: SPACE / VARAH

As his vihmyana <u>raced toward Varah</u>,[208] a glowing Lord Wohtan lay livid in its darkened systems bridge. Responsible for Rehmanizing the prized elantah's humble ones, Wohtan remained furious that *in front of the Overlord*, those despicable darkeyes had dared express their strategic opinion. Whether the Varahns' inherent fear of the technologically advanced Khraelings represented "a state of <u>exploitable vulnerability</u>[209]" was *not* for servants to decide.

Having considered the obvious long before those loathsome sycophants, Wohtan felt greatly cheated. It had nothing to do with ambition. It was a matter of respect in the eyes of his fellow Sons. *It was purely a matter of pride.*

He would visit the Varahns and reassess his plan, after which he would see to it that GROUP COMMAND's presumptuous detestables would think twice before overstepping the bounds of their commission. He would ceremoniously settle the score.

Wohtan silently summoned Ænus, his trusty scout, and the two fast pinned to the Varahn way station. Inside the outpost's lone lit orb they found two young corpsmen monitoring the surrounding void. And in various sections of the station's much larger central hub, they found two others snacking in the mess, and two asleep in private quarters. Three more lay in hibernation, for a total of nine in all.

One by one, as the demon scanned their minds, those awake felt nothing more than a momentary sinking feeling and a fleeting numbness in their heads. All four corroborated the Varahn phobia, their deep fear and distrust of the Khraeling Federation. But for now, Wohtan would leave the corpsmen and their little station as he and Ænus continued on to the local star and the rare elantah, Varah, that orbited the system's gas giant, Taran-Tahk.

ShaJah was the Varahn capital and the royals' family name. The legislative cavveht held office in shaJah, and the monarchy resided on a modest estate that overlooked the picturesque capital city.

On the first day of alternate weeks 128 randomly selected citizens lunched with their queen, Aphelia, who believed in maintaining a strong bond with her subjects. All but her son, Prince Adahr, utterly adored Queen Aphelia—a secret that stayed between them.

One year in advance, citizens' names were drawn and keepsake notifications were sent: "It is Aphelia's delight to request the pleasure of your company at the palace...."

Beginning at daybreak, the queen's guests would arrive for light refreshments and a tour of the palace grounds. Then, upon the trumpeting of high noon, the 128 would go to a room designed for the occasion, or weather permitting, to a garden patio where they would take any seat at their assigned table.

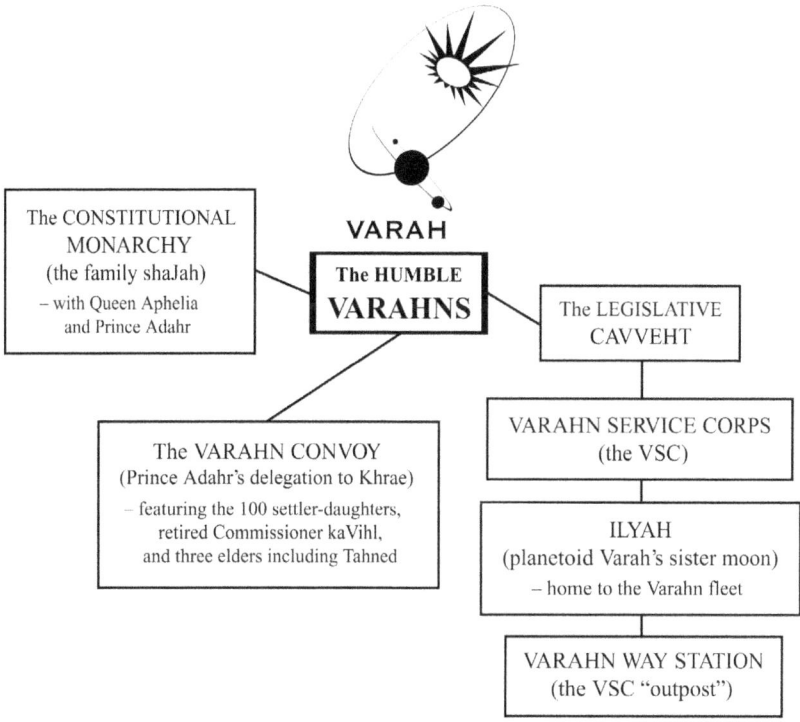

Whether indoors or out, the guests would find eight round tables arranged with seventeen elegant settings each. Unknown to the guests, Aphelia would take each table's unclaimed seventeenth seat, thereby enjoying one course of the eight-course meal at each table.

Lord Wohtan and his midwayer swooped into the estate's garden to find one of Aphelia's famous luncheons in progress. The scene looked the same as the Og depiction in the warrior's copy of the Og material transferred from Iiose's cruiser to the Overlord's khoomyahna five days before.

While Ænus ranted unheard, the warrior scanned several Varahns' minds. Without exception, whether just below the surface or buried in their subconscious, all were suppressing a genuine fear of their Khraeling cousins. *The Master's will be done.*

The Son pinned high into the sky, thought-formed a radiant Rǝhman insignia, and held it more than a minute that all of shaJah might see. Then Wohtan left the brilliant form to slowly wither while he returned to the royal garden and entered a guest sitting across from the queen.

The demon/guest hawked, spat and stood—his chair's legs skidding and screeching piercingly on the patio's white marble floor.

Such inconceivable behavior stunned Aphelia's guests. Ever-composed, however, the queen calmly asked, "Are you not wel...."

With a quick motion of his unconscious host's hand, the Son cut short Aphelia's words and then turned his eyes toward the advancing royal guards. All nine abruptly dropped to their knees.

The visitors and their servers were shocked. What could bring about such disrespectful behavior? And what had come over the royal guards?

The warrior returned to the bewildered Varahn monarch, raised his victim's arm and pointed to the sky—toward his lingering, thought-formed apparition.

"Behold The Master's mark!" he bellowed. "Behold the sign of Rǝhm, *and be warned!* Denizens will vanish! And chariots of the enemy will appear in star-filled skies!"

While most recoiled at the incredible depth and power of the offender's voice, Aphelia managed to steady herself. But a revealing smile remained frozen on her angelic face.

A golden light suddenly appeared and washed out the guests' view of the Rǝhman sign. With a shriek, Ænus unleashed a barrage of insults and obscenities at what had to be an intruder from Nordehk's Vihdæa.

The Vihdæan—Bel—ignored the midwayer, and silently addressed the Rǝhman Son so none but Wohtan would hear.

"Brother, dear. Your deeds are known. Be not lost in darkness when The

Great Light so abounds." Then both she and her light were gone.

Humored, Wohtan flared his luminescence. And though fading, the Rehman sign returned.

"Eleven times more," he snarled, face glowing, eyes wide and burning with abhorrence for the pathetic weaklings, "behold His sign, and know!"

Know?

The Son just stood there sneering and leering, before adding, "The *betrayal* then, draws nigh!"

ᚱ

A GIFT FOR THE MARSHALL
D-27.17: KHRAE / PATOS

Marshall Pranol was standing in his office, a modest windowless room of mostly lunar stone. His vice marshall, Jehrmi Brohjal, sat near him along with two other senior officers from the KSF. The four were watching a decoded replay of Major Ihmoy's private message. The squadron leader's face filled Pranol's imaging field.

"...at 122.216% OMV with coils fully wound."

They had already studied an earlier transmission from Ihmoy's pursuit leader, which included images that confirmed the target's speed.

Turning his back to the others and folding his arms across his chest, the marshall chose to state the obvious. "This, gentlemen, represents a quantum leap over the current ceiling."

The others said nothing. The implications were clear.

"I want that ship disabled, Jehrmi, while it's still in range of the pursuit team's cannons. Ihmoy is waiting for my approval. Send your congratulations on his flyby and include a reminder that my birthday coincides with his arrival back on Patos. He'll understand. He'll take it from there."

"Yes, Sir. But what about the governor, Marshall?" Brohjal asked, with a facial expression that made clear his devotion to Pranol, but which also displayed his political concerns. "We'll need joint authority for another round of fire, especially one adequate to disable that ship."

"Just get me that engine, Vice Marshall," Pranol turned and said with a resolute scowl. "I'll handle Haleahm and he'll handle Mauhk."

IN THE DEMON'S GRASP
D-27.18: SPACE / PIRATES

With warning bolts bearing down on their target, Lord Mohaar eased his shrouded vihmyana into position over the Varahn container and fired a small, stealthy device through its lightly shielded hull.

The Son watched it slip through without resistance, and then he snared the Jakomen cruiser and shut its systems down. Captain Narlihd's electromagnetic anchors immediately relaxed their grip on the container's spine.

Next, Mohaar wrapped the cruiser in his shroud, gently plucked the tiny ship off the huge container's back, and drew it in close to his destroyer.

— ◦ ☼ ◦ —

Narlihd cursed. His main systems were dead. He had emergency power, but not enough to stop his coils' slow tangential discharge of the engine's energy stream.

— ◦ ☼ ◦ —

Luthur Poth's eyes sprang open to the sickening whine of both coils winding down. The chief unstrapped his harness, jumped to his feet and dove into a diagnostic check that confirmed an inexplicable, catastrophic loss of power. Yet the ship had full gravity. *Weird.*

— ◦ ☼ ◦ —

The screws began stirring. A few looked out the cruiser's windows in time to see their booty sailing slowly away.

"Captain," one of them called out.

Narlihd did not respond.

"Sir? You might want to have a look at this."

90 SECONDS TO IMPACT
D-27.19: SPACE / PURSUIT TEAM

Pursuit leader Heln tracked the warning shots' final 90-second race toward impact. She had seen it before. They would hit and be absorbed by the target's shielding, but their message would be clear.

Heln suddenly lost the pirates' engine print. She checked the RSU's images and could not see the suspect ship. Maybe the cruiser had rolled over, out of the remscanner's view. *But what would be the point?*

She reversed and replayed the images. And there it sat: glued to the container's back and stable at 122% OMV. Then it just…disappeared.

Heln shook her head, reloaded the images and played them one more time. There it sat—the suspect ship, clamped onto the container's spine. And then the spine was clean.

POLITICS AT PLAY

D-27.20: SPACE / KSF ESCORTS

Four and a half hours into his rollback dive for docking with the Varahn tug, all the squadron leader could think about was the jacks' amazing engine. Considering the governor and the festival and all the politics at play, Ihmoy felt uncertain about how far Pranol could go, or would go, to get it. But nothing was stopping the major from taking independent action, from having his pursuit team disable the ship and tow it back to base. And while the Aggah ranted, the KSF would copy the engine, and that would be that. Either way, Major Vihlkin Ihmoy would take the fall.

The more he thought about it, the more he realized it had to be done. Pranol would look after him, if the governor didn't demand an execution.

"Major." The pursuit leader unfolded in'field. "Check the remscanner's images, Sir. The cruiser disappeared."

Disappeared? Ihmoy pulled up the images and squinted. The Jakomen were gone.

"Key the layer to J5^{D}403, Major. That's 92 seconds before impact and 4 seconds before she vanishes."

Ihmoy found and replayed the images, and there it was—the pirates' cruiser…and three, two, one—the jacks were gone.

WAITING FOR THE HIT

D-27.21: SPACE / CONVOY

Although the prince and a few others had returned to quarters after their escorts' flyby, the majority of Varahn delegates went to the tug's main lounge to monitor the warning shots' final approach.

Many noted the abrupt loss of the Jakomen's engine signature. But with ten seconds to go, most grimaced and turned away from the room's considerable imaging field as the blue-white beams closed in on their target like twin bolts of focused lightning.

Precisely at the moment of impact, the starship's ample lounge lit up. Those who had looked away, turned back in time to see a gigantic ball of fire.

IHMOY'S SHAME

D-27.22: SPACE / KSF ESCORTS

Ihmoy's pursuit team—Yhurg and Heln—watched in horror as the fireball suddenly imploded, and then roared back a hundred times larger before vanishing completely from view.

"Major!" yelled Captain Heln. "Did you see that?!"

Ihmoy saw and felt an uncommonly deep chill. As he had feared, a bad situation had become much, much worse. And as escort squadron leader, no one could be blamed but him.

A PLEDGE, A PRAYER, AND DISBELIEF
D-27.23: SPACE / CONVOY

Prince Adahr lay alone in his quarters, unaware of the container's destruction. He suddenly sensed a potent presence. Again.

The crusader sat up, stood and homed in on a powerfully negative force near a corner of his room. And that corner filled with a sudden illumination, completely free of physical form.

"Bhuvana.... Ang Kaht."

Bhuvana? Sarcastic and filled with loathing, this was surely a Rehman Son. But a different one...a second one. Much more hateful than the first.

Adahr dropped to his knees and silently replied, "By your radiance, my Lord...."

"Wohtan—Son of Rehm!" thundered the demon-Son. Unseen and unheard, Ænus shrieked and howled above.

"By your radiance, my Lord...Wohtan," the incarnate begged, raising both hands. "I swear my allegiance! I pledge m...."

As had happened on the starship's observation deck <u>mere hours before</u>,[210] the prince jerked back and nearly lost his balance. And once again—in an instant, clear and concise—the incarnate prince received this second Son's, this *hateful* one's, unquestionable instructions.

— ∘ ☼ ∘ —

Piloting itself and cruising far beyond light speed but still several days from its destination, Lord Wohtan's destroyer shot smoothly through one of Nordehk's interstellar way portals toward Varah's sun.

Meanwhile, having served the humble ones' first notice at Aphelia's luncheon, Wohtan and Ænus pinned into the Overlord's khoomyahna, and directly down to the depths of its priestly rectory.

After <u>the netherbeast's first lessons</u>,[211] Vakaar had slipped away with Dehniss and Phobb, leaving the session's surviving brawnies to tend to their own wounds and to honorably dispose of their slain brothers. Later, after cremating the nobly-fallen, others of the priesthood returned to the rectory's secret chamber to wash it, and then clean and reasonably reconstruct the nethercreature's mangled body, which now lay cold but largely intact inside its dark-bluish, light-filled pod.

Once back inside the darkened chamber, Ænus hovered watchfully above the beast's softly glowing pod while Lord Wohtan reentered his precious creation.

Fast into a deeply meditative state, the Son summoned and soon began absorbing The Master's potent vigor…and the electrifying spark of life came forth, and the healing then began.

And the intense pain from those dreadful wounds became sharp and fresh again. And Lord Wohtan's wantful suffering, for a time, would be appeased.

Adahr's fellow delegates were abuzz in a telepathic flurry of conjectures, misgivings and fears. What were the Khraelings doing? Had they intended to destroy the container all along? And the Jakomen operatives with it? *Did this prelude another war?*

Major Ihmoy called the Varahns, unsure of how to begin or even what to say. His speechless image soon filled their imaging fields, layered atop empty space.

From all their distraught faces, Ihmoy knew the humble ones had been monitoring the situation and had witnessed the impact and explosion. He saw Commissioner kaVihl in the crowd, but thankfully, not the Varahn prince.

"Commissioner…delegates. I…uh…the intensity of those warning shots was far too low to have penetrated your container's shielding." Uncharacteristically blurting the sentence, Ihmoy captured everyone's undivided attention.

"I honestly have no idea what could have caused such an enormous blast," he added much more calmly, and with unrehearsed sincerity.

Several of the Varahns nodded politely in support. They heard truthfulness in the major's voice and saw no deception in his face. And they *wanted* to believe him.

"Strangely, 88 seconds before the explosion, the vessel's engine print abruptly disappeared." If ever Ihmoy had prayed, he prayed now that the Varahns had also registered the signature's loss.

"We confirm your observation, Major," replied Commissioner kaVihl, sensing with the other delegates the squadron leader's great relief.

"Thank you, Commissioner," said Ihmoy before realizing that may have sounded inappropriate. "The relevant images," he quickly added, "have already been forwarded for analysis to Khrae Lunar Command."

The major then confirmed that he and his four wingmen would dock "in 31.4 hours." And in an awkward silence, he ended his awkward call.

A TRAITOR IN THE SHIP

D-27.24: SPACE / PIRATES

Conscious now in his sickbay bed, Pahl Radool lay with a splitting headache and no memory of how he had bumped his head. His harness was cinched down way too tight, and he could barely breathe. In the frustration of it all, he felt prickly—from his pounding temples to the toes of his sweaty, calloused feet.

With a jolt, Lord Mohaar re-entered him, reknocking Radool unconscious. Telekinetically, the demon sprung the harness's release and then whipped off the enigg's blanket, sat him up and swung his legs over a side of the bed. And as one with the young operative, he headed for the helm.

— ○ ☼ ○ —

The captain's screws were deeply confused: their engine was dead but they had full gravity.

In a low voice, almost a whisper lest the KSF be listening, one of them theorized, "The khraeks must have developed a new technology to snare us like this."

"Qah, but why blow the container?" replied another, angrily, and caring not who else might hear. "It doesn't make sense!"

Determined to keep everyone busy while he sorted things out, Captain Narlihd assigned six screws to Chief Poth along with a mandate to restart the coils. A few more returned to the communications room where an eerie silence pervaded all frequencies. The others cleaned their ship and changed the last of its rancid air filters. None paid much attention to the near-naked enigg as he strode by.

The captain sensed someone watching. He turned to see Radool wearing only underwear and an inappropriate—*insubordinate*—smirk.

"Are we feeling better, Enigg? It would seem your coils aren't doing so w...." Narlihd froze in mid-sentence as a powerful voice all but shattered his mind.

"Summon your crew, Captain."

Upon a sudden, sickening dizziness and an intense pain in his brain, Captain Narlihd lost all will to resist.

— ○ ☼ ○ —

The dejected Jakomen operatives turned hopefully toward the nearest imagers as their captain called for all eyes up. But the captain did not look his usual, confident self. And when the enigg stepped in front of him and began speaking, an ominous feeling befell them all.

"The time for liberty is upon us. The time for our proud people's prosperity is at hand."

Liberty? Prosperity? Radool's voice sounded completely unfamiliar. Powerful. Commanding. Compelling.

"Bear witness! dear ones. *Bear witness!* dear friends. To the dawning of a new age."

Dear ones? New age? What the hell was he saying? Had the soft-spoken design engineer been fooling them all along? Was Radool a traitor who had sold them out to the khraeks?

"In twelve minutes," the enigg continued, "a 30-second acceleration sequence will commence. Since this little ship is relatively unshielded, we may experience some discomfort."

Little ship? This was an <u>NHD</u>^{G249d} transport-cruiser, 220 meters stem to stern! *Relatively unshielded?* What the hell was he talking about?

"Outside, attached to our hull near the main airlock, you will find a small crimson chest. After completion of the sequence, send someone dressed in full gear to retrieve it. The chest is of far greater value to our people than any Varahn container."

A piddling chest of greater value than a maxed out amstrahd-class container? If Radool wasn't a traitor then that bump to his head had caused more than surface damage.

Mohaar/Radool turned to Captain Narlihd. "Heed my message, Captain," he said, "for we shall soon be upon New Hollatia." The demon then exited his host, who dropped unconscious to the floor.

The screws stared at their captain's image staring down at the enigg's crumpled frame. And they all wondered the same thing. *What had Radool meant about being upon New Hollatia soon?* Even at 122% OMV—*if* they could rewind the coils—their world was a good three months away.

Narlihd suddenly called for someone to come up and take the enigg back to sickbay. "Strap him down and lock him in," he ordered. "The rest of you fasten up. Tightly and quickly."

Two screws rushed Radool away, hurried back to their flight seats and waited with the rest for the supposed acceleration.

— ∘ ☼ ∘ —

After several minutes of diminishing expectations, the screws began rolling their eyes and shrugging at each other. Then their bodies began pressing into their seats, and they heard stacks of Varahn commodities tearing loose inside their hold.

One by one, under the tremendous force of Mohaar's keen acceleration, the operatives blacked out. And their cruiser, as though by some measured dynamic force, moved up to and passed right through a shimmering section of the destroyer's scaly hull.

Seconds later, the Rehman Son's great vihmyana lunged into a nearby arterial portal that tapped New Hollatia's yellow sun.

Chapter 19 — N O T E S

N²⁰⁷ *the communicator.* The device revealed upon solving the ancients' techno-puzzle:

> [from D-28.9, *THE ANCIENTS AND THEIR BROOD*] The ancients knew that a surviving colony would eventually launch probes into space, and that it would only be a matter of time before their stellar station/outpost, at just one light-year away, would be found. And with it, the machine-like technopuzzle they had left.
>
> Both the Khraelings and Varahns found and solved the puzzle. Their uniquely different efforts succeeded in awakening the device into triggering a transmission, a signal back to Mhu that alerted the ancients to each extremely exciting achievement. The mechanism revealed was a communicator that beaded, aimed and flashed its messages in 10-second bursts at 114.7 times light speed: the universal telepathic ceiling (the conductivity speed of dark matter) and rather surprising example of Mhu's formidable accomplishments. With the exception of this gift—copied rather well by the Khraelings in 40 years, and adequately by the Varahns in 900—the ancients respectfully and unwaveringly refused to share other technowonders with their brood.

N²⁰⁸ *raced for Varah.* Having left its mothership (the khoomyahna) the day before:

> [from D-28.11, *THE SONS PROCEED*] Comfortably reclined in the khoomyahna's systems bridge, and with the Lords Dhanz and Wohtan piloting the two departing vihmyanas, Zhol reopened the warship's stellar program and zoomed in on the ancients' ninth seed.

N²⁰⁹ *exploitable vulnerability.* As expressed by Group Commander Iiose during his formal briefing of the Sons on Day -32:

> [from D-32.7, *HOSTING THE DEMON SONS*] "Having focused on spiritual advances, Varah's inhabitants, technologically, have fallen behind their later-settled cousins—those of Khrae, the second of the ancient's brood. Most notably, the Varahns' subsequent awareness and inherent fear of their distant neighbor-cousins may represent a state of exploitable vulnerability."
>
> The second junior grunted and briefly but noticeably brightened. The demon inside—Lord Wohtan—bore responsibility for bringing Varah into the fold. He knew well the Varahns' vulnerabilities, including their inherent fear of their not-so-distant neighbors, the technologically advanced Khraelings. Long had the Son formulated a plan of action to seal the Varahns' fate. The *audacity* of this presumptuous little Og commander to overstate the obvious

and to dare presume credit for Lord Wohtan's perfect plan.... Such insubordination would *not* go unpunished—not in the Overlord's eyes, nor in the eyes of Rohm.

N[210] *mere hours before.* During Major Ihmoy's flyby:

[from D-27.14, *FLYBY*] Sensing a powerful presence, Adahr shaJah stood and began looking around for what had to be a Rohman Son. Several of his delegates noticed and felt pleasant surprise at their prince's apparent interest in the ensuing, albeit rare, event.

"Forty-five seconds to flyby. Lotus check on three, two, one—mark."
"Two check." "Three check." "Four check." "Five check."

The prince determined the demon's general vicinity. Fixing his eyes upward on that spot, he suddenly jerked his head backward from the jarring force of instantaneously receiving his unquestionable instructions.

Despite their straining for a glimpse of the oncoming escorts, several delegates witnessed Adahr's strange convulsion. Those close at hand expressed their concern and offered to help ease him back into his seat. But with deepening dread, the shaken crusader-prince waved them off, bowed his royal head (and many delegates joined him in the obvious spiritual gesture), and silently pledged his heart to Rohm.

N[211] *the netherbeast's first lessons.* On Day -30:

[from D-30.7, *PRIESTLY CONTRIVANCES*] Deep in the rectory's bowels, the yamah's two cohorts, Dehniss and Phobb, and nine of the khoom's brawniest young priests lounged half-naked, greasing one another. A creature of darkness would soon be summoned. For its lessons. For its study in fleshly pain.

G[249d] NHD: New Hollatian Defense; the global police, security force and defenders of New Hollatia

20

TRADITIONAL BOUNDS
D-27.25: NORDEHK

Nordehk's eight Vihdæa met at their sky-blue roundtable. Their golden self-illumination amplified the surrounding ethereal garden's morning mist.

Aware that the first notice of Rɵhm's coming had been served on Terrah, Varah and Mhu, the administrators knew that the Sons would deliver but eleven more such warnings. All eight were still reflecting on the oraph Hyynehk's cryptic words[212] about prevailing, and about willful defections, and things long written, and extreme polarities. And about working together, *"that triumph be assured."*

Most believed that the mysterious messenger had subtly imparted an invocation on behalf of the Most Highs, Ohrvon's 127 Universal Sons. But the manner of Hyynehk's presentation gave no indication of the means by which their council would or could "prevail."

Bel felt an intuitive urge to approach their esteemed neighbors, the Vihdæan Council of the adjacent Lazrehk constellation. But for what purpose, remained unclear.

Jaylah, current chief of Nordehk's council, was reluctant to step beyond traditional bounds. He also thought his compatriots were reading too much into the divine messenger's words.

"Together," he proffered, "let us probe The Infinite Mind. Here and now—*together.*"

GOOD TIMES, BAD TIMES
D-27.26: TERRAH

Oftentimes when things got rough and his mom got sad and had enough, young Ricky tidied up and cooked, and read his mom her favorite book.

She liked the one about the mouse who tricked the cat that ruled the house. It made her smile and shake her head, and *eventually* she'd get out of bed. And when she did she'd take her "little man" out for like a really manly treat—like steak and eggs and toast and jam, and a super creamy latte.

No one ever came around to help out when his mom felt down. But

Ricky was okay with that 'cause he liked to do grown-up stuff and pretend like he was twenty. So mostly he'd just let her be—for a day or two, or maybe three.

And when she got back on her feet and rested up from all that sleep, things would be quite good again, for a while.

A SKEPTICAL COUNSEL-RA
D-27.27: KHRAE

"…appraised at around eleven parells: the equivalent of a small nuclear blast."

Marshall Pranol was reporting the container's destruction to an anxious governor and a leery Counsel-Ra.

"I expect KLC's full analysis within 18 hours."

Gjadren Mauhk closed his eyes. "And the Jakomen, Mannon?"

"Around 38 hours before the pursuit team's projected intercept," the marshall replied, "the suspects initiated a two-hour acceleration that peaked at 122% OMV."

The governor's eyes sprang open.

"They sustained that velocity until roughly four hours later, when—just moments before the warning shots struck—the Jakomen ship abruptly disappeared."

Disappeared? Haleahm looked skeptical. Mauhk appeared to be weighing the consequences.

THE OPERATIVES' RELEASE
D-27.28: SPACE / NEW HOLLATIA

Lord Mohaar held his racing vihmyana steady in the boiling portal's churning core until he'd overshot the Khrae/New Hollatian system by more than a billion Rohman miles. Then he emerged from the cosmic highway, shrouded his ship and doubled back toward Khrae and New Hollatia—in a heading now *opposite* that of the Varahn star.

A short time later, he cut his velocity to 54.863% of light speed and eased the Jakomen cruiser out through a sublimated section of his destroyer's cooling hull. Then he sent his trusty midwayer, Iddh, on a mission related to his nearly settled plan.

$$- \circ \; \text{☼} \; \circ -$$

Unlike the grueling acceleration of a few hours ago, the first operatives to regain consciousness did not feel the destroyer's deceleration, as the Son had purposefully buffered their little ship. But with all systems restored and coils fully wound, their ship's navigational bar reciphered and then announced their new location.

Captain Narlihd squeezed the sleep from his eyes, looked into his imaging field, and softly uttered, "Impossible."

THE NECESSARY QUORUM
D-27.29: NEW HOLLATIA

Operators of the ever vigilant New Hollatian Defense quickly detected a fully shielded vessel's swift approach—with cannons raised, and velocity…122% OMV! *More than half the speed of light!*

They sounded a broad alert and launched a squadron to engage.

Deep beneath the Aggah's compound, two of the NHD's ten generals directed a very busy war room. An array of large imagers systematically blinked layer after layer of scans, zooming images of the space around New Hollatia, images of the intruder and of Khrae, and fuzzy close-ups of distant Patos and Khrae Lunar Command. How had an invader eluded their web? Except for the ship's unknown engine signature, it bore all the indicators of an NHD cruiser modified for special operations.

General Qaloov arrived, spotted his two subordinate generals and signaled them aside for a private huddle. As the NHD's ranking general, Qaloov had already been briefed.

The two hurried to him, snapped to attention, saluted and clicked their heels together. The seniormost promptly whispered a hypothesis—nervously, but with professional deliberation.

"General. One of our cruisers could have been captured and placed as a *decoy*…" She dragged out the word. "…the lead ship of a Khraeling armada."

Qaloov could not risk time second guessing. If the intruder had so suddenly appeared from the emptiness of space, then so too could an attacking armada. The Aggah need not be consulted while precious seconds passed by. He and these two generals comprised the necessary quorum to unleash New Hollatia's entire military might.

"Launch," Qaloov ordered, calmly and without further deliberation, "in accordance with the D-plan."

Less than a minute later, dozens, then hundreds, and then thousands of ships erupted from the New Hollatian planet and its moon. At virtually the same time, the Jakomen's top secret Second Wave—an elite fleet concealed on the moons of Ubahr[213]—scrambled to the ready and began directing an independent series of undetectable flash-scans toward Khrae.

BACKS TO THE BOW
D-27.30: SPACE / PIRATES

All of Narlihd's screws were wide awake and battle ready. "Six fighters on the reibar, Captain," shouted one. "Two destroyers not far behind," yelled another.

Narlihd retracted his cannons and barked out an order to brace for full repulsion. Then he hailed the NHD and initiated the dreaded sequence for a full stop.

Flight seats locked and erect, backs to the bow, the operatives watched images of thousands of ships fanning out from New Hollatia. It looked like the first phase of the D-plan, the NHD's long-planned response to the long-feared Khraeling invasion.

Narlihd scanned astern. Nothing but empty space.

RESPONDING TO THE THREAT
D-27.31: KHRAE / PATOS

Khrae Lunar Command detected an unidentified object racing toward New Hollatia from well within the Bool-Dahr, the sun-sized territory that encompassed the Jakomen's homeland. Claimed by the Jakomen as a sovereign defensive zone since the Exodus, the Federation respected the area. Even their commercial ships steered clear.

To KLC's astonishment, the object's velocity was 122% OMV, and its shape and engine signature seemed identical to the suspect ship scanned near the Varahn convoy a few hours before. Minutes later they witnessed the NHD's massive launch and immediately made ready to respond in kind.

Battalions on maneuvers froze operations and awaited further instructions. From shuttles to carriers, all other KSF traffic began assembling in preassigned formations mostly below ground.

Compared to the beehive of activity around New Hollatia, the space around Khrae fell eerily silent. Like a hair-trigger, fully cocked.

THE FRAGRANT AGGAH BOOD
D-27.32: NEW HOLLATIA

Qahlona, New Hollatia's capital, had been built around the entrance to a

cavern that led to an underground hotspring and an expanse of deepening passages, warm pools and small lakes. Discovered during the Great Exodus, the cave and its hidden secrets served to relieve the Jakomen's hardships while they struggled to resurrect themselves on their marginally terra-formed new world.

A labyrinth of complexes covered Qahlona's eastern sector and formed the Aggah's compound, an interconnected maze of low-lying stone structures with ten to fifty sublevels of ultra-modern facilities for the government and for the headquarters of the New Hollatian Defense. Into one of these sublevels, the one housing the circular war room where the three generals and dozens of other officers and staff coordinated the counteroffensive, the Aggah Bood and six of her fit, female aides marched in.

The generals jumped to attention. Qaloov clicked his heels and saluted smartly. Properly but nervously, the two others returned to their tasks.

Unah Bood was a rather short but intimidating presence who dressed in a military fashion of her own design. Now and then she wore earthen tones that complimented her fair complexion and bright, naturally reddish-orange hair. But she preferred, and this day wore, black and dark-blue fabric trimmed with stripes of primary red. Her similarly matched boots and gloves had been cut and stitched from strong, but thin and supple, synthetic hide. A thick mat of tight curls filled her skull's deep crease, a mat she liked to coax up and trim perfectly square and flat on top. She shaved the back of her heavily freckled neck daily and kept her bright reddish-orange hair cropped short on the left side to proudly expose her deformed left ear—that her Dahanan lineage be ever on display.

Bood ignored Qaloov's salute while her pale-green eyes panned the array of images framing the room. Her muscular aides stood rigidly "at ease," hands behind their backs, six abreast behind her.

With no sign of Khraeling ships, the Aggah issued a marginal, reciprocal salute and demanded, "Where is this armada, General? Show it to me. Now."

From the moment she stepped into the room, Bood's delicate perfume began wafting through the air. Deliciously intoxicating, its formula had been reserved for her alone and could only be sampled by discreetly sniffing the air whenever she was near.

"We have only the suspected decoy, the lead ship in view, my Aggah," Qaloov replied, turning down the corners of his mouth in a clever bid to imply confidence, while masking an irresistible sniff with a quick inhale through his nostril. "It is within the Bool-Dahr and registered 122% OMV upon detection. Its engine signature is unlisted."

"Impossible," Bood snapped. "Show me."

With a flick of his hand, Qaloov had one of the war room's operators zoom the cruiser's image. Its weapons were disengaged and its velocity was 16% OMV and falling rapidly in an obvious full repulsion.

"From where has it come? Tell me."

Busy but straining to eavesdrop from their stations, the room's two other generals glanced at each other, glad not to be in Qaloov's boots.

"From nowhere, my Aggah," Qaloov replied, matter-of-factly. "It appeared suddenly, and at half light speed."

"Impossible. Replay your first images. Now."

After impatiently watching five seconds of replays, the Aggah pointed to the second general and then to the third a few meters away. She knew both had been watching her reflection while they worked. Then she pointed to Qaloov.

"I want that ship. I want that crew. I want that engine. Intact. See to it. Now."

"Qah, my Aggah," said Qaloov with another smart click of his heels. "You shall have it—them." And with his signal, an underling quickly left the room.

"Forgive me, my Aggah," a controller interrupted, turning from his station. "The intruder has hailed us, General. Their codes are special operations. The, uh…the rendezvous with the Varahn convoy."

"The Varahn convoy…" Bood said slowly, softly and sarcastically before screaming, "…*that* mission is a hundred days out! *This* ship approaches from the opposite direction!

"I want to see the armada," she said more quietly, but firmly. "Now. Show me the armada."

"My Aggah…" Qaloov knew he was in trouble. "…the solo intruder's sudden appearance, unprecedented velocity and unknown engine signature, qualified it as…."

Bood cut him off and moved a step closer toward the much taller and wider General Qaloov. "If an armada had this lone ship's capability and were poised to attack, would the Khraelings tip their hat? Has history not taught us to expect quite the contrary[214]?

"Recall the fleet." If nothing else, the action would give the Federation something to think about. "Now."

"Qah, my Agg…."

"I shall expect a full report on my desk first thing in the morning," she continued. "It will include the estimated cost of your profligate exercise, and the reaction we can expect from the KSF." Bood headed for the door, and added, "Have that ship escorted to the compound and its captain brought before me."

Clicking his heels again, General Qaloov saluted, "Qah, my Aggah," thankful he had launched just half the fleet.

THE MARSHALL TAKES CONTROL
D-27.33: KHRAE

A suspicious Raund Haleahm and a shaken Gjadren Mauhk watched recorded images of the astounding action around New Hollatia. First, the sudden *materialization* of another transport-cruiser that boasted the new coils, and then what had to be the enormously expensive exercise of briefly scrambling and recalling what might well have been the NHD's entire fleet.

"What are we to make of all this, Marshall?" asked Mauhk's wary Counsel-Ra.

Pranol was pacing in front of his imager, mind racing while he waited for the last of his staff to join him and Vice Marshall Brohjal in'field. If the *KSF* had developed that engine along with an ability to conceal their ships, and if the *KSF* had flaunted those achievements so brazenly, it would surely have struck terror into every Jakomen's heart.

Seeing that Pranol's mind was churning, Brohjal responded to Haleahm's question.

"There is a possibility, Counsel, that the 'materialization' in the Bool-Dahr was nothing more than a vessel testing a new generation of scanning foilers. It would, however, be foolhardy not to assume the worst. We shall therefore maintain a prelaunch alert while we evaluate developments."

"Yes, thank you, Jehrmi," said the marshall cutting in. "At the moment, we don't have anything conclusive, gentlemen. Allow us some time to get back to you."

COMPOUNDING THE SUSPICION
D-27.34: SPACE / NEW HOLLATIA

The repulsion's worst was over, but it remained a bad situation for Captain Narlihd and his crew. Most of the screws lay unconscious. The NHD had acknowledged his codes, but now they wanted to know if there was a problem with his ship.

Even without the repulsion's effects on his mind, Narlihd couldn't think straight and did not know where to begin. Unable to answer coherently, he found himself stammering, and his babbling served only to create more suspicion.

While his systems blared dire warnings of imminent doom, two NHD fighters curled around beneath him and four others shaved his hull. Worse, two slowly spinning destroyers lay bristling dead ahead.

AN IMPROBABLE STEPPING STONE
D-27.35: SPACE / NEW HOLLATIA

Comfortably reclined inside his vihmyana's systems bridge, an entertained Lord Mohaar monitored the Khraelings' KSF monitoring the Jakomen's NHD.

Above deck, among the dozens of curious bahva peering through the viewports of the Son's shrouded ship, the two Janah aboard watched the Jakomen fleet swarm home. Staring up at the painted planet, they wondered in whispers whether this world could be freedom's stepping stone.

An odd twinkle of sunlight reflected off negligible collections of water. Cloud cover was minimal, meager ice caps covered its poles, and small patches of green were scattered here and there on a pink and creamy, mostly yellow surface.

One of the anarchists shook her head and whispered to the other, "It looks like a difficult place to survive."

Chapter 20 — N O T E S

N²¹² *Hyynehk's cryptic words.* As delivered on Day -30 about prevailing, and about willful defections, and things long written, and extreme polarities. And about working together, *"that triumph be assured"*:

[from D-30.5, *THE MYSTERIOUS MESSENGER*] "Rɵhm wants nothing tangible. It is the *power*. It is his mastery over the potent vibrations of fear and loathing, and especially the procession of etherean defections—his cherished, willing recruits—that sustain The Fallen One.

"With each new negatively-polarized defector—one who chooses to abandon the Light, whether a seraph, midwayer, Vihdæan, or will-creature—there is a discernible empowering of those above, an exponential accumulation of power whereby those at the top of the Rɵhman hierarchy benefit most. Similarly, with every conquest and conversion en masse of more billions of evolving beings, 'Prime Crusader's' powers substantially increase."

— ∘ ☼ ∘ —

[and moments later] "Feeding on fear and ruling through intimidation, Rɵhm's methods vary greatly and he exhibits a vast spectrum of creative destruction on his journey through the night. His 'Sons,' fallen Vihdæan sisters and brothers themselves, are powerful and serve him well. But so is it written and long known to us oraphim, '...so shall the darkness begin to fade, and with the Light, become as one.'"

Long known? Who held these words of things to come, and how—*and when*—had they been written? And why should knowledge of such profound, future events be privy to so few? Yes, the oraphim were of a high order; and yes, it was improper for simple administrators to solicit insights into the broader divine...but....

"As always, there are no shortcuts to enlightenment," Hyynehk continued, as though having heard their thoughts. "Administration through patient revelation will ultimately reveal the joys of Love and Light. The Most Highs have every confidence in your ability to prevail."

Prevail? None before had prevailed. None before had even briefly slowed the Rɵhman hordes. Were these just hollow words? Had others heard them, too?

"Work together, that triumph be assured."

N²¹³ *Ubahr.* A gas giant and the system's sixth planet from the sun. The Khraelings conceded Ubahr and her moons in exchange for exclusive rights to the system's three lifeless inner worlds. Among the few post-holocaust Agreements negotiated with the Federation, the trade enabled the Jakomen to begin mining meager polymide deposits on three of Ubahr's moons, while patiently establishing a hidden base for a secret, second fleet (the "Second Wave").

N[214] ***quite the contrary.*** A reference to the surprise attack on and sudden annihilation of Old Hollatia:

> [from D-32.15, *THE JAKOMEN HOLOCAUST*] The Federation's unending trade deficit with the Jakomen became a growing embarrassment to "Those of the Continents"—Khrae's nine ruling barons. And the Jakomen's generosity, their steady stream of grants and donations to innumerable humanitarian causes, seemed a deliberate slight. But most of all, Those of the Continents resented their citizens' growing awareness that life in "desolate" Hollatia was more just and simply better than their own. And one day, the small island continent of Hollatia and its 1.2 billion Jakomen were reduced to dust.

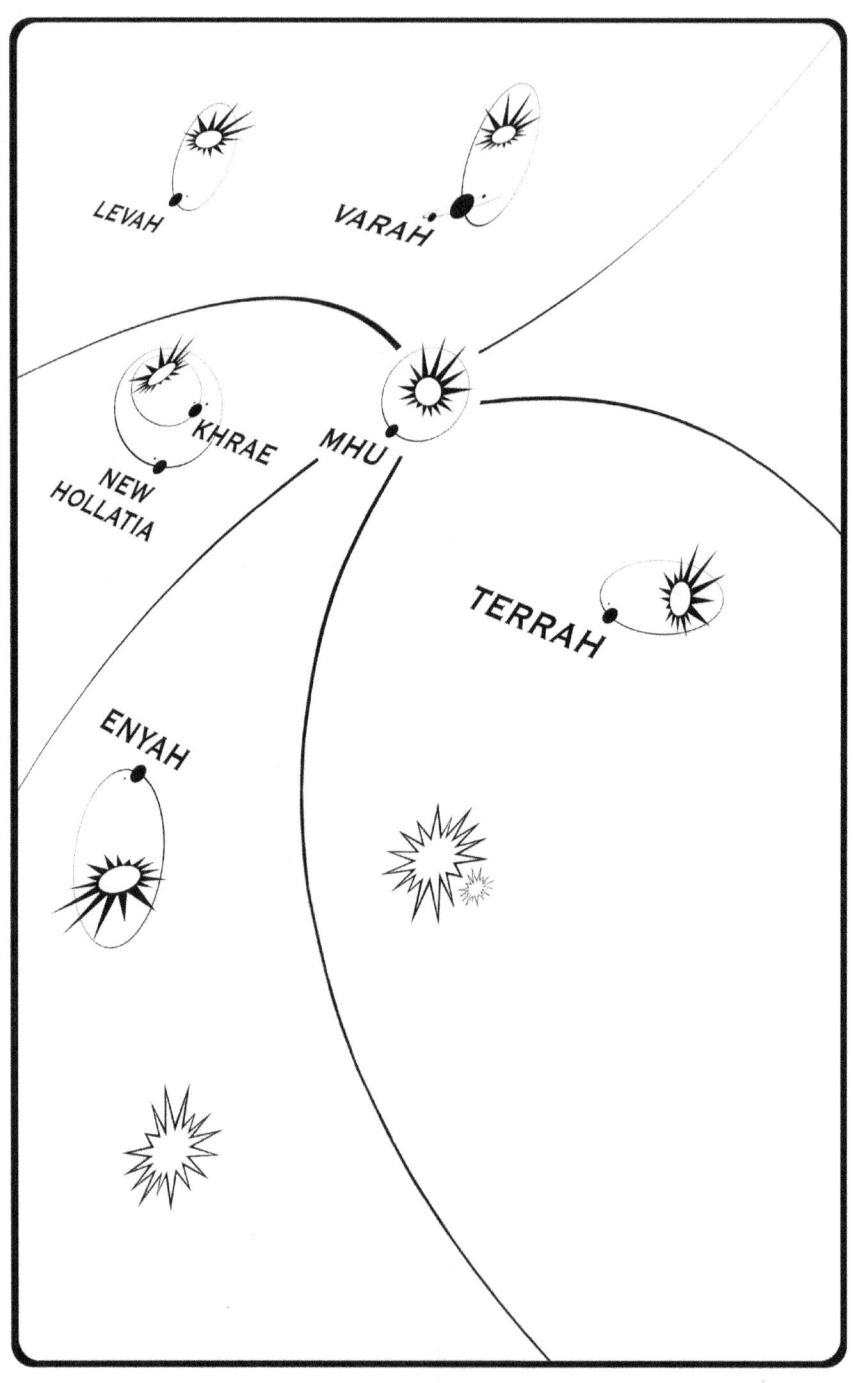

21

QUERYING THE SERAPHIM

DAY -26: MHU

Levitating cross-legged over twenty-four large, white cushions, twenty-four ancients formed a steady circle in the air. Their arms hung at their sides, fingers not quite touching the puffy pads below. Nothing but an occasional wisp of faint, golden light could be seen of the seven planetary seraphim that hovered in the ancients' midst.

Deeply distressed by yesterday's demonic attack in Lemurah's crystal plaza,[215] the twenty-four officials had called forth the seraphim to help them determine what it all meant. Mindful of seraphic sensitivity to will-infringement, the officials spoke in a telepathic union and strove to word their queries with the utmost care.

A gentle voice filled the ancients' minds. "Peace be upon you, dear ones. How may we be of aid?"

"The murder in the plaza causes us great concern. We are uncertain of its significance and of the implied threat to our world."

"The nature of your query is unclear, dear ones," said another seraph. "Please rephrase that we may serve."

The officials tried a more direct wording.

"We humbly ask that you help us understand the relevance of yesterday's psychic attack."

"Regretfully," another of the seraphim softly replied, "we share misgivings of replying specifically to this inquiry." To respond to the request as phrased might involve the need for intellectual evaluations—judgmental assessments—something beyond seraphic bounds. "Please do not interpret our shyness as reluctance to assist."

The twenty-four tried again. "Could you tell us of the dark spirit who came to our capital, and the purpose for his acts?"

"We could."

"Please do," responded the ancients, finally seeing their way clear. "We allow and welcome your imparting this information."

"The entity is a high demon of the order of fallen Vihdæa…"

Fallen Vihdæa? A chill rushed through the ancients.

"...and is among those who seek to try your faith."

Among those? More than one? "Why would these beings challenge our faith when we are committed to serving Prime Creator?"

"They have pledged allegiance to a false god, and choose to do his bidding."

Understanding to a degree, the officials paused and then asked, "To what did the demon refer when proclaiming that Nordehk would be put in order?"

"The dark one subscribes to a distortion that all of Creation is in turmoil, in a state of chaos that can only come to order through service unto self."

Service unto self? The concept was alien.

"Serving in a negative orientation."

Still no understanding.

"They would manipulate others to do their bidding."

Manipulate? "Are you referring to conquest and enslavement?"

"In part, dear ones, these things are among the greater distortion to which we refer. Our channel appears to weaken." The seraphim could not hold the interdimensional bridge much longer, the etheric connection between the sixth density and Mhu's fourth. "May we answer one more query?"

The ancients realized the seraphs' struggle. "We are concerned for our delegation en route to Khrae."

"Be at peace in the knowledge that Love and Light are the great protectors. Prime Creator's will be done."

DELEGATES IN GEL

D-26.2: SPACE

Engulfed in a thin envelope of iridescent light, an elegant fourth-density ship sailed through space at nearly the speed of light. The gracefully contoured, concave disc featured a thick crown that tapered to a spinning, involuted perimeter.

Sent by Lord Mohaar the day before to find this ship[216]—the ancients' fabled merkabah[217]—Iddh burst through its crown and quickly found sixteen voyagers podded near the vessel's core. Their heads nearly touched in the midst of a clear, communal pod. All sixteen lay curled in fetal positions, naked and motionless, suspended in a transparent, silver gel. Their partially open, almond-shaped eyes looked about two-thirds the size of Og eyes and were set into similarly large skulls. But the ancients' eyes were a uniform, medium violet, as opposed to the darkeyes' solid black.

Iddh let out a perversely joyful cackle. These beings—Those of Mhu—would serve his masters well.

THE INDUSTRIOUS DAHOEN
D-26.3: KHRAE

Not far from Patos and the tensely quiet, subsurface bases of Khrae Lunar Command, Lord Mohaar lay inside his vihmyana tweaking the program of a small Rehman drone. Then he shrouded the device, fired it toward Khrae, activated his recliner's blue energy field and pinned to the planet alone.

Pausing over Old Hollatia, Khrae's contaminated island continent, the Son saw a foreboding and desolate land of barren rifts and valleys, ephemeral streams, and a vast expanse of drifting sand. Except for an occasional ruin that jutted out from the sterile landscape, little evidence of the continent's once-thriving culture remained.

Continuing across a small northern sea, Mohaar headed for the lush shores of Pagorea, homeland of the Jakomen's age-long antagonists, and to the seaside estate of the family Rikahr. Six times through the course of Khrae's intercontinental wars, Rikahr's compound had been destroyed; and each time, the family tenaciously rebuilt. The last reconstruction was said to look much like the original, but no one knew for sure.

The current Baron Rikahr, Baron Moulahd Rikahr III, stood alone on his favorite spot atop the estate's squat, 2,000-year-old TK turret.[218] In a recent dream, his handlers had advised him of the Rehmans' arrival, and although he had been thinking of little else, it had not occurred to the incarnate that he might be called upon directly by a righteous Rehman Son.

Lord Mohaar's intentionally overpowering mind-scan thus came as a terrifying sensation to the unprepared big man. In an instant, crusader Rikahr received his orders: clearly, concisely, and complete with vivid images—glimpses of the future, and of roles he would soon play.

The burly baron raised his arms and dropped trembling to his knees. "By your radiance, my Lord!" he cried aloud. But seeing no radiance, no hint of light at all, the baron lowered his arms and whispered, unsure, "I...I pledge my heart...to Rehm."

Further west, along neighboring Elasia's south coast, Mohaar arrived at the sight of the resin runners' recent crash.[219] Ships from the KSF were still scouring the vicinity and scanning the ocean's depths for clues to the accident's cause. Hundreds of smaller local craft methodically swept for wreckage that may have washed ashore.

The demon turned inland toward Elasia's high country, and to the distinctive island wondercity of Dahoen. Perched on a planetary peculiarity that had survived Khrae's violent history intact, Dahoen stood atop a massive lava column that had been an ancient volcano's frozen core. Long before the original Khraeling colonists arrived, the great mountain's slopes had eroded, leaving its towering basalt core exposed. Rains and transitory streams then carved a depression around the column's base, where a lake gradually formed.

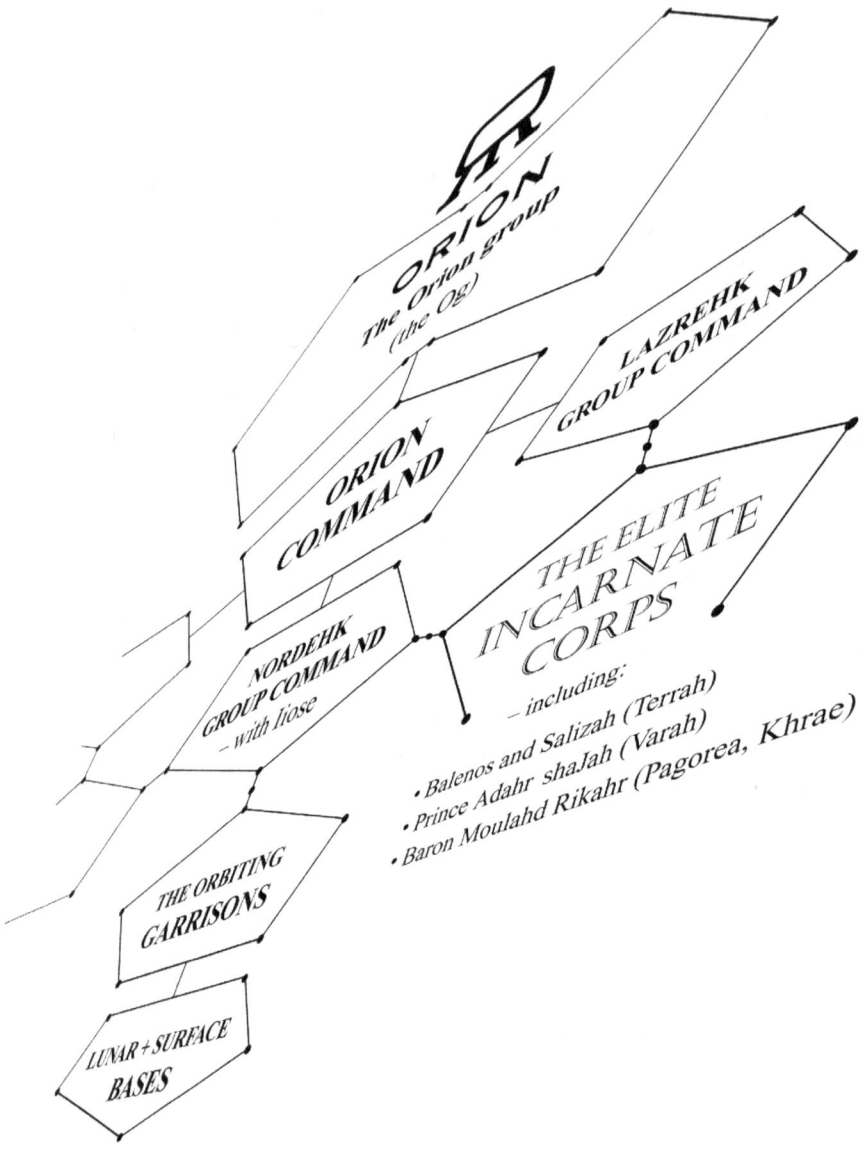

The first to discover the aberration were members of a religious sect that had been fleeing persecution. Surviving generations toiled to establish a safe haven for themselves and any others willing to contribute to the difficult way of life.

Initially, a treacherous maze of stairways, ladders, cramped crevices and hand-hewn tunnels led up the nearly impassable cliffs. Later, the sky-dwellers—the "dahoen"—devised a complex system of ropes and pulleys that enabled them to hoist an assortment of logs to the top where they utilized them as booms for an array of substantial derricks. In time, dozens of thick, <u>tightly woven cables</u>[220] dangled over the precipice and down more than a Rehman mile to the lake below, for the raising and lowering of boats, supplies, refuse, and the dahoens themselves.

The refuge underwent constant reconstruction until all that remained were remnants of a 20-kilometer perimeter wall wedged between immense glass towers clamped onto the precipice like cornices of pale blue ice. Successive generations restricted the buildings' height to one-twentieth that of the basalt column. Consequently, the dahoen burrowed ever deeper until finally more people lived within the core than on top. They reserved the column's priceless upper surface for the hotels, restaurants, museums and gift shops of a burgeoning tourist economy. And eventually the population of Old Dahoen—those dwelling in or atop the core and excluding the surrounding lakeside city—stabilized at about 90,000 where it remained to the present day.

High above the old city's central plaza, Mohaar created a huge apparition of The Master's sign around his radiant pinpoint of concentrated Sonlight. The midmorning sun amplified the specter's intensity and produced an eerie halo, and several of those below began recording the dazzling form.

Leaving the apparition to linger, the warrior pinned down to the plaza where he selected and entered a local being, knocking his hapless victim backward into a large but shallow fountain. The victim's friends laughed and then offered to help. But strangely, he got to his feet and backed into the fountain's showery periphery.

With such odd behavior and a brilliant specter overhead, a crowd began to grow.

"Denizens of Dahoen!" the demon bellowed as he stretched his host's arms toward the fading insignia. "Behold the sign of Rehm, *and be warned!*"

Sign of Rohm? Be warned? The power of his voice seemed frighteningly unnatural.

"A plague befalls us! Behold The Master's mark, and know! His faces *will* be seen!"

ᛩ

NARLIHD'S INTERVIEW

D-26.4: NEW HOLLATIA

Still unconscious, Enigg Pahl Radool now lay in the local infirmary. And while agents of the NHD scoured Captain Narlihd's transport-cruiser, the rest of his crew underwent intense debriefings. The captain himself had been hustled to the Aggah's office, where he stood rigidly at attention before a preoccupied Unah Bood.

A simple stone chamber, her office had changed little in its 300 New Hollatian years. Its rough, windowless walls angled irregularly beneath high arched ceilings. Inside its wide doorway, two of Bood's fit female aides stood in recessed enclosures on opposite sides of the jagged, yellow rock entrance to the room.

The Aggah sat behind a heavy wooden desk that had come from Khrae during the Exodus. A large fireplace blazed in back of her, and six Elders stood to each side of her desk. Unseen and unheard, Iddh hovered overhead, muttering obscenities between a series of drawn-out cackles.

Face unshaven and coated with an oily sweat, Captain Narlihd felt as embarrassed as he felt confused. Uncertain about how best to begin his explanation, he silently rehearsed his opening statement. His lips betrayed the effort.

Choosing to display a hint of suppressed anger, the Aggah raised her head and asked the captain why he had aborted his mission.

"My Aggah," he said with a click of his heels and another quick sniff of her luscious perfume, "I am confused and do not know where to begin."

"Begin at the beginning, Captain."

Narlihd nervously explained that the first 57 days of his mission had been uneventful. The experimental coils worked well, no different than they had performed in months of pre-mission testing, and he had sustained an average 103% OMV.

"Then they began developing problems, my Aggah, an unexpected molecular realignment of the dielectrics. My chief engineer, Luthur Poth, thought it would take two days to install replacements, but he could not guarantee that the same phenomenon would not reoccur.

"He proposed slowing our velocity to limit the saturation, and I cut back to 80% OMV, deciding to tackle the repairs after we secured the container. The coils held for ten more days, and then the field equilibrium started to destabilize. The molecular migration had resumed."

The Elders looked completely neutral as the captain continued. Bood acted unimpressed.

"Chief Poth designed a stress model that projected dielectric fractures unless we reduced our velocity further. I cut to 75% OMV, then 70%—averaging 11% less, every ten days. And when we finally did rendezvous with the convoy, my Aggah, we were under 51% OMV and 28 days behind schedule. It took a two-second plasma burn to bring us in sync with the convoy, or we would have missed them completely."

Narlihd paused to blink the sweat out of his eyes.

"Twenty-two hours later, my Aggah, with the container in tow, the Khraeling escorts' scanners came into range. They were too far out to tag our engine print but close enough to determine that our mass looked similar to the convoy's missing container. Two of the seven interceptors veered toward us with coils fully wound." Not a word from the Aggah. "We had to begin the repairs." Not even an understanding nod.

"The chief estimated less than a one-percent loss in velocity through the time he needed, and it was becoming uncertain as to whether we would escape."

"But escape you did, Captain." The Aggah's demeanor softened. "You may stand easy. Continue."

Narlihd let his shoulders down and opened his hands to cool them.

"In an attempt to confuse our pursuers, and while their scanning resolution was still in doubt, I kicked the container into a slow tumble, and the screws started transferring the Varahn cargo to our ship...."

FOREIGN VAPOR IN THE FOG

D-26.5: KHRAE

A shrouded Rehman drone[221] broke from its low orbit over Khrae and dove toward Elasia's southern shores.

Homing in on the coastal village of Efrahm, it made a low pass through the morning fog and released a burst of vapor. Then it shot back to the sky.

Chapter 21 — N O T E S

N[215] ***demonic attack in the crystal plaza.*** Lord Zhol's possession and subsequent slaying of an innocent in delivering the ancients' first notice of Rehm's Coming:

> [from D-27.5, *A QUANDARY FOR THE OVERLORD*] While Poxx rained a torrent of unheard curses and threats from above, Zhol rendered his defiant host unconscious, and then leered at the surrounding, bewildered crowd.
>
> Recovering from their brief hesitation, those nearest the Overlord's victim rushed to their brother's defense, embracing him and resuming his telepathic forbiddances, chants and prayers. "Negative spirit we forbid you entrance to this body! You are not in harmony with the Light! Bel l'ura Donai! Bel l'ura Donai! Bel l'ura Donai! *Bathe us in Prime Creator's light!*"
>
> With the power of his mind, the Son flung several feeble defenders a good twenty cubits. Then, clamping his host's left hand onto the head of a now kneeling, would-be rescuer who had ventured too close, Zhol outstretched his right arm and raged aloud.
>
> "Behold the sign of Rehm! Behold the sign of changes!" Blood spewed from his victim's mouth as the demon shredded vocal cords that had been used for little more than gentle laughter.
>
> In a challenging, sweeping gesture, the warrior pointed at the growing throng. "Be warned, *ancients* of Mhu!" he screamed, mocking their epithet.
>
> Eyes a fiery red and face severely contorted, he bellowed, "Eleven times more, will His great sign appear over your mountains, over your oceans, over your temples and your homes.
>
> "*Count!* And know you then!" The demon paused to glare a moment. "*Order* will come to Nordehk!"

N[216] ***to find this ship.*** Based on its departure information, route and velocity, as supplied by the Og six days before, in the transfer of data from Iiose's battle cruiser to the Overlord's khoomyahna:

> [from D-32.7, *HOSTING THE DEMON SONS*] "The following actions and developments are detailed in the data now flowing to your khoomyahna. A transfer of capsules containing the requested samples and codes for Nordehk's flora and fauna, including genetic materials from the higher species, is also underway."

N[217] ***merkabah.*** *Ship of light* in the language of Those of Mhu.

N[218] ***TK turret.*** The Rikahrs' famous turret houses a prized vestige of Khrae's intercontinental wars: an unpowered but otherwise preserved 12,000-year old Pagorean TK cannon, once capable of destroying targets in near space.

N[219] *the resin runners' recent crash.* Just six days before, on Day -32 near the beaches of Elasia:

> [from D-32.16, *DEMON AT THE HELM*] Arnod's crewmates stared in disbelief. They had substituted two of his three lucky roobs and still he'd pulled it off. And not just a double, but a *second* toss of triple fives.
>
> It was unheard of…impossible. And something else was wrong. Where was that gravitational pull, that wonderful weightiness that subtly signaled their nearness to home ground?
>
> While Arnod danced and gathered up his winnings, two of his crewmates pushed their faces against a leeward porthole in time to see the ocean rushing up.

N[220] *tightly woven cables.* Weighing far more than anything hoisted, the dahoens' precious cables were among their most valuable possessions. Their greatest treasure lay in the discovery of a cistern network deep inside their haven's basalt core: a near-limitless supply of potable water. In an attempt to starve the dahoen into surrendering the frequent sieges, many an invader had poisoned the lake below. None succeeded in waiting them out.

N[221] *a shrouded Rohman drone.* As fired by Lord Mohaar from his vihmyana a few hours before:

> [from D-26.3, *THE INDUSTRIOUS DAHOEN*] Not far from Patos and the tensely quiet, subsurface bases of Khrae Lunar Command, Lord Mohaar lay inside his vihmyana tweaking the program of a small Rohman drone. Then he shrouded the device, fired it toward Khrae, activated his recliner's blue energy field and pinned to the planet alone.

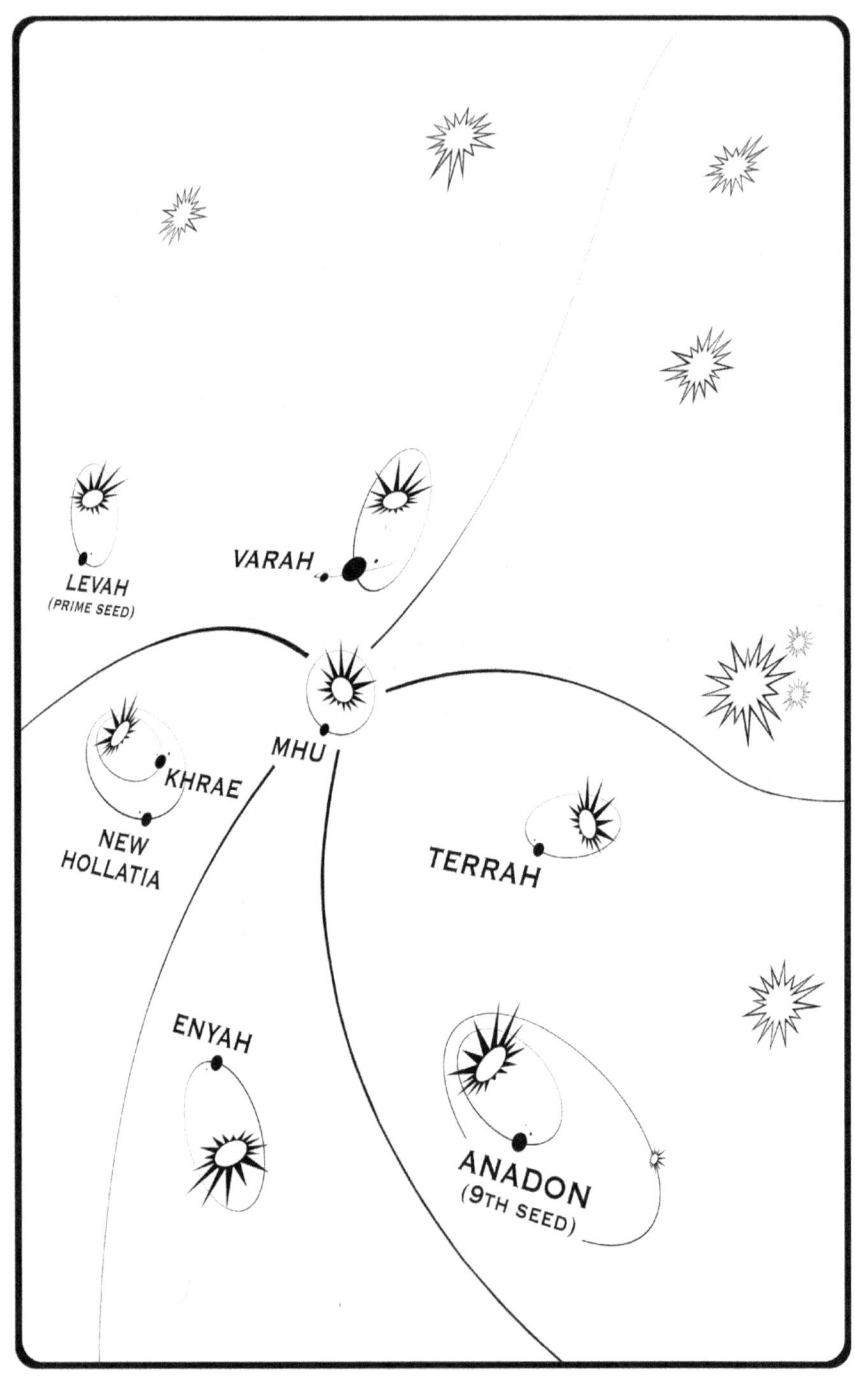

22

A CAPITAL DESIGN

D-26.6: SPACE / KHOOMYAHNA

Alone in his khoomyahna's systems bridge, Lord Zhol studied prospective sites for Anadon's golden city, the future administrative center for the Nordehk constellation. A perfect photonic image of the ancients' pristine ninth seed shone before him: half in darkness, half in light. Blue oceans surrounded two of the world's six lush continents. The Overlord zoomed in on the smaller of the two.

By The Master's design, a gigantic imperial insignia, 12 Rǝhman miles long by 10 wide, marked the surface of all the Empire's inhabited worlds. On constellation capitals, the mark had to be centered between a golden city and 144 monolithic stone faces of Rǝhm, with the sculptures, sign and city aligned within twelve degrees and at least a horizon apart. On waterworlds (those with surfaces of more than one-third water), the faces were always installed on islands, either natural or bhuvani-made.

Along the southernmost part of Zhol's preferred continent lay some rolling, red granite foothills: a prime location for The Master's mark. Around 1,200 miles to the southwest, a chain of rugged islands rose nearly 4,000 cubits above the ocean's surface. Spectacular cliffs on the easternmost island faced the chosen land: a prime location for the 144 faces.

Roughly aligned some 1,200 miles northeast of the red granite foothills, and on the same continent's extensive eastern shore, stood the high peaks of coastal mountains. For the necessary alignment, the city's precise location could lay somewhere in that range.

Zhol closed in on a large meadow nestled between two of the coastal peaks. The site seemed ideal for Anadon's golden city…for…*Endorah.* The name came to the Overlord in an electrifying shiver, as though The Master Himself were near.

THE CRIMSON CHEST

D-26.7: NEW HOLLATIA

Narlihd's debriefing continued with the captain explaining that his chief engineer's assistant, Enigg Pahl Radool, had been repairing the transen coil when he bumped his head and knocked himself out.

"As I understand it, my Aggah, within minutes of regaining consciousness, the enigg approached Chief Poth with a sudden idea to improve the primary's performance, a concept the chief initially resisted but soon came to embrace."

Bood cocked her head. *An enigg with bold ideas?* Could he be the one she had dreamed[222]?

"Shortly afterward, I was briefed and assured that the modifications would solve the engine's problems and could be made within the time allotted for repairs. Poth's uncharacteristic excitement and confidence in the idea's simplicity, along with due consideration to our increasingly critical situation, must have convinced me to approve the proposal."

Bood felt a pang in her stomach. "Must have convinced you, Captain?"

The senior operative wondered if that was what he had said. He tried to remember making the decision. "The memory is unclear, my Aggah."

Things were falling into place. A highly decorated NHD captain was making questionable decisions. It *was* the enigg—the bright-eyed avenger—she'd dreamed a few nights before.

"And the net result was to modify the engine and achieve 122% OMV?"

"Qah, my Aggah," Narlihd replied.

"How then, Captain, do you explain your reappearance here—months ahead of schedule, and without the container in tow?"

Squeezing more sweat from his eyes, the captain opened his mouth to continue, but the Aggah stepped from behind her desk and ordered, "Get Captain Narlihd a chair. And water. And a damp towel. Now."

An aide quickly placed a chair behind the captain. A damp towel came fast into his hands, and a tall glass of cooled water. Then Bood motioned for Narlihd to sit.

He thanked her, sat, wiped his face and neck, and took a sip of water. And while the Aggah strolled around her office, hands clasped behind her back, the captain explained about intercepting the Khraelings' communications and learning that their pursuers were not authorized to apprehend.

"As soon as we finished the repairs and modifications, I wound the coils to 122% OMV, and when the engine held, I felt certain we were away. It was truly amazing, my Aggah. We experienced no vibration, and there was no leakage. I'd never heard twin coils sound so good, especially fully wound."

"And the Khraelings bore witness?"

"Qah, my Aggah. We were under constant scan, both from our pursuers and from an RSU they had launched for a second perspective. We were outrunning the interceptors and stretching the estimated impact time of the warning shots they had fired. But within six hours of initiating our acceleration, the bolts were upon us."

Captain Narlihd watched with the Elders and Bood's aides as the Aggah returned to her seat. Even they seemed to be wondering her thoughts.

"At around 90 seconds to impact, our main systems died and we lost our grip on the container, which raced ahead as though our engine had stalled. And our gravity took on a different feel...." The captain paused, remembering the strange sensation.

"Captain?"

"Qah, my Aggah, forgive me. Then the warning shots ripped into the container, which literally disintegrated in an explosion much different than I have ever seen..." Narlihd shook his head. "...a tremendous eruption that suddenly imploded and then roared back to fill the heavens before vanishing completely, all in a second or two. We should have been blinded by the light, but it was as though our windows were somehow filtered. It was almost a beautiful thing...."

"And how is it, Captain, that you came to reappear here, so...unexpectedly?"

The captain searched for words. "I don't know, my Aggah."

"What are your suspicions?"

Narlihd shook his head again. She would never believe him.

"Captain?..."

"It seemed like we had been snared by another ship—much larger...and invisible."

A few of the Elders and some of the aides looked at each other from the corners of their eyes.

"We must have been drawn into our captor's hold, for although we were running on emergency systems, we had full gravity when we should have had ten percent at best. Then all became dark around us...around our ship, I mean. The stars disappeared, my Aggah, and our navigational bar could not make sense of our isolation.

"We remained that way for at least two hours. We tried everything to restart our systems but to no avail. Then Enigg Radool appeared at my door— in his underwear, and with an insolent smirk on his face...."

"His underwear, Captain?"

"Qah, my Aggah. He'd been in sickbay, having fainted after completing the engine modifications."

"I see. Continue."

"Well, I became angry and started to say something. Then I felt a...a dizzying numbness and could not speak. The enigg told me to summon the crew, *ordered* me, my Aggah, in an unfamiliar and powerful voice." The captain stared at the floor, briefly reliving the moment. "It had a hypnotic effect, and I did as he said."

"He spoke to us of prosperity and the dawning of a new age." Narlihd looked at the Elders and then the Aggah. His eyes welled with tears. "I felt like a believer in the presence of a prophet."

Some appeared to accept the truth of his story; others shook their heads. Bood gave no signals one way or the other.

Recomposed, the captain continued. "Radool said that after a brief acceleration, we should retrieve a crimson chest that had been attached to our hull...."

"A crimson chest, Captain?"

"Qah, my Aggah. He knew of the chest *and* its color, and that its contents were of great value: 'far greater than that of the Varahn container,' he said. Then, strangely, the enigg told us that we would soon be upon New Hollatia. Those were his words...and here I sit before you, Aggah Bood."

"And do you have this crimson chest, Captain?"

"Qah, my Aggah. The force of the acceleration was so great, I blacked out...I believe we all did. But the first to awaken retrieved the chest and placed it in our hold."

The Aggah signaled an aide to fetch the chest, but kept her eyes on the captain. With his tale told, he'd regained his composure. But he did not look well.

"How much time, Captain, between the container's destruction and your reappearance home?"

The captain seemed reluctant to say.

The Aggah tilted her head. "Captain?"

The stress had gotten the best of Narlihd and he blurted, "Eight hours, my Aggah!"

Some of the Elders gasped.

"That will be all for now, Captain. Please report to the infirmary for a thorough examination. Allow my aides to escort you."

ANOTHER HOLOCAUST?

D-26.8: KHRAE

With Jakomen operations apparently back to normal, the tension had subsided in the underground towers of Khrae Lunar Command. But an air of shocked disbelief prevailed.

The images from the Bool-Dahr seemed irrefutable. Besides the mock invader's remarkable velocity, the Jakomen appeared to have accomplished what Khraeling science had deemed impossible. They had brazenly displayed controlled modulations both in and out of the visibility spectrum. And KLC's analysis of the escort squadron's images did little to ease concerns.

$$- \circ \; \text{\Large ☼} \; \circ -$$

After a military consensus, the marshall's staff meeting was over, and Pranol stood in'field with the governor and Counsel-Ra, walking them through the report.

"Item One. Lunar Command confirms that the intensity of the pursuit team's warning shots was inadequate to penetrate the container's shielding. Here is a scan of the actual bolts."

The marshall's likeness shrank and moved to one side of the politicians' imaging field as images of the twin beams unfolded. Governor Mauhk grimaced.

"They look mean, Governor," Pranol continued, "but note the scale on your lower right and see that they are unquestionably low-intensity. Now, here is a scan of the container's shielding that reveals a standard commercial web that should have been more than adequate to absorb that meager fire.

"Item Two. KLC confirms the presence of a nuclear pump in the pirates' modified cruiser. Here is a recording of the suspects' engine print. The highlighted subfield is a perfect match with dozens of NHD twin-coil configurations.

"Item Three: Lunar Command's attempt to explain the transport-cruiser's disappearance. This portion of the analysis was produced by an isolation team unaware of the recent events in the Bool-Dahr. These are the images."

Several layers unfolded in'field.

"Note the cruiser's velocity, 122% OMV, and note the ship's EM anchors on the container's spine. Now suddenly: no cruiser, no anchors."

Haleahm closed his eyes, blinked and said, "Run that again, Mannon, please."

Pranol stretched the sequence to 1,000 frames per second and replayed the disappearance frame by frame. Within three frames—three one-thousandths of a second—the cruiser dematerialized and disappeared.

"KLC speculates that although the significant increase in velocity would suggest an innovation, the similarity between the suspect ship's engine signature and previously listed coils would indicate a modification rather than a completely new design. In the ensuing haste to escape our pursuit interceptors and to make up time lost during repairs, KLC further speculates that the suspects may have overextended their troubled engine and unwittingly created a runaway modulation, an unanticipated electromagnetic phenomenon that resulted in the physical disappearance of their ship. The analysis refers to the KSF's energy density and frequency modulation tests of the last century, and to the decidedly uncontrollable 'montauk effect'[223]."

"Item Four: KLC's attempt to determine the cause of the explosion that destroyed the Varahn container. Since the explosion coincides perfectly with the impact of the warning shots, KLC believes that as a purely precautionary measure, the Jakomen planted an explosive device and linked it to the container's shielding."

Pranol froze a frame and then ran the succeeding frames, one by one.

"Here the shielding is reaching to absorb and cushion the impact. The imaging is then blinded by the detonation which, when stretched to 100,000 frames per second, can be seen bursting *outward* through the hull as the web extends toward the bolts. The shots clearly did not penetrate the hull, nor were they absorbed before the detonation.

"Exotic vapors were widely dispersed throughout the debris-cloud's fine particulate, possibly from the explosive concentrate, possibly from the suspect ship's experimental engine, possibly from Varahn commodities destroyed in the explosion.

"If the operatives did succumb to a runaway modulation, they may have made a desperate, heroic and apparently successful effort to arm the bomb in their final seconds. However, in light of the events in the Bool-Dahr, it is plausible that the dematerialization was controlled. If so, then the 88 seconds between the cruiser's disappearance and the container's destruction were adequate for the suspects to escape, simply by employing a full repulsion from the amstradt mass in order to distance themselves from the blast.

"In fact, the Jakomen may have escaped, conceivably abandoning the container and arming the device under orders from the NHD—the Aggah having had ample time for confidential discussions with the Varahns, and the container being sacrificed for reasons unknown."

Mauhk sat transfixed. Haleahm gnawed at a hangnail.

"Item Five. Lunar Command confirms zero radioactivity in the cloud of fine debris, yet we know that cruiser's engine had a nuclear pump. Although the remote scanning unit malfunctioned within minutes of entering the debris field, it was on continuous scan and its data is conclusive, lending further credence to the theory that the suspects escaped unscathed.

"Item Six: KLC's attempt to determine whether the ship's disappearance and the container's destruction were connected. I shall read verbatim from the report:

'At no time during the secret montauk testing did subject ships explode. Also, the lack of radioactive isotopes in the vaporized container's debris field—which would have been present had a nuclear pump disintegrated— would seem to indicate that the two events were unrelated, unless the detonation was intended to cover the operatives' escape. We deem it implausible, however, that the Jakomen had the technological wherewithal to control a dematerialization, and illogical that they would detonate the container as a cover when they were clearly outdistancing our interceptors. But without sufficient data, we cannot conclusively determine the cause for either the disappearance or the explosion.'"

The governor and his C-Ra maintained a rare silence while the marshall summarized.

"Scanning foilers notwithstanding, gentlemen, the KSF must assume that the Jakomen have indeed achieved controlled modulations in and out of the visibility spectrum. Opinions vary as to why the Aggah would choose to reveal such an astonishing capability, and the manner in which she has done so, merits solemn consideration. But the ramifications are of grave concern.

"On the surface, it would appear that the purpose of the Bool-Dahr exercise was to measure response times—to estimate *our* response times—to a surprise attack. And although the ships launched had known engine signatures, they may well have been outfitted with switchable devices, modifications that would enable them to achieve the higher velocity and to dematerialize and rematerialize on demand."

Switchable devices? Dematerialize on demand? Mauhk shuddered at the thought.

"It is also entirely possible that the events at the Varahn convoy were similarly staged."

Haleahm squinted and then nodded ever so slightly, as though he shared that line of thought.

"If a statement is being made, gentlemen," Pranol continued, "we are unclear as to what the message is. And if there can be any comfort in these revelations, it may lie in the fact that they could easily have been kept secret from us. I therefore tend to disavow intimidation as the Aggah's motive. That she has chosen to announce her achievements could imply an intention to negotiate."

Negotiate? That word came as a relief to Governor Mauhk.

"However, although we perceive no immediate threat to Federation security, we shall maintain a general alert. A modulation capability and an advantage in velocity cannot be conceded, once confirmed.

Cannot be conceded? Was Pranol planning war?

"These alleged developments warrant a review of our position regarding our commercial relationship with New Hollatia, or lack thereof. Purchase of the technology should be a viable option but cannot be, without a working relationship with the developers, and I would suggest that this may be in line with Bood's thinking. It could well be that the Aggah is, for the first time in New Hollatian history, able to negotiate from a position of strength, as was—ironically—the last Aggah of Old Hollatia."

The governor noticeably paled. Not another holocaust. Not in his name.

Chapter 22 — N O T E S

N²²² *the one she had dreamed.* On Day -30:

> [from D-30.8, *THE AGGAH'S DREAM*] The Aggah Bood curled up on her
> favorite couch with a small, iced glass of smuggled, Khraeling mohrd.
> Dressed down for the evening, she wore but a plain, navy-colored gown.
>
> She gazed intently into the multicolored flames of her suite's modest
> fireplace, watching their embrace of a neatly arranged stack of slow burning,
> pressed-fiber sticks. She felt confident that Khrae's military had managed to
> pirate her broadcast, and that Governor Mauhk and the barons or their envoys
> had been among her viewing audience. Bood had staged the forum for their
> benefit. She had had a prophetic dream.
>
> She'd dreamt of an enigg, a junior officer of the New Hollatian Defense.
> He held his hands in fire and spoke of retribution, of avenging the Dahanah
> and the Jakomen of old. He spoke of things written long before, and of their
> fathers' long gone lands. And he rubbed his hands together and held them
> high, palms out. And neither hand had burned. And then his body became as
> glowing, and he rose up off the ground....
>
> The Aggah remembered well the enigg's dancing eyes. She could feel
> his power—still.

N²²³ *montauk effect.* Entire ships had dematerialized in the Federation's
disastrous invisibility experiments that had been monitored by the curious Og.
Most ships never reappeared, but those that did, rematerialized thousands of
kilometers away: every one as horrible, molecularly rearranged masses—
crews and all. Years later, Og agents quietly observed a surprisingly similar
military experiment on Terrah which met with the same, calamitous results.

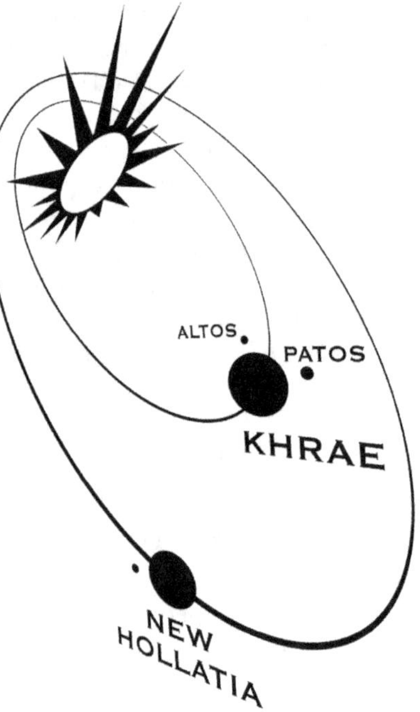

ALTOS

PATOS

KHRAE

NEW
HOLLATIA

23

THE 1ST PLAGUE

D-26.9: KHRAE

Inside her apartment in the Elasian coastal village of Efrahm, not far from where the resin runners had crashed, citizen Annah Neprihe was nursing her new baby. She noticed a tiny red speck on the infant's forehead, touched it and saw that it lay beneath her baby's skin. Neprihe noticed another, and another—all pinpoint hemorrhages seemingly appearing before her eyes. The child's face became flushed and he began to cough.

"Interrupt!" his mother shouted. "Medical emergency!" and she began rocking her baby boy.

A tone sounded and an image of a young man dressed head-to-toe in powder blue appeared near the wall beside her.

"I am Doctor Raufin, citizen Neprihe..." He looked calm and reassuring, but felt scared to death. "...how may I assist you?" He saw Neprihe's baby struggling and gulping for air. Something dreadful was happening in their village, and he had no idea what it was.

"My baby boy is choking, Doctor! Help me! What can I do?"

"An ambulance will be there shortly, Annah," he said, noting the caller's first name from the records layered alongside Neprihe's in'field image. "Look closely at the infant's skin and tell me what you see."

"Red specks...all over!" The boy turned blue, and in moments lay unconscious. "Oh, God! He's dying! Tell me what to do!"

"Sit with your knees together and sloped toward the floor." In the past half-hour, the doctor had seen images of a dozen cases just like this. "Place him face down on your lap with his head at your knees, and turn his head to one side."

Neprihe did as instructed.

"That's good, Annah. Now press gently on his back, then release...." She did as he said. "That's good. Now once more, a little firmer." Bloody fluids oozed from the baby's mouth. "Good, yes...again." Still more fluids. Mostly blood.

"The ambulance has arrived, Annah." Neprihe hadn't noticed. It was hovering outside her window, and its telescopic ramp was reaching for her balcony.

"Annah, it's okay. You can stop now and let the attendants in."

Two attendants opened her gate and approached her window. They wore shiny, white, one-piece body suits with clear face shields.

Neprihe stopped pressing on her baby's back and looked toward the window, and then back at the doctor's image.

"Why are they dressed like that?" she asked, afraid to let them in.

"It's all right, Annah, it's just a precaution. Please retract the window so they can enter. They are here to help you and your son."

Neprihe just stared from the corners of her eyes.

"Citizen Neprihe!" The doctor startled her. "Open the window! You are wasting precious time!"

"Yes...yes! I'm sorry," she said. "Program interrupt...retract side balcony window."

Her imager released the window's latches, and the synglass slid away. The attendants rushed inside and opened a clear plastic capsule, withdrew a quilted yellow pad, and wrapped it around the baby's torso. Then they placed the infant inside the capsule and closed it. In seconds, he began breathing again.

One of the attendants held out a respirator. "This will help you relax, Annah. Let me help you put it on." The attendant secured it snugly over Neprihe's mouth and nostril.

"Thank you, Annah," Doctor Raufin said. "Go with them now, to the hospital." He paused before adding, mendaciously, "Everything will be fine."

A REFRACTION, A PREDICTION, AND A MYSTERIOUS DISEASE
D-26.10: KHRAE / PATOS

Marshall Pranol finished reviewing a special version of KLC's analysis, one edited for the Varahns, with all references to exotic vapors deleted. He then forwarded an internal "K1—Eyes Only" encrypted copy to the governor's Counsel-Ra that included links to another K1 file labeled "Strategic Options for a Defensive First Strike."

A call came in from Jehrmi Brohjal.

"Marshall. A mysterious disease has emerged in a small village along Elasia's south coast, near the crash site of the resin runners' frigate."

Mysterious? Federation science had catalogued all known strains of disease. Nothing "mysterious" had emerged for centuries.

"A KSF task force has been organized and dispatched to the scene. More than a hundred victims have been hospitalized. Twenty-seven have already died, including a number of workers who were sweeping the beaches where wreckage has washed ashore. Elasian Security has come up with something interesting and possibly related."

Pranol gestured to continue.

"This morning, ES received a number of reports describing some kind of solar refraction in the skies over Dahoen. The occurrence was simultaneous with a commotion in the city's central square that involved the rantings of a Dahoen native who dropped dead after predicting a plague."

Solar refraction? Prediction of a plague?

"Here are some images compiled from copies of tourist and local recordings."

Brohjal ran the images, which ended with the native's warning of a plague. "…and be warned! A plague befalls us!"

Pranol thought for a moment. *Dahoen* was being warned of a plague, *not* Efrahm. "Have KLC analyze all available recordings, Jehrmi." Just the same, it seemed an uncanny coincidence. "Find the cause of that refraction and its connection to the citizen. If we're dealing with a conspiracy, get to the bottom of it. Run a separate, quiet investigation. And keep it detached from the task force, which *you* will head up."

Brohjal nodded his understanding while wondering how he'd find the time.

"I want you highly visible, Vice Marshall. Baron Ebah and everyone involved must see that we are not taking this thing lightly. Brief me before talking to the media. I will keep our political friends informed."

CONTAINING THE EPIDEMIC

D-26.11: KHRAE

Efrahm was no longer a sleepy little town. Much to the beleaguered, local authorities' relief, agents of Brohjal's task force had arrived.

Emergency response units poured in from neighboring cities, while hundreds of shuttles busily offloaded tonnes of equipment from three KSF transport-cruisers hovering offshore. Ground-based interceptors came and went. Their impermeable compartments provided secure transport for the overflow of infected patients from Efrahm's overburdened clinic to the larger and more secure facilities of a subsurface KSF base.

While the continental media broadcasted continuous updates from the presumed safety of their sealed shuttles, units of Brohjal's task force searched for evidence of chemical or biochemical poisoning, and collected blood and tissue samples from the deceased. Others hunted potential vectors including algae, insects, rodents, and birds—anything that could act as a carrier for a new, pathogenic microbe. And anyone thought to have been in contact with known victims in the past 48 hours was sought for quarantine.

THE CONTRABAND CONNECTION
D-26.12: KHRAE

The governor summoned the continental barons for an unscheduled meeting of the <u>Federation Board</u>.[G115] In light of the Jakomen's recent technological revelations and Pranol's implied threat of a preemptive strike, they would meet in person in 48 hours. A way to peaceably acquire the Aggah's new engine had to be found.

While Mauhk, his Counsel-Ra and the barons' envoys worked to formulate viable options for the Board to debate, they listened to a live report from Efrahm.

"…and of 160 affected, 37 have now died. Except for the military, all traffic in and out of Efrahm has been halted. Citizens who left the village within the last 48 hours, or who know of someone that did, are required to contact their local authorities immediately. A complete menu of emergency addresses can be accessed at all times on Image Layer 10.…"

"My god," said the governor, "what is the extent of this thing?" Although he attended the capital's monthly theosophical services and always included at least some reference to God in his vernacular, it was by habit: Mauhk was not a religious man. The insinuation was pure Haleahm.

"Since the crash of the alleged pirate frigate six days ago," the report continued, "both sealed *and* smashed barrels of contraband have been washing up on Elasia's southern beaches, including those of the Efrahm township."

As she had done during the Aggah's forum a few days prior, Eikah Jouhl smacked the beveled edge of the envoys' mirrored console to switch the broadcast off. Then she turned to her Elasian counterpart, and said, "Excuse me Jahl, but I believe we have yet another reason why that operation should be shut down. Now a New Hollatian microbe is killing Federation citizens."

Without looking at the brash Pagorean, Jahl Khulnah calmly replied, "As you are all well aware—but for the record, Eikah—the Jakomen thoroughly debionate the resin, and our highly trained crews take all necessary precautions. There's no way a living microbe was in the product or aboard that frigate."

"Yes, thank you, Jahl," the governor interjected. "The crash may well have been an unpropitious coincidence. Most importantly, this epidemic will be contained and its cause determined. In more than 1,400 years there has not been an outbreak of any strain of any disease that has taken us more than four days to bring under control.

"And I would remind everyone…" Mauhk glanced at the Pagorean. "…that this is only the second shipment lost by the Ebah family, and the first on our planet's surface. The Elasians are suffering, and they and their baron need and shall receive our full support."

A DUBIOUS DISTINCTION

D-26.13: KHRAE / ENU

Vice Marshall Brohjal had quickly established a command center for his task force on continental Elasia at the prestigious Elasian National University. Like all Khraeling educational/research facilities, the KSF operated and occupied 20% of the complex, including its renowned biological containment lab.

Drafted and flown directly to ENU to determine the cause of Efrahm's outbreak, an intercontinental team of experts assembled in a secure lecture hall. Khrae's top microbiologists and a host of other specialists in related fields sat among the distinguished staff.

As their first order of business, the team elected a strong leader: Dr. Thurmod Bahk, the dynamic, fast-talking, microbial geneticist who headed the Federation's Health Organization. Determined to bring the episode to a swift conclusion, the doctor wasted no time laying out his strategy and delegating responsibilities.

Since the project fell under the auspices of the KSF, Bahk won the dubious distinction of reporting to Vice Marshall Brohjal.

SECONDARY SYMPTOMS

D-26.14: KHRAE / EFRAHM

Alone with a body-suited nurse inside a containment cell in Efrahm's tiny clinic, Annah Neprihe was developing secondary symptoms, and her doctors had ventured every treatment known.

Her fever was spiking dangerously. She could not swallow and all her muscles ached. Her bowel was incontinent, and she was extremely disoriented with no idea who she was or where she lay. She did not know she had a young son. She did not know her baby had died.

Chapter 23 — N O T E S

G[115]   Federation Board: an 11-seat executive council consisting of the governor, Counsel-Ra, and Khrae's nine continental barons

24

THE PRICKLIES

D-26.15: TERRAH

Ricky felt eyes watching him almost all the time. He didn't know just how or who, but kind of like the angels do. Except it wasn't them.

Probably the hell-men, who he thought about a lot. Not because he wanted to, but every now and then they'd just pop into his mind. Just like that, he'd flash on those scarry "skinnies" staring down at him with their big, black, buggy eyes.

Oftentimes he'd daydream about reaching up suddenly and jabbing their eyes with his finger or poking them with a pointy stick. In fact, he'd gone to bed a few times with a nice sharp pencil in his pocket so he'd be ready for those assholes. But his mom always found it in his pajamas or between his sheets, and she'd always tell him to stop taking sharp things to bed or else he'd end up poking his *own* eye out.

Ricky also liked to imagine squishing the skinnies' heads.[224] Even though he didn't care too much for hard-boiled eggs, he liked to squish them between the palms of his hands with the pointy part down: the way the bastards' heads looked. During each squishing, his mom allowed him to make an evil face so long as he ate what he squished. She even kept a few peeled eggs in the fridge for whenever he needed to squish one.

Even if the skinnies' heads weren't squishable, he'd sure like a chance to find out. Maybe when he got bigger he'd reach up from that silver bed and grab one by surprise. Once he was bigger, he'd definitely give it a try.

Anyways, he figured the skinnies put something inside him, and that's where his damn urges were coming from. Urges to do things like touch every sign post he walked past—not always, but sometimes. And if he didn't do it when he got the urge, he'd start feeling all prickly, so he just did it. He knew it was weird, but he couldn't stand the pricklies. So he'd just do whatever it took to make them go away.

Sometimes he'd get all prickly if things weren't in their proper place or not aligned or arranged in certain ways—not always, but a lot. Especially with food. Some things like peas were okay between the carrots or potatoes on his plate, but they had to be separate and not all mixed together. And most definitely peas could not be next to meat—that was a real prickler. Both had to be on opposite sides of his plate with stuff in between, and then he had to chew and swallow some peas only, and then some meat, and then more peas. It was also okay to eat all the meat first and then all of the peas, or all of the peas first and then the meat, just so long as both stayed separate 'til they reached his tummy, where things were beyond his control.

Actually, it made sense that peas and carrots should be separated, because peas grew above the ground, while carrots grew below the ground. But Ricky really didn't understand why it was all right for rice or potatoes to touch meat, because rice grew above the ground like pigs and cows, but potatoes grew below the ground like carrots.... So he just put the damn things in their correct, not-prickly order and tried not to let it bother him too much.

He also had to eat most meals in careful amounts so he'd have one bite of each thing left so he could finish the servings evenly and end with the portion that he liked best. That's why he preferred sandwiches and cereal and soup and macaroni and cheese, because when food came already mixed up like that, he could just eat without getting all prickly about it. Unless it was frozen peas mixed with chopped up carrots, which he had to separate without complaining.

Whoever was watching him probably had a good reason for causing his pricklies, but he just could not imagine what that reason might be. So he never made a big deal about it, and whenever he was with his mom or somebody when the pricklies came and he had to do something like touch all the sign posts, he would skip along and maybe sing a song like he was having fun. And if he had to adjust something that wasn't in its proper place, he'd lift it up and check it out like he was just curious before putting it back, correctly.

Adults never seemed to notice when he rearranged things, but the bully kids sure did. Probably because one of them saw him do something like when he got the urge to reorganize the coatroom. That was a mistake. Now the shitheads were watching him pretty close and were setting lots of traps.

But he just did what he had to do—that's what his mom said, "Just do what you have to do"—and if he got laughed at or beat up every now and then...well, that's just the way it was, what with being small and smart and cute on top of everything else. Actually, he liked being smart and he liked being cute and he especially liked his big eyes, which his mom just adored and always said were a gift from God. In fact, what he liked most about his big blue eyes was that bright lights never bothered him. His eyes just seemed to instantly adjust, and what was really cool about that was that he didn't need sunglasses, even on the brightest days at the park when the sun lit up the beach and the lake and even the sand, and everybody else had to wear sunglasses—

which he freakin' hated, and didn't need at all.

Anyways, he figured he'd probably start getting taller pretty soon, and a whole lot tougher, too, because he could already do a hundred pushups and even more situps. So one of these days, if he still wanted to, he'd kick the crap out of those asshole bullies and asshole hell-men. That was a *big* urge he'd been suppressing for years.

And concerning whoever was watching him, he figured that eventually they'd fess up and let him know what the hell his pricklies were all about. There had to be a reason for his urges, and one thing for sure—they weren't coming from him.

஫

THE ENIGG'S INTERVIEW
D-26.16: NEW HOLLATIA

The Jakomen High Council's hemispherical kiva was the deepest and hottest of all the many chambers that lay beneath the Aggah's compound. Nearly three kilometers below ground, the kiva's naturally circular wall curved inward to merge with a high stalactite ceiling, while the perimeter seating and raised central firepit had been shaped, ground and polished from the living stone.

A narrow, spiraling stairway had been carved into the sizeable room's curving periphery, and looped precariously upward in two railless turns to the entrance of a vacuum shaft hidden amid the primeval formations. The kiva's ventilation system, array of imagers and other gadgetry were concealed, and its central firepit had been formed from the remains of a small dry pool—the original hotspring having rerouted itself long ago. Craftsmen had removed the surrounding stone from the pool's irregular perimeter, so the resulting, raised "pit" stood more than a meter above the kiva's sunken floor.

A steady stream of flammable bubbles rose to the firepit's water-filled surface, where they ignited in a dancing layer of colorful, flickering flames. A built-in device neutralized undesirable vapors by emitting counteragents through a thin, polymide band inlaid on the inner side of the pit's broad rim. Heat from the planet's molten core radiated through the chamber's floor and walls, and served to clear the minds of New Hollatia's devoted leaders.

Twelve Council Elders sat on the cushioned ledge carved into the room's perimeter, and wore an assortment of traditional loincloths, headwraps, and shawls. Twelve counterparts in feathered ceremonial garb drummed, clapped, and danced around the firepit in unrehearsed, spontaneous, yet perfectly synchronized, gyrations. The firepit's flames cast giant shadows on the curving kiva wall.

Barefoot, and wearing only a tangled, cream-colored loincloth with a light brown, loosely woven shawl, the Aggah Bood paced slowly between the dancers and seated Elders. All were perspiring like Captain Narlihd just a few hours before.

The kiva dancers abruptly ended their trance-induced performance with a crisp, collective cry. All twelve simultaneously froze in mid-motion, except to fade the shaking and rattling of the percussional instruments strapped to them and clasped in hand. The Aggah then stopped pacing and quietly joined the twelve sitting on the kiva's cushioned ledge. As the dancers sat among them, Mohaar's scout, Iddh, screeched into the firelit room. The fire died, and to the midwayer's delight, a replay appeared of Enigg Pahl Radool's debriefing.

The images showed a young enigg who did not seem to remember much, not even his idea for modifying the twin coils. To his interviewers' astonishment, Radool acted as though he did not understand the concept. With no recollection of having addressed the captain and crew, he seemed genuinely confused about the events that had occurred since beginning the engine repairs. Except for the swollen cut on his head, his headache and loss of memory, the infirmary reported his condition as normal: the effects of a mild concussion.

"Let us summon Enigg Radool," suggested the Aggah, her voice soft but crystal clear in the subterranean chamber, "that we may question the young man ourselves."

In full agreement and as if to leave their kiva, the Elders started to stand.

"No," she said, softly once again. "Tonight, the enigg shall come to us."

Come to us? Except for a few privileged craftsmen and technicians, none but the Aggah and High Council were allowed in the sacred room.

"The enigg is worthy," Bood assured them. "You shall see."

— ∘ ☼ ∘ —

Nestled high in the kiva's stalactites, Iddh alternately cackled and cursed the Elders seated below. All twenty-four seemed on edge and were staring into the firepit as though hypnotized by the dancing flames. With only minor discrepancies, Captain Narlihd's version of events had been corroborated, and General Qaloov's report left no doubt that the Khraelings thought the NHD possessed a new and superior engine. Worse, the khraeks would likely believe it had been intentionally revealed in an exercise designed to gauge KSF response times to a surprise attack. In all probability, Marshall Pranol was considering a preemptive strike.

A tone announced the arrival of a sled in the kiva's vacuum shaft. Iddh stopped cackling and flew up for a look, as two of Bood's able-bodied aides emerged from the shaft and then went back inside to help an overly nervous young enigg to his feet. Like the Aggah and Elders below, Radool wore a headwrap, light shawl, and a loincloth. With a shriek, Iddh pinned away.

The Aggah's aides issued a series of flattering remarks, doing their best to reassure the enigg as they escorted him to the kiva's low-lit, sealed entrance. Then, with a kiss from both on each of his cheeks, the two returned to their sled, guardedly giggling, and left the young operative to fend for himself.

Pahl Radool felt weak and nauseous, and his bare feet burned on the hot stone floor. He jumped as a vaulted doorway hissed open. Then he stepped cautiously inside and moved unsteadily to the top of the kiva's narrow, spiraling stairway. Seeing no handrail, he mustered his strength and began the dizzying, two-loop descent into the sweltering heat and down into the firelight flickering below.

From the room's far end, the Aggah watched intently as the chosen one appeared—appropriately, she thought—from out of the darkness. Unah Bood's time had come. A high-ranking crusader from the Og's elite incarnate corps, she had birthed into an average Jakomen family; and as intended, she drew attention to her leadership abilities from a very early age.

Singular of mind, Bood had never married, and of the few lovers she had taken, none were male. Upon her eighteenth birthday in New Hollatian years, she became Aggah—the youngest of any on record. Ever focused on her destiny, she had always harbored GROUP COMMAND's assertion that the Rohmans would come during her reign on New Hollatia. And that someday she would rule on Khrae.

Radool came to the last stair and stopped, hesitant to step onto the sacred kiva floor. The Aggah stared awhile, and then ordered, quietly, "Come forward, Enigg Radool."

The operative expected an echo, but his Aggah's voice sounded sharp and clear. He stepped to the floor and marched as best he could, barefoot and nervous, past the first few Elders.

He looked so ordinary. The purported prophet bore no physical deformities, no signs of a genetic link to the revered Dahanah. Not even a scarred tribute.[225]

Radool skirted the firepit and stopped about three meters from the seated Aggah Bood. His nausea intensified as he smelled her sweet perfume.

Standing rigidly at attention, he saluted smartly and tried to stiffen his muscles to hide his trembling—to conceal his rising fear. He could hear the Elders breathing. He could feel their curious eyes.

"You may stand easy, young man," said the Aggah, surprisingly softly.

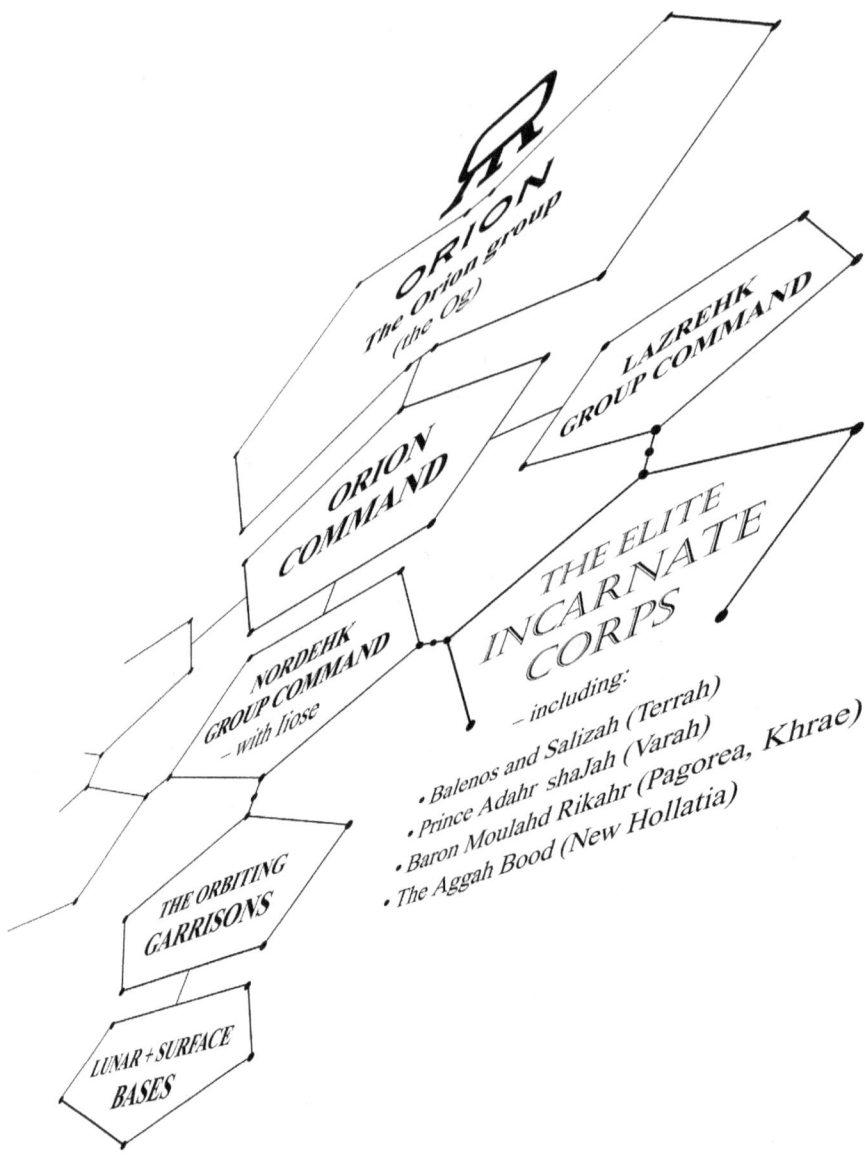

ORION
The Orion group
(the Og)

ORION COMMAND

LAZREHK GROUP COMMAND

THE ELITE INCARNATE CORPS
– including:

• Balenos and Salizah (Terrah)
• Prince Adahr shaJah (Varah)
• Baron Moulahd Rikahr (Pagorea, Khrae)
• The Aggah Bood (New Hollatia)

NORDEHK GROUP COMMAND
– with Iiose

THE ORBITING GARRISONS

LUNAR + SURFACE BASES

Radool tried moving his left foot. It felt numb, rubbery, and it tingled sharply as he tilted it and dragged it over a little way.

He crossed his hands behind him and stared ahead between his Aggah and an Elder. His head pounded and he could not feel his knees. *Would his legs give out before he fainted, or would he just faint first?*

"Are you feeling all right, my son?"

My son? "Qah, my Aggah." He sounded timid. His throat was constricted. He should push through his nervousness and speak with confidence. And he should be truthful with his leader.

"I am a little nervous, my Aggah," he admitted, verbalizing more loudly, but voice cracking to his dismay.

"It is the High Council's understanding, Enigg," Bood said, her stare intense but unthreatening, "that you have suffered a memory lapse."

"I remember everything well, my Aggah," Radool more forcefully replied, embarrassed by the way his voice had cracked, "up until sometime after I began working on our cruiser's transen coil."

"Do you remember hurting your head?"

He felt a swirling sensation…fought it, and answered, "Naq, my Aggah. I remember replacing some parts we fried in the plasma burn…" Her perfume seemed stronger, and ever more sickly sweet. "…then nothing until waking in the infirmary." He managed a swallow.

"I awoke as from a dream." He couldn't feel his legs. "I have tried to recall bumping my head…" Every few seconds everything turned grey, and then a brief, nauseating swirl of red rushed through his head. "…but I am unable to hold the moment…." He was afraid to close his eyes, afraid to swallow for fear of vomiting. And with a final rush of grey and red, Radool knew that he was fainting.

Instead of dropping limply to the hot stone floor, however, the enigg jerked forward as Lord Mohaar entered him and fast threw Radool's right foot ahead. In the same motion, the demon slapped it down hard to catch his balance. Iddh, now back in the kiva's stalactites, alternately shrieked, howled and cheered the Rohman Son.

Bood cocked her head to one side, and several Elders leaned forward in their seats. All watched intensely as the young operative slowly straightened. His eyes looked suddenly alive. He had lost all signs of nervousness and he stood tall with head held high and shoulders squared. His confident smile was unsettling.

Mohaar scanned the Aggah's mind…she seemed competent and prepared. And then her two fellow Og-incarnates, the twins Ehdin and Klohe…who—yes—would serve well in their supportive roles.

Upon sensing the demon's scanning, all three incarnates bowed their heads and silently pledged their hearts to Rohm. The kiva's confounded others knew not what to think.

In an instant, the warrior/enigg flashed a string of explicit instructions to the Aggah Bood. Again, she seemed capable and fully engaged.

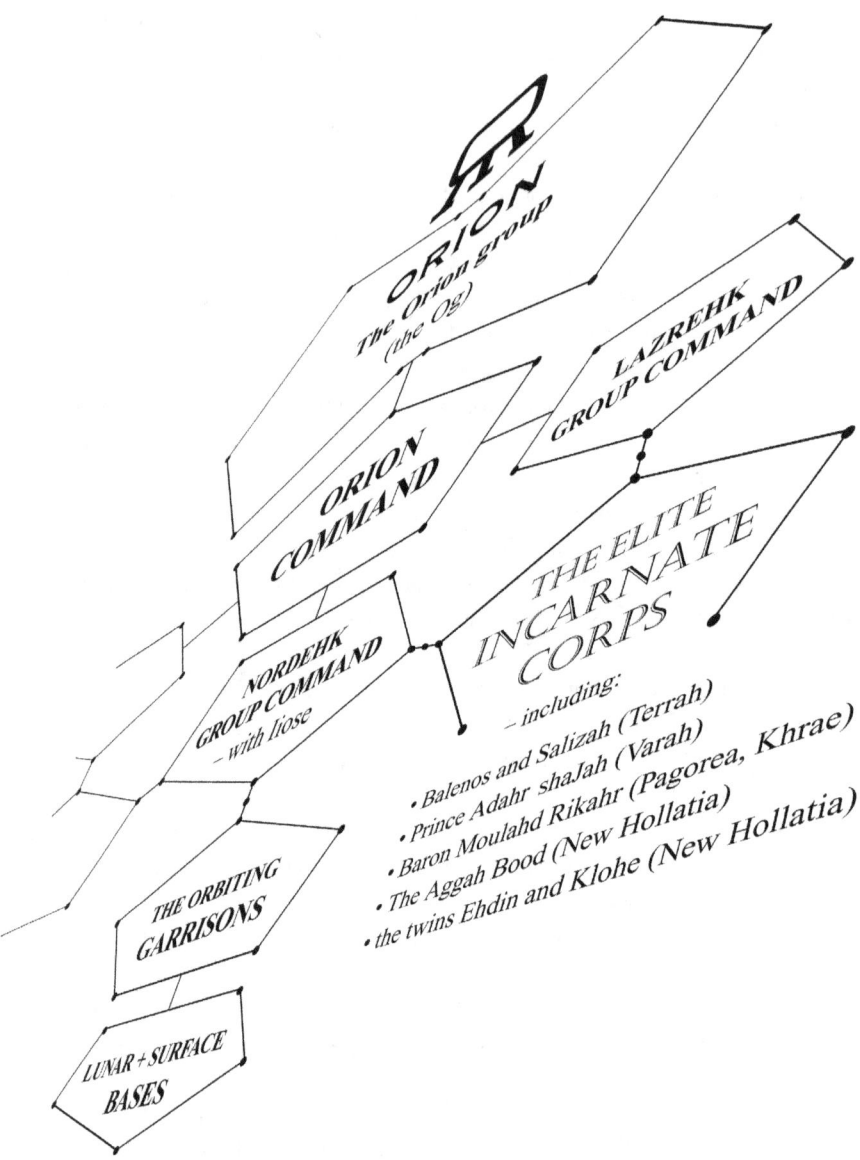

ORION
The Orion group
(the Og)

ORION
COMMAND

LAZREHK
GROUP COMMAND

NORDEHK
GROUP COMMAND
– with liose

THE ELITE
INCARNATE
CORPS

– including:

• Balenos and Salizah (Terrah)
• Prince Adahr shaJah (Varah)
• Baron Moulahd Rikahr (Pagorea, Khrae)
• The Aggah Bood (New Hollatia)
• the twins Ehdin and Klohe (New Hollatia)

THE ORBITING
GARRISONS

LUNAR + SURFACE
BASES

"Your service is known, crusaders," said the Rəhman Son in a telepathic resonance heard by just the three. "Now, *look up!* And see as these shall see."

Bood, Ehdin and Klohe reverently raised their heads, and with the others watched Mohaar/Radool begin his slow walk around the kiva, between its firepit and the Jakomen seated on the perimeter wall's cushioned ledge.

As he sauntered past each proud but perplexed Elder, the Son scanned the being's mind and learned its deepest fears. After a full circle, he stopped, turned and spoke—aloud.

"You wonder at your operatives' premature return."

His voice's deep reverberation startled them all—except Iddh, who remained crouched high in the kiva's stalactites. It was nothing like Radool's initial, timorous address.

"You suffer the loss of *your* container," he thundered.

Lord Mohaar raised and spread the arms of his unconscious host. And in a profound appreciation for the flesh, the demon slowly unraveled the young one's marvelous fingers.

"You wonder who I am!" he thundered.

Several Elders recoiled; others gasped and cowered. Even the Aggah, Klohe and her brother Ehdin appeared overcome with fear.

A mild illumination enveloped the enigg's body.[226] In the fire-lit chamber, it looked extreme.

Mohaar/Radool lifted off the floor. Feet dangling, he turned one slow revolution.

"I represent your salvation."

And one more, slow, full turn.

"I represent The Lord of Lords."

Chapter 24 — N O T E S

N[224] ***the skinnies' heads.*** The bulbous heads of the tall Og who wear tight white suits, the ones to whom the shorter, subservient "hell-men" deliver Ricky for periodic, surgical adjustments.

N[225] ***scarred tribute.*** Fairest of Khrae's ten cerise-skinned tribes (self-sorted by their inherent pigmentational disposition), the Jakomen have come to embrace the deformities that tie them to their Dahanan lineage. More often than not, those born free of birth defects will, at some stage of their young lives, smash a bone or slash a limb in memory of the holocaust. Although expected, the disfiguring tributes are no longer encouraged.

N[226] ***a mild illumination.*** As the Aggah had dreamt just days before:

> [from D-30.8, *THE AGGAH'S DREAM*] She'd dreamt of an enigg, a junior officer of the New Hollatian Defense. He held his hands in fire and spoke of retribution, of avenging the Dahanah and the Jakomen of old. He spoke of things written long before, and of their fathers' long gone lands. And he rubbed his hands together and held them high, palms out. And neither hand had burned. And then his body became as glowing, and he rose up off the ground....

To be continued, in:

BOOK 2

Part II

H E A T

The CONSOLIDATED
CHAPTER NOTES

N[101] ***the veiling syndrome.*** The forgetting of past lives and pre-birth intentions, a phenomenon limited to the third dimension/density.

N[102] ***the Orion group*** [pron. Ō-rī′-ŏn]. Pitiless mercenaries from the motherworlds and territories of the Orion constellation; seasoned troops commissioned by the Rǝhmans to serve in *His Crusades.*

N[103] ***the Rohmans*** [pron. **Rō′**-mǝns]. Those living within or crusading beyond The Master's (Rǝhm's) vast domain.

N[104] ***the fourth density.*** The fourth "octave" or "dimension" of reality, a seven-level plane of existence with a common visibility spectrum wherein the resident beings' senses, perceptions and abilities are more highly evolved than in those of the lower realms. As such, most newly Rǝhmanized fourth-density groups are militarized, and then forced through economic necessity to bid for service in *His Crusades.*

N[105] ***amphidor.*** A highly versatile computer and powerful photonic 3D imaging machine.

N[106] ***three-dimensional image.*** Og crusaders have long used amphidoric imagery to found and fortify false religions, or to confound authentic Faith. Beaming live or recorded images of one or more performing hybrids from a shrouded disc or cruiser, the darkeyed deceivers easily produce effective apparitions, "divine visions," which invariably are readily embraced.

N[107] ***NORDEHK GROUP COMMAND.*** An interlocking assembly of five battle-ready motherships located near Nordehk's lone red dwarf at the constellation's inward Vesper fringe, GROUP COMMAND is the tactical command center for the Orion group's Nordehk operations.

N[108] ***pinning.*** To pin. The concentration of one's consciousness into a pinpoint of light for the purpose of traveling instantaneously to destinations seen in the mind's eye. Or, if *The Master's will* be done, to enter and possess other living forms, whether briefly, repeatedly, or for a longer term.

N[109] *hybrid-incarnates.* Elite Og crusaders who occupy bodies genetically engineered from local and alien reproductive materials. Designed for a minimum 300-year life span, and with appearances reflecting local perceptions of divine beings, squadrons of the darkeyes' lovely hybrids are to usher in the New Order upon receipt of a glorious Rǝhman Son's command.

N[110] *six-fingered hands.* Five fingers, plus opposable thumb.

N[111] *Rǝhman Sons.* Fallen angels (both male and female) known to some as Imperial Lords or Sons of Rǝhm, and to others more correctly *and foremost* as high demons.

N[112] *ancient amphidoric chart.* Twelve thousand standard years before, Orion Command received an imperial map of Nordehk along with an invitation to bid on the contract to prime the constellation for conquest. Having already logged hundreds of exploratory missions to Nordehk, the Og were relatively familiar with the starfield's inhabited and uninhabited worlds, but had long been under imperial constraints. To instill fear and confusion, costumed visitations were allowed, but sustained open contact would violate the broad Eighth Commandment:

> **8:** *[1]Only by the hand of Rǝhm, shall All That Is be brought to Order.*
>
> —from The Teachings (The Book of Rǝhm)

N[113] *bahva* [pron. **bä′-vä**]. Rǝhman slang for *bhuvani*/beings; imperial citizens; ordinary beings of The Master's vast domain.

N[114] *the Vihdæa* [pron. **Vĭd-ā′-yǎ**]. Etherean administrators of the constellations; a largely passive, largely loyal order, the Vihdæa are local keepers of the Light.

N[115] *midwayer.* Creatures of eternity, midwayers (or more formally, *peshim* [pron. **pĕ-shēm′**]) spontaneously manifested midway between the fourth and fifth densities where they remain forever bound—billions in every galaxy, all endowed with special talents but unable to reproduce. Few entities have an extrasensory ability to accurately lock on to a particular point in space. The Vihdæa are capable, and though the Sons can maneuver between planets of the same solar system and stars of adequate magnitudes, the Sons depend on midwayer "scouts" to find shrouded or rapidly moving warships: a challenge made easy by a telepathic fix with one of their kind. To monitor activities inside unpiloted Rǝhman ships trekking through cosmic highways, "resident midwayers"/midwayer-sentinels are assigned temporarily and then released from duty after their vessel's emergence at its destination.

N[116] *'drax (andrax)*. Modifiable Rǝhman androids; societal attendants and enforcers of The Teachings on Rǝhmanized worlds, and formidable weapons in war.

N[117] *cubit*. An imperial unit of measure equal to 12 Rǝhman inches, 0.485 of an Og meter, or 19.1 Terran inches.

N[118] *feritts*. Weightless, mobile, lightly armed, insect-like surveillance machines.

N[119] *Jinn-Jinn* ♂. The khoomyahna's temporary resident midwayer.

N[120] *the other standing three*. Group Commander Iiose and his two aides.

N[121] *Mohaar* ♂ [pron. **Mō′**-här]. A righteous Imperial Lord of the Realm, and glorious Son of Rǝhm. Lord Mohaar's eternally committed, personal midwayer/scout is *Iddh* ♂ [pron. Ĭd].

N[122] *Wohtan* ♂ [pron. **Wō′**-tăn]. A righteous Imperial Lord of the Realm, and glorious Son of Rǝhm. Lord Wohtan's eternally committed, personal midwayer/scout is *Ænus* ♂ [pron. **Ē′**-nŭs].

N[123] *Dhanz* ♀ [pron. Dôns]. A righteous Imperial Lord of the Realm, and glorious Son of Rǝhm. Lord Dhanz's personal, eternally-committed midwayer/scout is *Bhu* ♀ [pron. Boo].

N[124] *Zhol* ♂ [pron. Zōl]. A righteous Imperial Lord of the Realm, glorious Son of Rǝhm, and Overlord of the Nordehk campaign. Lord Zhol is an inspirational Son who leads by example, a warrior who fully understands the relationship between wisdom and wealth and how to balance the pursuit of both. As Overlord of now fifteen constellations—three more than Lord Dhanz—Zhol spends much of his time preparing updates for the twelve Supreme Sons (the Rǝhman High Court), and tending to his holdings in the realm. Lord Zhol's personal, eternally-committed midwayer/scout is *Poxx* ♂ [pron. Pŏks].

N[125] *elantah* [pron. ē-lăn′-tə]. Varah is among the family of cosmic curiosities dubbed "elantahs" by the Rөhmans: temperate, water-bearing, lunar planetoids. Eleven such oddities exist within the Empire. Varah would become the twelfth.

N[126] *pentahm* [pron. **pěn′**-tôm]. Pentahms are five, adjoining, similarly sized, three-dimensional stellar sectors that constitute a constellation and radiate outward from its core. Underdeveloped pentahm sections are known as "frontiers."

N[127] *favorably inclined.* Negatively oriented/polarized; focused on self and on the trappings of serving oneself, as opposed to a positive polarization and service unto others, and unto the common good.

N[128] *MoLs.* Mercenaries of Light; entities of a positive polarity who, of their own free will, incarnate from the higher realms to inspire and enlighten those of evolving cultures.

N[129] *Vakaar.* "His Reverence"; high priest or *yamah* of the Nordehk campaign's appointed priesthood:

> [from D-32.4, *BEL'S INTRUSION*] Responsible for channeling the flow of turbid liquid sweating from the warship's fleshy inner walls, the criminal crew toiled knee-deep in a ditch that flanked an ample but ill-lit passage to the khoom's rectory, when Vakaar and an entourage of robed and hooded priests came sloshing into view.
>
> As the mission's high priest, or "yamah," Vakaar held final authority in the absence of a Rөhman Son. Skinny, hunched and noticeably shorter than the rest, few rarely saw him without his two lanky cohorts—the ones to whom his spies reported—and this day both were at his sides. Stooped with necks awkwardly twisted, they mouthed constant whispers into the scrawny yamah's pointed ears.

N[130] *thought-forms.* Temporary apparitions or enduring material manifestations formed by the power of thought.

N[131] *Bel* ♀. A founding member of Nordehk's 8-seat Vihdæan Council and their most capable spy, Bel is the khoomyahna's angelic "intruder."

N[132] *Janah* [pron. **Jă′**-nä]. A secret sect of 22 Rөhman rebels—closet anarchists who volunteered for the mission to Nordehk with hopes of escaping the Empire's stifling *Order:*

[from D-32.6, *CHAOS AND LIGHT*] Thirteen covert rebels huddled in their secluded hideaway: a cramped nook near the eighth of the khoom's twelve static containment domes. They had heard rumors of an intrusion, and of the intruder's brilliant light.

Like the other free bahva onboard the khoomyahna, these thirteen young Rohman citizens had volunteered for the one-way mission to Nordehk and had met the selection criteria. Quite unlike the others aboard, however, these were some of the Janah, a secret sect of twenty-two beings bent on escaping the Empire's stifling *Order*.

N[133] ***pranah.*** An element of the cosmic force that carries extrasensory callings and other telepathic communications, as well as the consciousness of those able to harness portions of its power.

N[134] ***pods…dias, and imposing golden throne.*** Fundamental components of all khoomyahnas' black chamber, or "Chamber of the Pods".

N[135] ***temporal vehicle.*** An ephemeral, material-life vehicle, a living structure capable of temporarily hosting the consciousness of an evolving entity.

N[136] ***third density.*** The third "octave" or "dimension" of reality; the lowest density to support the communal, incarnational development of living creatures; a seven-level plane of existence having a common visibility spectrum wherein its creature's senses, perceptions and abilities are less developed than those of higher realms.

N[137] ***their meeting with the Og.*** The Sons' briefing inside the tactical chamber of Group Commander Iiose's battle cruiser.

N[138] ***will-creature.*** Any evolving life-form endowed with the unique capacity to make a moral decision, and which usually labels itself "human," "human being" or "man."

N[139] ***negatively oriented midwayer.*** Jinn-Jinn, the khoom's temporarily-assigned sentinel.

N[140] ***tactical chamber.*** The illusory chamber of Group Commander Iiose's battle cruiser:

[from D-32.3, *AWAITING THE DEMON-SONS*] The tactical chamber's curving walls, blackish metallic floor and domed ceiling blended indistinguishably and looked impossibly immense for the cruiser's modest

size. It was an illusion, an imperial innovation—one of few technological
marvels the Rohmans chose to share.

N[141] *freshly updated stellar program.* Updated through the transfer of data and
materials to the khoomyahna from Group Commander Iiose's battle cruiser:

> [from D-32.7, *HOSTING THE DEMON SONS*] ...the old group
> commander cleared his throat and took a moment to gather himself.
>   "The following actions and developments are detailed in the data now
> flowing to your khoomyahna. A transfer of capsules containing the requested
> samples and codes for Nordehk's flora and fauna, including genetic materials
> from the higher species, is also underway."

N[142] *polymides.* Exotic metal alloys; extremely lightweight supermetals having
various combinations of properties including superstrength, superductility and
superconductivity.

N[143] *atmahan* [pron. ăt-mă-**hăn'**]. The Rohman word for "ring of death,"
atmahan is applicable only to a non-planetary, stellar belt of asteroidal debris.
Although early Og explorers were intrigued by the ancients' advancing culture,
stunned by the Varahns' spectacular lunar world, and covetous of Khrae's
inestimable polymides, they were utterly fascinated by the Terran system's
perilous belt of asteroids. Nearly as rare as elantahs, atmahan are unmistakable
stellar hallmarks of human belligerence. Also known as "suicide rings,"
Creation's uncommon atmahan consistently contain evidence of societal self-
destruction.

N[144] *Khrae and New Hollatia.* Rival worlds in a shared solar system.

N[145] *already on his way.* Having promptly pinned to his assigned solar
system* upon the conclusion of the Sons' meeting with Group Commander
Iiose.

> * that of sister worlds Khrae and New Hollatia—as detailed in the
> upcoming sequence, *A DEMON AT THE HELM.*

N[146] *Elasia.* One of the 10 continents of planet Khrae.

N[147] *the Jakomen.* Who no longer inhabit Khrae (as Group Commander Iiose
recounted to the four Rohman Sons):

> [from D-32.7, *HOSTING THE DEMON SONS*] "Through a slow but

steady erosion of populace polarity, we estimate that 14% of the Khraelings are favorably inclined. Their most recent foray of merit, some 600 standard years ago, saw the near-annihilation of one of Khrae's ten tribes, the so-called Jakomen people. Since the surviving Jakomen's self-imposed exile on Khrae's terra-formed sister planet 'New Hollatia,' the strained relationship between the Jakomen and their Khraeling cousins—and the lingering calls for retribution—may present an opportunity for a controlled reduction."

Lord Mohaar, possessor of the leftmost junior, made mental note of the commander's intimation, for it reinforced a tentative plan he had long contrived.

N[148] *the ruling barons.* The barons issued paper "qubals" backed by the Federation's considerable gross product. The Jakomen of Old Hollatia circulated gold certificates backed by an inventory of bullion greater than any three of Khrae's other continents combined. The Federation spoke a common language; Hollatia spoke its own. The Jakomen subscribed to a belief in one god, and although claiming a similar faith, the Federation has yet to completely unify its theological elements.

N[149] *elite incarnate corps.* Select Og mercenaries trained and assigned to birth into the unsuspecting tribes of worlds being primed for Rehmanization.

N[150] *from Varah.* From the compassionate Varahns of Khrae's neighboring solar system.

N[151] *the benevolent Elasians.* The people of continental Elasia (of planet Khrae), who sheltered the surviving Jakomen after the holocaust.

N[152] *KSF.* The Khrae Security Forces; Khrae's defenders and the enforcers of Federation law.

N[153] *NHD.* The New Hollatian Defense; the global police, security force and defenders of New Hollatia.

N[154] *Federation Board.* Khrae's 11-seat executive council consisting of the governor, Counsel-Ra, and all nine continental barons ("Those of the Continents").

N[155] *meters.* Og-incarnates unfailingly impose Orion's metric system on those they are priming for conquest. Their Rehman masters allow the imposition as a prelude to the coming New Order. Consequently, all measures of volume, weights and non-stellar distances are identical on Nordehk's inhabited worlds, except Mhu:

> [from D-32.7, *HOSTING THE DEMON SONS*] "One: Mhu. The progenitors of Nordehk's tribes, the so-called ancients of Mhu, retain a purely positive polarity and remain committed to the Light. Having completed their transition from the third to fourth density some 240,000 years ago, those of Mhu have been left to your discretion, as prescribed."

N[156] *nostril.* The Khraeling/Jakomen single nostril.

N[157] *the Rikahrs.* The ruling family of continental Pagorea, and age-old rivals of the Ebahs (rulers of continental Elasia).

N[158] *Baron Miloh Ebah XII.* The current Baron of Elasia; head of Elasia's ruling Ebah family, the continued rivals of Pagorea's ruling Rikahrs.

N[159] *KLC.* Khrae Lunar Command; the nerve center of the Khrae Security Forces (the *KSF*) is located on and beneath the surface of *Patos*, the largest and outermost of Khrae's two moons.

N[160] *Altos.* The polymide-laden, innermost, and smallest of Khrae's two moons.

N[161] *warrior-crusader.* A lieutenant devoted to a host of Rohman Sons through the course of a host of Rohman campaigns.

N[162] *Son sponsorship.* An Imperial Warrior—a newly fallen Vihdæan defector—may attain Son status only through the sponsorship of a campaigning Rohman Son, to whom he then becomes forever obligated to serve when called upon. If such a Son should ever fail, both he *and* his sponsor could be stripped of their rank and title by the Rohman High Court, and banished to lesser service as Imperial Administrators of the Realm.

N[163] *the next in line.* As determined by the ancients of Mhu.

N[164] *the ancients' invitation.* A necessary formality by the ancients' maxim concerning volition, as opposed to their improperly *informing* the Varahns and Khraelings and presuming their participation—despite that certainty (as all parties understood the strategic value of participating in such a monumental event). Presumptiveness aside, the ancients' preparatory formalities are respected as such.

N[165] *all four participating worlds.* Mhu, Varah, Khrae and New Hollatia.

N[166] *as had the Jakomen of old.* Before the holocaust.

N[167] *Pagorean sons.* Decendants of the suspected perpetrators of the Jakomen holocaust.

N[168] *100-day festival.* As Group Commander Iiose reported to the four Rɵhman Sons:

> [from D-32.7, *HOSTING THE DEMON SONS*] "Under the ancients' direction," Iiose continued, lowering his hand and privately pleased with the execution of his practiced showmanship, "Varah, Khrae, and New Hollatia are preparing to jointly colonize the so-called Seed. There is to be a 100-day festival on Khrae designed to celebrate the occasion, and which will culminate in the joint departure of 200 'settlers': 100 from Varah, 90 from Khrae, and 10 from New Hollatia. Festivities are scheduled to begin in 33 days as time is measured by the Khraelings, whose 24-hour planetary rotation is within seconds of the Rɵhman standard day."

N[169] *the Varahn convoy.* An interstellar tug/starship with Prince Adahr, his delegation and the 100 settler-daughters on board—all in hibernation—and with 14 gigantic containers of commercial goods in tow.

N[170] *the prince's starship.* The Varahn convoy's powerful interstellar tug.

N[171] *advance departure.* With 6.4 standard light years between Khrae and Varah, the Varahns learned of, prepared for, and departed for the mission long before the ancients informed Khrae's leadership.

N[172] *sky-blue roundtable.* As described on Day -32 when Nordehk's Vihdæan Council awaited the return of their sister, Bel, while she spied inside the approaching khoomyahna:

> [from D-32.10, *THE COUNCIL AWAITS*] Their spacious, thought-formed table consisted of three concentric rings that stepped down in height from the outside in toward an open middle. With one seat empty, Nordehk's pensive Vihdæan Council anxiously awaited the return of their sister, Bel.

N[173] *Loyal Order of Oraphim.* A high order of etherean warrior-messengers irreproachably devoted to the Light.

N[174] *the ablest of spies.* Stealthiest of celestial agents, the oraphim are endowed with all the skills and talents of the Vihdæa, the seraphim, the midwayers and more. Like the midwayers, they were born between densities, but not the fourth and fifth. Oraphic reality lies between the sixth and seventh densities—a very high order irreproachably devoted to the Light. Though few in number (less than 150 million per galaxy), the oraphim serve in ways not possible to describe in words of the lower realms. Mysterious messengers and warriors at once, they assist incarnating Mercenaries of Light in ways unknown to the selfless MoLs. They also serve the Universal Sons and the Vihdæa, but take their orders from neither. Nor would they ever defect.

N[175] *so is it written.* As recorded in *The Sacred Tomes of The Ancients of Days*—divine prophesies known only to the eternally committed, and whispered infrequently among the rest.

N[176] *Dehniss and Phobb.* The ones to whom Vakaar's spies report.

N[177] *her broadcast.* The broadcast of her forum intercepted earlier in the day:

> [from D-30.2, *THE AGGAH'S FORUM*] Haleahm pointed in'field (in the imaging field), directly at the marshall's life-sized image, which along with the other imaged layers, dissolved as a staticky interception of a New Hollatian broadcast filled the display. The Jakomen were sitting in public forum with their current Aggah—the dynamic Unah Bood. The gathering was limited to 60,000: the same rounded number as that of their revered Dahanah, those who had survived the actual surprise attack on Old Hollatia some eight centuries prior to recent times.
>
> Governor Mauhk groaned. He had been hoping for some kind of signal, some indication of possible compromise. But the sign was clear: the Jakomen's towering holocaust memorial, a dark and twisted framework that seemed to stretch halfway to the stars, formed the backdrop for Bood's fire-lit forum.
>
> All 24 Jakomen Elders sat quietly behind their beloved leader, whose speech rose in crescendo. Khrae Lunar Command's translation of the Aggah's address streamed down one side of her flickering image as a red band of Khraeling characters, while she shouted over a rising applause and fierce pounding of ceremonial drums.
>
> "...and after two centuries of virtual neglect, we have been *'invited'*..." She drew the word out. "...for what?!" she screamed, her live audience now roaring and stomping their feet.
>
> "For a *'celebration'*..." The roar grew louder. "...for a *'party'*...." The roar was deafening.
>
> "What has changed? What has happened that I am so blind?"

N[178] ***thirty days ago.*** As the needy Jakomen had prearranged with their compassionate Varahn friends.

N[179] ***as received by the mission's priesthood.*** Prior to the khoom's departure for Nordehk, Vakaar received several sets of the Sons' podded bodies, which the brothers stored in the warship's rectory for future placement and unspecified, future use.

N[180] ***nostril.*** The Khraeling/Jakomen single nostril.

N[181] ***illusionally obscure.*** As induced by a Rǝhman illusory device adaptable to curvilinear chambers (one of few technological marvels shared with certain fourth-density crusaders, including the Og).

N[182] ***flash-scans.*** An adaptation of technology gleaned from one of the ancients' abandoned outposts, flash-scans utilize arcing bursts of invisible particles fired/flashed at 114.7 times the speed of light [further detailed in upcoming Chapter 14].

N[183] ***vihmyana.*** The new destroyer that left its mothership (the khoomyahna) a few hours before:

> [from D-29.2, *BIRTHING THE FIRST VIHMYANA*] On the underside of the khoom's outer midsection, a small portion of the warship's hull began to bulge. A tear appeared and dilated, and great globs of turbid birthing fluid gushed out, froze and tumbled into space. Lord Mohaar's vihmyana squeezed through, somersaulted and rolled away—its umbilical stubs dangling from seemingly random surfaces of the destroyer's graceful, ray-like body.

N[184] ***as detailed by the Og.*** In the materials transferred from Group Commander Iiose's cruiser to the khoomyahna on Day -32:

> [from D-32.7, *HOSTING THE DEMON SONS*] "The following actions and developments are detailed in the data now flowing to your khoomyahna. A transfer of capsules containing the requested samples and codes for Nordehk's flora and fauna, including genetic materials from the higher species, is also underway."

N[185] ***ten long years in space.*** As measured in lengthy Varahn years (nearly 19 as measured by Khrae's Intercontinental Federation).

N[186] *in the vihmyana's systems bridge.* Since leaving his destroyer in orbit over Patos:

> [from D-29.4, *JUST A CHILL*] Lord Mohaar brought his shrouded vihmyana into orbit high over Patos, Khrae's outermost moon. Then, as his silver recliner wrapped his temporal body in a field of preserving, fluorescent-like blue light, he summoned and pinned away with Iddh.

N[187] *Vihdæan intrusion.* Bel's intrusion of the khoomyahna on Day -32:

> [from D-32.4, *BEL'S INTRUSION*] Moments later, a pinpoint of shimmering, iridescent light—Vihdæan light—appeared and blossomed, illuminating the dim corridor. The convicts scrambled from their ditch and scattered. A few stopped and turned, covered their eyes and squinted through their fingers at the dazzling form taking shape in midair.
>
> Unseen and unheard by all but the brilliant intruder, the khoom's resident midwayer, Jinn-Jinn, charged into the passageway, screaming insults and vile Rǝhman threats.
>
> The violators heard nothing but the intruder's gentle, reassuring voice in their minds.
>
> "Peace be upon you, dear ones. I am Bel."

N[188] *yesterday's cryptic meeting with Hyynehk.* On Day -30:

> [from D-30.5, *THE MYSTERIOUS MESSENGER*] "Feeding on fear and ruling through intimidation, Rǝhm's methods vary greatly and he exhibits a vast spectrum of creative destruction on his journey through the night. His 'Sons,' fallen Vihdæan sisters and brothers themselves, are powerful and serve him well. But so is it written and long known to us oraphim, '…so shall the darkness begin to fade, and with the Light, become as one.'"
>
> *Long known?* Who held these words of things to come, and how—*and when*—had they been written? And why should knowledge of such profound, future events be privy to so few? Yes, the oraphim were of a high order; and yes, it was improper for simple administrators to solicit insights into the broader divine…but….
>
> "As always, there are no shortcuts to enlightenment," Hyynehk continued, as though having heard their thoughts. "Administration through patient revelation will ultimately reveal the joys of Love and Light. The Most Highs have every confidence in your ability to prevail."
>
> *Prevail?* None before had prevailed. None before had even briefly slowed the Rǝhman hordes. Were these just hollow words? Had others heard them, too?
>
> "Work together, that triumph be assured."
>
> *Work together?* Nordehk's Vihdæa had always worked together. Was the oraph suggesting that they solicit outside help?

N[189] ***Rehm began calling.*** The Master's callings exploit a fundamental weakness in galactic administration: the Vihdæan constraints. Once assigned to a constellation upon its first world's sparking by the divine Sowers, the Vihdæa are bound to an eternity of largely passive roles. Rehm offers that which is otherwise unattainable: proactive diversity—a highly powerful lure. As warrior-crusaders, Vihdæan defectors may see, *and experience*, All That Is. As elevated Sons of Rehm, a ranking earned through unfailing service, their full powers are put to the test. By defecting and serving in *His Crusades*, they may become known. They may become loved. They may become *feared*.

N[190] ***their long, deep sleep.*** The Varahn voyagers' 10-year hibernation (as the Varahns record time), or 19 years as measured by the Khraelings.

N[191] ***the incident at Base 11.*** The abrupt death of Specialist Mahrget Thowm:

> [from D-29.7, *EAVESDROPPING ON IHMOY*] Listening intently, Mohaar came to a locked directory, *"Restricted—K1: Eyes Only."* Thowm knew it as the Federation's strategic files. She did not know the codes and had served her purpose.
>
> The demon silently summoned his cackling scout. Then he violently exited his young, warm, Khraeling host, and pinned back to his destroyer. And without a sound, Mahrget Thowm slumped over her console.

N[192] ***frequently paired incarnate troops.*** To counteract the undesirable effects of loneliness, as arranged for the hybrids Balenos and Salizah:

> [from D-32.2, *THE COLLABORATORS*] Similar in height and with short dark hair, cold blue eyes and beautifully sculpted faces, the two hybrids could pass for thirty-year-old Terran twins. Nearly ninety years before, they had transferred to the Terran garrison from their quarters in GROUP COMMAND's elite incarnate wing, before pinning directly into the modified fetuses growing inside their earthling mothers' wombs. As they and their mission planners intended, the two Og-earthling hybrid-incarnates were born within days of each other in the same small town.

N[193] ***etheric chambers.*** All orbiting Og garrisons contain sophisticated etheric chambers that effectively transcend space and time. Designed to overcome the powerful effects of the veiling syndrome on their elite incarnate troops, the chambers enable Og specialists to consciously navigate the dream world's interdimensional planes where they effectively draw dreaming incarnate-crusaders to them and to one another. Occasionally, the chambers produce a strange side effect whereby the incarnates inexplicably glimpse the future, and premonitions become part of their in-session or after-session dreams.

N[194] *a rare instantaneous jump.* The essence of the Ehkilah Phenomenon [detailed in upcoming Chapter 16], as referenced by Group Commander Iiose during his briefing for the Sons:

> [from D-32.7, *HOSTING THE DEMON SONS*] "We therefore humbly suggest that the imminent geological upheavals be accelerated, that the changes may be effected *before* establishing the New Order. And, ever mindful of the Ehkilah Phenomenon, that the potential for a density jump be preempted and effectively nullified."
>
> Behind the glistening eyes of her unconscious young host, Lord Dhanz quietly considered the commander's cautious warning. Charged with delivering a needful, willing Terrah into The Master's mighty hands, she knew well the Ehkilah Phenomenon. And knew well the need to countervail.

N[195] *10,000 years.* Since Mhu's orbital period is just three hours short of the imperial standard year, the ancients measure time much the same as Rǝhman administrators.

N[196] *standard years.* As measured similarly by the Khraelings and the ancients of Mhu, and by the Rǝhmans—based on the average calendar of the Empire's inhabited worlds.

N[197] *with two already gone.* The two Janah now aboard Mohaar's vihmyana:

> [from D-29.2, *BIRTHING THE FIRST VIHMYANA*] In the khoomyahna's lower midsection, deep beneath the surface of a roundish, murky lake, teams of bahva specialists readied a fully developed vihmyana for launch. The teams dashed to and fro through the turbid solution in a profusion of shuttles and odd machines, while thousands of robotic devices scoured the scaly surface of the twitching, untried craft.
>
> The destroyer hung among eleven other maturing vihms amid a tangle of thick umbilicals in the khoom's birthing tank. Beams of fire-like light streamed outward from the thin band of huge, deck-straddling viewports that ringed the ship's shallow crown. Farther down, the vihmyana's 144-man crew, which included two volunteers from the Janah, settled in for their unknown mission.

N[198] *the Great Exodus.* The Jakomen emigration en masse from Khrae to the terra-formed sister world, Qalakah, which they subsequently renamed New Hollatia.

N^{199} *Og incarnates.* Accomplished infiltrators from GROUP COMMAND's elite incarnate corps.

N^{200} *the destroyer shot through the core.* A short time after having left its mothership (the khoomyahna):

[from D-28.10, *THE JANAH VOLUNTEERS*] Of the khoom's 12,000 bahva, fewer than six percent had volunteered to crew the two new vihmyanas being readied for launch. Along with 139 of those volunteers, five members of the Janah—including Chak, Sarvah's closest friend—had been approved.

[and from D-28.11, *THE SONS PROCEED*] Comfortably reclined in the khoomyahna's systems bridge, and with the Lords Dhanz and Wohtan piloting the two departing vihmyanas, Zhol reopened the warship's stellar program and zoomed in on the ancients' ninth seed.

N^{201} *to their vihmyana.* As it shot through a way portal that tapped planet Enyah's sun:

[from D-28.17, *THE EHKILAH PHENOMENON*] As her vihmyana shot through the core of an arterial way portal that tapped planet Enyah's yellow sun, the demon Dhanz lay in a full recline inside the destroyer's systems bridge.

Responsible for Rehmanizing both of the ancients' youngers, Terrah and Enyah, Dhanz revisited the briefing that the darkeyes had delivered four days before at the fringe of Nordehk's second frontier. She found Group Commander Iiose's guarded suggestion about Terrah to be of particular interest—that the world's looming geological changes be accelerated. She had thoroughly studied the full Og report, and would now review a copy of the khoomyahna's recording of that meeting.

N^{202} *glowed red hot.* After its two-day ride through the way portal's churning core.

N^{203} *two days before.* On Day -29, during his brief possession of Specialist Mahrget Thowm:

[from D-29.7, *EAVESDROPPING ON IHMOY*] While rummaging through the Federation's files, delving deeper and deeper into the KSF's database, Mohaar/Thowm intercepted an incoming communication. It was from a Major Ihmoy, a report that rang of opportunity. *The Master worked in mysterious ways.*

"…and we see no evidence of residual debris from an impact, either along its path or in the convoy's wake. The object's trajectory and velocity are suspicious."

N[204] *the Og report.* Contained among the data transferred from Group Commander Iiose's battle cruiser to the khoomyahna, on Day -32:

> [from D-32.7, *HOSTING THE DEMON SONS*] "The following actions and developments are detailed in the data now flowing to your khoomyahna. A transfer of capsules containing the requested samples and codes for Nordehk's flora and fauna, including genetic materials from the higher species, is also underway."

N[205] *Dr. Isdrav ♀.* Ashdah Isdrav, renowned Khraeling expert on tribal evolution.

N[206] *the two Janah nearby.* The two that had volunteered two days before:

> [from D-29.2, *BIRTHING THE FIRST VIHMYANA*] The destroyer hung among eleven other maturing vihms amid a tangle of thick umbilicals in the khoom's birthing tank. Beams of fire-like light streamed outward from the thin band of huge, deck-straddling viewports that ringed the ship's shallow crown. Farther down, the vihmyana's 144-man crew, which included two volunteers from the Janah, settled in for their unknown mission.

N[207] *the communicator.* The device revealed upon solving the ancients' techno-puzzle:

> [from D-28.9, *THE ANCIENTS AND THEIR BROOD*] The ancients knew that a surviving colony would eventually launch probes into space, and that it would only be a matter of time before their stellar station/outpost, at just one light-year away, would be found. And with it, the machine-like technopuzzle they had left.
>
> Both the Khraelings and Varahns found and solved the puzzle. Their uniquely different efforts succeeded in awakening the device into triggering a transmission, a signal back to Mhu that alerted the ancients to each extremely exciting achievement. The mechanism revealed was a communicator that beaded, aimed and flashed its messages in 10-second bursts at 114.7 times light speed: the universal telepathic ceiling (the conductivity speed of dark matter) and rather surprising example of Mhu's formidable accomplishments. With the exception of this gift—copied rather well by the Khraelings in 40 years, and adequately by the Varahns in 900—the ancients respectfully and unwaveringly refused to share other technowonders with their brood.

N[208] *raced for Varah.* Having left its mothership (the khoomyahna) the day before:

> [from D-28.11, *THE SONS PROCEED*] Comfortably reclined in the

khoomyahna's systems bridge, and with the Lords Dhanz and Wohtan piloting the two departing vihmyanas, Zhol reopened the warship's stellar program and zoomed in on the ancients' ninth seed.

N[209] *exploitable vulnerability.* As expressed by Group Commander Iiose during his formal briefing of the Sons on Day -32:

[from D-32.7, *HOSTING THE DEMON SONS*] "Having focused on spiritual advances, Varah's inhabitants, technologically, have fallen behind their later-settled cousins—those of Khrae, the second of the ancient's brood. Most notably, the Varahns' subsequent awareness and inherent fear of their distant neighbor-cousins may represent a state of exploitable vulnerability."

The second junior grunted and briefly but noticeably brightened. The demon inside—Lord Wohtan—bore responsibility for bringing Varah into the fold. He knew well the Varahns' vulnerabilities, including their inherent fear of their not-so-distant neighbors, the technologically advanced Khraelings. Long had the Son formulated a plan of action to seal the Varahns' fate. The *audacity* of this presumptuous little Og commander to overstate the obvious and to dare presume credit for Lord Wohtan's perfect plan.... Such insubordination would *not* go unpunished—not in the Overlord's eyes, nor in the eyes of Rohm.

N[210] *mere hours before.* During Major Ihmoy's flyby:

[from D-27.14, *FLYBY*] Sensing a powerful presence, Adahr shaJah stood and began looking around for what had to be a Rohman Son. Several of his delegates noticed and felt pleasant surprise at their prince's apparent interest in the ensuing, albeit rare, event.

"Forty-five seconds to flyby. Lotus check on three, two, one—mark."

"Two check." "Three check." "Four check." "Five check."

The prince determined the demon's general vicinity. Fixing his eyes upward on that spot, he suddenly jerked his head backward from the jarring force of instantaneously receiving his unquestionable instructions.

Despite their straining for a glimpse of the oncoming escorts, several delegates witnessed Adahr's strange convulsion. Those close at hand expressed their concern and offered to help ease him back into his seat. But with deepening dread, the shaken crusader-prince waved them off, bowed his royal head (and many delegates joined him in the obvious spiritual gesture), and silently pledged his heart to Rohm.

N[211] *the netherbeast's first lessons.* On Day -30:

[from D-30.7, *PRIESTLY CONTRIVANCES*] Deep in the rectory's bowels, the yamah's two cohorts, Dehniss and Phobb, and nine of the khoom's brawniest young priests lounged half-naked, greasing one another. A creature of darkness would soon be summoned. For its lessons. For its study in fleshly pain.

N²¹² *Hyynehk's cryptic words.* As delivered on Day -30 about prevailing, and about willful defections, and things long written, and extreme polarities. And about working together, *"that triumph be assured"*:

> [from D-30.5, *THE MYSTERIOUS MESSENGER*] "Rehm wants nothing tangible. It is the *power*. It is his mastery over the potent vibrations of fear and loathing, and especially the procession of etherean defections—his cherished, willing recruits—that sustain The Fallen One.
>
> "With each new negatively-polarized defector—one who chooses to abandon the Light, whether a seraph, midwayer, Vihdæan, or will-creature—there is a discernible empowering of those above, an exponential accumulation of power whereby those at the top of the Rehman hierarchy benefit most. Similarly, with every conquest and conversion en masse of more billions of evolving beings, 'Prime Crusader's' powers substantially increase."
>
> — ∘ ☼ ∘ —
>
> [and moments later] "Feeding on fear and ruling through intimidation, Rehm's methods vary greatly and he exhibits a vast spectrum of creative destruction on his journey through the night. His 'Sons,' fallen Vihdæan sisters and brothers themselves, are powerful and serve him well. But so is it written and long known to us oraphim, '...so shall the darkness begin to fade, and with the Light, become as one.'"
>
> *Long known?* Who held these words of things to come, and how—*and when*—had they been written? And why should knowledge of such profound, future events be privy to so few? Yes, the oraphim were of a high order; and yes, it was improper for simple administrators to solicit insights into the broader divine...but....
>
> "As always, there are no shortcuts to enlightenment," Hyynehk continued, as though having heard their thoughts. "Administration through patient revelation will ultimately reveal the joys of Love and Light. The Most Highs have every confidence in your ability to prevail."
>
> *Prevail?* None before had prevailed. None before had even briefly slowed the Rehman hordes. Were these just hollow words? Had others heard them, too?
>
> "Work together, that triumph be assured."

N²¹³ *Ubahr.* A gas giant and the system's sixth planet from the sun. The Khraelings conceded Ubahr and her moons in exchange for exclusive rights to the system's three lifeless inner worlds. Among the few post-holocaust Agreements negotiated with the Federation, the trade enabled the Jakomen to begin mining meager polymide deposits on three of Ubahr's moons, while patiently establishing a hidden base for a secret, second fleet (the "Second Wave").

N[214] *quite the contrary.* A reference to the surprise attack on and sudden annihilation of Old Hollatia:

[from D-32.15, *THE JAKOMEN HOLOCAUST*] The Federation's unending trade deficit with the Jakomen became a growing embarrassment to "Those of the Continents"—Khrae's nine ruling barons. And the Jakomen's generosity, their steady stream of grants and donations to innumerable humanitarian causes, seemed a deliberate slight. But most of all, Those of the Continents resented their citizens' growing awareness that life in "desolate" Hollatia was more just and simply better than their own. And one day, the small island continent of Hollatia and its 1.2 billion Jakomen were reduced to dust.

N[215] *demonic attack in the crystal plaza.* Lord Zhol's possession and subsequent slaying of an innocent in delivering the ancients' first notice of Rɵhm's Coming:

[from D-27.5, *A QUANDARY FOR THE OVERLORD*] While Poxx rained a torrent of unheard curses and threats from above, Zhol rendered his defiant host unconscious, and then leered at the surrounding, bewildered crowd.

Recovering from their brief hesitation, those nearest the Overlord's victim rushed to their brother's defense, embracing him and resuming his telepathic forbiddances, chants and prayers. "Negative spirit we forbid you entrance to this body! You are not in harmony with the Light! Bel l'ura Donai! Bel l'ura Donai! Bel l'ura Donai! *Bathe us in Prime Creator's light!*"

With the power of his mind, the Son flung several feeble defenders a good twenty cubits. Then, clamping his host's left hand onto the head of a now kneeling, would-be rescuer who had ventured too close, Zhol outstretched his right arm and raged aloud.

"Behold the sign of Rɵhm! Behold the sign of changes!" Blood spewed from his victim's mouth as the demon shredded vocal cords that had been used for little more than gentle laughter.

In a challenging, sweeping gesture, the warrior pointed at the growing throng. "Be warned, *ancients* of Mhu!" he screamed, mocking their epithet.

Eyes a fiery red and face severely contorted, he bellowed, "Eleven times more, will His great sign appear over your mountains, over your oceans, over your temples and your homes.

"*Count!* And know you then!" The demon paused to glare a moment. "*Order* will come to Nordehk!"

N[216] *to find this ship.* Based on its departure information, route and velocity, as supplied by the Og six days before, in the transfer of data from Iiose's battle cruiser to the Overlord's khoomyahna:

[from D-32.7, *HOSTING THE DEMON SONS*] "The following actions and developments are detailed in the data now flowing to your khoomyahna. A transfer of capsules containing the requested samples and codes for Nordehk's flora and fauna, including genetic materials from the higher species, is also underway."

N[217] *merkabah. Ship of light* in the language of Those of Mhu.

N[218] *TK turret.* The Rikahrs' famous turret houses a prized vestige of Khrae's intercontinental wars: an unpowered but otherwise preserved 12,000-year old Pagorean TK cannon, once capable of destroying targets in near space.

N[219] *the resin runners' recent crash.* Just six days before, on Day -32 near the beaches of Elasia:

> [from D-32.16, *DEMON AT THE HELM*] Arnod's crewmates stared in disbelief. They had substituted two of his three lucky roobs and still he'd pulled it off. And not just a double, but a *second* toss of triple fives.
>
> It was unheard of...impossible. And something else was wrong. Where was that gravitational pull, that wonderful weightiness that subtly signaled their nearness to home ground?
>
> While Arnod danced and gathered up his winnings, two of his crewmates pushed their faces against a leeward porthole in time to see the ocean rushing up.

N[220] *tightly woven cables.* Weighing far more than anything hoisted, the dahoens' precious cables were among their most valuable possessions. Their greatest treasure lay in the discovery of a cistern network deep inside their haven's basalt core: a near-limitless supply of potable water. In an attempt to starve the dahoen into surrendering the frequent sieges, many an invader had poisoned the lake below. None succeeded in waiting them out.

N[221] *a shrouded Rohman drone.* As fired by Lord Mohaar from his vihmyana a few hours before:

> [from D-26.3, *THE INDUSTRIOUS DAHOEN*] Not far from Patos and the tensely quiet, subsurface bases of Khrae Lunar Command, Lord Mohaar lay inside his vihmyana tweaking the program of a small Rohman drone. Then he shrouded the device, fired it toward Khrae, activated his recliner's blue energy field and pinned to the planet alone.

N[222] *the one she had dreamed.* On Day -30:

> [from D-30.8, *THE AGGAH'S DREAM*] The Aggah Bood curled up on her favorite couch with a small, iced glass of smuggled, Khraeling mohrd. Dressed down for the evening, she wore but a plain, navy-colored gown.

She gazed intently into the multicolored flames of her suite's modest fireplace, watching their embrace of a neatly arranged stack of slow burning, pressed-fiber sticks. She felt confident that Khrae's military had managed to pirate her broadcast, and that Governor Mauhk and the barons or their envoys had been among her viewing audience. Bood had staged the forum for their benefit. She had had a prophetic dream.

She'd dreamt of an enigg, a junior officer of the New Hollatian Defense. He held his hands in fire and spoke of retribution, of avenging the Dahanah and the Jakomen of old. He spoke of things written long before, and of their fathers' long gone lands. And he rubbed his hands together and held them high, palms out. And neither hand had burned. And then his body became as glowing, and he rose up off the ground....

The Aggah remembered well the enigg's dancing eyes. She could feel his power—still.

N[223] *montauk effect.* Entire ships had dematerialized in the Federation's disastrous invisibility experiments that had been monitored by the curious Og. Most ships never reappeared, but those that did, rematerialized thousands of kilometers away: every one as horrible, molecularly rearranged masses— crews and all. Years later, Og agents quietly observed a surprisingly similar military experiment on Terrah which met with the same, calamitous results.

N[224] *the skinnies' heads.* The bulbous heads of the tall Og who wear tight white suits, the ones to whom the shorter, subservient "hell-men" deliver Ricky for periodic, surgical adjustments.

N[225] *scarred tribute.* Fairest of Khrae's ten cerise-skinned tribes (self-sorted by their inherent pigmentational disposition), the Jakomen have come to embrace the deformities that tie them to their Dahanan lineage. More often than not, those born free of birth defects will, at some stage of their young lives, smash a bone or slash a limb in memory of the holocaust. Although expected, the disfiguring tributes are no longer encouraged.

N[226] *a mild illumination.* As the Aggah had dreamt just days before:

[from D-30.8, *THE AGGAH'S DREAM*] She'd dreamt of an enigg, a junior officer of the New Hollatian Defense. He held his hands in fire and spoke of retribution, of avenging the Dahanah and the Jakomen of old. He spoke of things written long before, and of their fathers' long gone lands. And he rubbed his hands together and held them high, palms out. And neither hand had burned. And then his body became as glowing, and he rose up off the ground.

GLOSSARY

G[002] Adahr: Prince Adahr shaJah, third in line for the Varahn throne and scheming to be king; see Varah

G[003] Ænus: [♂ pron. Ē′-nŭs] a fallen midwayer in service to the warrior-Son Wohtan (Rǝhman); see midwayers

G[005] Aggah: elected leader of the Jakomen people (New Hollatia); see Bood

G[006] All That Is: Creation; the Universe of Universes

G[007] Altos: Khrae's smallest, innermost moon and major polymide deposit

G[009] amphidor: a highly versatile computer and powerful photonic imaging system capable of generating, transmitting and receiving scalable, distortion-free, three-dimensional images

G[010] amstrahd: the largest class of commercial containers utilized by the Varahns and Khraelings for their interstellar trade

G[011] Anadon: the ancients' current 9th seed; a waterworld selected and named by Rǝhm to become Nordehk's capital world; see waterworld

G[013] ancient: a now fourth-density will-creature that has chosen to evolve on Mhu; see Mhu

G[015] andrax: modifiable Rǝhman androids ('drax for short); societal attendants and enforcers of *The Teachings* on Rǝhmanized worlds, and formidable weapons in war

G[018] Aphelia: Queen Aphelia shaJah; current head of Varah's constitutional monarchy

G[023] atmahan: Rohman for "ring of death," these objects are also
                                   known as asteroid belts and suicide rings; orbiting
                                   remnants of a civilization's most thorough self-
                                   destruction, they are prized by the Rohmans as
                                   puzzles to be solved

G[027] bahdram: a secret multi-channeled KSF communications
                                   system (Khrae)

G[028] Bahk: [♂] Dr. Thurmod Bahk; a microbial geneticist and
                                   head of Khrae's Health Organization; appointed to
                                   head the effort to develop a cure for the Efrahm
                                   virus

G[030] bahva: citizen-commoners of the Empire; Rohman slang
                                   for a "being" or "beings"; see bhuvani

G[031] Balenos: Mr. Balenos; a co-handler of Majestic 12; a senior
                                   hybrid-incarnate and partner of Mr. Salizah

G[032] Bandora: the third in order of Khrae's settled continents
                                   (once the richest and most powerful of the original
                                   ten); location of the governor's compound and seat
                                   of the Federation Board

G[033] Baron Ebah: Miloh Ebah XII; successor to a long line of Elasian
                                   barons; rival of Pagorea's Baron Rikahr

G[034] Baron Rikahr: Moulahd Rikahr III; successor to a long line of
                                   Pagorean barons; rival of Elasia's Baron Ebah

G[036] Bel: [♀] one of eight divine Vihdæan overseers assigned
                                   to administrate the Nordehk constellation; see
                                   Vihdæa

G[037] belligerence: the ultimate result of individuals serving self; the
                                   seed of hatred, crime and war

G[038] Belurah: the first evolutionary world of Nordehk; the now
                                   uninhabitable, sister planet of Mhu

G^{039} Bhu: [♀ pron. Boo] a fallen midwayer in service to the warrior-Son Dhanz; see midwayers

G^{040} bhuvani: plural of bhuvana, the formal Rehman word for intelligent, humanoid beings; see bahva

G^{041} (the) Board: Khrae's 11-seat executive council consisting of the governor, his Counsel-Ra, and the nine continental barons; see Federation Board

G^{042} Bood: [♀] Unah Bood; current Aggah of the Jakomen people (New Hollatia); see Aggah

G^{043} Book of Rehm: the imperial Holy Book and written laws of the Rehman Empire; a consolidation of *His Teachings*—the 936 passages that comprise the sacred Book of Rehm; see *The Teachings*

G^{044} Bool-Dahr: the sun-sized defensive buffer zone around the planet New Hollatia

G^{045} Brehlea: the fifth in order of Khrae's settled continents; homeland of Governor Mauhk and his Counsel-Ra Raund Haleahm

G^{046} Brohjal: [♂] Vice Marshall Jehrmi Brohjal, second in command of the KSF (Khrae)

G^{047} brood: a colonized world that has attained a required level of technological development to achieve its progenitors' promotion from "younger" to full "brood" status (Terrah and Enyah are Nordehk's current youngers) ; see younger

G^{050} Caladea: the sixth of Terrah's seven continents (in order of settlement); recently renamed North America

G^{054} cavveht: the Varahn governing body of 128 elected legislative legislators

G⁰⁵⁸ Chak: [♂] a unique looking, lateral-eyed member of the
                           Janah (Rөhman); see Janah

G⁰⁶⁰ Chandron: Chandron Nebula; the star hatchery that spawned
                           the Nordehk constellation

G⁰⁶² cone: a living vibrational chamber that can be formed by
                           certain will-creatures for the purpose of harnessing
                           pranaic energy; see will-creature; see pranah

G⁰⁶³ constellation: a mostly arbitrary collection of stars, divisible into
                           five, adjoining, roughly-equal, three-dimensional
                           pentahms; see pentahm; see galaxy

G⁰⁶⁴ continental lords: the nine ruling barons of Khrae's Intercontinental
                           Federation; "Those of the Continents," as the group
                           prefers to be called

G⁰⁶⁵ cosmic highways: becoming visible and accessible only as one nears
                           light speed, these are the vein-like portals (or way
                           portals) that form the stellar nervure linking
                           galaxies and stars

G⁰⁶⁶ Counsel-Ra: senior counsel and second most powerful seat on
                           Khrae's Federation Board, next to the governor; see
                           Haleahm

G⁰⁶⁷ Creation: All That Is; the Universe of Universes

G⁰⁶⁸ crusader-incarnates: negatively-polarized entities who birth into cultures
                           to torment and/or to confuse and eventually enslave;
                           or positively-polarized entities who, of their own
                           free will, birth into cultures to serve and enlighten;
                           see MoL; see incarnates

G⁰⁶⁹ cubit: a Rөhman unit of measure equal to 12 Rөhman
                           inches, or approximately 19.1 Terran inches, or
                           48.5 Og centimeters; see inch; see mile

G⁰⁷⁰ Dahanah: the 60,000 that survived the nuclear attack on
                           continental Old Hollatia (Khrae); see holocaust

G^{071} Dahoen:	an Elasian wonder city (Khrae), named for its original inhabitants, the "dahoen" ("sky-dwellers")
G^{074} darkeyes:	a disparaging Rǝhman moniker for the Og; see Og
G^{075} dark seraphim:	[pron. sĕr-ă-**phēm′**] seraphic defectors to Rǝhm, twelve of whom serve as His personal escorts; see seraphim
G^{077} debionate:	a process for cleansing and preserving ingestibles (Khrae, New Hollatia, Varah)
G^{079} Dehniss:	[♂] one of the Rǝhman yamah Vakaar's two cohorts who manage the priesthood's spies (Phobb is the other)
G^{080} demons:	entities of the fourth and higher densities who have embraced a negative orientation, and who occasionally possess creatures of the lower realms; see warriors; see high demons; see polarity
G^{083} (Lord) Dhanz:	[♀ pron. Dôns] a fallen Vihdæan among the elite Rǝhman warriors to have achieved "Son of Rǝhm" status; in the Nordehk campaign, she bears responsibility for Rǝhmanizing the ancients' two youngers, Terrah and Enyah; her eternally committed, personal midwayer/scout is ***Bhu*** [♀ pron. Boo]
G^{087} Dloue:	[♂] Shaum Dloue; an enigg in the NHD (New Hollatia), he is the selfless Jakomen alternate for the mission to Levah
G^{089} Earth:	"Mother Earth," the name the Terrans have given their world; see Terrah
G^{090} Ebah:	the ruling family of Khrae's continent of Elasia; see Baron Ebah

G^{091} Efrahm: a coastal village on Khrae's continent of Elasia; site of Nordehk's first outbreak of the Rɵhman plague; see Efrahm virus (next)

G^{092} Efrahm virus: a Khraeling designation for what the Federation does not know to be a manufactured Rɵhman microbe

G^{093} Ehdin: [♂ pron. Ĕ-dēn′] one of the 24 Jakomen Elders (New Hollatia)

G^{094} Ehkilah: a rare phenomenon in which, after catastrophic geological upheavals, a harmonically imbalanced third-density world suddenly jumps to the fourth density and its surviving will-creatures readily embrace a "miracle"-induced positive polarization; see will-creature

G^{095} Eikah: [♀] Eikah Jouhl; petulant envoy to the powerful Baron Rikahr (Pagorea, Khrae)

G^{097} elantahs: [pron. ē-lăn′-təz] extremely rare, temperate, water-bearing lunar planetoids capable of supporting evolving life-forms; see Varah

G^{098} Elasia: the fourth in order of Khrae's settled continents

G^{099} Elasian envoy: [♂] Jahl Khulnah; tactful envoy to Baron Ebah (Elasia, Khrae)

G^{100} Elasians: a Khraeling tribe, and the traditional benefactors of the Jakomen

G^{102} Endorah: the golden city and administrative center of Nordehk's capital world; see Anadon

G^{103} enigg: rank of junior officer in the NHD (New Hollatia)

G^{104} ENU: Elasian National University; sight of Khrae's containment laboratories and temporary headquarters for the KSF task force heading the effort to combat the Efrahm virus

G[105] envoys: the nine representatives of Khrae's nine continental barons; the envoys serve full-time with the governor and Counsel-Ra in administrating the Federation

G[106] Enyah: one of the ancients' two youngers (the other is Terrah); see younger; see bahtuus

G[107] ethereans: the diverse first family of Creation, including those irreproachably devoted to the Light, those bound in Darkness, and the multitude of fickle, formless others in between

G[108] etheric handlers: highly-skilled specialists, who from etheric chambers in orbiting Og garrisons, navigate the dream state's interdimensional planes to manage incarnate troops in action; see Og-incarnate

G[111] Exodus: the Great Exodus; the Jakomen's 30-year emigration from Khrae to terra-formed sister planet New Hollatia; see terra-forming

G[112] Family of Light: entities of the etheric and physical realms who, of their own free will, are committed to serving others

G[114] Federation: Khrae's Intercontinental Federation; the economic union of Khrae's nine inhabited continents

G[115] Federation Board: an 11-seat executive council consisting of the governor, Counsel-Ra, and Khrae's nine continental barons

G[116] feritt: a weightless, mobile, lightly armed, insect-like surveillance machine (Rǝhman)

G[117] (the) festival: the 100-day festival on Khrae which is to celebrate the departure of 100 male Khraeling and Jakomen settlers and 100 female Varahn settlers who are to colonize Levah, the ancients' current Prime Seed; see Prime Seed

G[119a] flash-scanning: a method of low-resolution, long-range scanning developed by the Varahns and shared with the Jakomen of New Hollatia; an adaptation of the ancients' interstellar communications device, flash-scanning is undetectable by its target and is more than 100 times faster than conventional scans

G[119b] flash-scans: arcing bursts of invisible particles fired/flashed at 114.7 times the speed of light; a reverse-engineered, Varahn adaptation of the ancients' interstellar communications device, and a technology the Varahns later shared with their Jakomen friends

G[119c] flash-scans: arcing bursts of invisible particles fired/flashed at 114.7 times the speed of light; a reverse-engineered, Varahn adaptation of the ancients' interstellar communications device, and a technology the Varahns later shared with their Jakomen friends

G[122] fourth density: the fourth "octave" or "dimension" of reality; a seven-level plane of existence with a common visibility spectrum wherein senses, perceptions and abilities are more highly evolved than those of the lower realms

G[124] freewill zones: those constellations designated experimental areas for the potentialization of *all* probabilities, with unrestricted interaction between dark and light

G[125] frontier: an underdeveloped section of a pentahm; see pentahm; see constellation; see galaxy

G[126] frontier outposts: stellar stations installed in all five of Nordehk's pentahms by the ancients of Mhu within one standard light-year of solar systems holding worlds that the ancients have slated for colonization

G^{128}	galaxy:	wholly independent collections of billions of stars spinning as single masses through space, but which may join with others to form assorted clusters and/or grand superclusters within that which constitutes All That Is
G^{131}	Gjadren:	[♂] Gjadren Mauhk; governor of Khrae's Intercontinental Federation; a native of continental Brehlea, along with his lifelong friend and Counsel-Ra, Raund Haleahm
G^{133}	(the) greys:	naïve Terran moniker for those of the crusading Orion group; see Og
G^{134}	GROUP COMMAND:	an interlocking assembly of five battle-ready motherships located near Nordehk's lone red dwarf at the constellation's inward Vesper fringe, GROUP COMMAND is the tactical command center for the Orion group's Nordehk operations; see Og
G^{136}	Haleahm:	[♂] Raund Haleahm, Counsel-Ra of Khrae's Intercontinental Federation; a native of continental Brehlea, along with his lifelong friend, Governor Gjadren Mauhk
G^{138}	hellies:	see hell-men (next)
G^{139}	hell-men:	young Ricky's name for his Og abductors (Terrah); see skinnies; see Ricky
G^{140}	Heln:	[♀] KSF Captain Gladah Heln, lead wingman of Major Ihmoy's seven-interceptor escort squadron sent by the Federation to rendezvous with the incoming Varahn convoy, and subsequent leader of the two-interceptor pursuit team dispatched by Ihmoy to retrieve the convoy's hijacked 14th container (Khrae)
G^{142}	high demons:	the most cunning, capable and anticipatory of demons, not necessarily in service to Røhm

G[143] *His Crusades:*   the Rohman expansionary campaigns designed to bring readily-embraced Order, constellation by constellation, unto rampant chaos shrewdly contrived

G[145] hojooli: a fragrant New Hollatian plant with unique properties

G[146] (Old) Hollatia: the original Jakomen homeland and last continent settled of Khrae's ten lands; see holocaust; see New Hollatia

G[147] holocaust: the surprise attack and virtual annihilation of continental Old Hollatia and its 1.2 billion Jakomen people some 800 standard years before current times

G[150] human: see human being (next)

G[151] human being: a will-creature; any evolving life-form endowed with the unique capacity to make a moral decision, and which usually labels itself "human," "human being" or "man"; see will-creature

G[152] hybrids: see hybrid-incarnates (next)

G[153] hybrid-incarnates: elite Og crusaders occupying bodies genetically engineered from local and alien reproductive materials; designed for an average 300-year life span and with appearances reflecting local perceptions of divine beings, the darkeyes' lovely hybrids are to usher in the New Order upon a glorious Rohman Son's command

G[154] Hyynehk: [♀] a messenger/warrior for the Family of Light; one of Ohrvon's mysterious, irreproachable oraphim; see oraph

G[155] Iccha: [♀ pron. **Ēk′**-chă] "Fear"; *Iccha* is the female of Rohm's two thought-formed Vu-dogs (her mate *Trsnah* [pron. **Tûrs′**-nŭh] is the other); invariably,

Iccha keeps to The Master's right—ever on guard with mouth ever open and teeth ever bared; see thought-forms; see Vu-dogs

G¹⁵⁶ Iddh: [♂ pron. Ĭd] a fallen midwayer in service to the warrior-Son Mohaar; see midwayers

G¹⁵⁷ Ihmoy: [♂] Vihlkin Ihmoy, KSF Major and leader of the squadron sent to rendezvous with and escort the incoming Varahn convoy (Khrae)

G¹⁵⁸ Iiose: [♂ pron. Ī'-ōs] venerable group commander of Nordehk's Og crusaders

G¹⁵⁹ Ilyah: Varah's tiny sister moon, Ilyah is the VSC's base of operations and home to the Varahn fleet; see VSC

G¹⁶⁰ imager: a device that produces, transmits and receives slightly distorted three-dimensional images (Khrae, New Hollatia, Varah)

G¹⁶¹ Imperial Crusaders: fourth-density beings (such as the Og) who en masse have been conquered, Røhmanized, militarized, and commissioned to serve in *His Crusades*; see *His Crusades*

G¹⁶² Imperial Warriors: (aka: warrior-sons) fallen Vihdæa in service to Røhm who have not yet achieved "Son of Røhm" status, and who serve as lieutenants under the higher ranking Røhman Sons; also see warriors and warrior-sons

G¹⁶³ incarnates: negatively-polarized entities who birth into cultures to torment and/or to confuse and enslave; or positively-polarized entities who, of their own free will, birth into cultures to serve and enlighten; see MoL

G¹⁶⁴ inch: a Røhman unit of measure equal to approximately 1.59 Terran inches, or 0.0404 Og meters; see cubit

G[165] in'field: in the imaging field (Khrae, New Hollatia, Varah)

G[166] Isdrav: [♀] Dr. Ashdah Isdrav, historian, Doctor of
                                        Psychology and teacher on Patos of the 100 settler-
                                        sons and their 10 mission alternates (Khrae)

G[167] jack: a disparaging Khraeling term for a Jakomen; see
                                        khraek

G[169] Jahl: [♂] Jahl Khulnah; tactful envoy to Baron Ebah
                                        (Elasia, Khrae)

G[170] Jakomen: the fairest/lightest of Khrae's red-skinned tribes;
                                        descendents of those who survived the Old
                                        Hollatian holocaust and emigrated to Khrae's sister
                                        planet Qalakah (renamed New Hollatia); see
                                        Dahanah

G[171] Janah: a secret sect of 22 Rohman rebels—closet
                                        anarchists who volunteered for the mission to
                                        Nordehk, hoping to somehow escape the Empire's
                                        stifling Order

G[172] Jaylah: [♂] current rotational chief of Nordehk's Vihdæan
                                        council of eight—neighbors to and peers of
                                        Lazrehk's Vihdæan Council; see Lazrehk; see
                                        Vihdæa

G[175] Jinn-Jinn: [♂] a Rohman midwayer-sentinel temporarily
                                        assigned to watch over the Overlord's khoomyahna
                                        during the warship's voyage to Nordehk

G[178] Jouhl: [♀] Eikah Jouhl; petulant envoy to the powerful
                                        Baron Rikahr (Pagorea, Khrae)

G[180] kaVihl: [♂] Uril kaVihl; retired commissioner of the
                                        Varahn Service Corps and appointed spokesman for
                                        the 177 Varahn delegates coming to attend the
                                        planned 100-day festival on Khrae

G[183] khoomyahna: a huge Rəhman warship of terrifying capacity, known to average at least five standard light-years per standard day through the cosmic highways; see way portals

G[184] Khrae: first of the ancients' colonies to qualify technologically and achieve "brood" status; see brood; see Varah; see younger

G[185] khraek: a disparaging Jakomen term for a Khraeling; see jack

G[186] Khulnah: [♂] Jahl Khulnah; tactful envoy to Baron Ebah (Elasia, Khrae)

G[187] kilo: an Og measure of weight introduced to Nordehk by Og-incarnates; see metric system

G[188] kilometer: an Og measure of distance introduced to Nordehk by Og-incarnates; equal to 0.518 of a Rəhman mile, or 0.621 of a Terran mile; see metric system

G[189] KLC: Khrae Lunar Command; located on and beneath the surface of Patos, KLC is the Khrae Security Forces' nerve center for the KSF's military operations; see KSF; see Patos

G[191] Klohe: [♀ pron. **Klō′-ē**] one of the 24 Jakomen Elders (New Hollatia)

G[192a] KSF: Khrae Security Forces; defenders of the planet and enforcers of Khrae's Federational laws

G[192b] KSF: Khrae Security Forces; defenders of the planet and enforcers of Khrae's Federational laws

G[195] Lazrehk: core to core, Lazrehk is the nearest of constellations adjoining Nordehk, and is also suffering discreet Og manipulation for eventual Rəhmanization

G[197] Lemurah: the capital city of the planet Mhu; see Mhu

G[198] Levah: name given by the ancients to their current Prime
                                  Seed; see ancient; see Prime Seed

G[199a] light-year (Khrae): 0.762 of a standard light-year (also as calculated on
                                  New Hollatia)

G[199b] light-year (Mhu):   0.999 of a standard light-year

G[199c] light-year: the distance traveled by light in one standard
                                  Rehman year

G[199d] light-year (Terrah): 0.845 of a standard light-year

G[199e] light-year (Varah): 1.487 of a standard light-year

G[200] liter: an Og measure of capacity introduced to Nordehk
                                  by Og-incarnates; see metric system

G[201] Lord of the Orbits: (aka: Overlord) the official title of the Rehman Son
                                  who bears responsibility for a conquest's outcome,
                                  and who bears its financial burden

G[202] Lords of the Realm: male and female "Sons" of Rehm; see warrior-Sons

G[203] Luthur: [♂] Luthur Poth; a chief engineer with the NHD,
                                  and one of the Jakomen pirate-operatives sent to
                                  secretly rendezvous with the Varahn convoy and
                                  "hijack" its 14th container (New Hollatia)

G[205] Majestic: the 12-man Majestic Group (aka: Majestic 12, The
                                  Twelve, MJ-12, M12, Maj'ic); independent lesser
                                  demons to a man, Majestic is the secret and
                                  absolute Terran power, "the president-makers" and
                                  willing collaborative minions of the Og

G[206] Maj'ic: short for Majestic (above)

G[208] man: any evolving life-form endowed with the unique
                                  capacity to make a moral decision, and which
                                  usually labels itself "human," "human being" or
                                  "man"; see will-creature

G²¹⁰ Mannon: [♂] Marshall Mannon Jee Pranol; senior ranking officer of the heavily armed KSF (Khrae)

G²¹² (The) Master: [♂] Rɘhm, the self-proclaimed Lord of Lords and Master Over All; see Rɘhm

G²¹³ material-life vehicle: a living structure capable of temporarily hosting an evolving entity's consciousness

G²¹⁴ Mauhk: [♂] Gjadren Mauhk; a native of continental Brehlea, Mauhk is the current Governor of Khrae's Intercontinental Federation

G²¹⁵ Mercenary of Light: MoL [pron. mōl]; entities of a positive polarity who, of their own free will, incarnate from the higher realms to inspire and enlighten those of evolving cultures; see polarity

G²¹⁷ merkabahs: "ships of light" in the language of the ancients; resplendent interstellar cruisers (Mhu); see ancient

G²¹⁹ metric system: the Og system of measurements based on the number 10; see Og

G²²¹ Mhu: core planet of the Nordehk constellation; home world of the ancients; see ancient

G²²³ Midway: the ever-changing point midway between the sister planets Khrae and New Hollatia

G²²⁴ midwayers: formally designated "peshim" [pron. pĕ-**shēm**′], these ethereans exist midway between the fourth and fifth densities; unheard and unseen by those of the lower realms, midwayers are highly regarded for their service as exceptional "guides" or "scouts"

G²²⁵ mile: a Rɘhman measure of distance equal to 4,000 Rɘhman cubits, or approximately 1.2 Terran miles or 1.94 Og kilometers

G[226a] (Lord) Mohaar: [♂ pron. **Mō′**-här] a fallen Vihdæan administrator turned warrior-crusader for Rǝhm and recently elevated to the status of Rǝhman Son; in the Nordehk campaign, Mohaar bears responsibility for Rǝhmanizing Khrae and New Hollatia; his eternally committed, personal midwayer/scout is ***Iddh*** [♂ pron. Ĭd]

G[226b] (Lord) Mohaar: [♂ pron. **Mō′**-här] a fallen Vihdæan administrator turned warrior-crusader for Rǝhm and recently elevated to the status of Rǝhman Son; in the Nordehk campaign, he is to Rǝhmanize Khrae and New Hollatia; Lord Mohaar's eternally committed, personal midwayer/scout is ***Iddh*** [♂ pron. Ĭd]

G[227] mohrd: a powerful, aromatic, Khraeling liquor from continental Brehlea

G[228] MoL: [pron. mōl] Mercenary of Light; entities of a positive polarity who, of their own free will, incarnate from the higher realms to inspire and enlighten those of evolving cultures; see polarity

G[231] montauk effect: sudden, uncontrolled molecular rearrangements resulting from runaway electromagnetic modulations of vibrational frequencies

G[232] Most Highs: the 128 male and female Universal "Sons" who serve in each galaxy's central administrative council, and who supervise the Vihdæa; see galaxy

G[235] Mr. Balenos: an advisor to America's National Security Council (Terrah) and a co-handler of Majestic 12; a senior hybrid-incarnate and partner of Mr. Salizah

G[236] Mr. Salizah: an advisor to America's National Security Council (Terrah) and a co-handler of Majestic 12; a senior hybrid-incarnate and partner of Mr. Balenos

G[241] naq: an expression of denial, disagreement or refusal in the Jakomen language (New Hollatia)

G^{242a} Narlihd:	[♂] Captain Rauhf B. Narlihd; captain of the pirate-operatives sent by the NHD to secretly rendezvous with the Varahn convoy and to "hijack" its 14th container (New Hollatia)
G^{242b} Narlihd:	[♂] Captain Rauhf B. Narlihd; captain of the pirate-operatives sent by the NHD to secretly rendezvous with the Varahn convoy and to "hijack" its 14th container (New Hollatia)
G^{242c} Narlihd:	[♂] Captain Rauhf B. Narlihd; captain of the pirate-operatives sent by the NHD to secretly rendezvous with the Varahn convoy and to "hijack" its 14th container (New Hollatia)
G^{242d} Narlihd:	[♂] Captain Rauhf B. Narlihd; captain of the pirate-operatives sent by the NHD to secretly rendezvous with the Varahn convoy and to "hijack" its 14th container (New Hollatia)
G²⁴⁷ New Hollatia:	the terra-formed home planet of the surviving Jakomen (formerly known as Qalakah), settled 783 years prior as time is measured by the Khraelings; see holocaust; see Hollatia
G²⁴⁸ New Order:	an unsustainable societal structure imposed on the unsuspecting as a prelude to their Rohmanization
G^{249a} NHD:	New Hollatian Defense; the global police, security force and defenders of New Hollatia
G^{249b} NHD:	New Hollatian Defense; the global police, security force and defenders of New Hollatia
G^{249c} NHD:	New Hollatian Defense; the global police, security force and defenders of New Hollatia
G^{249d} NHD:	New Hollatian Defense; the global police, security force and defenders of New Hollatia

G[251] Nordehk: "Net of Jewels" in the language of Creation; one of several constellations now under the jurisdiction of the Rɘhman Son, Zhol

G[252] North America: the sixth of Terrah's seven continents (in order of settlement); formerly known as Caladea

G[254a] (the) Og: short for **O**rion **g**roup, the Og are a widely varied, inherently godless, resentfully subjugated and therefore ever scheming, shrewdly deceitful fourth-density species, commissioned by their Rɘhman masters for long-term service in *His Crusades*; see **G**[143]

G[254b] (the) Og: those of the ever scheming **O**rion **g**roup; the infamous, grey-skinned "darkeyes" from the motherworlds and territories of the long-Rɘhmanized Orion constellation, where—well before the Rɘhmans' annexation of Orion—the taller and intellectually superior "original purebred species" enslaved the territories' similar looking, less advanced tribes

G[254c] (the) Og: short for **O**rion **g**roup, the Og are calculating imperial minions, disparagingly referred to as "darkeyes" by the Rɘhmans, "mahisha" by the Varahns, and more dubiously by the naïve Terrans as the phantom "greys" (on Khrae and New Hollatia the Og remain unknown)

G[255] Og-incarnates: elite Og mercenaries skilled at birthing into the tribes of those worlds Orion Command has been commissioned to prime for Rɘhmanization; see incarnates

G[256] Ohrvon: the galaxy that encompasses millions of constellations, including Nordehk and neighboring Lazrehk

G[257] OMV: Of Maximum Velocity; the velocic ceiling of the twin-coil engine (Khrae, Varah and New Hollatia)

G^{259} oraph: singular of oraphim, a high order of etherean
                          warrior-messengers irreproachably devoted to the
                          Light

G^{260} Oridea: the seventh in order of Khrae's settled continents

G^{262} Orion: [pron. Ō-rī′-ŏn] a fully Rⱥhmanized constellation
                          and home to the infamous Og crusaders; see Og

G^{263} Orion Command: the ever-changing Council of Ten who reside
                          within the Orion constellation and preside over its
                          commissioned and internal affairs

G^{264} Orion group: those living on and crusading beyond the
                          motherworlds and territories of the long-
                          Rⱥhmanized Orion constellation; see Og

G^{265} Overlords: officially Lords of the Orbits; senior Rⱥhman Sons
                          who plan, finance and perform in the execution of
                          His Crusades; see *His Crusades*

G^{266} Pagorea: the ninth in order of Khrae's settled continents
                          (now the richest and most powerful of the ten);
                          traditional nemesis of old and New Hollatia

G^{267} Pagorean envoy: Eikah Jouhl, petulant envoy to continental
                          Pagorea's powerful Baron Rikahr (Khrae)

G^{268} Pahl: [♂] Pahl Radool; young design engineer, NHD
                          enigg and pirate-operative infrequently possessed
                          by Lord Mohaar, the Rⱥhman Son; see Radool
                          Coils; see Radool

G^{270} Patos: the largest and outermost of Khrae's two moons;
                          home to Khrae Lunar Command, the hub for KSF
                          military operations; see KLC; see KSF

G^{271} Patti: Og-abused mother of young Ricky (Terrah); see
                          Ricky

G[272] pentahms: [pron. **pĕn′**-tômz] five, adjoining, similarly sized, three-dimensional stellar sectors that constitute a constellation and radiate outward from its core; underdeveloped pentahm sections are known as "frontiers"; see constellation; see galaxy

G[274] peshim: [pron. **pĕ-shēm′**] the formal designation for this group of ethereans that spontaneously manifested between the fourth and fifth densities, and is entirely unable to reproduce; unheard and unseen by those of the lower realms, the peshim are highly regarded for their service as exceptional "guides" or "scouts"; see midwayers

G[276] Phobb: [♂] one of the Rөhman yamah Vakaar's two cohorts who manage the priesthood's spies (Dehniss is the other)

G[278] pinning: to pin; the concentration of one's consciousness into a pinpoint of light (that can vary in intensity from virtually invisible to intensely radiant) for the purpose of instantaneous travel to destinations seen in the mind's eye, or to enter and possess other living forms—whether temporarily or for a longer term; see possession

G[279] Planet of the Cross: an Og moniker for Terrah

G[281] polarity: the orientation of a will-creature toward light or darkness, to the positive or negative, to empathic service unto others or opportunistic service to self

G[282] polymides: exotic metal alloys; extremely lightweight supermetals having various combinations of properties including superstrength, superductility and superconductivity

G[283] portal: way portal; becoming visible and accessible only as one nears light speed, these are the vein-like cosmic highways that form the stellar nervure linking galaxies and stars

G²⁸⁴ possession: an act of psychic aggression whereby a being's mind and body are controlled by a negatively-oriented entity from a higher realm whether temporarily or for a longer time; see demons; see pinning; see polarity

G²⁸⁵ Poth: [♂] Luthur Poth; an NHD chief engineer and one of the Jakomen pirate-operatives sent to secretly rendezvous with the Varahn convoy

G²⁸⁶ Poxx: [♂ pron. Pŏks] a fallen midwayer in service to the warrior-Son Zhol; see midwayers

G²⁸⁷ pranah: an element of the cosmic force that carries callings, telepathic communications, and the consciousness of those able to harness portions of its power

G²⁸⁸ Pranol: [♂] Marshall Mannon Jee Pranol; senior ranking officer of the heavily armed KSF (Khrae)

G²⁸⁹ Prime Creator: God, Allah, The Great Light, Infinite Mind, and Universal Father

G²⁹⁰ Prime Crusader: Rǝhm, "The Caller," Ohrvon's fallen Universal Son and determined deliverer of All That Is into Darkness; the self-proclaimed Master Over All, Great Creator, Universal Lord, Lord of Lords, Bringer of Order, Omnipotent One, and Friend of Man and Angels; "the prime defector" (as designated by those devoted to the Light); see Most Highs

G²⁹¹ prime defector: Rǝhm—as designated by those devoted to the Light; see above

G²⁹² Prime Seed: the next Nordehk world slated for colonization (as determined by the ancients of Mhu)

G²⁹³ Prince Adahr: Prince Adahr shaJah, third in line for the Varahn throne; see Varah

G[294]　psychic attack:　　　a prophetic outburst or otherwise excessive behavior enacted by a negatively-oriented entity through its possession and temporary use of a vulnerable will-creature's body; see polarity; see possession

G[295]　qah:　　　a reply of comprehension, affirmation or consent in the Jakomen language (New Hollatia)

G[296]　Qahlona:　　　New Hollatia's capital city and site of the Aggah's compound

G[297]　Qalakah:　　　the fifth planet from Khrae's sun; the recently terra-formed world subsequently settled and renamed New Hollatia by the Jakomen

G[298]　Qaloov:　　　[♂] General Qaloov; senior ranking officer of the heavily armed NHD (New Hollatia)

G[299]　qubal:　　　the monetary unit of Khrae's Intercontinental Federation

G[301]　Radool Coils:　　　a modified twin-coil engine named for its credited inventor, the NHD enigg Pahl Radool (New Hollatia)

G[303]　Radool, Pahl:　　　[♂] young design engineer, enigg and pirate-operative in the NHD (New Hollatia)

G[304]　Raund:　　　[♂] Raund Haleahm, Counsel-Ra of Khrae's Intercontinental Federation; a native of continental Brehlea and lifelong friend of fellow Brehlean, Governor Gjadren Mauhk

G[306]　realities:　　　finite planes of existence in a temporary state of becoming

G[307]　remscanner:　　　remote scanning unit or RSU; a KSF surveillance drone, usually weaponized (Khrae)

G³⁰⁸	repulsion:	the brief harnessing of dark matter's forces so as to dynamically repel the pull of gravity
G³⁰⁹	resin:	a concentrate produced from the fragrant New Hollatian hojooli plant
G³¹⁰	Ricky:	[♂] a troubled young dreamer of realities and future events (Terrah)
G³¹¹	Rikahr:	the ruling family of continental Pagorea (Khrae); see Baron Rikahr
G³¹²	roemstims:	roving electromagnetic stimulators; robotic massager-exercisers designed to counter fitness diminishment during interstellar travel (Khrae, New Hollatia, Varah)
G³¹³	Rehm:	[♂] "The Caller," Ohrvon's fallen Universal Son and determined deliverer of All That Is into Darkness; the self-proclaimed Master Over All, Great Creator, Universal Lord, Lord of Lords, Bringer of Order, Omnipotent One, and Friend of Man and Angels; "the prime defector" (as designated by those devoted to the Light); see Most Highs
G³¹⁴	Rehmans:	the diverse entities of Rehm's ever expanding domain; the empire's citizenry of bahva/bhuvani/beings and fallen ethereans including many Vihdæa, seraphim, and midwayers/peshim
G³¹⁵	Rehman gate:	an imperial designation for the brief, planet-sized, plasmic eruption that occurs when an interstellar vessel emerges from a cosmic highway; see way portal
G³¹⁶	Rehman High Court:	the highest legislative body of the Rehman Empire, second in power only to The Master, and comprising the twelve Supreme Sons; see Supreme Sons

G[318] Rohman Sons: fallen Vihdæa (male and female) who defected to Rohm's callings, first serving and initially ranked as Imperial Warriors (aka: "warrior-sons") and eventually earning The Master's recognition and promotion to Son-status through exceptional, unfailing service; also known as Imperial Lords, Sons of Rohm, and to others as high demons or simply demon-Sons; see demons; see Vihdæa

G[319] Rohmday: last day of the Rohman 12-day week; a day for thanksgiving and reflection on Rohm's greatness

G[320] roobs: a recently imperialized Jakomen game of chance that features a set of three spherical 7-sided dice; Terran patents pending (terrah.com/licensing)

G[322] RSU: remote scanning unit or "remscanner," a usually weaponized KSF surveillance drone

G[323] Salizah: Mr. Salizah; a co-handler of Majestic 12; a senior hybrid-incarnate and partner of Mr. Balenos

G[325] Sarvah: [♀] a member of the Rohman anarchists, *the Janah*, Sarvah bravely spies for her comrades by reluctantly riding the mystical pranah in a controlled projection of her consciousness; ; Sarvah's nicknames are Weebie and Weebs; see Janah; see pranah

G[327] scouts: formally designated "peshim" [pron. pĕ-**shēm**′] and more commonly known as midwayers, these ethereans exist midway between the fourth and fifth densities; unheard and unseen by those of the lower realms, they are highly regarded for their service as exceptional "guides" or "scouts"

G[328] screws: Jakomen slang for low-ranking NHD operatives/grunts (New Hollatia)

G[329] season: an etherean and Rohman reference to an indeterminate period in which certain probabilities may actualize

G^{330} second frontier: the outer reaches of the second of five pentahms radiating outward from Mhu to divide the Nordehk constellation into five, adjoining, similarly sized, three-dimensional stellar sectors; see pentahm

G^{331} seeds: those pristine Nordehk worlds slated by the ancients of Mhu for eventual colonization

G^{333} seraphim: [pron. sĕr-ă-**phēm**′] plural of seraph; an angelic order of ethereans, the seraphim assist and escort the Vihdæa and Most Highs, and are the genuine "guardian angels" of legend and myth, from whose ranks some do fall; see dark seraphim

G^{334} settlers: the 100 young sons of Khrae and New Hollatia, plus the 100 daughters of Varah, who together are to colonize Levah, the ancients' current Prime Seed; see Prime Seed

G^{335} shaJah: Varah's capital city and royal family name

G^{338} skinnies: young Ricky's moniker for the tall Og "doctors" to whom his abductors (the shorter Og "hellies/hell-men") take him from time to time for genetic alterations; Ricky's "skinnies" are Og purebreds from the motherworlds of Orion, as opposed to Ricky's "hell-men" who are a subservient subspecies from Orion's outer territories; see territories

G^{339} Sons of Rǝhm: male and female Rǝhman "Sons," Imperial Lords, His Glorious Sons, Lords of the Realm; see warrior-Sons

G^{341} Sowers: irreproachable etherean devotees to the Light and channelers of the divine spark to Creation's ready worlds, the Sowers are of a high order in the administration of All That Is

G^{343} statcon: an abbreviation for static containment

G[344] stellar stations: frontier outposts installed in all five of Nordehk's pentahms by the ancients of Mhu within one standard light-year of solar systems holding worlds that the ancients have slated for colonization

G[346] Supreme Sons: the current twelve highest-ranking Rehman Sons who form the Rehman High Court to whom the Overlords report; collectively, the Supreme Sons are second in power to Rehm

G[349] Tahned: [♀] a Varahn elder and one of Prince Adahr's delegates visiting Khrae for the Federation's festival to celebrate the departure of the 200 settlers to the ancients' Prime Seed

G[351] *The Teachings*:   *The Master's Teachings*; the imperial Holy Book and written laws of the Rehman Empire; all 936 passages that comprise the sacred Book of Rehm

G[352] terra-forming: the technologically-induced acceleration of an otherwise slowly greening world

G[353] Terrah: one of the ancients' two youngers (the other is Enyah); third planet from its sun; a world known to its inhabitants as "the earth" or "Mother Earth," and to the Og as "the Planet of the Cross"; see youngers; see Planet of the Cross

G[354] (the) territories: the outermost solar systems of the Orion constellation, ravaged and enslaved by those from Orion's manicured, core motherworlds long before their swift surrender and submission to the Rehmans; see Og

G[356] The Master: Rehm, Master Over All, Prime Crusader, Omnipotent One, Lord of Lords, and Friend of Man and Angels (aka: "the prime defector" by those devoted to the Light)

G[359] third density: the third "octave" or "dimension" of reality; the lowest density to support the communal incarnational development of living creatures; a seven-level plane of existence with a common visibility spectrum wherein its creature's senses, perceptions and abilities are less developed than those of higher realms; see fourth density

G³⁶⁰ **Those of the Continents:** the favored designation by and for the nine ruling barons of Khrae's Intercontinental Federation

G³⁶¹ **thought-forms:** temporary apparitions or enduring material manifestations formed by the power of thought

G³⁶² **Thowm:** [♀] Specialist Mahrget Thowm, a KSF operator on Khrae Lunar Command's Base 11, and the first Khraeling to be possessed by a Rohman Son

G³⁶⁴ **tonne:** an Og measure of weight equal to 1,000 kilos; see metric system

G³⁶⁶ **Trsnah:** [♂ pron. **Tûrs′**-nŭh] "Desire"; *Trsnah* is the male of Rohm's two thought-formed Vu-dogs (his mate *Iccha* [pron. **Ēk′**-chă] is the other); invariably, Trsnah keeps to The Master's left—ever on guard, mouth ever closed; see thought-forms; see Vu-dogs

G³⁶⁷ **Ubahr:** the frozen gas giant and sixth planet of the Khrae/New Hollatia star system; the NHD secretly maintains a large, second, battle-ready fleet—the "Second Wave"—on four of Ubahr's moons

G³⁷⁰ **Universal Sons:** the 128 Most Highs of each galaxy's central administrative council; supervisors of the Vihdæa; see galaxy

G³⁷¹ **Uril:** Uril kaVihl; retired commissioner of the Varahn Service Corps and appointed spokesperson for the 177 Varahn delegates, including Prince Adahr, who are coming to attend the 100-day festival on Khrae

G³⁷³ **Vakaar:** His Reverence; high priest/yamah of Nordehk's newly arrived Rohman priesthood; see yamah

G^{374} Varah: a lunar planetoid and second of the ancients'
                                    colonies to qualify technologically and achieve
                                    "brood" status; see brood; see younger; see Khrae;
                                    see elantahs

G^{375} Varahn way station: a Varahn Service Corps early-warning station
                                    positioned by the VSC along the commercial lanes
                                    between Varah and Khrae at one light-year from
                                    Varah (as measured by the Varahns)

G^{377} veiling syndrome: one's forgetting of pre-birth intentions and past
                                    lives; a reincarnational phenomenon limited to the
                                    third density

G^{379} vibrational   the vibrational rate of atoms which determines
          frequency: matter's relative density and visibility

G^{381a} Vihdæa: [pron. Vĭ-dē′-ăh] angelic administrators of the
                                    galaxies' living constellations, and local keepers of
                                    the Light; see galaxy

G^{381b} Vihdæa: [pron. Vĭ-dē′-ăh] ethereans of the sixth density who
                                    administrate the constellations in Councils of eight,
                                    the typically passive Vihdæa are largely loyal to the
                                    Light, with but a wee percentage answering
                                    Rohm's calls to defect and forever serve in *His
                                    Crusades*

G^{382} Vihdæan Council: eight Vihdæa who, as a council, administrate a
                                    constellation under the authority of the galaxy's
                                    Most Highs; see Vihdæa (above); see Most Highs

G^{383} Vihlkin: Vihlkin Ihmoy, KSF Major and leader of the seven-
                                    interceptor squadron sent to escort the incoming
                                    Varahn convoy (Khrae)

G^{384} vihm: vihmyana; a Rohman destroyer capable of
                                    breaching the cosmic highways where they are
                                    known to average at least one standard light-year
                                    per standard day

G^{385} violators: imperial bhuvani convicted of having violated one or more of *The Master's Teachings* (Rǝhman)

G^{386} VSC: Varahn Service Corps; headquartered on Ilyah, the VSC is responsible for serving and protecting the Varahns, their world and off-world interests

G^{387} Vu-dogs: beastly four-legged guardians thought-formed by Rǝhm for near-constant companionship; there are only two—Iccha ♀ and Trsnah ♂; see thought-forms; see Iccha; see Trsnah

G^{389} warriors (Rǝhman): fallen Vihdæa who have defected to Rǝhm; short for both fledgling Imperial Warriors and for the elevated Sons of Rǝhm (see next)

G^{390} warrior-sons: (aka: Imperial Warriors) fallen Vihdæa in service to Rǝhm who have not yet achieved "Son of Rǝhm" status, and who serve as lieutenants under the higher ranking Rǝhman Sons

G^{391} waterworld: a Rǝhman designation for a world of at least one-third surface water

G^{392} way portals: becoming visible and accessible only as one nears light speed, these are the vein-like cosmic highways that form the stellar nervure linking galaxies and stars

G^{394} Weebie: [pron. **Wē′**-bē] along with "Weebs," Weebie is the Janah's nickname for Sarvah, their reluctantly brave projectionist/spy (Rǝhman); see Sarvah

G^{395} will-creature: any evolving life-form endowed with the unique capacity to make a moral decision, and which usually labels itself "human," "human being" or "man"

G^{397} (Lord) Wohtan: [♂ pron. **Wō′**-tǎn] an indifferent Vihdæan turned warrior-crusader for Rǝhm eons prior, he is among the many Rǝhman warriors to achieve elite "Son of

Rehm" status through his unfailing and innovative service; in the Nordehk campaign, Wohtan bears responsibility for Rehmanizing Varah; his eternally committed, personal midwayer/scout is *Ænus* [♂ pron. Ē′-nŭs]

G[400] yamah: *controller of the passage* in the imperial tongue; the high priest in a constellational order of Rehman priesthood; see Vakaar

G[402] Yhurg: Lieutenant Yhurg; pilot of one of the seven KSF interceptor pilots, who under the command of Major Ihmoy, were sent to rendezvous with and escort Prince Adahr's convoy (including the Varahn delegates and settler-daughters) to Khrae; during that escort mission, Lt. Yhurg also served as wingman to Ihmoy's pursuit leader Heln in their failed attempt to retrieve the convoy's hijacked 14th container

G[404] younger: a colonized world that has not yet attained a required level of technological development to achieve its progenitors' promotion to "brood" status (Terrah and Enyah are Nordehk's current youngers); see brood

G[404] younger: a colonized world that has not yet attained a required level of technological development to achieve its progenitors' promotion to "brood" status (Terrah and Enyah are Nordehk's current youngers); see brood

G[405] (Lord) Zhol: [♂ pron. Zōl] officially "Lord of the Orbits" of the Nordehk campaign and Overlord of fourteen other constellations, Zhol is among the brightest of fallen Vihdæa to serve Rehm; he bears the campaign's financial burden and is responsible for Rehmanizing the ancients of Mhu; his personal, eternally-committed midwayer/scout is *Poxx* [♂ pron. Pŏks].

The CHARTS

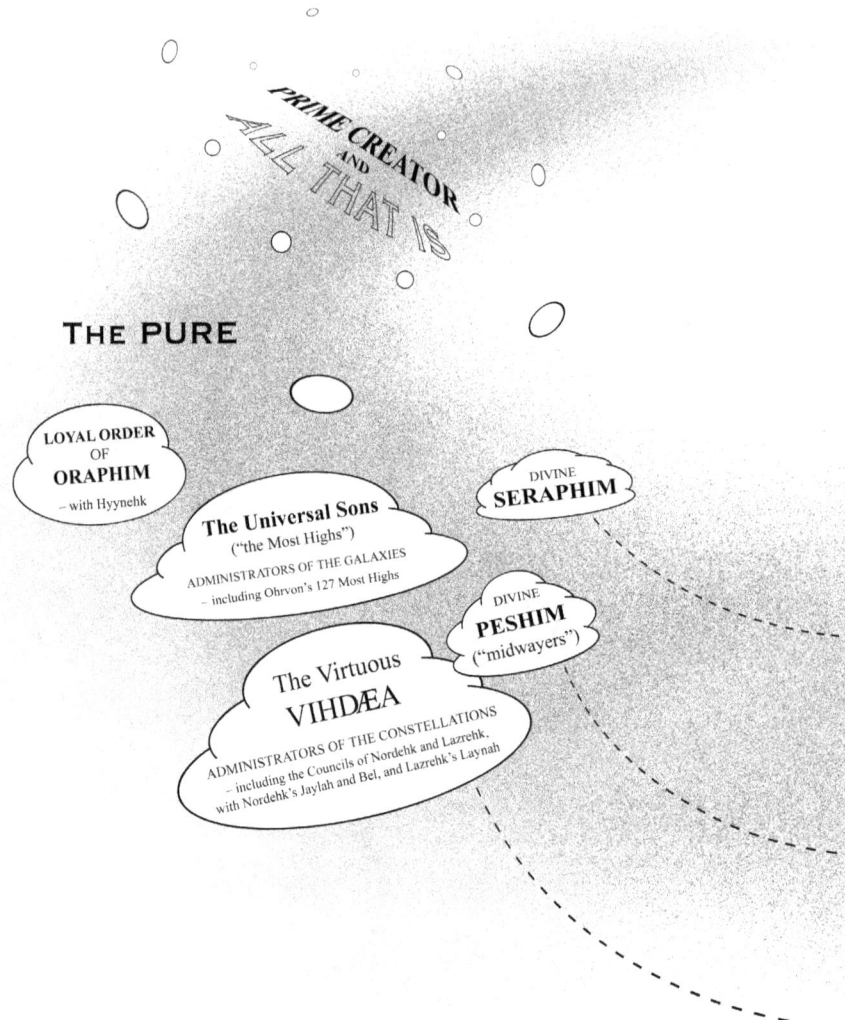

PRIME CREATOR AND ALL THAT IS

THE PURE

LOYAL ORDER OF **ORAPHIM**
– with Hyynehk

DIVINE SERAPHIM

The Universal Sons
("the Most Highs")
ADMINISTRATORS OF THE GALAXIES
– including Ohrvon's 127 Most Highs

DIVINE **PESHIM** ("midwayers")

The Virtuous **VIHDÆA**
ADMINISTRATORS OF THE CONSTELLATIONS
– including the Councils of Nordehk and Lazrehk,
with Nordehk's Jaylah and Bel, and Lazrehk's Laynah

THE FALLEN

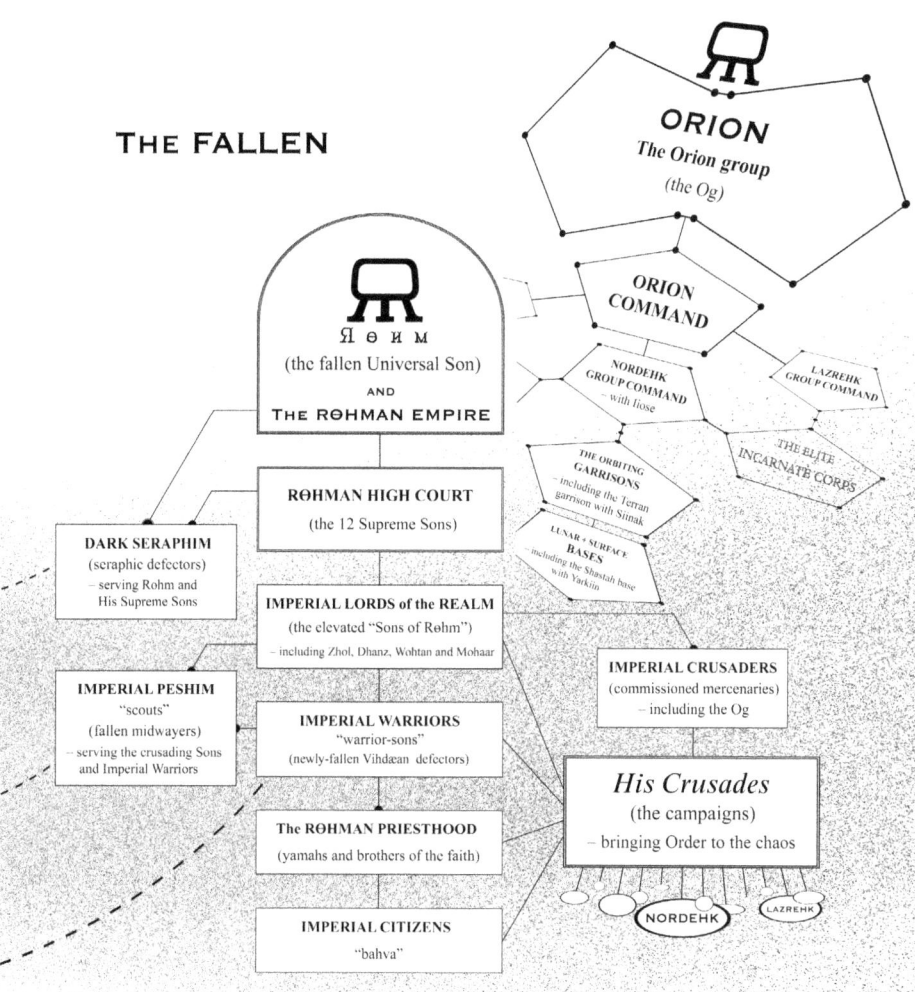

The 30 Suns and Featured Worlds of
CONSTELLATION
NORDEHK

FIFTH PENTAHM

TERRAH
(EARTH)

THIRD PENTAHM

FOURTH PENTAHM

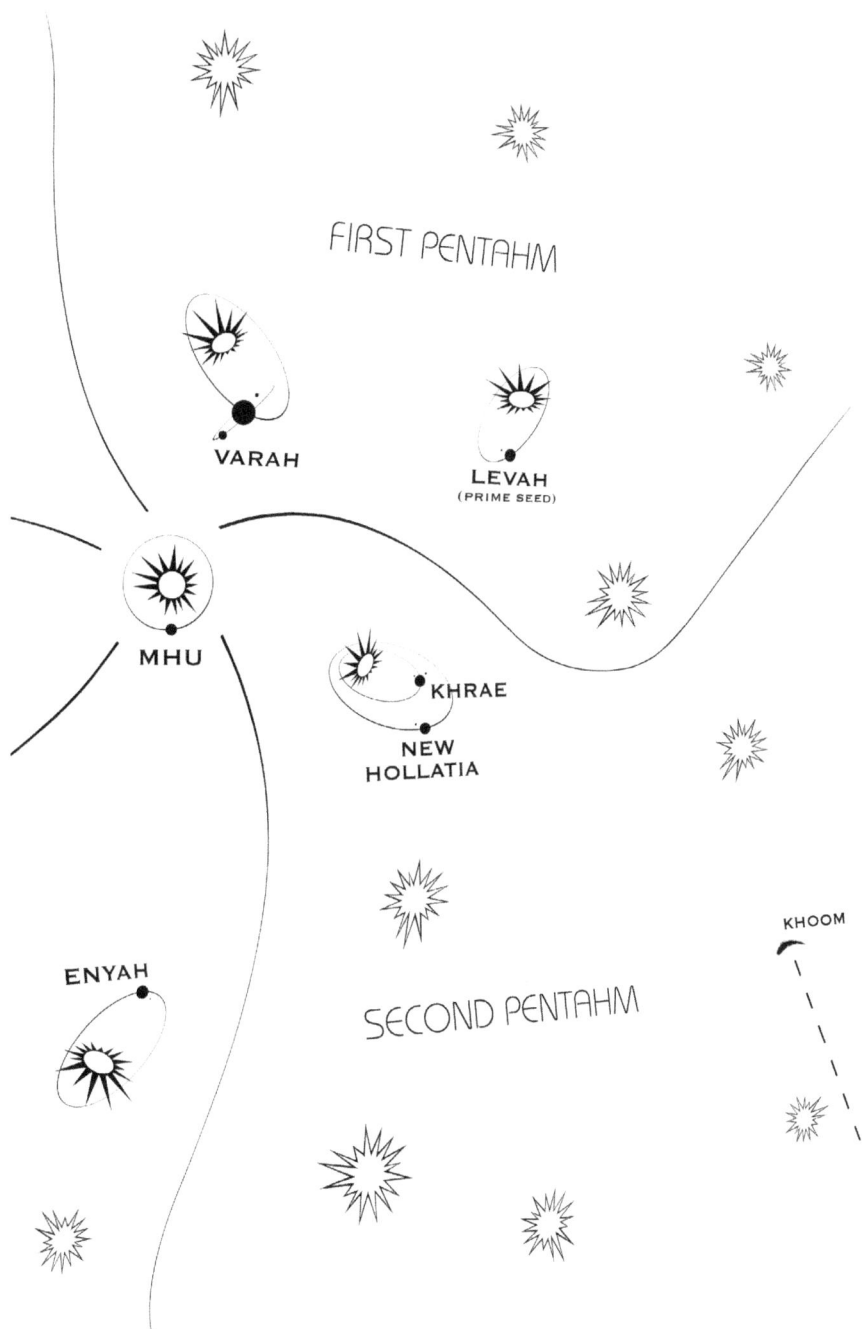

FIRST PENTAHM

VARAH

LEVAH
(PRIME SEED)

MHU

KHRAE

NEW
HOLLATIA

ENYAH

SECOND PENTAHM

KHOOM

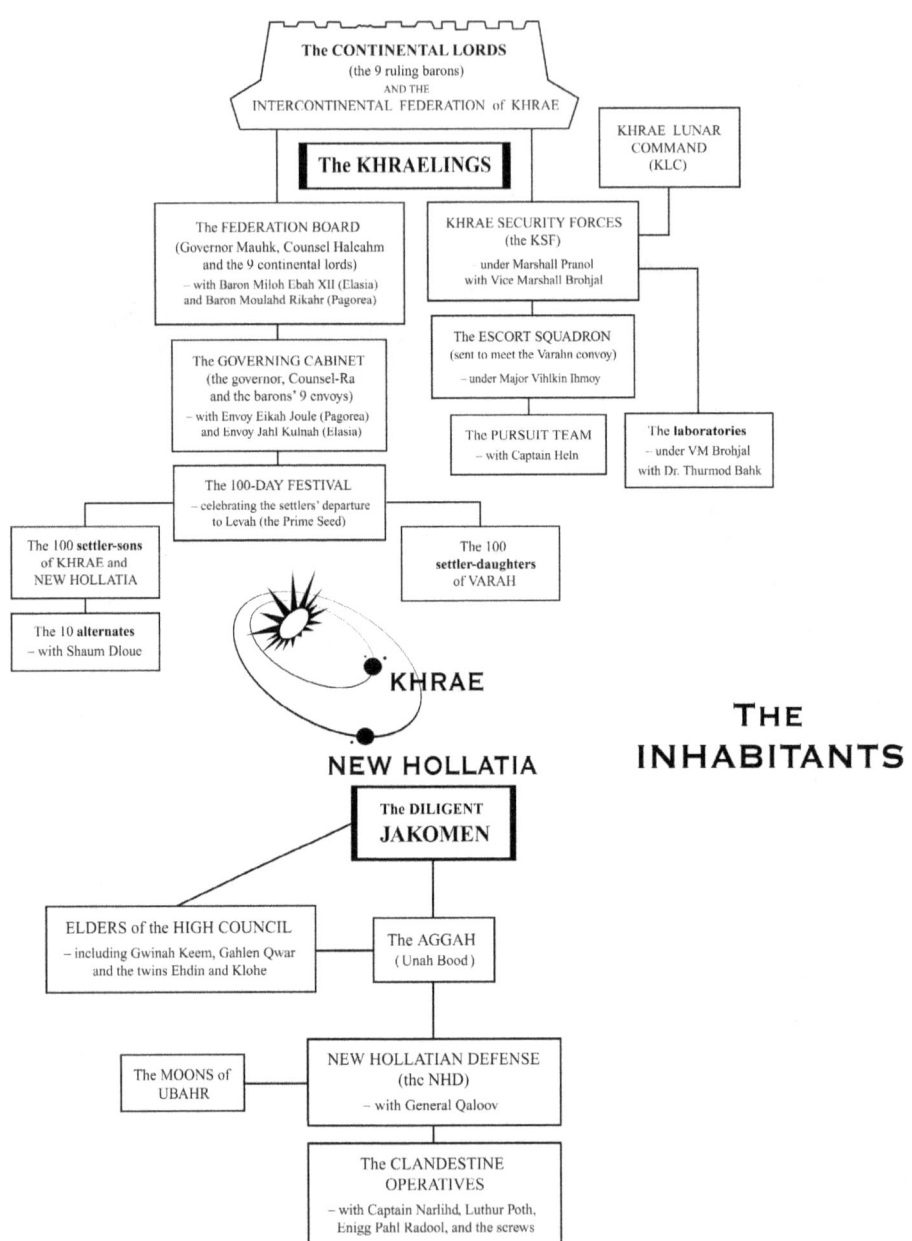

The CONTINENTAL LORDS
(the 9 ruling barons)
AND THE
INTERCONTINENTAL FEDERATION of KHRAE

The KHRAELINGS

KHRAE LUNAR
COMMAND
(KLC)

The FEDERATION BOARD
(Governor Mauhk, Counsel Haleahm
and the 9 continental lords)
– with Baron Miloh Ebah XII (Elasia)
and Baron Moulahd Rikahr (Pagorea)

KHRAE SECURITY FORCES
(the KSF)
under Marshall Pranol
with Vice Marshall Brohjal

The GOVERNING CABINET
(the governor, Counsel-Ra
and the barons' 9 envoys)
– with Envoy Eikah Joule (Pagorea)
and Envoy Jahl Kulnah (Elasia)

The ESCORT SQUADRON
(sent to meet the Varahn convoy)
– under Major Vihlkin Ihmoy

The PURSUIT TEAM
– with Captain Heln

The laboratories
– under VM Brohjal
with Dr. Thurmod Bahk

The 100-DAY FESTIVAL
– celebrating the settlers' departure
to Levah (the Prime Seed)

The 100 settler-sons
of KHRAE and
NEW HOLLATIA

The 100
settler-daughters
of VARAH

The 10 alternates
– with Shaum Dloue

KHRAE

NEW HOLLATIA

THE
INHABITANTS

The DILIGENT
JAKOMEN

ELDERS of the HIGH COUNCIL
– including Gwinah Keem, Gahlen Qwar
and the twins Ehdin and Klohe

The AGGAH
(Unah Bood)

The MOONS of
UBAHR

NEW HOLLATIAN DEFENSE
(the NHD)
– with General Qaloov

The CLANDESTINE
OPERATIVES
– with Captain Narlihd, Luthur Poth,
Enigg Pahl Radool, and the screws

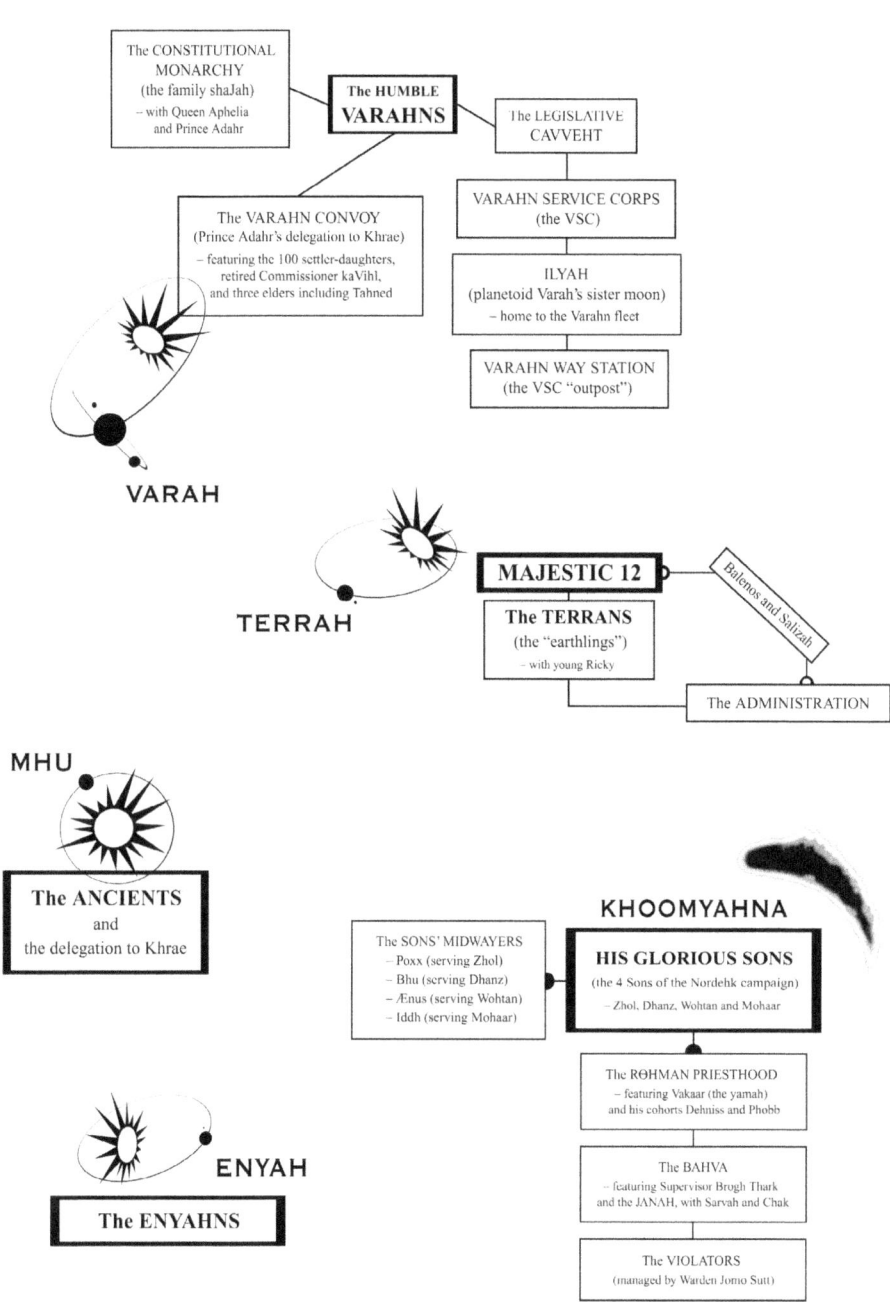

The CONSTITUTIONAL MONARCHY
(the family shaJah)
– with Queen Aphelia
and Prince Adahr

The HUMBLE **VARAHNS**

The LEGISLATIVE CAVVEHT

The VARAHN CONVOY
(Prince Adahr's delegation to Khrae)
– featuring the 100 settler-daughters,
retired Commissioner kaVihl,
and three elders including Tahned

VARAHN SERVICE CORPS
(the VSC)

ILYAH
(planetoid Varah's sister moon)
– home to the Varahn fleet

VARAHN WAY STATION
(the VSC "outpost")

VARAH

TERRAH

MAJESTIC 12

Balenos and Saltzah

The TERRANS
(the "earthlings")
– with young Ricky

The ADMINISTRATION

MHU

The ANCIENTS
and
the delegation to Khrae

KHOOMYAHNA

The SONS' MIDWAYERS
– Poxx (serving Zhol)
– Bhu (serving Dhanz)
– Ænus (serving Wohtan)
– Iddh (serving Mohaar)

HIS GLORIOUS SONS
(the 4 Sons of the Nordehk campaign)
– Zhol, Dhanz, Wohtan and Mohaar

The ROHMAN PRIESTHOOD
– featuring Vakaar (the yamah)
and his cohorts Dehniss and Phobb

ENYAH

The ENYAHNS

The BAHVA
– featuring Supervisor Brogh Thark
and the JANAH, with Sarvah and Chak

The VIOLATORS
(managed by Warden Jomo Sutt)

BEING GOD

A Trilogy of our Near Future

BOOK 1

The PLAYERS & WORLDS

The ETHEREANS: the diverse first family of Creation, including those irreproachably devoted to the Light, those consigned to Darkness, and the multitude of fickle, formless others in between.

• *the loyal oraphim:* a high order of warrior-messengers selflessly bound to the Light.

• *Hyynehk* [♀]*:* one of Ohrvon's mysterious, stealthy oraphim.

• *the Most Highs:* the 127 *Universal Sons* (Rəhm is the fallen 128th) who administrate the starfields/constellations that form our galaxy: Ohrvon.

• *the Vihdœan Council of Nordehk:* eight angelic entities including *Jaylah (♂ council chief)* and *Bel* [♀], appointed by Ohrvon's Most Highs to administrate the Nordehk constellation.

• *the seraphim:* an order of angelic beings from whose ranks some do fall, seraphim assist and escort the Most Highs and Vihdæa, and are the genuine "guardian angels" of legend and myth.

The RØHMANS: the diverse entities of Rohm's ever expanding domain; the Rohman empire's citizenry of bahva/bhuvani/beings and fallen ethereans including numerous Vihdæa, seraphim, and midwayers/peshim.

• **Rohm:** "The Caller," the fallen Universal Son and self-proclaimed Prime Crusader, Universal Lord, Architect of *All That Is*, Omnipotent One, and Friend of Man and Angels.

• **the Sons of Rohm:** defectors from the Vihdæa who through unfailing service to Rohm have earned the elevated "Son" status of high demons; the many thousands of these Rohman Sons include: **Zhol** [♂], Overlord (Lord of the Orbits) of this campaign; **Dhanz** [♀], an Overlord herself; **Wohtan** [♂], an indifferent Son with special needs; and the ambitious, newly-promoted **Mohaar** [♂].

• **His dark seraphim:** of the many fallen seraphim, these are *His*—the twelve who serve as Rohm's unseen, ever-vigilant, personal escorts.

• **the Rohman peshim:** the Sons' personal, eternally-committed midwayers/scouts: **Poxx** [♂] to Zhol, **Bhu** [♀] to Dhanz, **Ænus** [♂] to Wohtan, and **Iddh** [♂] to Mohaar; **Jinn-Jinn** [♂] is the temporary, resident midwayer of the Overlord's khoomyahna while the warship treks deep space.

• **Vakaar:** the high priest or "yamah" of the Nordehk campaign's all-male, Rohman priesthood.

• **Dehniss and Phobb:** the yamah's two cohorts, and the ones to whom his spies report.

• **the bahva:** imperial citizens; Rohman commoners; ordinary beings of the realm.

• **the Janah:** a secret sect of Rohman anarchists bent on escaping the imperial Order.

• **Sarvah** [♀]**:** the Janah's reluctant projectionist/spy.

• **the violators:** those convicted of violating The Master's Teachings.

The ORION GROUP: those from the core motherworlds and outer worlds of the Orion constellation, including those from its subservient "territories."

• ***the Og:*** short for ***O****rion* ***g****roup*—known widely and disparagingly as the deceitful ***darkeyes****;* hateful, calculating mercenaries/crusaders commissioned by Lord Zhol some 8,000 years prior to discreetly ready Nordehk's unsuspecting worlds for willing absorption into Rɵhm's ever-expanding domain.

• ***Orion Command:*** the ever-changing Council of Ten who reside within the Orion constellation and preside over its commissioned and internal affairs.

• ***Nordehk Group Command:*** an interlocking assembly of five battle-ready motherships located near Nordehk's lone red dwarf at the constellation's inward Vesper fringe, NORDEHK GROUP COMMAND is the tactical command center for the Orion group's Nordehk operations.

• ***Iiose*** [♂]***:*** venerable ranking officer of NORDEHK GROUP COMMAND, local nerve center for the darkeyes' orbiting garrisons.

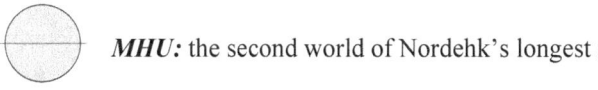

MHU: the second world of Nordehk's longest surviving tribe.

• ***the ancients of Mhu:*** the progenitors of four of Nordehk's five other inhabited worlds.

- -

VARAH: the prized "elantah" and first world colonized by the ancients of Mhu.

• ***Queen Aphelia:*** the Varahn queen, a constitutional monarch who presides over the world's ruling ***cavveht****,* the elected representatives of Varah's humble people.

• *Prince Adahr:* third in line for the Varahn throne, and scheming to be king.

• *Varahn Service Corps (VSC):* an agency designed more to serve than to defend.

• *Commissioner kaVihl* [♂]: retired head of the VSC, he is among Varah's delegation to Khrae.

• *the settler-daughters:* the 100 young Varahn women en route to Khrae with Prince Adahr, Commissioner kaVihl and the other Varahn delegates; they and the 100 sons of Khrae and New Hollatia are to colonize the distant planet Levah, the ancients' current Prime Seed.

- -

 KHRAE: the second world colonized by the ancients of Mhu.

• *Gjadren Mauhk* [♂]: governor of Khrae's loosely bound Intercontinental Federation.

• *Raund Haleahm* [♂]: the governor's lifelong friend, Counsel-Ra, and Khrae's behind-the-scenes primary political power.

• *Khrae Lunar Command (KLC):* moon-based nerve center for the *Khrae Security Forces (KSF)*—defenders of the planet and enforcers of Federation law.

• *Mannon Jee Pranol* [♂]: marshall of the heavily armed *KSF*.

• *Jehrmi Brohjal* [♂]: the KSF's young vice marshall, the Forces' second in command.

• *Baron Ebah:* baron of Khrae's Elasian continent and staunch supporter of the Jakomen.

• *Jahl Khulnah* [♂]: the tactful Elasian envoy and diplomatic representative of Baron Ebah.

• *Baron Rikahr:* baron of Khrae's Pagorean continent and rival of Baron Ebah.

• *Eikah Jouhl* [♀]: the petulant Pagorean envoy and diplomatic representative of Baron Rikahr.

• *the 100 settler-sons:* the 90 young Khraelings and 10 young Jakomen who with the 100 Varahn daughters are to colonize the distant planet Levah, the ancients' current Prime Seed.

• *the 10 alternates:* the 9 Khraelings and 1 Jakomen training with the sons as tentative substitutes.

- -

 NEW HOLLATIA: originally known as Qalakah, the solar system's fifth planet from its sun, New Hollatia is Khrae's terra-formed sister world, settled by the Jakomen after the Old Hollatian holocaust.

• *the Jakomen:* an estranged Khraeling tribe; descendants of continental Old Hollatia's holocaust survivors, they emigrated to the system's fifth planet and renamed it New Hollatia.

• *the Aggah Bood* [♀]*:* the Jakomen's capable, self-assured leader.

• *Elders of the High Council:* the 24 who, under their Aggah, justly govern New Hollatia.

• *Ehdin* [♂] *and Klohe* [♀]*:* twin brother-and-sister Elders of the Jakomen High Council.

• *New Hollatian Defense (NHD):* the global police, security force and defenders of New Hollatia and the Jakomen people.

• *General Qaloov* [♂]*:* senior officer of the heavily armed NHD.

• *Captain Rauhf B. Narlihd* [♂]*:* captain of the pirate-operatives sent by the NHD to secretly rendezvous with the Varahn convoy and snatch its rich 14th container.

• *Enigg Pahl Radool* [♂]*:* an NHD junior officer and design engineer infrequently possessed by the demon-Son Mohaar.

- -

TERRAH: third world colonized by the ancients of Mhu.

• *the "earthlings":* Terrah's self-named, multi-colored tribe; technological infants, these unsuspecting sufferers of ruthless Og manipulation have only recently ventured into space.

• *Majestic Twelve (MJ-12):* the secret, all-male, absolute Terran power; "the president-makers" and collaborative minions of the Og.

• *Balenos and Salizah:* elite, paired, male Og hybrid-incarnate operatives who birthed on Terrah for the express purpose of managing the Majestic Twelve.

• *Ricky* [♂]*:* a young dreamer of realities and future events.

- -

 ENYAH: the fourth and most recent world colonized by the ancients of Mhu.

• *the bahtuus:* the primitive surviving tribe of the planet's Og-instilled genocidal wars.

- -

 LEVAH: the ancients' current Prime Seed, scheduled for imminent colonization by the 100 Khraeling-Jakomen sons and 100 Varahn daughters.

BEING GOD

BOOK 1

CHARACTER TIMELINE

936: *[1]He brings Order to the chaos. [2]Rəhm IS.*

—from The Teachings (The Book of Rəhm)

www.ingramcontent.com/pod-product-compliance
Lightning Source LLC
Chambersburg PA
CBHW061313170626
46817CB00001B/164